SECOND THOUGHTS

When Panoyan was first jailed, Cavanagh had hoped he would accept some sort of guilty plea on reduced charges in exchange for testimony against his accomplice. But Stark reported back to Cavanagh that Panoyan's answer was he didn't think he was guilty of anything, and wouldn't take any plea. Trying to force a confession out of him by keeping him locked up—an old prosecutor's trick—clearly hadn't worked.

Now Cavanagh was swimming in the horrible problem of what to do about Panoyan. When the depositions started, the prosecutor had thought both defendants were 100% guilty. But all the punching Vinikoor and Stark had done to his case had in fact achieved its intended effect. Brian's certainty about Panoyan's guilt slowly dropped: 90% guilty . . . 70% guilty. And after his star witness, Patrick O'Brien's, deposition, it plunged below 50%—a very unsafe place for a prosecutor to be.

If Panoyan was guilty of *anything at all*, it certainly wasn't murder.

UNTIL PROVEN INNOCENT

ARTHUR JAY HARRIS

AVON BOOKS ◆ NEW YORK

UNTIL PROVEN INNOCENT is a journalistic account of the actual murder investigation of Dana and Rodney Williamson for the 1988 murder of Donna Decker in Davie, Florida. The events recounted in this book are true. The scenes and dialogue have been reconstructed based on tape-recorded formal interviews, police department records, and published news stories. Quoted testimony has been taken verbatim from pre-trial transcripts and other sworn statements.

AVON BOOKS
A division of
The Hearst Corporation
1350 Avenue of the Americas
New York, New York 10019

Copyright © 1995 by Arthur Jay Harris
Published by arrangement with the author
Library of Congress Catalog Card Number: 95-94486
ISBN: 0-380-77733-9

First Avon Books Printing: December 1995

Printed in the U.S.A.

RA   10   9   8   7   6   5   4   3   2   1

How often have I said to you that when you have eliminated the impossible, whatever remains, *however improbable,* must be the truth?

—Sherlock Holmes to Watson
The Sign of Four

Usually homicides are easy to solve. One person doesn't kill another for no reason.

—Detective Kelly Woodroof
Davie Police Department

◆ PREFACE

Davie, Florida, is an orange grove and horse town turned suburb.

At the turn of the century, it was virgin swamp. The development of Florida had been stunted throughout the 1800s by the Seminole Wars, then almost immediately following, the Civil War. Long before all the modern conveniences of land development were even imaginable, the summer heat and mosquitoes in the Florida swamps made the place unlivable to all but the Native Americans. An often repeated U.S. soldier's joke of the period suggested that if he owned both Hell and Florida, he'd live in Hell and rent out Florida.

But in the 1890s, Henry Flagler extended his Florida East Coast Railroad south to Palm Beach, then on to Miami, which incorporated in 1896. The first Florida land boom was on. Great dreamers, as well as con men, envisioned swampland as grand cities merely not yet built.

In 1906, a Colorado millionaire named R.P. Davie bought 27,500 acres of Everglades swamp west of Fort Lauderdale, which itself had only a few hundred residents. There were no roads west at the time; the only way to get there was via the New River.

In 1909, Florida's governor Napoleon Bonaparte Broward—whom Davie's county was named after—commissioned for the swamps to be drained for the future development of Florida's interior. It was done by creating a network of canals connected with Lake Okeechobee and the Intracoastal Waterway.

Davie, Florida, was incorporated in 1925 as an agricultural town. In 1930, a horseman who raced at Hialeah Park in

Miami discovered it and built up a breeding industry, which gave the town its Western feel.

From then on, Davie prided itself as a rough, tough cowboy town, complete with rednecks and a rodeo. It couldn't have been more different than genteel Miami Beach or Palm Beach, most of whose visitors never knew Davie existed.

Today, Davie is different. Although cows still graze on some of its acreage, equestrians share trails with bicycles and pedestrians, and some country roads remain two-laned; suburbia has transformed this little outpost. In 1960, the population had been 2,000; in 1980 it was 20,000; by 1990 it passed 50,000. As country towns go, it's now a suburb. As suburbs go, it's in the country.

In the mid-1970s, faced with a deteriorating downtown inappropriate to its new inhabitants, the town council voted for gentrification. But when they suggested tearing down the rodeo arena, dozens of angry cowboys stormed Town Hall.

City fathers compromised. They agreed to rebuild downtown anew; but following the 1960s example of "the Mouse that Put Orlando on the Map," they zoned in a 1860s Wild West theme. Once again in Florida, kitsch ruled the day.

The Decker homicide was the biggest case in the town's history. It happened in this atmosphere of conflict between those remaining few who were proud to be Davie rednecks and its many come-lately suburban slickers, who saw the town as charming.

What tipped off that the conflict might be an issue was a well-worn cowboy hat found next to Massachusetts-born Donna Decker, wife of a wealthy home builder.

I

"My Husband, My Baby"

✦ ONE

Friday, November 4, 1988
10:13 P.M.
Davie, Florida

The woman's breathless call to 911 interrupted a quiet Friday night in the horse country suburbs.

"1-6-5-1 Southwest 1-1-6 Avenue. I'm stabbed to death. Please."

Broward County Sheriff's Office dispatcher Andrea Guess took the call. On a screen in front of her was a myriad of information describing her caller: her phone number, address, city, the name the phone was listed under, and the nearest Emergency Medical Services (EMS) unit.

"Did somebody stab you?" she answered back calmly and efficiently.

"Yes . . . and my husband—my baby."

"Your husband? Is he still there?"

"Yes."

"Stay on the line," Guess ordered. Immediately she got on the radio, assigning the distress call to local police in the town of Davie. In the code language of police dispatch, she radioed out that the husband stabbed the wife, husband still 10-97—at large—with a Signal Zero knife—meaning he was armed. A call to EMS went out as well.

"I've got a woman in Davie. She said her husband stabbed her."

10:14–10:16 P.M.

Four Davie road patrol officers radioed back that they were close by and en route. They put on their lights and sirens,

5

cutting their sirens as they approached the quiet residential neighborhood. They were Robert "Dusty" Banks, William Bamford, David Pavone, and K-9 officer Greg Mize. A fifth officer, Sergeant Michael Allen, in charge of road patrol officers on the 3–11 P.M. shift, radioed from Davie police headquarters that he was en route as well.

When the dispatch operator came back to the telephone line, there was no response. Fearing that the caller was dead, she put out a Signal 5—meaning a murder had most likely taken place. It went out as "Two victims, one Signal 5."

10:18–10:19 P.M.

Believing they were responding to a domestic with a stabbing, the four road patrol officers all arrived at the scene, adrenaline rushing. It was a wealthy neighborhood, where police weren't often called. The ranch houses were set back from the street, a wooded acre apart from each other. The street was dark, and the officers searching for street numbers posted on the houses or mailboxes couldn't see them from the road. It wasn't at all obvious which house was 1651.

They spotted a lit-up house on the east side of the narrow street. The windows were open, and Mize and Bamford found the doors unlocked. They yelled for someone to come to the door; then, when no one did, they went inside, as far as the living room.

No one was home except for two pit bulls. It was the wrong house. The house number was even.

10:20 P.M.

Advised of the officers' arrivals, dispatch broke off the 911 telephone line, which had been silent for the previous seven minutes.

10:22 P.M.

Sergeant Allen arrived at the scene.

10:23 P.M.

The officers located 1651, across the street, by the number on the mailbox. There were three vehicles in the twenty-five-yard-long driveway. It didn't lead to an obvious front door.

Mize took charge of the scene. He ordered Banks and Bamford to set up a perimeter guard around the house, in case someone armed was still inside. Banks radioed that he was observing the front of the house—the northwest side—while Bamford covered the southeast side—closest to the street. Neither saw any open or broken doors or windows.

Mize and Pavone joined Bamford on the south side. Finding the front door, one of them knocked but got no answer. Bamford saw lights on inside the living room window but no activity.

There was another wooden entrance door to the house next to the garage. They knocked again on that door and got no response. When Mize turned the doorknob, it was open. There were no signs of forced entry.

Mize decided they should enter. He led, followed by Pavone, then Bamford and Sgt. Allen.

"Davie police!" Mize called out. "Anybody there?"

No response.

This might be more than just a domestic, they thought. All drew their guns, believing the suspect most likely was still in the house. It had only been minutes since the 911 call.

The foyer beyond the door was dark, but there was a light up ahead. On the right was another door. When they opened it, a huge dog jumped on its hind legs and pounded against the door. It startled Bamford, and he quickly closed the door.

Through the darkness they passed the first room, which looked like a home beauty shop, undisturbed. At the entrance to the main part of the house, which was partially lit, Allen and Bamford stayed behind, assuming a ready-to-fire position, guarding their colleagues' backs.

Now it was just Mize and Pavone. With Mize leading, the two men, back-to-back, tensely proceeded through a hallway on the left. Mize decided to go by the book and systematically "clear" the house, for their own safety. The hallway led to a bedroom and bath, but there was nothing disturbed there, either.

Returning to the main area they saw a long counter separating the kitchen from the large living room. The only light in the room was the indirect glare from a television that was on, the light moving with every scene change. Looking into the living room, one of them spotted a pump shotgun lying on a throw rug directly in front of the fireplace. The barrel was pointing toward them.

Nothing else seemed out of place, other than a coffee table that seemed to have been moved.

Then they heard the screaming.

It sounded like the cry of a baby. It came from the far side of the house.

They couldn't run toward the cry quite yet; first they had to clear the rest of the house. Against otherwise better judgment, they split up, Mize taking rooms back toward the master bedroom and Pavone checking the rooms nearer to the door where they had entered. They arrived at the master bedroom together, with Allen behind them. The door was partially open and they could hear the baby wailing.

What they found they couldn't have prepared for.

"Oh God, get rescue in here quick!" Mize screamed back to Bamford.

The room was lit. On the plush carpet was a two-and-a-half-year-old child curled up, lying next to his father's head. The father was on his stomach, facing the wall. He was immobile and helpless—his wrists were manacled behind his back to his ankles with yellow nylon rope. There were handcuffs on his wrists as well, and a black cloth gag stuffed in his mouth.

Looking closer, Mize saw he was unconscious and bloody. He had been shot twice, in the back of the head.

First thing, Mize removed his gag. Surprisingly, the man regained himself.

"My son's been shot! My son's been shot!"

Mize picked up the baby and started to run out of the house. But before he got much further than a step, he stopped, realizing that the perpetrator might still be in the house. He laid the baby back down next to his father and shouted at Pavone to keep looking through the rest of the house for the shooter or more victims. Then Mize untied the father, thirty-six-year-old Bob Decker, so that he could help his son. But for the moment Mize couldn't do anything about the handcuffs.

On the wood console waterbed was another man, the baby's seventy-six-year-old grandfather, Clyde Decker. He had been shot in the face, a large pool of wet blood next to him staining the salmon-pink sheet and dark red comforter. At arm's distance were fragments of violently shattered dentures. He lay on his back, head against the headrest, still conscious. Like his son Bob, his hands and feet were tied together behind him, all connected by a single cord.

There was confusion as to whether the child, Carl Decker, was injured. He hadn't been tied up, and Pavone didn't think anything was wrong with him. Bamford noticed only that he was holding the right side of his face.

When Pavone returned to the unlit hallway leading to the bedroom, he and Bamford found a door locked from the inside with light leaking out underneath. They called over Sgt. Allen, whose first thought was that a suspect could be hiding behind it.

Allen ordered Mize, the burliest officer there, to kick the door open while everyone else poised their guns once again. Mize placed his kick just under the door handle, breaking the door frame. The door swung open partially, stopped by something inside the door.

"Oh shit," said Mize.

He saw her first. They had found their 911 caller.

She was Donna, according to the brown plastic J.C. Penney salesman ID badge she wore on her dress. She lay face up on a strewn pile of papers and correspondence, her brown eyes wide open. There was blood all over her hands and the front of her pink dress, which was pulled up to her waist, revealing her hose and panties. Both ankles were tied: her right ankle with electrical cord, the plug dangling, her left ankle with natural colored rope. A very bloody telephone handle lay off the hook next to her on top of a color brochure entitled "Colorado Ski Country," inches from her foot, which covered a receipt from a tire store. There was blood on the Panasonic wall phone numeric pad as well.

Allen checked her pulse, but everyone who saw her knew it was too late. Her complexion had already turned pallid.

"She's gone," someone said.

10:26 P.M.

Allen radioed that there were two victims Signal 5—murder. Then he grabbed the shotgun lying in the living room and took it outside to the driveway. That was just in case the killer was still in the house, so that he wouldn't be able to use it on the police. It didn't appear as if it had been recently fired.

Bamford's first thought was that Donna Decker had been sexually assaulted, but her undergarments were intact. He saw a striking fear in her face and even in the clutched fingers of her bloody left hand, which still grasped a knotted dark pink terry bathrobe belt around her neck that she apparently had been able to rip from her mouth. Her blood was the adhesive that stuck a Visa card receipt to the same hand.

The room where she lay was a walk-in closet used as an office. It looked ransacked and was a disarray in itself. Receipts, canceled checks, account statements, bills, correspondence from an attorney about a mortgage loan, a package of papers from a title company—most with smudges or drops of blood on them—were scattered. Her left elbow pressed against the wall and a six-inch smudge of blood trailed from it. The back of the door was bloody too. A well-worn beige straw cowboy hat with a feather and a brown headband lay upside down on the floor next to her, just beyond the telephone.

The first Emergency Medical Services ambulance had arrived at 10:23, nine minutes after being called. They had idled in the driveway, awaiting instructions. Now police wanted them inside, even though they hadn't yet issued an all-clear signal. That didn't ever happen, thought paramedic Meyer Marzouca as he raced inside.

To get to the back of the pitch-black house, Marzouca ran crouched like a duck following armed officers. He passed the closet and saw the dead woman and figured that was it. Then an officer yelled "Over here!"—pointing to the bedroom.

When he entered the room, he was stunned; he had never seen anything like it. Focusing on the father, he almost tripped on the little boy, thinking he was a doll until doing a triple take. Even after Marzouca knelt beside him and turned him over, Carl still didn't look real, his color was so ashen.

Marzouca picked the child up, saw some blood trickling down from his nose, then realized he wasn't breathing. Marzouca did what came automatically to him—he shook the child. It worked: he pinked up and started breathing. Had Marzouca come in even a minute later, Carl would have suffered brain damage from lack of oxygen. Another minute or so later and he would have died.

"Don't hurt me! Don't hit me!" the child screamed. Then he vomited.

Sgt. Allen ordered Officer Paul Brugman to open Bob Decker's handcuffs with his police-issue keys, however to be careful not to contaminate them with his own fingerprints. But Brugman's keys didn't fit because the cuffs weren't police-issue. They were toy cuffs, he thought. The cuffs never were removed at the scene, but a few minutes later paramedic Ron Vargo snapped them apart at the chain with a bolt cutter.

Meanwhile, Bob Decker went in and out of alertness. Mize, back in the room, tried to get some details about the suspects before he was taken away. He asked, "Do you know who did this?"

"Yeah, I know who did it," Bob answered, without hesitation.

Allen ordered Mize to search the adjacent grounds and woods with his German Shepherd police dog, in case suspects were still nearby. Two or three other K-9 officers and their dogs joined the search later. But the animals picked up no scents, which probably meant that the perpetrators had left the scene using the asphalt driveway, which had been contaminated by all the police traffic.

Bamford, then later Mize too, was assigned to canvass the neighborhood. Not surprisingly, no one had heard anything, except for the Deckers' next door neighbor who said he had heard a sound at about 10 P.M. He thought a garbage can had been knocked over.

10:34 P.M.

That day, Detective Kelly Woodroof had felt the onset of a cold. Expecting a quiet night, he took a Drixoral, which he knew would help him get to sleep early.

It was not to be. At 9:30 P.M., he got an emergency call to come to the police department and interview a twelve-year-old male victim of a lewd and lascivious assault. At the station, Woodroof told his superiors he had no experience on that sort of case, and instead they should call in one of the detectives specially trained to handle sex crimes.

Just before 10:30, as Woodroof was ready to go home and take the sleep that his cold and the medicine demanded of him, Det. Gary Killam asked him to hold up for a minute. There had been a stabbing on the police radio. Minutes later, Killam drove Woodroof to the Decker house.

Mike Allen had had his differences with Woodroof in the past, but now he was very pleased to see him, so that he could relinquish control of the scene. Woodroof thought Allen looked like he was either going to cry or be sick.

"It looks like a professional hit," Allen said.

First thing, Woodroof radioed for backup from Broward County Sheriff's Office (BSO) crime scene detectives. At the same time, Mize put a BOLO (Be on the lookout) out for a blue Ford van with temporary tags stolen from the residence. Bob Decker had told him it might be gone.

10:39 P.M.

BSO Crime scene detectives radioed they were en route.

← Two

When he saw the man in the banged-up blue pickup truck who was barreling through the parking lot at fifty miles an hour and then flagged him down, Jay Greenfeder thought the guy was drunk. Definitely. Greenfeder was the outdoor security guard on duty at Sybar Plaza, a Davie strip mall which had a Walgreen's and a twenty-four-hour supermarket called Xtra. He first saw the truck as it turned into the mall entrance on Hiatus Road, a block short of State Road 84. Hiatus Road was a divided highway, and to make the left turn into the mall required illegally crossing the grass median, something the truck driver didn't seem to think twice about.

Greenfeder was the only guard on duty during the 4 P.M.– 1 A.M. shift that Friday night. It wasn't a high crime neighborhood, and nothing had happened earlier. Nor was the strip mall busy then.

When the man spotted Greenfeder walking around the parking lot in front of Walgreen's he hit the brakes and jumped out of the truck without bothering to park it in a space. For a moment the man seemed to think Greenfeder— dressed in his blue security outfit complete with handcuffs, flashlight, and radio—was a cop. Only after the man got closer did he realize that he wasn't.

"Call the police. I've just—my buddy and I have just been robbed," Charles Panoyan shouted frantically.

Greenfeder had been a security officer for eight years and a military policeman before that, so he was trained to be an observer. The man was shaking. He couldn't calm down and wasn't able to answer his questions. He was badly dressed in an old blue T-shirt that read "CRD Homes," baggy brown pants, and dirty work shoes. He was perspiring profusely, and you couldn't miss his extraordinarily bad smell. His dilated eyes were another indication to Greenfeder that he had been drinking.

"Where did it happen?" Greenfeder asked.

"You don't understand," burst out Panoyan, trying to get across the message that the crime was still in progress. Looking over his shoulder, he repeated, "I've just been robbed! You don't understand! They're following me! They have my tag number! They knew where I live! They're gonna get me!"

Greenfeder explained that all he could do was use his waist-mounted walkie-talkie to radio his dispatcher, and they would call Davie Police to respond.

"I need P.D. at Sybar Plaza. A man was just robbed," Greenfeder told the radio, and a moment later, the radio message came back that police were en route.

"They'll be here in a minute," Greenfeder told him, but that wasn't fast enough for the guy.

"I don't have a minute," he implored. "I need them now. Look, can't you do anything for me?"

"I'm not a cop. I can't leave my area, there's nothing I can do."

Panoyan looked behind again. "I don't care about you not being a policeman, let me have your gun."

"My gun? I can't give you my gun."

"Well, let me borrow it then."

"I can't do that." The guy was whacked out to think he'd let him borrow his gun, he thought.

"What's wrong with the police? Why haven't they come?"

"They're coming," Greenfeder said.

While they waited, Greenfeder asked what the robber looked like.

"I couldn't see his face. He had a stocking over it and he had a big white hat with black trim." That was all the description Panoyan could provide.

Greenfeder noticed that the man's hands were in his pockets. He was searching for something. A quarter, it turned out, so that he could call his wife. He said the robber had stolen his wallet and he didn't even have a quarter for the telephone.

Greenfeder volunteered a quarter and walked him over to the phone bank, next to the store's main entrance. But first he made the man move his truck into a parking space.

Panoyan had the same breathless telephone conversation that he had just had with Greenfeder. "Get the kids out of the house and drive away as far as you can!" Greenfeder overheard.

Panoyan then asked to use a bathroom, and Greenfeder said one was inside the sliding glass door and immediately to the left.

But before Panoyan got inside, a dark blue car with a white top pulled into the space immediately to the left of the truck. It struck Greenfeder as odd because the truck was the only vehicle parked in the entire section, and there were spots much closer to Xtra, where the two men who got out quickly walked toward.

One was a tall black man, the other white. They didn't touch the truck, but Greenfeder noticed they made eye contact with Panoyan as they walked into the store, then immediately turned their heads away. Panoyan had been paranoid that he had been followed; were these the men?

By the time Panoyan came out of the bathroom, Davie Police detective Jo Ann Carter had responded. She was assigned to narcotics, but was off duty that night, working security in police uniform for an apartment complex called Scarborough, just across the street from Xtra. She had heard the police radio calling all available units to the Decker home.

When the Xtra call came in—a possible robbery in progress—and Davie didn't have anyone left to send, she was asked to respond, since Davie police officers are technically on duty whenever they are inside town limits. She got into her marked police cruiser and drove across the street. It only took a minute. She routinely recorded the time of arrival with dispatch at 10:47 P.M.

Carter first found Greenfeder, in front of Walgreen's, who pointed out Panoyan, now running toward them. Greenfeder told her the robbery was elsewhere than the shopping mall.

Carter also saw the Panoyan was upset. He was jumping around like he was nervous or speeding, using his hands a lot. She stayed in her car.

"They're watching my house," Panoyan said.

"Who's watching your house?" asked Carter.

"I don't know."

"Why are they watching your house?"

"I think my friends are being robbed," he said. "They know where I live. They know the address. I have to get my wife and kids out of the house."

"Where are your friends?"

"At home!" said Panoyan, frustrated at having to explain everything.

"Where do they live?"

"Over there." He pointed south into the residential woods.

"Over there where?" It was equally frustrating for Carter, who didn't think Panoyan was making much sense.

"I don't know the address."

"How do you know what happened? Where were you?"

"I was there sitting at a table with my friend and he came in and told me to leave. They were watching my house."

"Who came in? What did he look like? What was he wearing?" asked Carter, desperate for coherent details.

"I don't know! He had something over his face!"

"Did he have any weapons?"

"A knife," Panoyan said.

Carter told Panoyan to get in the back of her cruiser so that he could guide her to the crime scene. At first Panoyan didn't want to go back. On Carter's prodding, he entered the car hesitantly, whining once more that he needed to call his wife again, that she was in danger. Before they left, Carter put on her bulletproof vest.

10:45 P.M.

Paramedics had taken twenty minutes to prepare Bob and Clyde Decker for transit; then they rushed them out of the house on stretchers. They passed Robert Banks, who was monitoring the door of the residence and writing down the names of everyone entering. Banks realized that no BOLO describing any suspects had gone out, so he asked both men for descriptions. He spent only a hectic moment with each before they left.

"Sir, I'm sorry. I know you're in a lot of pain," Banks

began, speaking first to Bob. "But I'd really like to get a description of this person out. Can you please answer a couple of questions for me?"

Both victims were able to talk coherently, but Clyde was in better shape, so Banks got most of his information from him. Banks asked if he would be able to recognize the suspect if he saw him again, and Clyde said yes. He also said that the shotgun—an Ithaca Deerslayer 12-gauge—found in the living room was his.

About 11:00 P.M.

It was less than a five-minute ride from Xtra to the crime scene, but Panoyan fidgeted and jumped around in the backseat of Officer Carter's car the entire time. Carter followed his directions until they spotted an ambulance near the house, then she trailed it the rest of the way. Only then did she realize that this was the same scene where everyone had been called to a half hour earlier.

In and around the Deckers' driveway there were two other ambulances and numerous police cruisers, blue police lights flashing. When Panoyan saw it, he began to get even more emotional.

"Oh my God. Oh my God. Is everybody all right?" He put his hands up to his head.

Carter had to open the rear door, and Panoyan got out immediately. He was stunned to see so much activity at the place he had just left minutes before. The front of the house was cordoned off with crime scene tape. He asked a group of neighbors what had happened.

"Bob went crazy. He stabbed his wife, shot his baby and his dad, and his dad took the gun away from him and shot him."

"No. That's wrong. That's not what happened," said Panoyan, now searching for an officer to tell his story.

Panoyan followed Carter until she saw Officer Bamford, to whom she turned over Panoyan. Then Corporal Russell Elzey told Bamford that Panoyan should speak to Greg Mize and Det. Robert Marseco.

While Bamford went to look for Mize and Marseco, he

suggested Panoyan might want to sit down, and for them to put him in a patrol car. But then he closed the door.

"Why am I locked in the back of a patrol car?" Panoyan asked.

"For your own protection," said Bamford.

"Nothing's going to happen to me in front of all these people."

"Well, you're probably right," said Bamford, reopening the door and letting him out.

A moment after Bamford walked away, Panoyan saw paramedics bring out a victim. To see who it was, Panoyan raced toward him, through the yellow "Do Not Cross" tape. "You can't go over there," said an officer. Panoyan broke his grip, but another blocked him before he could get much closer. All that he could see was that whoever it was, they were a bloody mess. Shocked, Panoyan tried to get information from the ambulance driver.

"I can't talk with you. I've got to go," the driver shot back.

11:08 P.M.

It wasn't until paramedics secured Carl on a stretcher that someone realized that he had been shot too, as his father had insisted. Remarkably, he had stayed calm, sitting next to his grandfather.

All three ambulances left the scene, carrying each victim to different hospitals. Fearing that Bob Decker was on the verge of death, Woodroof assigned Detective Gary Killam to follow his ambulance and take any statement at the hospital he could give.

Banks radioed a second BOLO, based on how the Deckers had described the suspect: white male, forty years old, medium to muscular build, about 165 pounds, wearing a hat, possibly straw, not a baseball cap, armed with a black revolver or black handgun. Subject last seen on foot in area.

The BOLO for the blue van with temporary tags was canceled when the vehicle was discovered in the driveway.

BSO crime scene detectives James Kammerer and John Alderton arrived.

11:09 P.M.

Robert Marseco was a narcotics detective, working undercover with Det. Gary Sylvestri. When they were called to the Decker house, they had been surveilling a nearby shopping mall parking lot (not Xtra), watching for small marijuana and cocaine transactions. As a result, they had arrived at the scene relatively quickly. Marseco had been inside the house and was the first to search the upstairs loft bedroom, accessible only by a ladder. It had been undisturbed.

After a while, it appeared to Marseco that he was only making the house more crowded, so he requested to go outside, where he walked to the edge of the long driveway leading to the house. When Carter spotted him standing there, she brought over Panoyan, who introduced himself as Charles.

While Marseco and Mize talked with Panoyan, Kelly Woodroof walked out of the house toward Mize's police car. The Drixoral he had taken two hours earlier made him thirsty. Since he didn't want to disturb anything in the house, the only water available was a gallon jug Mize kept for his dog. All night Woodroof would borrow the dog's tepid water.

On his way past Mize, Woodroof briefly talked to Panoyan. At that point, police still didn't have the names of the victims. Panoyan furnished him with that, then asked whether they were all right and if he could go inside the house. Woodroof told Panoyan he couldn't cross the crime scene tape, and didn't respond to how the victims were.

Panoyan continued talking with Marseco for about fifteen minutes. To Marseco, Panoyan appeared frightened. He said he was a friend of the people in the house, and he had been inside, in the living room watching television, when a six-foot tall man wearing a mask, gloves, and a cowboy hat entered the house carrying a .22. Beyond that description, Panoyan couldn't answer whether the man was white or black, nor estimate his weight.

"I thought it was a Halloween joke," Panoyan told Mize. "I started laughing." Halloween had been the previous weekend.

But then the assailant had pulled back the hammer of his pistol. He ordered everyone to lie down on the living room floor, then tied them all up. Then he led them all into the bedroom, where he further tied and handcuffed them all. But for some unknown reason, the assailant later removed Panoyan's handcuffs, untied him, then told him to leave.

But before he did, the masked man threatened him. Panoyan quoted him: "I know where you live and I have your family under surveillance."

"How did he know where you live?" Marseco asked.

"I don't know. He took my wallet," said Panoyan.

Panoyan asked Marseco a few times to let him call his wife. When Marseco walked away, he set in motion an order to send an officer to check on Panoyan's family.

Marseco told Lt. James Wollschlager, the shift supervisor, that Panoyan might be of value. Marseco repeated some of what he had said, including the reference that the assailant had been wearing a cowboy hat. Marseco himself had seen a cowboy hat in the room where Donna Decker's body lay.

Listening in were detectives Dennis Mocarski, Robert Spence, and William Coyne. Wollschlager ordered Spence and Coyne to take Panoyan to the police station in their unmarked Chevy Cavalier and interview him there.

Spence and Coyne had been the last two Davie detectives to arrive on the scene, at 11:18 P.M. Assigned to burglary investigations, they had worked a full day until 9 P.M., then had gone to dinner together.

Before the two men talked to Panoyan, they toured the crime scene and saw the body. Coyne noticed a Burger King bag full of food sitting on the kitchen counter. It would strike him later as suggesting a problem.

As Spence ushered Panoyan into his car, Panoyan spotted Carl Fitzgerald, a Davie officer he knew.

"Please call my wife. Carl Fitzgerald is my neighbor. Have him go to my house immediately," he pled with Spence.

After midnight, Officer Bob Frank did visit Panoyan's house, which was about ten miles from the Deckers. First he rang the doorbell, but no one answered. Then Panoyan's wife Darla, apparently watching, pulled up in the driveway behind the patrol car. She told Frank that her husband had called and told her to drive down the street and wait for police to arrive.

"Is everything all right?" she asked.

Frank told her about the shooting, although he didn't know many details.

"Was my husband involved?"

"He was there."

"Is he a suspect?"

"I don't know anything more than that," he said.

It didn't seem that anything had been disturbed at Panoyan's house, but Frank took a look around. Back sitting in his vehicle, talking to Darla, Sgt. Richard Rein—who had just come on duty during the midnight "Charlie" shift—called on the police radio and asked whether Frank had made contact with Darla.

"Don't tell her anything about the case. Her husband will phone her later," Rein said. Unknown to him, Darla heard that.

11:10 P.M. and after
Inside the house

Broward Sheriff's Office crime scene detectives Kammerer and Alderton's job was to document everything in detail of possible crime-solving value in and around the house. Their job was to be detached, not to make crime-solving conclusions.

Their task would take the next six hours. They began by inspecting the scene with Woodroof, who briefed them on what police knew. Then Alderton began looking for latent fingerprints, while Kammerer collected evidence and shot still pictures. In addition, BSO Deputy Robert Cerat shot video and sketched the crime scene.

Methodically, they started from the outside of the house, noticing no evidence of forced entry. On the otherwise clean kitchen table they noted a brown paper Xtra grocery bag with four six-packs of Bud Light cans, one six-pack of Miller Lite cans, and a bottle of Riunite wine. Next to it was the Burger King bag and a woman's brown and beige Gucci purse, its contents apparently dumped on the table. There was no wallet to be found.

In the main hallway leading to the front door, they found blood spatter on two walls, the front door, and the floor. The master bedroom closet, filled with clothes, had a corner of its carpet pulled up, revaling a Hayman floor safe built into the concrete floor. The safe was closed.

Besides the blood and shattered dentures on the bed in the master bedroom, there was also a box of papers and a closed photo album. On the floor were two leather belts, a bloody beige rope, a bloody brown sock lying on top of two manila file folders, a black jewelry purse, and two black straps apparently used to restrain the victims. There was also a pink-sheeted pillow with holes in it.

There were also bloodstains on the red carpet as well as in a blue jewelry box in an open drawer of the console bed. Elsewhere on the floor was a white analog alarm clock—showing the time of 6:31—and a Clairol makeup mirror, both with electrical cords that had been cut. The cradle of a white Cobra cordless phone was on the nightstand, but the handset itself was missing. Two of the three nightstand drawers, filled with rummaged clothes, were open.

Once observations were completed, Kammerer began collecting evidence. From the driveway he took the shotgun. On the chance that some of the blood might be from a wound to a suspect, he cut out bloody carpet squares from the master bedroom and the main hallway, and took a blood-soaked piece of an envelope and the bloody Panasonic telephone receiver from the hall closet. From the living room he collected some yellow rope and a check stub in the amount of $2,344.33. From the bedroom he picked up the denture fragments, the bloody sock, one of the belts, and the two black straps. He also took the clock, makeup mirror, and a cut plastic flexcuff—a thin plastic strip often used by police as disposable handcuffs. Later he also took into evidence the pair of metal handcuffs that Bob Decker had been wearing, after they were cut off at the hospital.

When Kammerer was done, he joined Alderton in dusting for fingerprints with black powder and a brush. That method won them five latents—two from the inside of closet doors in the master bedroom and three from a tall smoked drinking glass sitting on a pink file cabinet in the closet where Donna Decker was found. The prints were unidentified at the scene.

*   *   *

Outside the house, beyond the crime scene tape, the newspaper and TV press gathered in the postmidnight hours. For the press, the timing of the murder was bad; it had happened too late for TV to cover it live on the Friday night 11 o'clock news, and the deadlines had passed as well for the Saturday editions of the big morning papers—*The Miami Herald* and *Fort Lauderale Sun-Sentinel.* Instead, the story would break first in the area's least significant paper, a six-day morning daily called the *Hollywood Sun-Tattler,* which had the latest deadline because of their smaller press run and delivery area.

At 1:07 A.M., Assistant Broward County Medical Examiner Dr. James Ongley arrived to examine the body. No one had touched her in the three hours since Sgt. Allen and paramedic Ron Vargo had both felt for her nonexistent pulse. When Ongley lifted her, detectives watching, the scene was even more shocking. Blood had drenched the right side of the back of her dress encircling what looked like a knife cut. There was a similar cut on her lower left side, and almost as much blood. What seemed like a safe guess was that the cuts were made with the bloody wood-handled knife found on the carpet underneath her. On closer examination, the rusty knife had a brand name: "Old Homestead." Later it would be identified as belonging to the Deckers' kitchen.

At 2:40 A.M., Donna Decker's body was transported to the medical examiner's office.

◆ THREE

CHARLES PANOYAN
11:30 P.M.

Spence and Coyne drove Panoyan to the Davie police station, but they didn't turn on their tape recorder until almost two hours later. They took only a few basic notes of the preliminary interview, just Panoyan's full name—Charles Zarah Panoyan; his date and place of birth—October 31, 1940 in Beirut, Lebanon; and his current address, phone number, and wife's name.

Spence also asked if he had ever been arrested. Panoyan said he had been, four times; for grand theft auto, grand theft, carrying a concealed firearm, and shoplifting. (However, when police checked Panoyan's name on the FBI's National Crime Information Computer—a teletype—they found nothing. A possible explanation is that the NCIC system is notoriously incomplete, nor would they have shown if Panoyan was a juvenile at the time of those arrests.)

They quickly learned that Panoyan—this short and stubby man—was not someone who would answer a question in a sentence when the equivalent of a short story would do. Given his nervous, sweaty, and upset condition, the detectives must have wondered whether he would ever stop talking.

They turned on the tape at 1:22 A.M. Spence instructed him: "What I need you to do now is go back and explain to us what happened from the very beginning. Start from the time you got up today."

That was Panoyan's cue. He rattled off a monologue neither officer could stop.

"I got up today at 6:30 I guess, I went to work, I was

24

there at 7:30, I saw Bob and Grandpa Decker and I started painting, and while I was painting, Bob took my hat and put it in the paint and I took some ice cold water, threw it on him and he says, 'That's it, go home, you're fired!' " Panoyan laughed.

"I said, 'You can't fire me,' I says, 'I'm the owner of the company!' or something to that effect and he says, 'You're going home!' and I says, 'Okay, if I go home, I won't come back!' I says, 'Let me have my paycheck and I'll leave now.' And he says, 'Well, I don't have any money now.' He says, 'I'll pay you at 12:00,' I says, 'Okay, I'll work 'til 12.'

"So between that time we were name calling each other—just, you know, what we always do." He laughed again.

"And Bob took off, he said he was going to the bank. Grandpa Decker and I were talking about deer huntin' and I was still painting and I told him I'd be over tonight and bring him some deer meat, you know, tonight, he said, 'Okay.'

"And then I said, 'Bob, are you coming into work tomorrow [Saturday]?' He said, 'No, I'm taking a vacation.' I says, 'A vacation? What are you talking about?' And he said, 'Well, I just sold this place and I'm taking a vacation.'

"I said, 'Well, that's great. Well, what did you get for it?' He said, '$110,000' and I said, 'Man, that's fine' and he said he bought another lot and would be at work Monday morning.

"I says, 'Well, okay,' I says, 'How about 100? I want to put it in the bank.' He says 'Okay.' He gave me a hundred and, ah, he hadn't gotten paid yet, he wouldn't get paid 'til Monday. And so, ah, ah—I grabbed the hair on his chest and I reached back and I pulled it and I took off running and when I took off running I dropped a $100 bill and I went home, you know, I just started to drive off, I realized the $100 bill was gone and I said, 'Bob, where's my $100?'

"He had a big grin on his face and he said, 'What $100?' And I said, 'Well, you know what $100, the $100 that I lost!' Then he said, 'You didn't lose $100,' I says, 'I did too!' I said, 'Well, look, I gotta get to the bank, give me 100 bucks.' He gave me 100 bucks and said he'd pay me the rest Monday, and I said, 'Fine.'

"So I took off, went home, got cleaned up, got all the paint off of me, took the deer meat out of the freezer, went down to see Bob, he came in about—I came in about two minutes or a minute—he just practically pulled in, the engine was just turned off when he came in and we talked for about two or three minutes outside.

"Then I went into the house, and he went in the house first. He turned the alarm off, I went into the house, we sat down, we talked, he told me to keep away from him and I says, 'What do you mean, keep away from ya?' And he says, 'Just don't touch me' and I says, 'What do you mean?' I said, 'Don't touch *me!*' We started talking and we were laughing and joking and he said, 'Does your wife know you're here?'" Panoyan laughed again.

"I says, 'No,' and he says, 'Well, I'm going to call her!' and I says, 'Well, call her!'

"She wasn't home and I talked to the baby, to Jamie Lynn, and she says, 'What are you doing?' And I said, 'I'm gonna—I'll be working.' Bob went into the other room and answered his answering machine.

"He was in there and fooling around and then I started talking to Bob and he was ignoring me and I says, 'Bob, what are you doing ignoring me?' And he just had a blank look on his face and I heard some low talking in the back and I says, 'Speak up, Grandpa, I can't hear ya.'

"And there was still low talking and I could tell something was wrong, because the look on Bob's face.

"And I turned around and I saw this guy pointing a gun at Grandpa Decker and I said—well, I didn't say anything, I looked at Bob and Bob looked at me and we cracked up laughing. And the guy said something, I couldn't hear what he was saying, but he cocked the gun and when he cocked the gun we stopped laughing.

"He told us to get on the floor, and we got on the floor, he handcuffed me, he handcuffed the rest of us and took us into the bedroom, tied us up, took me out, tied me—tied my feet, and Donna came home when *Dallas* was on and she said, 'Hi,' and I said, 'Hi,' and she said, 'Where's Bob?'

"And I said, 'He's in the other room,' and she says, 'What's wrong with you?' And this other guy came in and he told her to freeze or do something and he took her into another room—it wasn't the bedroom—and came back in with me, hog-tied me, tied my hands, my feet, put it around my neck and went back in the other room.

"I tried to get loose, couldn't get loose—he came back to me, took, well, everything out of my pockets and he said, ah, what did he say? He said, 'We know where you live' and he started untying me and then he took the handcuffs off and he says, 'You go straight home, you're being followed, you're being watched.'

"I said, 'Okay.' I got in my truck, took off—while I was driving away I was looking around to see who was following me, I didn't see a soul following me, didn't see any lights, nothing!

"I pulled into that store and I notified a policeman or a guard and I told him there was a robbery in progress and I don't know if I'm being followed or not, but I've gotta call my wife, and he says, 'Yeah, go ahead.' I said, 'I don't have any money. Do you got a quarter I can borrow?'

"And he gave me a quarter, I called my wife, told her to get out of the house and call the police immediately, and she said 'Why?' and I said, 'Do what I told ya.'

"Then the police came, they said, 'What was happening?' and I told them there was a robbery going on at my friends' house and she said, 'What's his address?' I told them I didn't know, but I could tell ya how to get there and we told her how to get there and I seen an ambulance coming one way, passing us up, and she says, 'I think I know where we're going.'

"And I said, 'What are they doing?' And she said she didn't know and then when I got there, the place was swarming with people. I started to go up to the house and they told me I couldn't go in there and I said, 'Why?' And they didn't tell me, just then they took out somebody in the ambulance and I says, 'Who's he?'

"And I went to look and they told me 'No' and I went to look anyway and I couldn't tell who the person was. And then I waited in the police car until you guys came and then I came with you."

If ever a story raised more questions than it answered, it was this one. Coyne started him again at the beginning, just before they all walked into the house.

"Where was Grandpa?" asked Coyne.

"Him and I were outside with the baby looking at a toad and laughing at the toad, because the toad couldn't jump," answered Panoyan.

"Were they all in the car together when they got there?"

"Yeah. In fact, we were all standing outside for about five minutes, talking, looking at the toad."

"Did they say where Donna was at that time?"

"She was at work. She's a hairdresser and she works at, ah—Penney's on Hollywood Boulevard."

"You said when Donna came home, you were in the living room and you were already tied up," said Spence.

"Right," said Panoyan.

"And she just said hello?"

"Yeah, she didn't know I was tied up."

"Oh, okay. Were you sitting or were you standing?"

"I was sitting, my hands were behind me and my feet were tied and she said, 'Hi, Chuck' and I said, 'Hi,' and she said, 'Where's Bob?' And I said, 'In the other room.' "

"You didn't try to warn her that you were being robbed?" asked Coyne.

"I—this guy had a gun there. I started to say something and I looked up and I seen a shadow and I says, 'Man.' "

"Where was he at when Donna came home?" asked Spence.

"He was in the hallway."

"And she came into the living room?"

"Right."

"And is that when he approached her?"

"Right."

"Did she scream or anything?"

"No, didn't say a word."

"Did she try to run off?"

"No, she didn't do a thing, she did everything that guy told her to do. He took her into another room and I know it wasn't the bedroom. It was either the bathroom or utility room, I don't know."

"Okay, what did he tell Donna to do, do you remember?"

"No. I didn't hear nothing after."

"You didn't hear anything after he got her and took her to the other room?" asked Coyne.

"Right. The only thing I heard was doors opening and closing. I did hear a kidnapping, I did hear that."

"What do you mean by a kidnapping?"

"Well, I heard something kidnapping, I mean it's just a blur."

"You mean somebody saying something about kidnapping?"

"Right."

"Was that television on also, this whole time?"

"Yeah. *Dallas* was on."

"Was it on the TV you heard the kidnapping or was it somebody else?"

"I have no idea."

"You were sitting in the living room. Where were the other two guys?"

"In the bedroom."

"And why do you think you were taken out of the bedroom from them?"

"I have no idea."

"He didn't say anything?"

"He didn't tell me a word."

"Well, how did he tell you to go back out?"

"He grabbed ahold of me!"

"And what did he say?"

"I think he said, 'Come here.' I don't know."

"All right, so when all of you were originally in the living room when he first came in and he pointed the gun at you, did he say anything?"

"He wasn't talking, he was mumbling, he was whispering. I don't know exactly what he said. I followed whatever everybody did."

Spence returned the interview to the moment after the gunman took Donna.

"Okay. And then what happened after that, after you saw him take her in there?"

"Oh, he came back in here, he tied my hands, my feet, my neck."

"He tied your hands and feet up after he took her?"

"I was in the chair tied first, with my hands behind me. After he took her in the other room he came back, laid me down, tied my feet behind my back and put a rope around my neck and that's where I stayed.''

"Did you hear any gunshots at all?''

"I didn't hear a sound.''

"Anybody screaming?''

"No.''

"How long before he came back out of the room and back to you? Five minutes?''

"I don't know.''

"It was a long time, short time?''

"It seemed like a long time.''

"Then he came back out to you?''

"Yeah, he came back out to me, took everything out of my pockets, went through my wallet, didn't say a word to me and then he says, 'We got your house under surveillance.' I remember that word. He says, 'You do everything I tell you to do.' He says nothing was going to happen. He told me to get in my truck and drive straight home.' ''

"How did he know you had a truck?'' asked Coyne.

"Huh?''

"How did he know you had a truck?''

"My truck was there.''

"So were the car and the van.''

"Well, I don't know.''

"Okay, it's fine,'' spoke up Spence.

"He told me to get in, well, he said, 'Get in my truck.' ''

"Somehow he knew, right?''

"Yeah, he said, 'Get in my truck.' ''

"Okay. Then you left.''

"Then I left.''

"And you didn't see anybody following you.''

"That's what got me to wondering.''

"You expected somebody to be following you?''

"Car and lights. I expected lights. I went down the street, I turned and I kept looking, kept looking, didn't see a soul. I turned down the other street, kept looking, didn't see a thing and I says, 'Man, nobody's following me.' And then I see another, I did see lights but it wasn't coming from anywhere, where I had been turning. It was farther on down the road.''

"You're a hunter, right?'' asked Coyne.

"Yes."

"Handle guns all your life?"

"Yes."

"Pretty familiar with them?"

"Yes."

"Was the gun an automatic or a revolver?"

"Which one?"

"The gun he had."

"It was a revolver."

"Do you know about what caliber?"

"Twenty-two."

"How long was the barrel?"

"Four to six inches."

"Do you know if he had it in his right hand or left hand?"

"I didn't notice."

Panoyan recalled the phone call to his wife, Darla.

"All I told her was to get out of the house and she said, 'Why?' And I said, 'Somebody's probably watching the house,' but I wasn't sure. I said, 'Get the kids and get out.' "

"Okay, you called your wife again from here, right?" asked Spence.

"I told her to get out of the house and she says, 'Are you in trouble?' And I says, 'No, I'm not in trouble.' I says, 'I think *you* are.' And she said, 'Why?'

"I said, 'Is the police there?' And she said, 'Yes, they have gone.' I says, 'What do you mean gone?' I says, 'I want you out of the house.' And she says, 'What's going on?' And I says, 'I don't know.' "

"And she said, 'Somebody's been killed and ah, four or five people shot.' And I says, 'Who's been killed and who's been shot?' And she said she didn't know but the police officer said not to tell her anything.

"As far as I know right now one person's dead and four to five people are shot. I wish you'd ask her. She knows more about this than me."

Panoyan described the "masked man" as having a big build, about 6'1" to 6'3", two hundred pounds, wearing a stocking mask Panoyan believed was like women's nylon hose, dark clothing, dark long-sleeve shirt, dark brown gloves, and a white cowboy hat. But he couldn't tell whether he wore glasses or not, if he had facial hair, nor could he describe the man's accent. And he still didn't know if the man was white or black.

Panoyan tried to shift the interview to a man named "Warren," against whom Bob Decker had recently filed a police report. Warren had worked with Decker and Panoyan on a job site and had stolen a refrigerator, Decker had said in the complaint.

"About a year ago, Grandpa was talking about the riffraff [Bob] had working for him and said, 'It's a wonder Bob was still alive.' And I says, 'What are you talking about?' And he says, 'He works with a scurvy bunch.' And I said, 'You're calling me scurvy?' " Panoyan laughed. "And he says, 'No,' but he was just saying that Bob works with a rough bunch."

The cops wanted to come back to the events in the house. "You never saw but one person?" asked Coyne.

"Right," said Panoyan.

Panoyan described how the masked man restrained them all. He used handcuffs on Panoyan and the adult Deckers, as well as a "rough barby rope" on him. "It was about as big around as my baby finger and it had rough barbs on it," Panoyan said. "It was very, very rough. I kept feeling prickles, you know, sticking. It was rough like your mustache," he said, referring to Spence.

He said the assailant tied up Grandpa Decker first.

"He tied him up first, a seventy-six-year-old man?" asked Coyne, somewhat incredulously.

"Right. Right."

"And there was you and a thirty-five to thirty-six-year-old man in the room?"

"Right."

"But he tied the oldest one up first?"

"He was closest to him."

"Did he ever tie up the baby?"

"No. The baby was just as good as could be. He just did what we did."

Panoyan said the assailant tied up Bob and Clyde's feet in the bedroom, then Coyne asked how he did it. "You talk about one guy holding a gun with one hand on three people."

"You got it."

Then came a slip that indicated where Coyne's head was going. Perhaps it was intentional.

"What did you do with the gun?" he asked Panoyan, who seemed to have missed the question completely.

"Okay, well, what did he tell you? Did he tell you to sit or you just sat?"

"He pushed me down. He grabbed me by my hands and yanked me down and he grabbed—he pushed Bob down, he pushed Grandpa down."

"And all of you were handcuffed or tied up?"

"We were handcuffed and he started tying us."

"Three pairs of handcuffs?"

"Right. Bob and I were looking at each other. I couldn't see Grandpa, he was up on the bed. Bob and I—I think were on the floor."

Coyne pressed him on where the rope came from to tie the Deckers. Panoyan remembered that the assailant didn't use rope exclusively. In the closet he had found a suitcase strap and a blue or black cloth bathrobe belt. He used the cloth to tie up Grandpa.

Then the assailant yanked Panoyan up, hurting his wrist, and led him back into the living room, alone. That's when Donna came home.

"Where are you at?" asked Coyne.

"I'm sitting in the chair that I was originally sitting in."

"Okay, and what did he say to you?"

"He . . . he didn't say nothing to me. I saw the shadow of him with, ah, the gun pointing in my direction."

After the assailant took Donna and returned to Panoyan, he put him on his stomach, then tied his feet and hands with a single piece of rope, so that if he moved his legs he would choke himself. That was what he had meant by "hog-tied." Then the assailant left again.

"Well, what was he doing at that time?"

"Doors were opening and closing, that's about all."

"Did you hear any voices?"

"I didn't hear a sound."

"Then after that, what happened?"

"After that he came out and took everything out of my pockets, told me that my house is being watched, and I was being watched, to do exactly like I said and I wouldn't get hurt and he told me to go straight home, that I was being followed or watched. I drove out, backed up, drove out . . ."

"Did you see any cars?"

"I . . . I wasn't looking for cars. I was looking for lights."

"Well, when you got out to get in your car, you had to walk by cars, right, to get to yours?"

"I didn't see anything. You know, come to think about it, I was looking around too. I mean I was looking around to see who was following me."

"So you're out there looking to see if anybody's watching you . . ."

"I was out there, I mean, what I was doing was seeing if . . . if ah—I don't think, that's it, I don't remember if I— when I got in my truck that's when I felt safe."

"What happened to the meat? You said you brought some meat over tonight. What did you do with it?"

"He put it in the freezer."

"Who did that? Grandpa?"

"Yeah."

By 2:25 A.M., when the detectives finished taking the rambling statement, the investigation had found its focus: Charles Panoyan.

Coyne and Spence both felt that Panoyan knew more than he was saying. At the least they thought Panoyan was lying when he said he hadn't seen or known of the murder and the shootings.

Coyne returned to the Burger King bag, which had stuck out in his mind when he toured the crime scene. It had been neatly placed on the kitchen counter—not at all consistent with Donna Decker walking in on a crime in progress. If Panoyan was tied up on the couch, like he said, how could she not have seen that? The alternative explanation was that Panoyan had *not* been bound.

But most mysterious of all, why would someone let Panoyan go unharmed while attempting to murder the other four—including the baby? Especially if Panoyan was a witness?

It wasn't a normal home invasion, Coyne thought. There was something personal going on between the assailant and the victims. Just the manner in which the Decker males were shot—execution style, in the back of the head—implied this was a retaliation for something.

After the statement ended, Dennis Mocarski asked Panoyan if he would sign a consent to allow police to search his truck. The one-page waiver stated that he had the right to refuse to sign it and therefore demand that police obtain a search warrant. Panoyan signed and dated the page, noting the time as 2:25 A.M.

11:10 P.M. and after
At Xtra

In order to preserve the integrity of any evidence that might be found in Panoyan's truck, Sergeant Allen wanted to establish a chain of observance on it. He asked Jo Ann Carter to return to the Xtra parking lot. She got there within a few minutes of 11:10 P.M. Almost at the same time, Officer David Pavone arrived there too.

The truck—a dark blue 1979 Ford Club Cab in junkyard condition—was unevenly parked in an angle space not far from a lightpost. Carter looked inside the truck from the passenger side with her flashlight. Nothing in particular caught her attention, beyond the clutter of papers, trash, and odds and ends inside it. With Pavone there as well, she soon after left the scene and went back to her off-duty detail at Scarborough.

At about 3 A.M., Spence arrived at Xtra with the Consent to Search. Other Davie officers were there too. Inside the pickup, lying partly over the edge of the front passenger seat, he found a black nylon web gunbelt with a number of pouches. Sergeant Richard Rein, in charge of Davie's SWAT team, recognized the belt as similar to ones his SWAT team used.

When Spence took the belt and opened its pouches, he found two unusually shaped handcuff keys. They didn't fit his police-issue cuffs because they were too large. Spence took his find into Property. Back at the police station, detectives deliberately kept mention of it away from Panoyan.

At 4:20 A.M., Woodroof and Mocarski read Panoyan his Miranda rights regarding self-incrimination. At that point, it would be fair to say that the witness officially turned suspect.

Panoyan allowed himself to be further interviewed without an attorney present, and mostly repeated what he had told Spence and Coyne. However, these statements were not taped.

Panoyan did add a few details. After leaving work he had gone to Eastern Air Lines credit union, where he and his wife had an account; his wife worked for Eastern. However, the office was closed. From there he went home, made a few phone calls, went grocery shopping to buy dinner, then returned home. He recalled taking a shower, scolding his son for some misconduct and grounding him, then leaving again.

He also remembered that the masked man took Clyde Decker's wallet as he was handcuffing him. When the assailant asked Bob where his wallet was, Bob said it was in the safe. At that point the assailant took them all into the bedroom.

Sgt. Taylor ordered around-the-clock police guards at each hospital for the Deckers, believing they might still be in danger from their assailant once he found out that only one of the four was dead. Dr. Ongley, who had worked as a medical examiner in Miami, said he had seen this type of family homicide before. They were always drug hits, done by Colombians. He didn't know of anyone else who shot children point-blank.

When a fourth BSO crime scene detective, William Hawley, reported to the crime scene, he was sent out to photograph the surviving victims. At 12:31 A.M. he photographed baby Carl at Plantation General Hospital; then at 1:02 he took Bob Decker's picture at Humana Hospital Bennett; and then at 2:15 Clyde Decker's at Memorial Hospital in Hollywood. Responding back to the crime scene, Kammerer then sent Hawley to the Davie police station, where he photographed Panoyan at 3:49.

At Humana Hospital Bennett, emergency room doctors had Bob Decker awake and stable all night, although he wasn't talking very coherently; but then in the morning he suddenly deteriorated. Dr. Gary Gieseke decided he needed surgery immediately in case he had a blood clot.

Gieseke was right. He found a large vein that was bleeding. He removed bone fragments that had been driven into the brain, as well as the two bullets and a small metal fragment that had broken off from one. After the surgery, Gieseke handed the evidence in a clear plastic container to a Davie police officer who had stationed himself outside the door, watching the operation.

A cranial scan proved that Carl had been shot. The bullet, below his right ear in the back of the head, had broken into two pieces. Because Plantation General was unequipped to do neurosurgery, he was quickly transferred to Memorial Hospital in Hollywood.

On arrival at Memorial, Carl didn't seem to be in any distress, which had confused police and EMS workers. He was able to answer what his name was and how old he was. What was truly unbelievable was that a two and a half year old could even survive a point-blank gunshot. He did have some facial palsy on his right side. But when Memorial doctors reviewed the cranial scan, they decided surgery was riskier than doing nothing.

Woodroof had sent Det. Killam to the hospital to see if Bob Decker could talk. When Killam found he couldn't, Woodroof sent him to Memorial to see if Clyde Decker could say anything.

At 12:20 A.M., Killam found Clyde alert and in relatively good shape. He was clearly going to make it. But he was scared, and his face looked horrible. The bullet had ripped through the side wall of his nose, causing it to hemorrhage. To stop it, Dr. Robert Contrucci threaded gauze on a catheter through his nose, extending to the back of his nasal cavity.

Contrucci considered his patient lucky that he was found before he bled to death, and that he had been shot with a small caliber bullet; if the bullet had been bigger, or if it hadn't hit his dentures, it would have continued traveling into his brain. Instead, his biggest worry was whether a bullet fragment had contaminated Clyde's central nervous system.

Killam's biggest problem was trying to understand what Clyde was toothlessly mumbling in answer to his questions. All he could get was that the assailant was a white male wearing a stocking.

Killam was fortunate to leave when he did. Minutes after, Clyde sneezed and blew out some of his bullet fragments.

5:25 A.M.

Before Panoyan was allowed to go home, Woodroof and Mocarski asked for his boots. They had numerous splashes of
color on them that the detectives thought the crime lab should
check for blood. In the warm dawn air, Panoyan's wife drove
him home in his stocking feet.

6 A.M.

Sgt. Taylor led a briefing at the station before finally sending
his exhausted men home. They were already stretched far,
but it was likewise clear to everyone that their work was just
beginning. Sgt. Allen vocalized what everyone knew: that
this was one of the most violent, most challenging crime
scenes they had ever witnessed. But Woodroof disagreed with
him that it was a professional hit. If it were, why were three
shooting victims still alive?

Taylor made his assignments; all other priorities were to
be dropped. Dennis Mocarski was to be lead detective and
Woodroof was to work side by side with him. By rotation
among the detectives who handled crimes against persons,
Woodroof would have been designated lead, and in fact, he
had arrived at the scene an hour earlier than Mocarski. But
Mocarski had seventeen years experience as a New York City
cop before coming to Davie, and Woodroof had been a cop
just two years and had only led one homicide investigation
before. (On average, Davie experienced three to seven homicides a year.)

Spence and Coyne were ordered to further canvass the
neighborhood, then rummage through the papers scattered in
the Decker home for clues. Other officers were asked to vol-
unteer for overtime to fill out the 24-hour hospital watch for
each of the injured Deckers.

Then they discussed the problems they had with Charles
Panoyan. As Taylor saw it, the largest was the half hour
between Donna Decker's 911 call from the house and Panoyan's distress call from Xtra. It shouldn't have taken more
than five minutes or so to travel from the house to the shopping center.

Banks called Panoyan's story farfetched. If Panoyan

wanted to get to a phone, he could have pounded on a neighbor's door, and it wouldn't have even taken the few minutes needed to drive to the grocery. "There's no way," he said. "This guy's got something to do with this."

◆ Four

Saturday, November 5
6 A.M.

In the predawn, the first newspaper account of the story hit
the streets. The *Hollywood Sun-Tattler*'s front page had "One
killed, family hurt in Davie."

> Police investigating a domestic disturbance Friday
> night found one woman dead and three family
> members injured at their one-acre estate home in
> western Davie.
> The dead woman was identified as Donna
> Decker.
> She, her husband Bob Decker, about thirty, their
> two-and-a-half-year-old son Carl, and her father-
> in-law Clyde, in his fifties, were transported to
> three area hospitals.
> "This is a very peaceful, quiet area," said Louis
> Leadbetter, a neighbor. "We are all horse people."

7:30 A.M.

Roy Davis, a contractor and long-time mutual friend of both
Bob Decker and Chuck Panoyan, first heard about the murder
at about 7:30, when a plumber who worked for him called.
The plumber had read about it in the *Sun-Tattler*.

Davis called the Decker house to find out more, but the
answering machine picked up. He didn't know who else to
call, so he called Panoyan. Darla answered, and woke up
her husband.

"He told me that what I heard is true, that Donna is dead, and that he had been at the police department all night, they had been questioning him, he had just gotten home and gotten to sleep," Davis said later.

"He said he brought some deer meat over to Bob and that they were all standing there talking when the guy walked in. For some reason the guy brought Chuck back out or took them in the room first and left Chuck out in the living room. He mentioned how he was tied around the neck because as he moved around it would kind of choke him.

"Donna came walking in and she said, 'Hi, Chuck,' and he says, 'Hi, Donna.' She said, 'Where's Bob?' and that's when the guy grabbed Donna."

9:55 A.M.
Humana Hospital Bennett

Officer Leslie Mathis, working the overnight shift, had been assigned by Sgt. Rein to keep watch on Bob Decker at the hospital. He had arrived at 5 A.M. at the Intensive Care Unit and stationed himself outside.

At 9:55 A.M., twenty minutes before Bob Decker was to be transported to the operating room, he received a visitor. Daniel Guerrieri, an attorney, introduced himself as a close friend of the Decker family and said he had read about the shooting in the paper. He wanted to see Bob and "seemed very concerned that the police might be asking Decker questions," Mathis wrote. Mathis turned him away.

11:30 A.M.

Normally the lead detective drew the disagreeable assignment of attending the autopsy, but this time Kelly Woodroof, on two hours sleep, got it.

BSO deputy Bob Cerat was present as well. His job was not only to photograph the body but to gather any hair or fabric fibers that her assailant might have left. For comparison he took a hair sample from her head. He also clipped her fingernails; sometimes the crime lab found microscopic amounts of a killer's skin taken when a victim scratched him in self-defense.

In addition, Cerat took Donna's fingerprints, removed her clothing for evidence, then processed her skin for prints, using magnetic powder and a "magnetic wand." The results were negative.

Dr. Ongley, who had performed about 3,000 autopsies in five years on the job, counted six major stab wounds to Donna's five-foot, 100-pound body, plus a few minor ones. Three of them caused the most external bleeding—two to her left upper arm and one to the left side of her chest, which penetrated her lung.

Two other wounds to her back caused severe internal bleeding. One, on her upper right, deeply penetrated her lung and sternum; a second to her lower right back tore the liver and kidney.

Ongley guessed that she died from loss of blood four or five minutes after the stabbing. He couldn't say for how much of that time she had been conscious.

She was thirty-seven years old.

Late morning
Panoyan home

While Charles Panoyan slept, Darla noticed a strange car parked outside the window of their house. That was unusual because their home was so far out in the country; cars never parked alongside the road. She tried to shake her husband out of his deep slumber to tell him, but she was unsuccessful. Then she left the house with the kids.

He was awake an hour and a half later when their daughter Sharla asked him again about the car, which was still there. He walked outside toward it, and it took off.

But the car came back, parked only a bit further away. This time, Panoyan grabbed his hunting rifle in case he'd have to use it. In his car, he chased the surveilling car onto a main road where it wove through traffic to get away.

A few minutes later, Panoyan was amazed to see the car again. This time he called police; he lived in unincorporated Broward County, so the sheriff's office had jurisdiction. An officer arrived, talked to the car's driver, then told Panoyan that the car was just waiting for someone. Again the car left.

Incredibly, after the officer left, the car returned once more. This time Panoyan approached it with his gun drawn. Inside the car, an unshaven, casually dressed man pulled out his badge. He was Davie Det. Ron Marseco. He and Panoyan had talked together at the foot of the Decker driveway the night before.

Late morning
Humana Hospital Bennett

While Woodroof watched the autopsy, Dennis Mocarski arrived at Humana Hospital Bennett. He had hoped that Bob Decker would be in condition to talk, but instead he discovered he was in surgery. Mocarski left soon after.

12 noon
Near the Decker house

Det. Spence's canvassing of the neighborhood was largely unsuccessful. No one living next door or across the street from the Deckers had heard anything unusual or could provide any information.

However, while Spence was standing on the street in front of the Decker house, Daniel Metrick drove by and offered a tidbit. At about 7 P.M. the night before, he had seen Bernie Napolitano parked in a dead end two blocks away. He was alone, sitting in a small, white compact car. That was strange, Metrick thought, because Napolitano usually drove a white pickup.

Spence found Napolitano near his white Mitsubishi pickup, and asked what he was doing there the night before. He said he owned two acres of undeveloped land where the road came to a dead end, and that he was with his girlfriend in her car, feeding his horses. He had just finished doing some work on the property.

Napolitano told Spence that he hadn't seen or heard anything unusual that night. Spence noticed that Napolitano, a forty-seven-year-old man, fit the physical description they had of the gunman.

5:00 P.M.
Hollywood Memorial Hospital

The prognosis was improving for Clyde Decker, Bob's seventy-six-year-old father. The hospital had called Davie PD in the afternoon and told them Clyde would be able to speak to detectives. Mocarski and Woodroof rushed there once they heard the news. As would be the case for all the interviews they did together, Mocarski asked most of the questions, and Woodroof took notes.

They asked him to recount the evening from the beginning. Clyde remembered Panoyan—whom he referred to as "our hired help"—waiting in the driveway when they arrived home from dinner. Bob went in the house first, then Chuck, then Clyde and baby Carl.

After sitting and talking in the living room for a short while, Panoyan announced, "I better go get that venison and put it in the cooler," then he went outside.

"He came on in and handed it to me and I took it and I put it in the freezer. Well, then we came back out, sat down and was visiting. In they walked through the hallway," he said.

Despite his use of the word "they" Clyde described a single assailant as five and a half to six feet tall, solid build, 165 pounds, wearing a tight-fitting gray mask, a gray hat with a round rim, blue jeans, and a gray shirt or jacket. Unlike Panoyan, Clyde was certain the man had white skin.

The masked man ordered them all to lie face down, then with one hand holding his gun, used his other hand to handcuff first Clyde, then Chuck, then Bob. Clyde said Carl wasn't cuffed, but he was tied with white clothesline.

"Did it seem like Chuck or your son knew this individual?" asked Mocarski.

"Noooo, they kept looking at him. My son, I knew the way he looked at him that he didn't know him. And Chuck, I don't know."

"Hmmhhmm," reacted Mocarski.

Clyde said the gunman next took them into the bedroom,

one by one. "He took my son first in, laid him right beside the bed on the floor on his back, then tied his feet. He tied him up good and then he come and got Carl, took him and tied him to his feet."

"He tied Carl to your son's feet?"

"Yeah. Then he come and got me. But when he come out he asked me where I slept. Well, I usually slept up in the loft. There's a loft overhead by the fireplace. He says, 'Well, you come on in here. Get up on that bed.' He throwed me on the bed."

"Where was Chuck at this time?" asked Mocarski.

"Chuck was out in the chair with the handcuffs on. He told him to get up and get in the chair. I didn't see no more of him after that."

"Was he ever brought into the bedroom whatsoever?"

"No."

"He was never brought into your son's bedroom?"

"No."

That directly contradicted what Panoyan had told police little more than twelve hours before. It obviously didn't escape Mocarski and Woodroof.

Mocarski asked if they could, from the bedroom, see Chuck sitting on the chair.

"No, we couldn't. It was just far enough over."

"Could Chuck see into the bedroom from where he was sitting?"

"Ah, not too much, no. No, very little from where he was sitting. Well, he couldn't see in there at all, really."

Clyde said the gunman ransacked the bedroom drawers, stuffing jewelry into his pocket. He couldn't tell what the gunman was doing when he was outside the bedroom, but he remembered slamming noises from the rest of the house.

He also recalled he demanded Bob sign a paper he brought in from another room. To sign it, he had to remove one of Bob's handcuffs. In fact, minutes later, the same exercise was repeated. But Clyde didn't know what was on either paper.

"Was he saying anything to you at that time?"

"Oh, he was talking away about his—like I say, I'm ah—my hearing. I couldn't get what he was saying."

He remembered when Donna came home. "I looked at my

watch at 9:05 and thought that she could be there then and she would walk into something too.''

Clyde heard her holler ''Bob,'' then he saw her walk into the short hallway leading into the master bedroom. The assailant was in the bedroom and immediately grabbed her. She struggled, screaming the whole time as he put her in the office/closet.

''He tied her up. I don't know whether he tied her up before he put her in there or tied her up in there. I don't know. I couldn't see.''

''Did you hear anything from Chuck at that point?''

''I didn't hear his voice at all.''

The shootings came minutes after the papers were signed. He thought Carl was shot first, then Bob, each one getting two shots apiece.

''Did you hear the shot that you were shot by?''

''Oh yeah. He throwed the pillow right over just before he shot.''

''Was the shot loud?''

''Oh, I don't know. It was quite loud really, but that pillow, you know, muffled it pretty well.''

''After the shots were fired, did you hear anything from Chuck? Were you wondering?''

''Not at all.''

''Not at all,'' Mocarski repeated.

Clyde said he had recently given Bob two thousand dollars in cash for safekeeping.

''Did your son normally keep a large amount of money at home?''

''He done everything pretty much with cash,'' he answered.

Off the tape, Woodroof asked Clyde if his wallet was stolen. No, he said, contrary to what Panoyan had said.

6:25 P.M.
At the crime scene

Richard Ricketts, who had brought his children to the Decker house so they could play on the swings with Carl, was shocked when Officer Tim Alessi told him what had happened. Ricketts said he was Bob's close friend.

Alessi asked Ricketts if he knew anyone who might have forced Bob to sign some paperwork.

Ricketts said Bob had had problems with a black man named Warren in the past three or four weeks. He didn't know Warren's last name, but said he hadn't paid Bob rent, and he had stolen meat from them in the past.

6:45 P.M.

Woodroof and Mocarski returned to Humana Hospital Bennett to check on Bob Decker's condition. He was still unconscious, recovering from surgery. The detectives left their business cards with the head nurse.

7 P.M.
At the crime scene

Twenty-one hours after they were first called to the Decker house, police still controlled the crime scene. In fact, they would stay there for many more days.

BSO crime scene detectives George Miller and James Kammerer arrived at 7. Miller had brought a laser, which would be used to find, then photograph, latent fingerprints. But first he decided to try cyanoacrylate, commonly known as Super Glue. Heated to a gas, the toxic chemical adheres to surfaces and dries as white powder, revealing fingerprints when present.

Using the chemical, Miller, and Kammerer fumed the main entrance hallway, the office/closet, and the bedroom closet. Next, Miller used the laser, scanning with a four-inch diameter band of fluorescent light. He found one print on the front door not otherwise obvious to the naked eye. Kammerer then powdered, photographed, and lifted the print for evidence.

7:45 P.M.

Sharon Dupree and Robert Lee Kibler arrived at the crime scene in a car and said they were friends of the Deckers who had come to take the Deckers' dog George home with them. They said the Deckers had come to dinner at their house just Thursday.

George, a friendly St. Bernard, had been moved from the garage to a long chain in the backyard of the house. Officer Alessi got approval from Sgt. Taylor to allow them take the dog away.

◆ FIVE

Sunday, November 6
9:20 A.M.
Davie police station

Josephine Zazzo, Donna's older sister, told Woodroof on the phone that three pieces of Donna's jewelry were missing. Later, Woodroof issued a statewide BOLO for a half-carat diamond engagement ring, a gold wedding ring, and a pinky ring with diamond chips forming a letter "D." Perhaps some of it might show up at a pawn shop.

3:30 P.M.
Fort Lauderdale International Airport

Sgt. Taylor picked up Detective Gerald Todoroff, who was returning from a seminar. On their way back to the police station, Taylor briefed Todoroff so he could quickly be thrown into the fire.

Todoroff first went to the crime scene, where Mocarski and Woodroof were trying to find some order to the mess of papers strewn about by the intruder. Among other things, Woodroof had found an envelope containing $50 in cash.

Back at the detective bureau late that afternoon, Panoyan called. He had already called a few times before and just wanted to talk. Sgt. Taylor took the call.

"He called and said that he needed to talk to somebody, that he was scared, that he was worried, that he was having a difficult time coping with the stress from everything that had occurred. That he was afraid for his safety and the safety of his family," Taylor later said.

But Taylor was suspicious about Panoyan's motive. "You have to understand, I'm still thinking in my mind I don't know what Mr. Panoyan has done or what part Mr. Panoyan has played in this. I don't know if he has information that he's afraid to tell us. I don't know if he's withholding stuff.

"My concern is that he has information that can help us find the person who committed this. That he may be a legitimate victim himself and witness. That for some reason unknown to me, he's withholding this information," said Taylor.

That evening, Taylor sent Todoroff and Detective Gary Killam to Panoyan's house to talk with him. Todoroff was especially valuable in such a role because, as Taylor put it, "He's a person who's easy to talk to. He also was working on his [advanced] degree in psychology, but he's always had the ability to develop a rapport with people, to put them at ease."

The detectives arrived at 10:15 P.M. and stayed for two hours, talking to Panoyan and Darla. "He kept saying that this bad guy knew where he lived, and he was nervous about that. And by watching his behavior, he was nervous," Todoroff said.

Todoroff tried to reason with him, asking, "Why would they come after you now if they let you go that night?" Panoyan answered that they told him not to talk to the police.

Monday, November 7

"Occupant knew attacker, Davie police now theorize," stated a headlined story in *The Miami Herald*.

A savage attack that left a woman dead and sent three others to the hospital was not a random home invasion, police investigators have concluded.

"This house was chosen for a reason," Davie police spokeswoman Christine Murray said Sunday. "It was not a random hit."

There was a "relationship" between an occupant in the house and the attacker, Murray said, declining to elaborate.

Meanwhile, the newspaper in Donna's hometown of Lawrence, Massachusetts, ran a page one story calling the murder part of a jewel robbery. The *Lawrence Eagle-Tribune* added (though unpublished elsewhere) that Donna's killer intended to shoot her but ran out of bullets.

Morning
Davie Police Department

When Dennis Mocarski reviewed the crime scene videotape, he went "Holy shit!" They had forgotten about the cowboy hat next to Donna Decker. Mocarski asked Sgt. Taylor to have someone go to the house and fetch it for evidence, and Taylor assigned Todoroff and Killam.

9:56 A.M.
Humana Hospital Bennett

By Monday morning, Bob Decker was finally able to speak with police. Once again, detectives Kelly Woodroof and Dennis Mocarski arrived at the intensive care unit of the hospital.

Woodroof thought Bob looked pretty good, considering that a paramedic at the house Friday night had said he didn't think he was going to make it. Still, Bob didn't seem like he was there 100 percent. Not every answer he gave fit the question asked.

The one hour interview wasn't taped, but Woodroof took notes. "Do you know we're police?" Mocarski asked first, to make sure Bob was cognizant. He nodded in agreement.

"Do you know who did this?"

No, Bob said, contradicting what he had said at the scene.

"Do you know why someone did this?"

Again, he said no.

Bob had a question for the detectives. "What happened to Chuck?" he asked.

"He left and got out okay," answered Mocarski. "Do you think Panoyan was involved?"

"From the beginning," Bob said. He explained that he had felt weird about Chuck being there that night. Given a chance to think about it, he thought the gunman might have been

Chuck's electrician—at least their builds were similar, he said.

Bob had only met the electrician once, and believed he worked for either Tole Electric or Total Electric. He thought the man's name was Larry, that he was a long-time friend of Chuck's, and that he was "crazy enough to do something" like this.

Something else was out of the ordinary about Chuck's behavior that night. After the gunman took Bob, his father, and his son—but not Chuck—to the bedroom and tied them up, Bob had managed to hobble as far as the doorway. There he saw the gunman and Chuck talking.

Donna had already been apprehended. Right after that, Bob "could swear" that Chuck left.

Bob described the papers which Clyde had told the detectives he saw Bob forced to sign: they were legal-size white sheets, blank except for four lines drawn in ink and his and Donna's signatures on those lines. The assailant said something to him about taking him "further into court."

"Had you had a falling out with anybody?" asked Mocarski.

No, he said.

Bob said he did owe money to people, but no one was hurting for it. Mocarski asked about a man named Sam McFarland, whose name was on a bloody quitclaim deed found near Donna's body. Bob said he owed McFarland $15,000, but said he was a friend, and the debt hadn't created any serious problem.

But Bob did think that the blank paper was "connected somehow" to the motive for the crime.

All the while, the intruder kept saying he wanted their money and jewelry. He also seemed to know there was a safe in the house and asked where it was. Bob showed it to him, but it was empty—he never kept anything in it, he said.

"Do you think your wife had a boyfriend?" Mocarski asked. No, Bob said. Nor did he have a girlfriend on the side.

Had Donna told him about any threatening phone calls? No, she hadn't, and if there had been any, he was certain she would have said something.

Nor did he know who Bernie Napolitano was.

Mocarski asked who would benefit had all four of the Deckers had been killed, as apparently had been intended.

Bob couldn't give a good answer. He said he had no will, no business associates, and didn't own any property jointly with anyone. His creditors were McFarland and two mortgage agencies. The monthly payments on the mortgages were just $100 and $200.

12:50 P.M.
Hollywood Memorial Hospital

Mocarski and Woodroof revisited Clyde Decker to straighten up a few points. He remembered that the venison had been wrapped in white paper, labeled "steak." The package had weighed about a pound.

Panoyan had said the intruder asked for Bob's wallet, but Bob had said he didn't. Clyde agreed with his son.

Did Clyde know McFarland? Yes, and he seemed nice enough. He described him as heavyset, about six feet tall.

Outside Clyde's hospital room, Mocarski and Woodroof ran into Jo Zazzo and her husband Jim. The Zazzos had just visited Carl, who was also at Hollywood Memorial. Carl's first two days in the hospital had been awful. Although his condition was stable, he had cried, resisted the nurses, and called repeatedly for his mother. Only when Aunt Jo and his cousins had come to visit did he relax slightly.

3:20 P.M.
Wetz-Zz's Bar-B-Que Restaurant

Detective Todoroff met Don Wetz, the owner of the Cooper City restaurant where the Deckers had eaten before arriving home on the night of the assault. Wetz said he had known Bob Decker more than ten years. Decker had been a Friday night regular for the past three months, always coming in at the same time and always sitting at the same table. Wetz remembered seeing them on the night of the murder, but didn't notice anything suspicious in the restaurant that night.

4:45 P.M.
Humana Hospital Bennett

Woodroof and Mocarski returned to the hospital to ask Bob's doctor, Gary Gieseke, and the nurse in charge if they thought it was the appropriate time to tell Bob how the rest of his family had fared in the assault. When the detectives had talked with Bob earlier that day, he hadn't asked.

Dr. Gieseke said go ahead.

Mocarski, the older and more experienced of the two officers, felt that it was his obligation to do the talking.

"We need to tell you what is going on at this point," he told Bob when they walked in.

Woodroof remembered later that he would have given anything to be elsewhere. He hadn't had a total of ten hours sleep since the murder.

Mocarski's voice was shaking. Being a cop for a long time didn't make it any easier. He gave Bob the good news first: "Your father and your son survived, and they're both at Hollywood Memorial Hospital."

Bob looked relieved, but only for an instant. Then he realized from the way Mocarski had said what he just said, that the remaining news wasn't going to be as good.

"But Donna didn't make it," Mocarski said.

Bob cried. Woodroof realized that he had never before had to tell anyone that a loved one had died. He reminded himself of the professional detachment that he had been taught, but somehow the power of the moment had been vastly understated at the police academy.

"I wasn't sure, but I thought so," Bob said, when he could.

Before the detectives left, they asked Bob once again if he knew who might have done the crime.

Woodroof wrote Bob's answer in his notes: "Sam or Chuck crazy enough to do something like this."

6:15 P.M.
Davie Police Station

Armed with a number of leads and phone numbers from a list found in the house, Woodroof and Mocarski began interviewing Bob Decker's friends.

First was Roy Davis. He had since visited Bob Decker, as well as spoken to Panoyan by telephone the morning after the murder. He said he thought Bob knew who committed the murder, and that he was going to "handle this in his own way."

But pressed, Davis said he just felt that way—Bob hadn't said that to him.

Next was Richard Ricketts. He again suggested the gunman might be "Warren," who Bob had recently filed a police report against for grand theft of property in a house he had rented to him. Or it could be a subcontractor named Barry Drovie, with whom Bob recently had had payment disputes.

But by the end of interview, Ricketts concluded that Panoyan was most likely involved and could lead them to the gunman, whoever he was.

Next was Sam McFarland. He was very nervous and reluctant to cooperate. He also suggested that Warren had something to do with the case. Within the first twenty minutes, Mocarski provoked a confrontation, trying to get him to admit that he was the killer. Instead, McFarland just got up and left.

Tuesday, November 8
10 A.M.
Crime scene

Four days after the murder, Davie police decided it was time to relinquish the crime scene. But before they did, Todoroff, Mocarski, Woodroof, and other detectives made one last check of the house. After an hour of searching, Mocarski found another $75 cash hidden between papers in the closet, but that was all they found. While at the house, Woodroof got a message that Bob Decker wanted to speak with him and Mocarski again.

11:25 A.M.
Humana Hospital Bennett

Bob remembered that the intruder had found his Uzi semiautomatic handgun on the shelf of the office/closet and carried it with him around the house, pointing it. However, he didn't seem to know how to use it. Bob said he had recently purchased the gun and had a receipt for it from a gun dealer.

He also mentioned the name Steve Reagan, an electrician who used to work for Panoyan.

12:09 P.M.
Crime scene

Woodroof and Mocarski looked for the Uzi but didn't find it. At 1:30 P.M., they cleared the crime scene for the last time.

Time unknown
Hollywood Memorial Hospital

Carl had been crying for his mother for days. His attending physician, Dr. Yvonne Rutherford, knew someone was going to have to tell him about her death, and it couldn't wait much longer. Worse, his father obviously couldn't do it, nor his grandfather, nor was his aunt Jo Zasso up to it either. It would have to be her responsibility.

Rutherford knew that a two and a half year old wouldn't understand the concept of death. She struggled with how to present it. The best she could come up with was that his mother had gone away.

She wrote a poignant log in Carl's medical record that belied how emotional the episode was for her:

> Spoke with family about dealing with patient and mother's death. Spoke with child and family about how mother is in heaven and people in heaven cannot visit people on Earth because they are dead. Told him his mother loves him but got very sick and went to heaven. Encourage family to tell him his mother loves him, lives in heaven now, is not mad at him, and would visit if she could. Patient cried but is overall accepting this information well.

3:30 P.M.
Hollywood Memorial Hospital

Dr. Robert Contrucci performed surgery on Clyde Decker, removing multiple bone fragments as well as "a tremendous amount" of blood and mucus collected by the gauze in his sinus.

3:45 P.M.
Davie police

BSO crime scene detective George Miller told Woodroof that all their evidence was ready to go to the lab. Based on the blood spatter evidence on the lower portions of the foyer walls, and the absence of any other blood spatter in the house, he thought Donna Decker was probably stabbed in the foyer, in a prone or nearly prone position.

Six

CHARLES PANOYAN
Wednesday, November 9
9:30 A.M.
Davie police station

Earlier in the morning, Det. Todoroff had called Charles Panoyan to tell him he could pick up his shoes at the police department. They had come back from the crime lab after testing negative for blood. The technician guessed the brown marks were errant drops of wood stain.

Todoroff also told Panoyan when he came in, he could make an official report of the contents of his stolen wallet. He had lost six gas credit cards, a American Express Gold card, his driver's license, family photos, papers, business cards, and $100 cash.

In addition, Todoroff said they wanted his fingerprints so they could eliminate his prints from others found at the scene.

But until Panoyan arrived that morning, Todoroff didn't tell him the real reason police wanted him to come in: they wanted him to walk through the crime scene, explaining everything he could remember, on videotape.

The strategy worked: Panoyan said yes.

10:35 A.M.
Crime scene

Sgt. Taylor, cameraman, turned on the tape. The first scene was in the driveway. Panoyan remembered waiting at the empty house on the night of the murder until Bob Decker's car pulled up. True to form, Panoyan started babbling all sorts of details.

"I was standing back there, and he called me ugly and you look like—looked like I'd been in a flood or something like that, and I laughed and I called him a name and—I went up to here, we all went right up here and we were talking, they were talking about the dinner they had and everything. Then we all walked around over to here.

"And then something big jumped and there was a frog—toad—that went this way and Bob would go that way, it went this way, so when the toad jumped up to here, Bob kicked the toad and I said Bob, don't kick the toad, I said, you know, it's not right.

"And Carl started to kick the toad and I said, Carl, you know, don't kick the toad, and—Bob opened the door and he turned the alarm off."

Entering the house, Panoyan remembered Bob asked him to take his shoes off. Bob went straight to his telephone answering machine, then came out and played with Carl on the floor, tossing the baby in the air.

When Bob sat down, Panoyan said, "I got up, I grabbed ahold of him, and pulled the hair on his chest and started scuffling and he told me to sit down. He said I was gonna be leaving in about ten minutes anyway and I said, How come? and he said he was gonna watch *Dallas* and that was his favorite program."

A bit later, "Bob and I, we were leaning over talking and he was playing with the baby and all of a sudden from right there, he turned around and he looked straight that way and at this point you know, he was, you know, blank. And I looked at him and I said Bob, I says, you're ignoring me, and I said, 'Come on Bob.' I said, you're ignoring me and he didn't say anything.

"And I thought he was looking at Grandpa. I said, Bob, you're ignoring me, and he just had a stare and after the second time I said for crying out loud, you know—this isn't like him to do like that. I looked over to Grandpa, I heard a mumbling sound and I says, 'Grandpa.' I said, 'I can't hear you, speak up.'

"And I turned around to see, you know, why he was mumbling and this guy had a gun. Bob looked at me and I looked at him, he kind of grinned and started laughing and I started laughing and ah—he cocked the gun. The minute he cocked the gun we stopped laughing, stopped grinning, stopped doing everything, and he told us to get down on the floor.''

Advancing to when the masked man brought out handcuffs: "Bob and I were talking while he was handcuffing Grandpa.''

"You mean he cuffed Grandpa first?'' asked Todoroff.

"Right. Bob said, 'Do you know him? Does he look familiar?' and I said no. I said, 'Do you know him?' and he said no. Then he said shut up or be quiet or something.

"Then he came around to Bob, handcuffed him and then handcuffed me. Then he went over to Grandpa, took his wallet and his money and then he went over to Bob and said, 'Where is your wallet?' Bob and I were looking right at each other and Bob said, my wallet's in the safe. [The gunman said,] 'Why is your wallet in the safe?' and I was saying, Bob, you know, don't say anything about a safe. He asked for the combination and Bob said ah—the safe's open, he says, 'I'll take you to it.'

"The guy, he said, I don't care about the safe being open, or whatever, he wanted the combination, and Bob I think said he didn't know the combination. I mean, I think that's what he said, but that was crazy.''

"We don't expect you to remember everything,'' said Todoroff. "Just what you remember and what you feel comfortable with.''

"Well, I mean I remember, I mean, why would he tell the guy that, you know, the safe,'' said Panoyan.

"I don't know, you know, we'll find out sooner or later,'' said Todoroff.

"Then, Bob said it was in the bedroom, and the guy said, you know, get in the bedroom. It was a grumpy low voice—ah, I don't think, it didn't sound like a colored guy, but I mean if a colored guy can sound like a grumpy low voice, I don't know.''

"Did he take your wallet out there too?'' asked Todoroff.

"No—well, the minute he heard [the word] 'safe,' he forgot my wallet.

"At this point he said, 'Everybody in the bedroom.' He helped Bob up, helped me up, and Grandpa was laying there. He was being real rough and I said, 'Look, I don't think he can hear you, he doesn't have his hearing aid, he's hard of hearing,' and that didn't do anything to the guy.''

"So he was pretty rough to Grandpa?"

"Yeah, and he picked him up and Grandpa let out a moan, and ah, he took us into the other room."

Panoyan then repeated that he had been in the bedroom with the others, although Clyde Decker had since denied it. The videotape crew followed Panoyan into the bedroom.

"Grandpa and the baby were together, I was first, and Grandpa, baby, and Bob was last.

"I was, you know—I mean right next—right behind Grandpa all the way—he went down here and laid down." Panoyan pointed to the floor between the bed and the chest, under the window.

"Who did?"' asked Todoroff.

"Grandpa."

"Okay," said Todoroff.

"I mean this is, this is the part I don't, I barely remember."

"Okay."

"Barely. And it was dark, the lights were on, I think. All right, Grandpa was laying right here, the baby was laying right next to him.

"Right. And—it had to have been Grandpa 'cause Bob was the last one in and I was following the first one. And then I was laying right here"—Panoyan pointed at where he had been on the floor—"and Bob was on the bed laying right here. I was laying right here and I looked up and I seen, he had a big—it looked like there was a wardrobe or something over there, but I guess there isn't—but he got something from over there.

"And it was ah, a, ah—"

Panoyan paused for more then ten seconds. "Go ahead, Chuck, take your time," said Todoroff.

"It was a dark piece of—it looked like a bathrobe or something. And he—he was tying Bob's legs—while he was tying Bob's legs I—Can you handcuff my hands?" Panoyan asked Todoroff.

"We don't have any handcuffs, Chuck. Just do the best you can, it's all right," Todoroff answered.

"All right, I, I sat up like this and I seen him tying the

feet and while he was tying the feet, I was trying to get up, I remember that, I couldn't get up. And he wasn't saying anything, he was just tying his feet.''

"Was Bob allowing him to do this or was Bob fighting him off?"

"Bob didn't do a thing. Nothing. And—he came by with something else and tied Grandpa's feet and then he told me to get up and I couldn't get up and he grabbed ahold of me and yanked me up and I let out a cry, you know, an 'Ow' or something to that effect, and I got up.''

Walking back into the living room, he continued. "He took me in here, sat me down on the chair and tied my feet. As he—as I turned around I saw Bob coming in this way and I said, Man, I said, somebody's gonna get shot, that was the first thing in my mind 'cause he wheeled around and went like that''—Panoyan acted like he was pointing a gun—"and he told Bob, Bob to get back in there and don't move and don't make a sound, I heard that.''

"Let me just—when he came out, when Bob came out, could you tell whether his feet were still tied?" asked Todoroff.

"It, no—it looked like he walked out.''

"Okay, go ahead.''

"But I seen him tie his feet, I know I seen him—Bob walked out, he was, it looked like he was walking, 'cause he wasn't hopping.''

Panoyan said the intruder followed Bob back into the bedroom, came out again, and then Donna came home.

"I was looking over there, you know, to see what I could see—and ah, Donna came in, he was coming in this way when he saw Donna coming in, or heard the door close. I don't know if he saw her or not, but I was sitting right there.''

"Okay.''

" 'Cause I saw the shadow of a gun pointing right there, I seen the, I seen the, the body and it was pointing right at me.

"He ran back in here, pointed the gun at me in there, and Donna came in. She had groceries in her hand, she walked in, said 'Hi, Chuck,' and I said, 'Hi,' and she said, 'Where's Bob?' and I said, In the bedroom—he come out, I don't even know what happened to the groceries, everything went—went fuzzy, the lights came on in that room—and then he came in here and he hog-tied me right here."

Panoyan said the intruder grabbed Donna, but he couldn't recall exactly where, nor where he took her. He came back to Panoyan within a minute, and that's when he hog-tied him.

"Tied me right there and I get cramps—I got cramps for the last month or two, and it's from potassium. And I said, Man, if I get the cramps, I would have been dead, because there was nothing I could have done cause I didn't see him again for—a good half hour to an hour, not even an hour, half hour, forty-five minutes."

"Let me just ask you while I'm thinking about it. When Donna came in, did you hear any noises or yells or anything from the bedroom?" asked Todoroff.

"No noises, no yells, all I heard, I heard voices, and I couldn't tell if it was the TV.

"I heard a—while I was laying there I heard a kidnap. Now if that kidnapping was on TV, it was a TV kidnap. If it wasn't—"

"You heard the word 'kidnapping'?"

"I heard 'kidnap.' "

"Distinctly?" asked Todoroff.

"I heard it."

"So *Dallas* was on when you heard the word 'kidnapping,' " Todoroff put forward.

"Right. Now, I don't know if the kidnapping was in *Dallas,* I don't know if it was—I don't know."

When the intruder finally came back, Panoyan said, "He went into my wallet, got my wallet, stood over me, checked my pockets, took my money out of there, he was there for a minute maybe, and he said he knew where I lived, he knew—he knew my wife's phone work number, he knew my work number, and he said I was being watched, he said for me to go straight home, and I said—you know, yeah, okay."

"Wait. Okay, wait, he untied you and took the handcuffs off?"

"He untied me right there, helped me up, unhandcuffed me right here, and this is where he told me that I was being watched and followed, and my house was—he used surveillance, under surveillance, and I said ah, ah, I said okay and I walked out and I left. As I was driving off you guys came in."

"Did he hear any gunshots?" Sergeant Ed Taylor, holding the video camera, prompted Todoroff.

"Did you hear any gunshots?" Todoroff asked Panoyan.

"No, not one."

"Did anybody scream or anybody yell for anything?" Taylor asked directly.

"Nothing. In fact, he—he told us right here, he said nobody's gonna get hurt, he said, it was just—when he was, when, when he came in and we were all laying down he told us this was just a robbery and it would have been just a robbery if Bob hadn't have said 'safe' and that's in my mind, that, that triggered something. Because his, his whole being just, his voice, everything was different, either in my mind or his voice was different.

"Because while he was laying there talking, you know, Bob was talking about the safe, I said, Man, Bob, I said, you know, don't—keep your mouth shut, keep your mouth shut.

"And [why] he said safe, I'll never know."

"When you got there, you said it was just before *Dallas*, right?" asked Todoroff.

"It was about ten or fifteen minutes before *Dallas*."

"Okay, and then right before *Dallas* came on is when this guy came in," said Todoroff, trying to get it straight.

"It was exactly about seven minutes before *Dallas*," said Panoyan.

"Okay."

"Because Bob was saying I got fifteen minutes, ten minutes, five—no, he looked at the clock and he said seven minutes, and he said if I was real quiet, I, I can, I could watch it, you know, sort of laughing. I said, 'Gee, thanks, Bob.'"

"So after the bad guy came in, about how long do you think it was before Donna got home?—your best estimate."

"Ten minutes—not even ten minutes."

"Okay. And then after he put Donna wherever he put her, and he came back and released you and you left—about how long was that?"

"All right, I was—*Dallas* was still on, or *Dallas* was just over with, I don't remember. I, I don't remember."

Panoyan remembered seeing the intruder walk back and forth between the bedroom and the room he thought Donna was in, most likely, the bathroom. He also heard what sounded liké a file cabinet clanging as well as doors opening and closing. At one point he saw the intruder walk into the bathroom with what may have been a telephone cord.

"Did he say anything to you?"

"He didn't say a word to me, nothing. The only thing he ever told me is when he came to me—when he came to me, he didn't even tell me to get down, just grabbed me, put me down there, tied me, my, my hands—tied my legs, my hands, and had the rope around my neck, and I pulled on the rope just a little bit and I said, 'Man, this is crazy.' I started kicking my feet a little bit, and I said no, I said, 'I'm just gonna stay just the way I am.' "

They moved back outside. Then Todoroff and Sgt. Taylor entered Panoyan's truck so that they could all retrace his route to the Xtra supermarket, while videotaping the whole way.

"Now it's important that we do everything that you did when you left here, okay?" said Taylor. "You can talk as you go if you want and tell us what."

"I was looking in both mirrors," said Panoyan, backing out of the driveway. "I checked both mirrors to see if anybody was following me—nobody was following me.

"I stopped at the sign. I looked both ways, looked every way. I didn't see anybody following me, I didn't see any lights, I didn't see nothing.

"Stopped right here and I looked both ways, I looked every which way, I looked in the mirror and I looked everywhere, I didn't see any cars that even looked like they were following me. I went down here and I said, 'Man, this is crazy.' I says, I don't think anybody's following me, there were cars, you know, just standing cars, but I mean no lights, no, no, cars behind me.

"As I was pulling to the right I seen a car pull out, pulled out where we drove into, coming in this way, and—in my mind I, I was almost positive that guy wasn't following me because, you know, he was two blocks, three blocks over.

"And I still saw one car behind me, but that was, you know, quite a ways away. I knew that no other car that I could think of was following me except for that one car, and he was the car that turned about three blocks back, so I knew he wasn't—you know."

Panoyan drove the most direct route to Xtra.

"I seen a guy there, I jumped out, and I looked around me and I saw cars coming and I said, 'There's a home invasion robbery or robbery or something going on and I asked him to call the police. He called the police on his walkie-talkie, I think."

After the production was finished, Todoroff noted that Panoyan had driven 1.3 miles, with an average speed of twenty miles per hour—probably much slower than he had driven on the night of the murder. Still, it had only taken six minutes and five seconds to cover the distance.

11:55 A.M.
Humana Hospital Bennett

Woodroof and Mocarski spent another half hour talking to Bob Decker. They went over what he had said the day before, and Decker added some other points.

Woodroof had since pulled the Hollywood police grand theft complaint that Decker had filed against Warren Smith on September 26. Decker said Smith had stolen a refrigerator, a stove, and two air conditioners from a unit he had rented to him. Smith hadn't been found, although the refrigerator was recovered.

Smith fit the physical description of the gunman: 6'2", 200 pounds. But Decker said that he couldn't have been the gunman because Smith is black and the gunman was white.

They turned to Panoyan and Barry Drovie. Bob said Panoyan was suspicious because he never visited him on Friday nights. Also, he said Panoyan was having severe financial problems.

Bob said he had had a money dispute with Drovie, but he didn't consider it a real problem. However, that reminded him that Drovie had an assistant Bob didn't like who bore a physical resemblance to the gunman.

5 P.M.
Davie police station

Jo Zazzo called Woodroof to tell him that Donna's supervisor, Marguerite (at J.C. Penney), had told Jo that Bob had recently fired an employee, and that person had threatened to get even with him.

5:30 P.M.
Home of Doug Amos, Davie

Doug Amos was a friend of Bob Decker and a fellow contractor. He knew Panoyan, too. He told Todoroff that the houses Panoyan had built in Potters Park—the low-rent part of Davie—were probably causing him financial trouble.

He had just seen Panoyan and Decker together at a party about four weeks before. He knew that Bob had made Panoyan wait three hours while he got ready.

6:35 P.M.
Home of Trisha Tenbrock, Davie

A day or so after the murder, fourteen-year-old Trisha Tenbrock told her parents something she had dismissed at the time: that Donna had received a threatening phone call when Trisha was present two weeks before she was killed.

But unfortunately, Trisha had only little more to add for Todoroff. Donna had been home alone on the afternoon of October 18. Bob was out of town to drive his father from New York. Trisha didn't hear the caller's voice, but Donna told her that it was a man, and that he said, "I have a gun and I'm gonna shoot you."

Donna was very upset. Right after that the phone rang again, but there was a hang up. But Trisha didn't know if Donna had gotten any other similar calls.

8:50 P.M.

Using an address one of Bob's associates had given him, Woodroof drove to Miramar to visit Barry Drovie. Once there, Woodroof saw lights on in his house, windows open, and a dog in the garage, but no one responded to his knocking on the door.

Thursday, November 10
11:35 A.M.
Tole Electric Company

Working on Bob Decker's lead, Woodroof figured out that Panoyan's electrician friend, who fit the physical description of the gunman, worked for Tole Electric Company. On Woodroof and Mocarski's arrival, they were told the name of the man they were looking for was James Malcolm, who lived in North Miami.

12:35 P.M.,
Davie police station

Woodroof got Barry Drovie on the phone. Like Bob had said, Drovie considered their argument over payment to be minor. He volunteered to come into the station to answer questions. Asked for the name of his assistant, he answered Michael Dennis Benn.

Time unknown
BSO crime lab

Firearms examiner Patrick Garland was able to make some conclusions regarding the metal fragments surgically removed from Bob Decker and the pink pillow with a hole in it.

The two larger fragments were from copper-coated lead .22 long-rifle bullets. That didn't mean they couldn't have been fired from a handgun.

The pillow showed signs that it had been wrapped over the gun when it was fired. Generally, he said, that was done to muffle the sound of the gunshot, although it wasn't usually successful. Regardless, unless the windows were open, the sound of a .22 gunshot probably wouldn't have alerted anyone outside, anyway.

5:55 P.M.
Home of James Malcolm

North Miami was out of Broward County, so Mocarski and Woodroof were confused as to street addresses. A bit lost, they called Malcolm for directions.

When the detectives did arrive, they knew one thing for sure: at 6'1", 175, Malcolm fit the physical description of the gunman, as others had as well. But Malcolm said he hadn't heard about the murder until just moments before, when Panoyan had called him.

However, Malcolm said he had just spent a week in Utah hunting with Panoyan. There they shot the venison that ended up in the Deckers' freezer.

✦ SEVEN

Clyde and Bob Decker
Friday, November 11, 1988
12:05 P.M.
Decker home

Clyde Decker arrived home from the hospital in the morning, and detectives Todoroff and Killam and Sgt. Taylor lost little time before asking him to walk through the crime scene as they had with Panoyan.

At the same time, Mocarski and Woodroof were able to interview Bob Decker on tape at Humana Bennett for the first time.

Beginning with the elder Mr. Decker: Arriving at the house with Bob and Carl, he described seeing Panoyan parked in the driveway, walking in the house with him, and watching TV when the masked man entered. But this time Clyde neglected his earlier recollection that Chuck had gone outside to get the venison, which Clyde had said he put in the freezer.

He said the intruder handcuffed him first, then Panoyan, then Bob—all behind their backs. The intruder also tied Clyde's feet and Bob's feet, but not Panoyan's. He placed Panoyan on a living room chair and led Bob, then Clyde, into the bedroom.

Asked to describe the assailant, Clyde said he was between forty and forty-five, had a solid build, and wore a green jacket and pants, gray hat, gray tight-fitting mask, and cowboy boots.

As the videotaping moved inside the bedroom, Clyde remembered that the baby's feet were tied to Bob's feet.

70

"You are in the bed. Bob and the baby are on the floor and Chuck is still in the living room?" asked Todoroff.

"Yeah," agreed Clyde.

The intruder had used Clyde's belt to tie up his feet, but while the intruder was out of the bedroom, Clyde had worked it loose. "He seen my legs was getting loose so he went and got the electric clock, used the cord," and retied him.

"How did he get the cord off the clock?"

"He left the clock on it, dangling away."

"Did you ever see Chuck come into the bedroom at all?"

"Never. I didn't see Chuck at all no more."

Clyde apologized for his poor hearing. He hadn't heard the door open when Donna entered the house, although he did hear her "hollering" for Bob. That was just before she had seen the intruder, he figured.

"He grabbed her out there somewhere. He got ahold of her before she got to this door [pointing to the bedroom door from inside the bedroom], as far as I can see."

He saw Donna once more. This time when she came into the bedroom, she was tied up. "She went on out through here and she must have run right into him again, and from there on I didn't hear nothing until I heard her screaming after he shot us.

"He was done. She was the last one he took care of. He had already shot us. After the shots, we heard all this screaming."

Returning to the shooting: "I could see him bent over the baby with a pillow in his hands. He shot the baby. Then he come over and put the pillow on Bob and shot him two or three times. I don't know. I lost track of it.

"Then he done that and went around Bob and come in here and put it in me with a pillow over.

"The first time he pulled, it didn't go. Then, the next time, it did. He grabbed me by the throat and he choked the hell out of me. My teeth guard was all busted—blood. I couldn't hardly get my breath.

"I just thought I was a goner right there, but I finally gagged them up. He went on out.

"He just thought he had me, I guess, and he went on out and that is when the screaming started."

"After you heard her screaming, did you ever lose consciousness? Did you ever pass out?" Todoroff asked.

"Did I? Well, not really. I was kind of in a daze. When I carried the kid out, everybody wondered how I hung onto him, I guess."

Todoroff then posed a loaded question. "After you heard Donna screaming, did you hear them leave?" apparently referring to Panoyan as one of "them."

"No, I didn't."

They had laid still for a few minutes before the police came. "I didn't dare open my mouth. I finally said to Bob, 'Do you know whether he is gone or not?' He said, 'Yes, I'm sure he is gone.'

"He said, 'Is there any way that you can get off the bed? Is there any way at all to untie my feet to get the baby?' The baby was screaming.

"I couldn't get off the bed. My arms were all paralyzed, black and blue. I couldn't do much.

"We heard a knock on the door. Bob hollered twice to come in.

"We asked them to get the cuffs off as soon as they could because I was numb and he was numb, so they got them off right away. I sat up on the edge of the bed and took the belt and clock off my legs. They were working on him getting the handcuffs off and stuff. The baby was screaming quite hard.

"I hated to bend over because I was bleeding. I felt so sorry for the baby, so I got ahold of him. When the cops got ahold of him and took him, he started screaming all over again. I said, 'Would you please let me take him?' I hung onto him and carried him out there."

"What did you see as you carried him out?"

"I kept looking for Donna. I kept looking for Chuck. I just kept looking thinking I would see her somewhere. I wondered where Chuck was."

12:20 P.M.
Humana Hospital Bennett

Also starting at the beginning, Bob Decker remembered getting home from dinner at Wetz-Zz's restaurant at 8:45 and finding Panoyan parked dead center in his driveway. It seemed like he had been there a while because he had his arm and foot out the door.

Once inside the house, Bob gave him ten minutes before he had to hit the road. "I'm always kidding with him full-time. I'm kidding with him [when] I told him had about ten minutes to stay, *Dallas* was coming on, he had to go. He thought I was kidding."

"So you're saying you had about ten minutes to go—*Dallas* was coming on, so that must have been about ten to nine?" asked Mocarski.

"Right. I always watch *Dallas*. Everybody knows that *Dallas* is a big thing for me. I like *Dallas*."

"Is it unusual for Chuck to be at your house like this?"

"Yeah, it was. Today I found out that he had told my father that he was coming to bring some venison over. He had told us then, that day. Of course, I didn't know it and I didn't expect him."

Bob described what happened when he walked into the house.

"I turned on the TV and I went to the office and took out my wallet and my keys and set them on the counter there, inside the office. And I happened to be sitting there by the baby, kind of playing with him a little bit, and kind of playing with Chuck a little bit, you know—why was he over there? Did his wife throw him out tonight? And it was just kind of a kidding thing. That day he'd lost a hundred-dollar bill on the job which I had found right away, the second he lost it I found it, and we played a game with him that I was going to give it to him that night and it never even got that far."

Bob set the scene: He and the baby were playing in the living room with the baby's wrestling toys, his dad Clyde was sitting in the red recliner on the other side of the living room, and Chuck was closer, sitting on the brown recliner.

"Chuck got up and says, 'I'm gonna run and get the venison.' He run out to his truck and got the venison and come back in. He was gone a split second. I couldn't remember at the time, but he did go and he did get it. Between my wife coming home and him getting it, and then her being home and him not being here.

"He said it would be unfrozen if he didn't go get it quick.

I was watching *Dallas*. It had just come on, just that one second come on. And he was sitting there and in walks this guy right behind him.''

Mocarski asked how long after Panoyan returned with the meat that the intruder entered.

"We're talking seconds."

"Seconds?"

"Now, I don't know, I was watching *Dallas,* like I say, I turn off my lights when that *Dallas* comes on."

Chuck and Clyde had returned to their original places. "He come in on top of us right there, I seen him. I thought it was a joke, you know, it was somebody that he knew and I just, I laughed it off. And immediately he said, 'We're puttin' these handcuffs on.' ''

Bob's description of the intruder was more specific than Panoyan's or Clyde's:

"Work pair of boots, average work pair, good shape. Pair of blue jeans, mediocre, they were work blue jeans, cowboy. Had a denim type jacket on, work type blue jean, cowboy jacket type, wasn't too bad a shape, wasn't torn up too bad. It was dirty, but it wasn't torn up bad. Had a shirt under that, I couldn't tell too much on the shirt. I think it was yellow. And of course he had a on pair of stockings over his face, and he had a white straw hat on, between a whitish-yellow. And he had it pulled all the way down to here, right to his eyes."

Bob thought he was 30–40 years old, between 5'7" and 5'9", stocky and 170–190 pounds.

"Did you think of anybody when you first saw him?"

"No. The first thing I thought was it was a joke. What, we're getting robbed? Total joke. We're not getting shot. We're not getting robbed. He was shaking so bad with this gun, and it was an old .22, and when I looked at it, it looked like, you know, picking up that phone and holding it at me. You know, I wasn't scared a bit.

"It was an old, old gun. It looked like it was, you know, back in the 1700s. It was really old. He had all he could do to make the damn thing go off."

"How does he put the cuffs on?"

"I'm already sitting on the floor and he grabs the cuffs, turns us over on our belly. All of us get down on our belly."

"What kind of cuffs were they?"

"They were very rusty and very old and I heard him say something at one point, 'They're traceable.' That was the first time that he said he would call 911, would not shoot us, wouldn't hurt us, rob us and do what he was going to do and take the drugs and the money and leave."

"Why would he say he would take the drugs and money and leave?"

"I guess he thought he was getting a lot of drugs and money out of the house."

"In fact, do you have any drugs in the house?"

"None whatsoever."

Next the intruder wanted to see the safe.

"How did he know about the safe?"

"I don't know. I really don't know."

"Did he ask you about the safe?"

"He might have asked. Ah, Chuck might have said, 'There's a safe in the walk-in closet' or something. But I didn't say nothing. I pretended dumb all the way through everything."

"Did he ask you where your wallet was?"

"Yeah, he asked about that and I says, 'In the office.' That's all I said."

Mocarski clarified the difference between the office/closet and the walk-in clothes closet where the safe was. Inside the clothes closet, Bob said the intruder "makes me lay down on the floor. He pulls the rug there and of course it didn't move. It wasn't in that corner. It was in the other corner. That made him mad, real mad. So he jumps to the other corner. Then he uncovers it and sees that just the cover come off [there was an unconnected piece of metal that lay over the safe but under the carpet] and he says, 'Well, maybe the burglar alarm will go off on it and the police will come.' So he left it alone for a while."

(In fact, when police found the uncovered floor safe, it was closed.)

The intruder then dragged Bob back into the master bedroom proper. "This is where I was the rest of the night. I tried moving around a little bit, and when he'd see I was moving around he started tying me up more and more."

"Where was your father?"

"He was thrown on the bed. When I seen him first throw him on the bed I didn't like that 'cause he was just, he was pushing him around real hard."

Mocarski asked if he saw Panoyan after that.

"Chuck was in there for a split second, but not long. And then it acted like he was talking to him at the same time in the living room. And that's when I didn't see no more of him."

"Okay. All right. So . . ."

"Two minutes later my wife came home, said something to Chuck, and I heard the door shut. That's the last I heard of him.

"So you're saying a 'split second.' Are you talking three seconds, are you talking ten seconds—approximate?"

"Not even two seconds, maybe. He was in there and out of there."

"Okay. All right. Now, we have you, your son on the floor, we have your dad on the water bed—am I correct? What happened at that point?"

"He tied us up more and more. He pulled a string off, ah, I guess it was one of them light things, you know, a mirror with lights on it. He pulled that off and tied that around my feet. He pulled the string off the phone, it looked like. Couldn't tell if it was a phone or alarm clock, and tied my father's feet up. And then he tied a, ah, sock, first he tried shoving a sock in my mouth, almost gagged me to death.

"I kept saying to my son, you know, 'Stay here. Stay here.' "

Mocarski asked where the intruder went after everyone was restrained.

"First off he kind of looked through a couple of drawers in the bedroom where I was. Then he went [into the in-house] beauty shop. Then he was in, he was all over the house."

"Okay, but you couldn't see this."

"Everywhere. I could hear him."

"How long was he going through the house?"

"He was there approximately, total, over all, he was there one hour. Cause *Dallas* went off. I could hear *Dallas* going off."

"So the television was still on?"

"Yeah. Yeah, he left the television on."

"Okay. All right," said Mocarski. "He had gone through the drawers, this individual, and he goes back up into the closet and to the [beauty] shop and to the living room. At what point do you hear him talking to Chuck?"

"Ah, about maybe five minutes, would be ten minutes after he tied me up real tight."

"Okay."

"Five minutes, I'd say."

"Okay, did you ever overhear the conversation?"

"No, I couldn't hear what they were saying. They were whispering something."

"Were they whispering?"

"Kind of like a whisper."

"Okay. Was the conversation that Chuck was having with this individual before your wife came in or after your wife came in?"

"No, it was after."

"Okay."

" 'Cause she, I remember her saying, 'Chuck, what are you doing here?' "

"And did you hear a reply?"

"Never heard nothing."

"Okay, did it sound like she dropped anything?"

"Yeah, it, it was almost like she dropped everything she had in her hand and run in the living room, run in the—the bedroom I mean, where we were."

"Okay. This may be important. Did it sound like anything dropped?"

"Ah, I can't say, you know, I don't know what she was carrying. If she was carrying a bag of groceries she, she dropped a bag, if she wasn't, she didn't carry one."

"But did you hear anything drop?"

"Ah, I really, I didn't know what I was hearing. I was so tied up."

"Did you hear the door open when she came into the house?"

"Okay, I heard the door open. I heard her come in. Chuck was in the living room. He [the intruder] was in the bedroom and I says, 'Oh my God.' There was nothing I could do, I had already, you know, a split second had went out of my mind. She'd seen Chuck's truck outside. And she didn't see us in the ah, living room, I'm sure she would run in the bedroom and wonder what's going on.''

"So when she ran in the bedroom, what happened?"

"He grabbed her quick. Grabbed her right away and ah, took her into the bedroom. But he didn't even get to the bedroom when the door closed. I heard the door close and Chuck left.''

"Okay, I want to get this clarified. When she came into the bedroom, had Chuck gone already?"

"Yeah, he'd already gone. He, he like, he, he shut the door behind her almost.''

"Okay.''

"I mean you could hear there was a difference in doors.''

"All right, so you heard a conversation [between Panoyan and the intruder]. How long of a conversation—was it a long conversation?''

"No, very short.''

"Short conversation.''

"But whatever it was, it was, 'Okay, I'm leaving' or something, you know, it was very clear.''

"Okay, when she ran into the bedroom, what happened at that point?''

"Okay, he grabbed her and he tied her up right away with handcuffs, and he tied her up with string and just about anything he could get his hands on 'cause he was going frantic with her. She was going berserk and he was going frantic trying to tie her up. Chuck went out the door, of course, 'cause he—''

"You heard the door.''

"Yeah, I heard the door go shut.''

Bob described seeing the intruder tie up Donna in the bathroom.

"He did so many things, so many times. He had her in the living room, he had her in the office, he had her in the kitchen, he had her everywhere. She was, she was showing him around too, some, I could tell. Ah, just trying to get rid of him. He'd been looking through everything. Very perturbed that he didn't find drugs in the house.''

"At what point did this individual come to you with a paper?''

"With the paper was a few minutes later. I thought it was

kind of unusual, 'cause he, he calmed her down enough to sign it."

"Can you describe that paper to me?"

"All it was was a piece of paper. A blank piece of paper with four lines on it."

"Was it like typing paper?"

"Yeah, a typing paper. It was a vanilla paper with no lines whatsoever, but four lines off to the top a little bit, like you'd sign a deed exactly."

"Were those lines typed on the paper or were they drawn by freehand?"

"Oh, that I didn't, I couldn't tell."

"But you're saying that on this piece of paper there were four lines."

"Right."

"Two on the right side, two on the left side?"

"Yeah."

Bob said the papers had been handed to him placed on top of a manila folder, which Bob referred to as a "vanilla" envelope. Although the signed papers weren't found at the scene, a manila folder was left on the bedroom floor.

Mocarski asked if the papers he signed were folded. No, Bob said.

"He took them out of the vanilla envelope and laid them in front of me there and said, 'Sign this.' And when he looked at my, I didn't know, I didn't realize he had my ID, my, my driver's license up on the ah, sitting on top of the, ah, dresser. I was on the floor in the master bedroom."

"Okay. Who signed this piece of paper first?"

"She did."

"Okay. Then he came in and he asked you to sign the paper?"

"Yeah, he wanted me to sign it. I signed it quick."

"Okay, so . . ."

"My handwriting is terrible."

"Okay, so he uncuffed you once to sign . . ."

"He uncuffed me, ah, one side to make me sign it and I signed it quick. But he was pretty particular on that. He wanted that signed perfect."

"Then what happened?"

"So he says, 'Well, gonna do it aaalll over again!' "

"So he did it a second time," said Mocarski.

"So he went away. He was gone maybe a couple of minutes. A minute or two and he come back and he got her to sign it again."

"Donna's name was on the paper again?"

"Yeah."

"But it was not the same paper?"

"It was a different paper."

"Did you sign the second piece of paper?"

"Yes. And I didn't think an awful lot of it, other than right at this minute I wanted to get the hell out of that situation."

Decker described the guns he owned. He had an Uzi submachine gun he kept high up on a shelf in the office closet; a shotgun he had used for hunting (which he had kept since he was ten years old), also in the office, standing between two file cabinets; and a Smith & Wesson .357 pistol he kept in a briefcase in his van. The .357 was the only gun he kept loaded. All of the guns were legally registered.

Before the intruder had the Deckers sign the blank pages, he found the Uzi. Apparently he took it with him when he fled, as he apparently also stole the .357 from the van.

"He says, 'Cute, real cute,' he goes. I said, 'Oh my God. If he sees that and knows how to load that.' "

"Was Chuck there at that time?"

"No, I'm pretty sure Chuck was gone. Chuck was gone like by—I'm going to say thirteen or fourteen after, Chuck was gone."

"So about thirteen minutes after nine Chuck was gone?"

"Yeah," said Bob.

"Because *Dallas* had started," said Mocarski.

"Right. And he came in at exactly nine o'clock when *Dallas* started. I remember hearing the dum-ditty-dum-ditty-dum thing."

"Okay, so you heard the theme song from *Dallas* come on," said Mocarski.

"Right."

"Okay. And about thirteen minutes later Chuck is gone?"

"Gone. I don't know whether Donna was a little late too. 'Cause she's normally home at 8:30."

Bob described the shooting. "He came to shoot us. He

took a pillow and put it on my head and 'Pow pow,' and I was just, I jumped, I was ringing so from the shots."

"Do you know who got shot next?"

"I got shot first, then the baby got shot second, and my father third, and Donna was fourth."

"Okay."

"I could hear the shots. He shot six shots."

"Did he? Okay."

"And he worked that .22 so hard to shoot it, it was not even funny."

"Did you ever see him use the pillow on Donna or anything?"

"Pillow, no. I don't even know where she was."

"Once you were shot, your father was shot, the baby was shot, okay, what happened then? Can you remember anything?"

"I just laid there with my face down. Bleeding face down. I couldn't even move over and look at the baby."

"Do you remember if the lights were on at that time?"

"No, I could hear the detective. Two minutes went by and I could hear a detective outside calling, 'Is anybody in there?' And I kept screaming at him. I screamed at my father to scream because my father was as bad as I was. Finally, they come inside. I couldn't hear a thing, couldn't see a thing, I couldn't hear a thing."

The detectives tried to tie up some loose ends. Bob volunteered some theories on how Panoyan had gotten out of the house. "He snuck out, walked out, or the guy just let him out, one or the other. If he let him out, I'd rather shoot him. Whew!"

Once again, Bob suggested Barry Drovie's assistant as someone who might have been the masked man. The assistant drank all the time, beginning at 7 A.M., on the job site.

He said he would be able to identify the intruder's voice by the way he said "Cute, real cute," showing off the Uzi. He had a cowboy accent.

"Did it sound like he knew you?"

"No, no, he didn't know me. He, like the drugs and the money was the big thing and you know, between you and I—he did get a lot of money."

The intruder probably got $2,000 cash, Bob thought, which

was hidden under the Uzi in the office. It was his father's money, which he had wanted Bob to put in the safe.

"And dumb me, I didn't put it in the safe because I hadn't had nothing in the safe since I moved into that house. I was, you know, I been poor since I built that house. Hadn't had a dime in there."

2:10 P.M.
Home of Michael Dennis Benn

Benn was Drovie's assistant. He had an alibi, he told Woodroof. When the murder occurred, he was on duty at his job with the Oakland Park Fire Department.

→ Eight

Donna Decker was laid to rest on this morning, but her husband, only child, and father-in-law were unable to attend.

According to *The Miami Herald*'s story, Father Anthony O'Brien asked Donna's family and friends to pray that violent men learn the senselessness of their ways.

"The death of an innocent person is always difficult to understand, especially when the life has been taken by the callousness of someone else," the priest spoke.

"We do have a just God and people who commit crimes of this kind do eventually pay for their crimes. But that really is not for us to say. That is for God to decide."

Outside the church, Gerry Todoroff copied down all the license plate numbers of parked cars. Inside the chapel were Kelly Woodroof and Dennis Mocarski.

At about 10:40, Charles Panoyan walked in late with his wife. He sat beside Jim Westcott, a mutual friend of his and Bob's, but began crying. "He stayed maybe five, ten minutes," Westcott recounted. "He was crying so hard that he had to leave with his wife. I was trying to hold back my tears too."

When the service was over, Panoyan found Todoroff and Gary Killam. Out of all the Davie detectives Panoyan had spoken with, he felt the most comfortable with Todoroff, who had a kind manner. Todoroff wrote that Panoyan "was extremely distraught and appeared confused. He indicated that he was having a hard time with the aftermath of the offense. He plopped down on the grass and sat there as other mourners walked by. Chuck stated that he had taken some depressants prior to the funeral. We helped Chuck up, put him in his car, and his wife drove him home.''

To Todoroff, at least, there was no question that Panoyan's emotions were genuine.

Tuesday, November 15
2:40 P.M.
Hollywood Memorial Hospital

Carl had been having a terrible time. Physically, he was doing well; doctors reaffirmed their decision that he could survive without surgery to remove the bullet from his head. But they knew he would never recover from the loss of his mother.

In those first ten days, Bob had been unable to visit Carl since they were in separate hospitals. Aunt Jo Zazzo, realizing that she would now be forced to play more of a mother's role to Carl, had been a constant visitor with her husband Jim and daughter Chrissy, as had Clyde since his release four days before.

While Bob was in intensive care, he hadn't even been able to telephone Carl. But when he was finally able to call, Carl's reaction was hostile. He trembled and pushed the phone away. When a nurse tried to get him to take the phone back, he cried and screamed for his Aunt Jo.

That wasn't the first time Carl had shown hostility in the hospital. Playing with Chrissy in the playroom, he had suddenly become violent and began throwing toys at her. Another time, a nurse had seen him stabbing his ''Andre the Giant'' wrestling doll in the back and tying a scarf around its nose and mouth.

Later that evening, unable to sleep, Carl watched television and saw a man on TV holding a sword.

He screamed, ''Help! Change it! Change it!'' until a nurse ran in, turned the set off, and told him it was bedtime.

Time unknown
Broward Sheriff's Office crime lab

With the fingerprint submissions of Donna Decker and Charles Panoyan, the crime lab at last could begin its identification work.

At the crime scene, Sgt. Alderton had lifted two prints of value from a closet door and three of value from a water glass found next to Donna Decker's body. Since then, the crime lab had developed three more good fingerprints: two from the inside front door, and one from the Clairol makeup mirror. They also had one palm print on a check stub.

Latent examiner Jeanine McKenzie was able to identify the print on the mirror as Donna Decker's. Panoyan matched none of the prints. One down, eight to go.

Wednesday, November 16
11 A.M.
Davie police station

Knowing that Charles Panoyan felt most comfortable with Gerry Todoroff, Dennis Mocarski requested him to ask Panoyan to come in to the police station to answer more questions.

But what Mocarski really wanted was Panoyan's consent to take a polygraph. When Panoyan arrived he hesitated and wanted to call his attorney. That was news to the police that he had an attorney, and not good news either. Panoyan called, then handed the phone to Todoroff. The attorney—Panoyan's friend Jan Dubin—told the detective that he did not believe in polygraphs and had advised his client not to submit to one.

Todoroff wrote that the call was made at Kelly Woodroof's desk. "It should be noted that a specific handcuff key had been laying on top of Detective Woodroof's desk unbeknownst to me. I saw that Chuck had observed the key lying there and looked visibly shaken when he noticed it. After he hung up the phone, Chuck called me over and showed me the key. I stated, 'That's a handcuff key, what about it?' Chuck didn't say anything."

8:10 P.M.
Humana Hospital Bennett

Woodroof brought the cowboy hat to Bob's hospital room to see if he recognized it. He didn't; however, he added that his vision was blurry right then. He thought the assailant's hat was "more straw."

Thursday, November 17
9:20 A.M.
Hollywood Memorial Hospital

After thirteen days, at last both Carl and Bob were scheduled to go home. It should have been a happy occasion, but it only created more conflict. The day began when Jo Zazzo called the nurse, upset and crying because Bob planned to take Carl home. She wanted them both to stay at her house. It got Carl upset too; a few minutes later a nurse wrote that he called her an "asshole."

Midday was calm, but when Bob and Grandpa Clyde showed up at four o'clock with a police officer, the baby made a scene. He cried, "I want to stay here. I want Auntie Jo." After about ten minutes they were able to take him home.

✦ NINE

BOB DECKER
Saturday, November 19
4:13 P.M.
Decker house

Home at last, Bob Decker's prognosis was good. However, doctors told him he was going to have deficits for a long time: headaches and dizziness that caused him to veer from side to side when walking; some double vision; and speech problems that would make him sound drunk.

Police waited only a day before asking him to do a videotape walk through, as Panoyan and Clyde had already done. Once again, Gerry Todoroff asked questions and Sgt. Ed Taylor held the camera. Clyde was present while the tape rolled.

When Bob first saw Panoyan in the driveway that night, he told the officers, "I was kind of kidding about his wife, you know, did you have a fight with your wife or what happened? What are you doing here?

"It was 9:00. I always watch *Dallas* at 9:00 to 10:00, on Channel 4."

Inside the house, *Dallas* was just starting. "I heard him say something about venison and he went out to his truck to bring the venison in. Who took that and put it where? I don't remember that."

Clyde answered, "He handed it to me. I put it—"

"You put it in the house freezer," Bob cut him off. "He had a small package of venison meat, and he got up and put it in there and Chuck sat back down in the chair.

"The robber come in the second he was sitting down. The both of them had sat back down."

"As soon as Chuck sat down?" asked Todoroff.

"Yeah. I shaked it off as a joke almost. I thought it was a real joke."

"Were you talking to Chuck at that time?"

"Off and on. I told him he was going to be leaving in a minute or two because *Dallas* was coming on. This party was over. He was only here a couple of minutes, but it was just a joking thing all along because I thought it was weird that he was here."

"Why is that?"

"I just felt funny about it, you know. I see him twice a year [here at the house] for about two minutes. He come in like he made himself at home and was going to spend the night. It was very unusual, except that he had told him [Clyde] about this venison thing for a long time, saying he was going to bring him a package of venison from Utah.

"He went hunting a couple of weeks before. And—I really didn't think nothing of it other than, you know, he come over that night.

"Finally I got it out of him, something about his wife was arguing with the head people at the airlines down there. Of course, she has been with Eastern Airlines, which has been in trouble for quite a while.

"He [Chuck] went home and said, 'I'm not arguing with you after you argued with them.' I guess he left. Whatever happened—I don't know whether he come with this guy, he never seen him before, or whatever; but that split second— the door was unlocked and the guy came in."

The intruder had selected an unusual gun for a murder. Bob described it as a .22 revolver, "something that you would pick out of the garbage.

"He was shaking every second with it. Every second that thing was shaking like crazy."

"Like he was nervous?"

"Very scared, or on something or whatever. I don't know."

The intruder handcuffed Bob and Clyde, but Bob was uncertain if he cuffed Panoyan. "I did not see the handcuffs get totally both hands locked and everything with Chuck. I know he attempted, but I don't know how far he went with it."

"Right away, he was concerned with where the floor safe was. His exact words, I don't know exactly but they were something like, 'Which corner is the floor safe in? Is it hooked to the burglar alarm?' "

"Was there any conversation between you and Chuck?"

"No. Chuck and I never said another word the rest of the night."

The intruder dragged Bob into the master bedroom clothes closet where the floor safe was and found it under the carpet. But he didn't try to open it, guessing that it was connected to the alarm system. (It wasn't, Bob told the detectives.) Then he dragged Bob back into the bedroom proper and left him on the floor.

Next, "He brought my father in right away and threw him on the bed. I was upset. He was pushing him around already. Like this time here I am really convinced it is not a joke anymore at all."

While the intruder wasn't paying attention, Bob tried to get up to activate the panic feature on the alarm system. All he needed to do was touch the "test" button and any number, and the alarm would have gone off and rung for ten minutes. The intruder caught him trying to get up, then tied both he and Clyde tighter, using belts from the closet and electrical cords from the phone and makeup mirror.

"Did Chuck come into the bedroom?"

"Never. Never seen him in here."

That contradicted what Bob had told Woodroof and Mocarski, that Chuck was inside the bedroom for a "split second."

The intruder stayed busy rummaging through drawers in the bedroom, walking into the office/closet, and checking on Chuck in the living room. Before Bob was completely tied up as he would be later, he was able to stand and walk as far as the bedroom doorway. There he saw the gunman talking to Panoyan.

"He got him [Panoyan] up to the chair. I couldn't tell if he had handcuffs on or not. Boy, he come storming in here then. He is mad."

"Did he ever say anything like don't get up anymore?"

"Yeah. He kept threatening me. 'I'm going to shoot you right now.' That kind of thing."

Finally, the intruder "tied the hell out of me, my legs and

everything. He didn't want me to move no more. He went in that drawer there and got a sock and put a sock in my throat. I almost choked to death on that darn thing.

"My tongue was raw. I spit that out, luckily, then he put a rope around it—all the way around, and to me, I pretend it was still in there. I was able to still talk to Carl, to say, don't do this, stay here, stay here." Clyde had a sock in his mouth too.

"Could you hear anything from the other room?" asked Todoroff.

"Nothing."

"Did it seem to you like he was looking for anything specific?"

"The first thing he was very mad about is he was looking in all those drawers and bedboard and everything. He was looking for drugs and money.

"I says, 'Hey, I am going to tell you, you have got the wrong house when it comes to that. There ain't no money here and there is definitely no drugs because none of us take drugs at all. We don't mess with them.'

"That made him very mad because he didn't believe we didn't mess with drugs at all. He wanted drugs because he thought he was going to make some money. He started looking more and more and more."

This time Bob described the intruder as 5'8" to 5'9", very stocky, wearing blue jeans, a blue jeans jacket, ankle-length work boots, brown work gloves, brownish woman's nylon hose over his head, and a straw cowboy hat.

"Anything unusual about his voice?"

"No. I could tell he was a redneck. He was strictly a cowboy."

Donna had come in about the time *Dallas* went to its first commercial break. Bob didn't hear the door open, but he heard it shut behind her.

After talking briefly to Panoyan, Donna came to the entrance of the bedroom. "She seen him and right away she started to cry, you know, and 'Don't hurt us. Don't hurt us. What do you want? Do you want money?' "

"He was in the bedroom when she came in?"

"When she came in he didn't hear her. I don't know if

he expected her. He caught her by surprise. Well, I mean she caught him by surprise."

"What makes you say that?"

"Neither one of them knew either one of them was here until they seen us. Of course, it was too late. He already grabbed her the second he seen her.

"She was like in tears and about to cry, you know. 'Don't hurt my baby. Don't hurt us. I will pay you anything you want.'

"I knew better, because he was just going to do what he wanted to do, regardless. It didn't matter what you tried to talk to him. You couldn't talk to this man."

The intruder was about to take Donna to a room out of Bob's sight, then he heard a noise, "the very noise I heard before.

"Neither one of them left this room, but I heard the door open and shut quick. Chuck had went out the door and that upset me."

"Are you assuming that Chuck went out the door?" Todoroff asked.

"Yes. Well, I am like 99 percent sure. He would be the only one, probably."

"Did the robber hear that?"

"The robber didn't pay any attention at all. He was concerned with tying her up and getting her to shut up because she wouldn't shut up."

"During this part when he confronts her here, when do you hear the door open and close?"

"That second," said Bob. "I said to myself I was sure it was Chuck. I was sure he was gone. I called once or twice for Chuck and nobody would answer before that."

A few minutes later Donna reappeared in the same spot, her hands bound behind her with black nylon rope. She was wearing only one shoe.

"She was talking to us, trying to say, 'I will take the baby' or 'Are you okay?' or anything. Right away he grabbed her and yanked her right back out of here.

"I was too fully tied over here and not close enough. Even when I rolled, it was killing me to roll with the different ties and everything. I tried every God damned thing I could do to move."

"Did he take your wallet?"

"My wallet was in the office sitting above the phone with a set of keys. Then he also had my Uzi, which was just above that—Uzi submachine gun. Had a lot of slugs in it too. Was not loaded. He put the clip in it, and it looked like to me it was backwards, to tell you the truth. Maybe it wasn't, but it definitely looked like there was nothing in it."

"What other firearms or weapons did he have?"

"I had a shotgun in there, too, that I had just brought down from New York two weeks ago from my father's that I had when I was twelve years old."

"Did you see him carrying these weapons around?"

"He was carrying them around."

"All of them?"

"Yeah. He come in with the Uzi. 'Cute, real cute,' he said. 'Real cute.' "

After that Bob didn't see or hear Donna or Chuck again.

"No more noises out there. The TV was on and drowned everything out. Chuck was gone. He was gone for sure. I don't know if he took his truck. I couldn't hear his truck."

"You didn't hear the engines?"

"No. I couldn't hear that. He might have fired up by the time he hit the road and took off. Then again, he may not. He may have just run. He may have run and hid in the bushes, and when he seen nobody looking, he may have come back and got his truck."

At about 9:40, the intruder came in to deliver a message: "He come to me and says his mommy wants Carl to come with him. I said no way. He stays by me for sure.

"At that point I thought he was a little haywire. I could tell it wasn't no joke anymore. I was really scared. I didn't want him running with her. Then I know he would be crying. If he seen her, he would be crying his head off and as of this point, he didn't say a word. He stayed right by me, very quiet and very good."

"He was never bound?"

"No. That I am surprised of, now that I think about it."

"Well, after he says that, then what happens?"

"He came back and grabbed a pillow. I think he took it off that bed there. He put it over my head, my face was down like this and my back up. He put it on my head and he shot me—two shots.

"He shot the baby once and I pretended, I played dead because he would have kept on going.

"Luckily, it was that beat-up piece of shit .22. If he hadn't had that, I don't know what would have happened.

"I seen him shoot my father, the baby and me and everything, of course, but I was the first one. And I kept listening for him to go over there [pointing outside the bedroom, to where Donna might have been] to shoot.

"And, you know, I was kind of half blacked out a little bit too. Then it seemed like a few seconds later the medics come in and the police come in and seen me tied up."

"Did you ever hear anything from Donna after you were shot?"

"I heard a police officer say, 'She is really bad. I don't think she is going to make it.' Now, I didn't know if it was a bullet or it was a knife until two days ago. I found out from the other detective that it was a knife."

"You said you thought you might have blacked out?"

"I could have. I don't know. Because I wasn't all there. He shot, and the first time was the worst. Man, I really jumped. The second time it didn't do hardly anything."

"When you were being transported out of the house, did you see anything?"

"Nothing. No. It was gone by then. From that point I don't remember nothing from then on."

Todoroff returned to the pages Bob and Donna had signed. Bob described the papers as blank except for four lines hand-drawn with a straight edge, three-quarters of the way down the page. Donna's signatures were very shaky, and both times he signed on the line above hers. Vaguely he knew that he was signing a blank property deed. He said he had similar blank paper in his office, as well as a ruler.

"Is there anything else that you can think of that happened that night that might be important to our investigation?" Todoroff asked.

"Nothing. Just right from day one the only thing that I can remember is Chuck was very suspicious. It was weird how it happened, him coming and everything that night. I thought it was real strange because I see him every day, I don't need to see him at night.

"I was very surprised he came that night. The venison, personally, I could care one way or the other if I have it or not. Probably will get thrown out, who knows. I wouldn't have it, and if my father hadn't asked for it, he wouldn't have got it."

Wednesday, November 30
7 P.M.
Davie police station

Panoyan and his wife came to the station again to pick up his work boots. The last time he had come for them, he had forgotten to take them home once police took him to the Decker house to record his videotape walk-through.

Frustrated that their other leads were going nowhere, Mocarski and Woodroof reckoned that now was the time to spring what they had held back to see if Panoyan would break.

First, the detectives pointed out the inconsistencies in his story compared to the individual stories of Bob and Clyde Decker:

- Panoyan had said the intruder took them all into the bedroom, but both Deckers said he separated Panoyan from them at that point;

- Panoyan said it was Bob who mentioned there was a safe in the house, but Bob said he didn't, and the fact that the gunman knew about it meant that Panoyan must have told him;

- Bob said he saw the gunman whispering to Panoyan, but Panoyan hadn't mentioned it;

- Bob was all but certain that Panoyan left the house just after Donna walked in, but Panoyan said he didn't leave until just after *Dallas* ended.

Panoyan insisted that his account was correct. Both detectives accused him of complicity in the crime. He denied it.

Then Mocarski pulled out a photograph of the SWAT belt found in his truck and showed it to him. Panoyan looked at it, swore the belt was not his, he had never seen it before, and he had no idea what it was doing in his truck. His only idea of where it had come from was that he had picked up a hitchhiker earlier on the day of Donna's murder; perhaps that's whose belt it was.

Knowing that a handcuff key was found in the SWAT belt, the detectives asked him if he owned a pair of handcuffs. He said he did, but he had cut them in half. Mocarski asked Darla if she would return home, accompanied by Det. Spence, to look for the cuffs. They found them, but no key. In fact the cuffs were intact.

✦ Ten

December 1988

Detectives are fond of saying that most cases are solved in the first forty-eight to seventy-two hours after the crime. But if that time passes without an arrest, the chances of ever solving it diminish greatly.

A month into the case, the situation looked bleak. The rest of the detective bureau went back to their other business, and even Woodroof and Mocarski stopped spending full-time on the case.

However, they felt certain that Panoyan was the inside man for a robbery that turned into a murder. Therefore, they would have to wait until Panoyan led them to the gunman.

In the meantime, Woodroof and Mocarski did the little things. Neighboring Metro-Dade County Police had the ability to detect indented traces of writing; so on December 6, the Davie detectives gave them the manila folder that Bob Decker said the gunman placed underneath the blank documents for signing. But when the technicians saw it, they told Woodroof it was unlikely they would find anything because that type of cardboard wasn't soft enough to become indented by writing. They had had more success reading indented memo pad pages. Days later they reported their lack of success.

On December 7 they went to the school of Panoyan's twelve-year-old son Charles, Jr., and fourteen-year-old daughter Sharla to find if their dad had told them anything that he hadn't told police. Charles, Jr., said his father told him that he was gagged when Donna Decker had come home, then added that his mother said that if he were arrested, the family would have serious financial problems.

Later the same day they interviewed Darla Panoyan at her job at Eastern Airlines. They told her that her husband could be eliminated as a suspect if he took a polygraph, and she said that she could convince him to do so and would contact them. She never called back.

Another idea was to place Bob Decker under hypnosis. There were two reasons to try this: perhaps under hypnosis Decker would remember additional details of the incident, or possibly he was holding something back, such as involvement in the drug trade.

But this, too, produced nothing of value. In a session with a BSO hypnotist, Decker recalled nothing new besides a description of the gunman's cowboy-style belt, with decorative stitching and an oval silver buckle.

Woodroof felt most likely the gunman was James Malcolm. There were a lot of reasons to think so: Malcolm was the guy Bob Decker had thought of when he said the gunman reminded him of "Panoyan's electrician." He also fit the physical description. He was a hunting buddy of Panoyan, who in fact had been in Utah with Panoyan between October 20 and 27, just a week before the murder. On that trip they had shot the venison that Panoyan brought to Clyde Decker. In addition, Malcolm admitted that Panoyan had called him twice since the murder.

Going against the theory was the absolute lack of physical evidence or testimony.

Woodroof asked Malcolm to come to the Davie police station on the evening of December 22. Once there, Woodroof asked if he would take a lie detector test, which could be administered on the spot.

Malcolm balked, but Woodroof and other detectives insisted. "They convinced me by one thing that the guy said," Malcolm said later. "He said, 'If you're guilty of anything, don't take it. If you have nothing to hide, take the lie detector test.'"

Det. Charles Forrest administered the polygraph. He asked thirteen questions, but only seven were "relevant" questions spaced between innocuous "control" inquiries. Forrest asked:

"Regarding the murder of Donna Decker, do you intend to answer all of my questions truthfully?

"Did you kill Donna Decker?

"Did you shoot the baby?
"Are you involved with Chuck Panoyan in the murder?
"Do you suspect anyone in particular in the murder?
"Do you know for sure who is involved in the murder?
"Did you take part in the murder?"

Malcolm answered "yes" to the first and "no" to the rest, expressing some distaste that the questions were so accusatory. Forrest's conclusion was that Malcolm had been "nondeceptive," that is, he passed.

Just after the New Year, a man named Howard Leech called Davie police and was put through to Kelly Woodroof. The caller was a mechanical inspector for Broward County, and he knew Panoyan. In fact, Panoyan had spoken with him about the case, and Leech thought the police might be interested.

It was not until a month later that Woodroof made his way to Leech's home one evening. Leech said Panoyan mentioned that he hadn't told the police everything he knew about the homicide, although he didn't tell Leech what he had left out.

In addition, Panoyan told Leech that he was "sorry" that the murder happened, and that the assailant took an Uzi and several other guns from the Deckers.

The police administered more polygraphs On February 3, Det. Forrest asked the same relevant questions to Roy Davis, who also passed. However, Davis told Forrest that the last questions bothered him "because he feels that Bob Decker knows who murdered his wife and that Chuck Panoyan is involved," Forrest wrote in his report.

Forrest tested both James and Josephine Zazzo on February 7 to eliminate lingering doubts that a family fight might have provoked the murder. Both passed.

Next was Sam McFarland, the friend of Bob Decker's, who Mocarski had tried to provoke into admitting that he was the masked killer. Back then, McFarland had walked out. Forrest tested him on February 14, and his results in fact showed some deception.

But there was a problem. Forrest was a green polygrapher, with just a year and a half experience. Despite how the public perceives polygraphy, it does not provide cut-and-dried answers regarding truthfulness. Rather, it gives the examiner an opportunity to form opinions.

Two months later, on April 26, Mocarski decided he would no longer use Forrest. To polygraph Bob Decker, he instead employed BSO Det. Tom Eastwood, who had much more experience.

During Decker's discussion with Eastwood before the test, Decker asked why Panoyan had avoided taking a polygraph if he had nothing to hide.

When the test began, Eastwood asked Decker:

"Are you deliberately holding back any information from me about who attacked you and your family?

"Do you know the name of the person who shot you?

"Were you involved in any venture, legal or otherwise, that you haven't told me?

"Prior to the attack, were you involved in any relationship with any woman?

"Do you know of any reason why someone would want you or your family dead?"

All of Decker's answers were "no." Eastwood concluded that he had not been deceptive.

By June 1989, seven months had passed, and the police were as far as ever from an arrest. Hoping to put some renewed vigor into the case, Kelly Woodroof asked to become sole lead detective, and Dennis Mocarski agreed to bow out.

Immediately the investigation got moving again. On June 5, Woodroof took new taped statements from Bob and Clyde Decker, although they didn't provide any new details. Two days later he taped a statement from Roy Davis, who talked mainly about Panoyan's $4,500 unpaid debt to him. The same day Woodroof spoke to Dr. Ongley, the assistant medical examiner who told him that he had never found any visible marks on Panoyan's neck to support his story that his neck was bound with bristly rope.

On June 8, Woodroof went to the Broward County Courthouse to take a meeting with Assistant State's Attorney Brian Cavanagh, a homicide prosecutor. The two men and State's Attorney investigator Dave Patterson—a grizzled, streetwise, cigar-smoking retired Fort Lauderdale police homicide detective—had informally discussed the murder months before, while on a road trip to a federal prison in Sandstone, Minnesota. Back then the three were trying to break another case, involving the Outlaws motorcycle gang—which later ended up in federal court, where convictions were won.

Woodroof had said then he was frustrated because he felt he had the right suspects, yet not enough to pin it on them. After some talk, he convinced Patterson that he was on target.

Since there was no pending arrest, no prosecutor had been assigned to the case. Normally prosecutors in the homicide office didn't entertain such early meetings, but Cavanagh was known for being different and approachable in that respect.

Brian Cavanagh and Kelly Woodroof were similar in intensity and intelligence, but just as dissimilar in appearance. A hundred years ago they might have been enemies; even in America then, the Irish and the English didn't like each other much. Woodroof, in his early thirties, had a slight build, with thin light-brown hair. He joked that he reminded people of a cross between the Winnie the Pooh character Eeyore and Sherman, the sidekick boy who had a genius talking dog, Mr. Peabody, for a master, from *The Bullwinkle Show*.

Woodroof's game was soccer. On the other hand, Brian Cavanagh was a six-and-a-half-footer, built like a basketball power forward. As a youth he had been a lifeguard patrolling the surf of Long Beach (Long Island, New York). Now about forty, his wiry, curly brown hair was trimmed shorter, but he had grown a full blond mustache that he didn't like to trim, keeping it in a style that was popular at the turn of the last century. And while Woodroof never raised his voice and spoke in an understated tone that reflected his Vanderbilt University education, Cavanagh loved to be loud and to laugh from his belly.

Had you first met the two men together on an athletic field, and had to choose which was the cop and which was the prosecutor, you'd probably guess wrong. Brian had wanted to be a cop, like three generations of Cavanaghs before him, all New York City cops. His dad, "Big Tom" Cavanagh, and grandfather "Long Tom" Cavanagh, had been detectives who had solved some of New York's most difficult homicide cases from the 1930s to the 1970s.

Their substantial brainpower passed down to Brian, genetically and environmentally. But dad insisted Brian go to law school, so instead of taking a job offer as a cop, he enrolled at the University of Miami.

Woodroof had grown up in the sticks, a small town called Goodlettsville, Tennessee—home of country musician Bill Monroe—since swallowed up as a suburb of Nashville in the same way Davie had been overwhelmed by Fort Lauderdale. He joked that cops didn't run in his family. They were known for stealing livestock.

"It's not fair to say that all the Woodroofs were cattle thieves," he said, telling the story during a lighter moment. "But all the cattle thieves in Tennessee were Woodroofs."

At their meeting, Kelly briefed Brian on how far the investigation had gone and where it had stalled. He had hoped that Brian would say they had enough to ask a grand jury for indictments against Panoyan and Malcolm; but after a few days thought, Brian gave a firm no.

But Brian approved the idea of subpoenaing Panoyan's and Malcolm's recent telephone bill records and tapping their phones, and asked Woodroof to work with a second prosecutor, Charlie Vaughan, a native of the Alabama backwoods, who, unlike Woodroof, sounded unmistakably like he was from the South.

It isn't easy in the state of Florida to get a telephone tap. For the next three weeks, Woodroof organized his case into a long affidavit to present to a judge, arguing that all other investigatory avenues had been pursued unsuccessfully.

Phone records are less difficult to get. Knowing that he would at least get those, Woodroof figured out ways to "tickle the wire," that is, provoke some communication between Panoyan and Malcolm that would be recorded on their phone bills. The strategy had a chance of working because Panoyan and Malcolm lived a toll call apart.

On June 19, Woodroof went down the block from the Davie police station to Town Hall and spoke with a records clerk about property Panoyan owned. The clerk told Woodroof she knew Panoyan well because he came to Town Hall frequently.

Woodroof researched building permits and sales of properties that both Panoyan and Bob Decker had entered. He found that Panoyan was building a new home in Davie, and that the contractor was Sam McFarland.

He also found that Tole Electric had done the wiring on Panoyan's home. Malcolm worked for Tole Electric. On leaving, Woodroof deliberately said nothing to the clerk about not telling Panoyan that the police were inquiring about him, expecting the clerk to mention it to Panoyan the next time she saw him.

Later, when the telephone bills arrived, they showed that the tickle may indeed have caused a rewarding sneeze. Two days after Woodroof's inquiry, there was a fifteen minute call from Panoyan's phone to Malcolm's residence. That was followed by two more calls between them in the next two weeks.

Inspecting all the phone records of the two men since the murder, Woodroof found there was communication between them just after police talked to Malcolm the first time on November 10, 1988. Woodroof remembered that he and Mocarski had become lost in North Miami looking for Malcolm's home, called him asking for directions, then arrived about ten minutes later, at 5:55 P.M. When they got there, Malcolm said he had just talked to Panoyan, but told them Panoyan had called him.

The records showed otherwise. Malcolm called Panoyan at 5:48 and spoke for six minutes. That was a deception, Woodroof reasoned.

Then at 8:59 that same evening, long after police had left, Panoyan's phone called Malcolm's phone and spoke for ten minutes.

In all, there were thirteen calls between the two phones from November 10, 1988, to July 6, 1989. Ten were made from Panoyan's phone to Malcolm's phone.

On July 11, Brian Cavanagh agreed that they should ask a judge to authorize a "pen register, trap and trace" on the two phone lines prior to an approval of a full wiretap. Although they still wouldn't be able to overhear the content of the calls, they would get phone number of all incoming and outgoing calls, not just outgoing toll calls.

Hoping to show that Panoyan had severe money troubles, Woodroof got credit reports that listed all the financial institutions Panoyan dealt with, including mortgage brokers, credit card companies, banks, and credit unions. To get the actual records, he gave the addresses to Vaughan, who drafted subpoenas for a judge to sign.

On August 3, Woodroof delivered the cowboy hat to the BSO crime lab.

On August 29, Broward Circuit Court judge Robert W. Tyson, Jr., signed the trap and trace and pen register order.

On September 15, Woodroof brought Michael Gillette to the Davie police station to review Charles Forrest's opinions of the polygraph tests he had submitted to Malcolm and McFarland. Gillette had been Forrest's instructor.

Forrest had concluded that Malcolm was not deceptive, but McFarland was. Gillette, however, found that both were deceptive. In fact, Malcolm was "overwhelmingly deceptive" to the questions "Did you kill Donna Decker?" and "Did you shoot the baby?" McFarland had "significant reactions consistent with deception" to the questions "Did you have anyone in the house sign two blank legal-size papers on the day of Donna's murder?"; "Did you solicit someone to go to the Decker residence on the day of the murder?"; and "Do you know for sure who is involved in the murder?"

It took until September 19 for the trap and trace to become functional. Meanwhile, it became obvious to both the Malcolms and the Panoyans that the heat was on.

Although the financial institutions were ordered by subpoena not to reveal to their clients that their records had been sent to investigators, one of Panoyan's credit card companies mentioned it inadvertently.

Meanwhile, detectives had made a practice of driving by Panoyan's work site and writing down license plate numbers of parked vehicles. The officers were not told to be secretive, and after a while, Panoyan recognized them and waved whenever he saw them.

On September 20 and 21, Dave Patterson served subpoenas to Darla Panoyan and Sharon Malcolm—James's wife. Since the trap and trace could only determine which phone lines were communicating, investigators needed to know if the wives and children were friendly and spoke to each other on the phone. If they were, the phone bill records would be meaningless.

On September 26, both wives came to the courthouse, accompanied by their husbands. Woodroof, Cavanagh, and Patterson kept them for more than an hour each, but they kept up the conversations only long enough so that they could bury the single question they needed to ask.

Both women answered "no": they and their children never called each other.

Sharon Malcolm didn't have a lot else to say except that her husband sometimes wore a straw cowboy hat to do yard work.

On the other hand, Darla Panoyan had a lot she wanted to say.

It was one thing that police had made a mistake in suspecting that her husband was involved in the murder, but quite another that they could investigate her husband's friend when he had done absolutely nothing. Earlier in the morning, waiting outside for the investigators to prepare, she said she had apologized to both Sharon and James Malcolm.

Patterson asked Darla if her husband would consent to a polygraph, and flatly she said no. She said their lawyer told them that polygraphs "say what the police want it to say. We were told by one of the detectives that Jimmy took the test, and we were told he had failed the test. Now we know that Jimmy is not implicated in any way, so how has that helped Jimmy?"

"Do you know for a fact that Mr. Malcolm is not involved?" Woodroof asked.

"I can swear to you."

"How do you know Jimmy is not involved?" asked Patterson.

"Because I know for Jimmy to be involved you have to be saying my husband's involved, and that my husband arranged all this. There's just no way."

Woodroof asked Darla if there was any reason Chuck would willfully obstruct an investigation, given the discrepancies in the versions of what had happened in the house.

She said no. "I believe I did specifically talk to the detectives at one time, and I told them early on in the investigation that he is not a good witness. He just does not notice things.

He is not somebody who pays particular attention to things when they register. I told him before, I said, you want him to build a house or work for you, he is excellent, but as a general observer or repeating back what he saw, he is the worst. He's got to be one the worst witnesses you're ever going to get in any kind of a case."

Woodroof asked if Chuck had sought psychological help after the incident. "No," she said. "He should have earlier, especially that first day when he was completely overwrought. I mean the man was a basket case [then] and for quite a while afterward."

Had she seen her husband in tears over this?

"If he was broken down in tears, I mean actually tears, he didn't do it in my presence, but yes, he is very upset over what's happened with Bob. They used to be very good friends, and they're not anymore. Bob naturally is very confused about this whole thing, and Bob would prefer not to talk with Chuck. He doesn't understand it either. I mean, I can put myself in his place—if you're shot and somebody else isn't, you would wonder why. So you know that bothers him, but he is trying to just go on. It's hard."

Woodroof asked her if she had an opinion on what actually happened at the Deckers' that night.

Careful to qualify her answer as merely her opinion, Darla tried out a number of possibilities: Whoever it was "went there for money and drugs." Or, "Bob had borrowed some money and didn't repay it, but had borrowed from somebody who really meant business or had gotten into drugs."

She mentioned there were some threats of divorce between Donna and Bob, and that could have been part of it. "She may have been going out with somebody and stopped seeing him."

Just before the murder, Chuck had seen them at a weekend party. All was not well:

"Apparently Bob had been drinking and Charlie wanted to drive home and Bob wouldn't allow him to drive home, and they were in Donna's car and Bob got on the expressway and I guess decided to play cat-and-mouse with somebody on the expressway. They were going back and forth and Charlie told Donna to make sure [her] seat belt's fastened and get down in case anything happens. Then by the time they got home, Bob wheeled in the yard. I guess he smacked into a tree or something and Donna got on his case for putting a dent in the car. I know there's been problems, and I know conceivably when there's problems, it could happen."

She had one last idea: "Another thing, perhaps—to kind of muddle up the case—if you wanted to try to put blame or try to confuse the case, let one person go and maybe the blame will go that way and confuse the issue, more or less."

"I see," said Dave Patterson.

"This is your idea?" asked Brian Cavanagh.

"My idea," said Darla.

Woodroof tried using the media to generate new leads. In the first week of October, he planted stories in *The Miami Herald, Fort Lauderdale Sun-Sentinel,* and on two Miami television stations.

"I want some results," Bob Decker told the *Sun-Sentinel* on October 4, his voice cracking as he recalled the horrible night eleven months before. The story appeared the same day Decker closed on a new house in Port St. Lucie, about a hundred miles up the coast.

"Hopefully, somebody knows something," he told *The Herald.* "Maybe the guy who did it has a wife and kid. I know he's got a heckuva complex. He wanted to wipe out a whole household."

The family posed for pictures. Decker said he hadn't been able to work because the gunshots caused him to lose any coordination on his right side. Carl had recovered physically, except that he had lost all hearing in his right ear.

Woodroof told *The Herald* that he believed the crime was an "inside job." The paper contacted Charles Panoyan, who commented, "I've got nothing to say."

But as an investigative tool, Woodroof considered the stories a failure. They produced no new leads.

On October 13, Detective Bob Spence—half of the team that took Panoyan's first statement on the night of the murder—ran into him at Town Hall. Panoyan said hello, and Spence feigned extreme surprise that he wasn't in jail.

That made Panoyan very nervous. He said he was trying to restart his business, and Spence responded that the business would probably be very temporary. Then he left.

That succeeded in tickling the wire again. When Woodroof got the records, he found a thirty-five-minute call from Panoyan to Malcolm that evening.

Woodroof said later that applying for a wiretap was the hardest thing he had ever had to do in police work. To prove it was necessary, Woodroof had to detail his entire investigation to show all the reasons to believe that Charles Panoyan and James Malcolm were involved in the murder.

He wrote that so much phone traffic recorded between Panoyan and Malcolm was not normal, even though they were friends.

"Rather, this contact is indicative of an active and continuing conspiracy to avoid detection and prosecution for the murder of Donna Decker, as well as other crimes connected with that incident," he stated.

In addition, the subpoenaed financial records "yielded evidence that Panoyan was suffering financial difficulties at the time of this incident, which is valuable in proving motive.

"Every lawful means of gathering information or evidence has been tried, without providing evidence useful in the prosecution of the assailant in this matter. Further, Your Affiant does not believe that the passage of time will provide any further evidence."

If Kelly Woodroof later had wanted any words in the investigation back, they would have been that last sentence.

II

◆

LEFT FIELD

✦ ELEVEN

On Monday November 15, 1989, officer Bill Coyne approached Kelly Woodroof.

"Do you want to know who committed the Decker homicide?" he joked.

Woodroof did want to know. Late Friday afternoon on November 13, a call had come to Broward Crimestoppers—the citizens' tip line to police that paid rewards on arrests—that would change the tenor of the case. But it would take Woodroof more than a month to realize its significance.

The tipster was anonymous, yet he was uncertain at first of the names of the victims, referring to the case as "the Davie murder." But he did offer details police hadn't heard in a year and nine days of investigation: the assailant was named Dana Williamson, he had red hair, and he knew the victims because he had been to their house before to buy drugs. In all, he said, there were three or four persons involved in the murder.

The tipster added that Williamson had been convicted years before of killing two children. He had left the area after this most recent murder, but before then he had lived in Miramar. Just before he left, HRS (Florida's Department of Health and Rehabilitative Services) had removed his children from the house.

The caller also knew who Charles Panoyan was and said that police were barking up the wrong tree by harassing him. Panoyan was not involved and was a "good guy." It was coincidental that he was at the scene of the crime. Williamson recognized him and for some unknown reason freed him.

Because the call had come in after the Crimestoppers office had closed for the day, it had been answered by a regular

Broward Sheriff's Office dispatcher, who in this case was the wife of Bill Coyne—the other half of the team that interviewed Panoyan on the night of the murder.

Coyne was at home taking care of his daughter when his wife called to tell him that the tipster was on the line. He told her to get all the information she could. Since she knew the case, she in fact helped the caller on some specifics that he didn't know, such as the name of the victims.

Calls to Crimestoppers are advertised as confidential, but since this call had come in through central dispatch, Coyne knew it had been recorded. Later he would make arrangements to preserve the tape.

The tip was a bit of a shock to Woodroof. Could any of it be true? He called Bob Decker. He said he had never heard the name Dana Williamson. Nor had he sold drugs to him, nor anyone else, nor did he use them.

Woodroof then called Brian Cavanagh, who promised to look up the name Dana Williamson in court records. Meanwhile, Woodroof ran his name through the Florida Crime Information Computer (FCIC). By the end of the day, they had a discovery: the tipster was correct in that Dana Williamson had been convicted for a manslaughter in 1975. In fact, the crime had been unusual in its brutality: Williamson, then just fifteen, and a friend had killed a four-year-old boy in Davie.

"I think it's a crank call," Woodroof told Cavanagh. "It sounds like some nut, rehashing old stuff."

Cavanagh agreed, but told him he'd have to follow it up, for no other reason than to cover themselves when a defense attorney would ask at trial whether it had been pursued.

Higher on Woodroof's priority list was Panoyan's wiretap. Later the same day he learned that a monkey wrench was about to be thrown into it.

Davie officer Jim Wachtstetter—a friend of Panoyan's for a few years—told Woodroof that Panoyan had just reminded him once more if he wanted to join him on his annual fall deer hunting trip out west. He was leaving the next day, November 16, and would be gone two weeks.

Woodroof's head sank. He was certain that a judge was about to approve the wiretap, and tape could be rolling within the next two weeks. Brain Cavanagh had finally acceded to

bringing the case against Panoyan to a grand jury sometime
in December—they would pass for now on trying to indict
James Malcolm—and the plan was to highlight whatever they
got in the wiretap.

On Tuesday at 10 A.M., Woodroof passed by Panoyan's
house to see if his truck was there. It wasn't. But Woodroof
found it in front of a house in Davie that Panoyan had just
finished building and was for sale.

Woodroof called his supervisor, Lt. John Sciadini, to ask
if he would come to the scene and pose as a buyer. The real
purpose of the subterfuge was to find out what Panoyan's
vacation schedule was.

Woodroof picked Sciadini because Panoyan had never seen
him before, and he dressed plainclothes as an officer. While
the lieutenant got a tour of the house, he discovered that
Panoyan had changed his plans. Now he was going out of
town on the day after Thanksgiving (November 24) and
would be gone a week.

Back at the office that afternoon, Woodroof found another
arrest for Dana Lewis Williamson. This one wasn't quite as
hot—it was for driving with a suspended license in neighboring Pembroke Pines. But the date was interesting: September 2, 1988—just two months before the murder. The
computer offered only cursory information, but that included
Williamson's description: white, 5' 10", 160 pounds—which
was within the broad limits of what the witnesses said.

Woodroof requested Williamson's booking photo from
BSO and a copy of the report from Pembroke Pines police.
A driving violation sounded like it could wait, so he put it
on his rainy day list.

Relieved that Panoyan's new vacation plans would not in-
terfere with the state's plans to indict him for first-degree
murder, Woodroof met with Brian Cavanagh on November 20.
They picked a grand jury date: December 20. During the
meeting, Cavanagh asked him to apprise the Deckers and the
Zazzos of their decision; they would need Bob and Clyde's
testimonies. Cavanagh also wrote himself a note referring to
Dana Williamson as "the red-herring crimestopper tip" that
needed to be explored.

On Monday, November 27, back from his own week-long
Thanksgiving vacation to see family in Tennessee, Woodroof

called Panoyan's house himself, posing as a buyer. Darla Panoyan answered and told him that Chuck would be back the next day. To confirm that, Woodroof had Det. Gary Sylvestri call at 9:30 P.M., Tuesday, posing as an insurance salesman. Charles Panoyan took the call.

Without amending his wiretap affidavit to mention the Crimestoppers tip—leaving in the sentence that the passage of time wasn't likely to produce any new lines of investigation—Woodroof and Brian Cavanagh submitted the request to Broward Circuit Court judge Patti Englander Henning on Friday, December 1. She promised to read the twenty-eight-page document over the weekend; she signed it on December 4.

Finally the wiretap was in business. It was authorized to run for thirty days, beginning the day it was signed.

As cumbersome as had been the process to get the wiretap order, the actual intercept was a bigger pain. For one thing, a detective had to be present whenever the monitor and tape were on. This was so not only to take notes, but to minimize the intrusion on any calls between Panoyan and an attorney or calls that had nothing to do with the investigation, like those made to and from Panoyan's children (which the monitors found to be the majority of calls).

Using a listening post in a room in the Davie Police Department, the monitors started snooping at about 6 P.M. weekday evenings, when they knew Charles Panoyan would be home. They also kept a surveillance unit near his house, which informed them whenever Panoyan left.

On the evening of Tuesday, December 5, they tried tickling the wire once more. Dave Patterson and Bob Burns—another state attorney's office investigator—went to Panoyan's house to serve him with an "invitation" to testify to the December 20 grand jury.

Grand jury invitations are left-handed compliments. Grand jury witnesses who are subpoenaed by the state of Florida have immunity from prosecution regarding any criminal act they may be questioned about. The theory is the state cannot compel self-incrimination. But someone who accepts an invitation to testify to a grand jury is not compelled; therefore, he waives his right to self-incrimination. Accepting a grand jury invitation can be like voluntarily walking into a line of fire.

In addition, Patterson planned to ask Panoyan if he would give a blood and hair sample submission. If he refused, a judge could order him to submit. Malcolm was to receive the same requests.

Darla Panoyan told the investigators that her husband would be home in a few minutes. They waited outside. When Charles Panoyan arrived, they served him in his driveway.

"Why are you still picking on me?" Panoyan asked Patterson.

After explaining that he could speak to an attorney before talking further with them, Patterson answered, "Because of your inconsistencies in the statements that you've made to the police and to other people."

"What do you mean, 'inconsistencies'?"

"Well, like the gun belt being found in your truck."

Panoyan asked him to clarify what he meant, and Patterson recited some of the explanations Panoyan had offered in the past months: "I never saw it"; "A hitchhiker may have left it in my truck"; "It could have been Bob Decker's, Bob Decker had one like it in his garage"; "My truck was left unguarded that night, and somebody could have been along and put it inside of my truck"; and, "I may have bought it at a garage sale."

Patterson then asked him why he thought he wasn't hurt that night.

"At the beginning, I thought the whole thing was a joke," Panoyan said.

"Well, when did you realize it wasn't a joke?"

"When I saw the blood," he said.

"When was that?"

"When the ambulance people brought them out of the house and put them into the ambulance."

Patterson got in one last question: "Can you explain, if you thought it was a joke, why you called the police, and why it took you thirty minutes to get to that shopping center when it's, like, a four or five-minute drive?"

"You're twisting my words around," said Panoyan, ending the conversation.

*   *   *

As soon as Patterson left, so did Panoyan. On his way out, he spotted the undercover police surveillance unit and approached it. They said they were in the area watching suspected drug dealers.

Panoyan excused himself by saying he had to go make a telephone call at a public phone because his phone at home was tapped.

"How do you know it's tapped?" one of them asked.

"I just know it is," he said.

Panoyan then drove to the nearest bank of pay phones, at Everglades Holiday Park, a campground on the edge of the Everglades. The surveillance officers—one was from Davie Police, the other from BSO—followed him.

At the phones, Panoyan asked why they were following him and then asked to see their badges. They answered that they were just doing their job and asked if they could watch him dial.

Perhaps Panoyan might have called Malcolm had the surveillance officers not been so overt. Figuring that a pay phone would record a toll record the same as a private phone, he said he called his wife, so that he could talk to her outside the presence of the children. Woodroof did later subpoena the toll records for the public phone, which showed no long-distance calls to James Malcolm.

Woodroof never did figure out how Panoyan knew that his phone was tapped. Maybe he just guessed right. But as a result, the wiretap was just about useless.

Most of the interesting talks intercepted concerned Charles and Darla Panoyan's invective against the police and state attorney's office. On December 7, Darla called a friend in north Florida and told him that her husband's lawyers had advised him not to submit to a police blood test, nor to appear in front of the grand jury because "the grand jury is one-sided and handled and managed by the state attorney, and they can really twist everything.

"We've got a friend in the state attorney's office in Dade County, [and] he said every once in a while innocent people go to jail. Can you imagine Chuck shooting a child? I think what they think is Chuck planned a robbery and something went wrong. Donna raised a commotion and got stabbed."

Right after that, Darla took a call from a friend named Winston. He said he understood the investigator's point of view because Charles "was the only one left standing, so he must have known who did it."

"What can we do?" Darla sighed. "We've got to let it run its course. They had to know he didn't do it. If they knew Chuck real well, they'd know there's no way."

Winston said he was worried because Bob Decker thought Panoyan was involved.

"He still thinks Bob's his friend. I say this guy can never be your friend and treat you the way he has. I'm afraid for Charlie. Bob and his friend would go after somebody that screwed him."

In an outgoing local call the next day, December 8, Charles Panoyan summarized his story, as he saw it.

From Woodroof's contemporaneous notes:

"A buddy of mine—a guy came in and stabbed his wife. Two nights ago [sic] I was served a voluntary subpoena to the grand jury. I called my lawyer and he said don't do any of it. . . . Somebody's following me. I'm gonna get shot. Let me go. . . . He just let you go? He let me go. Basically . . . they said I was their prime suspect. I told them I was a victim.

"They found a web belt in my truck—[a] web military belt with a small pouch with a handcuff key in it. I don't remember a belt. I'm more worried about getting shot right now than the grand jury."

On December 10, "Winnie" made another call and this time talked to Charles Panoyan. Giving Panoyan advice, Winnie said, "You've got to stay away from talking to those cops. You can't trust cops. You can't trust 'em, ever. Look, let me tell you something—they're not particular whether they get the right person. While they're screwing around with you, the one who did the thing . . . I'll call you later."

Then in a later call, Darla told a friend: "If he had been involved I could accept it and work with that. First-degree murder punishable by death in the electric chair. I feel so bad for him. We've got a lot of people praying for us. We're hoping for a fresh start in the new year, [but] it's looking less and less possible. This is the type of crime they won't solve unless a miracle happens."

Satisfied that the rest of the thirty days would produce nothing more of value, Woodroof and the team decided, after eight days, to end the wiretap on December 11. At the time Woodroof considered it a total failure.

✦ TWELVE

The grand jury appointment on December 20 would go on, however. Looking up that rainy day list, Woodroof remembered the Dana Williamson lead. From the Pembroke Pines police report, he had an address for Williamson (or at least an old one): 1711 SW 99th Terrace, in Miramar.

On December 19, Woodroof decided to take a ride. He took Det. Gary Sylvestri with him. It was 8:30 P.M. when they arrived at the Williamson address.

No one answered Woodroof's knocks. But while lingering, a neighbor bringing in her plants noticed the guns and badges on the belts of the plainclothes detectives. Woodroof approached her.

"This is about the Decker case, isn't it?" she asked.

The neighbor's name was Ginger Kostige (rhyming with "hostage"), an attractive blond approximately forty years old. She invited them into her house across the street. Inside was her husband Russell.

The stunned detectives introduced themselves. "Why do you assume we're here on a murder?" Woodroof asked.

Russell answered. They had read about it when it happened. "When we heard that Panoyan was connected, we thought Dana might be involved as well."

Woodroof felt the ecstasy that comes from finding a new and crucial piece of a puzzle. *They knew Panoyan, too.* Then he felt the dread that came from knowing that at least part of the puzzle—the James Malcolm part—as he had believed it must be wrong.

The Kostiges had a few more surprises. There was a close relationship between Panoyan and Dana's father, Charlie Williamson, who had also lived in the house across the street. However, everyone left the house soon after Dana and his wife Sandy moved to Ohio—Cleveland, she thought—where Sandy's family lived. That was a year ago, around Christmas. They even recalled Panoyan at the house around Thanksgiving 1988.

Ginger also remembered that Dana used to wear a beige straw hat.

When Woodroof got home at ten o'clock that night, he rushed to call Brian Cavanagh at his home.

"I have good news and bad news," he said. "The good news is that Williamson leads right back to Panoyan." The bad news was they would now have to postpone the grand jury hearing that had been scheduled to begin that very next morning.

Woodroof also had a message from the office that a call had come from Dana's sister, Dawna Williamson Roppoccio. Woodroof called her back, and they spoke briefly. She told him that Dana had left town within a couple of days of Thanksgiving a year before. At first he left his wife behind, telling Dawna that he wouldn't take her because "she knew things that could put him away for a long time." Dana had been in prison before and flatly stated that he would not go back.

Dawna volunteered she knew something like that herself: In 1987, Dana had told her he had a way to make extra money: it involved guns and drugs and helping a friend get money that was owed to him.

The next afternoon, Woodroof picked up the Pembroke Pines police report he had neglected for a month. As soon as he saw it, he couldn't believe he had waited so long.

There was a second man in the blue 1985 Mercury Cougar with Williamson at 11:30 on the night he was arrested in September 1988. Dana was wearing a "camouflage jumpsuit," and they were talking together, parked on the side of a dark road.

It was Charles Panoyan. The Cougar was his car.

At 5 P.M., Woodroof and Sylvestri met with both Dawna and Vernon Williamson, Dana's younger brother, at their aunt's house. Dana wasn't talking with either of them, but earlier that day, a local real-estate agency told them that he was now living in Cincinnati.

Dana left Florida in a hurry a year before, sometime around November 8–12, they guessed. Later that month, HRS took temporary custody of his two daughters, then placed them with their aunt. After that, Dana briefly returned to pick up the girls, Sandy, and their possessions, and took them north. Rodney, their oldest brother, was probably with them too.

Woodroof had photographs of the cowboy hat left at the murder scene, identified as belonging to the masked gunman. He showed them to Dawna, Vernon and Charlie Williamson, their bedridden father.

Dawna thought it looked like his work hat. Vernon said he had seen Dana with hats that style, and that it might possibly be his hat.

Charlie Williamson, who had suffered a paralyzing stroke, had no use of his voice and needed an alphabet board to communicate his answers. He was a bit more tentative, saying that it looked like a hat Dana had worn, that it was the right color, but the hat since had disappeared.

Dawna told the detectives that Dana generally dressed in blue jeans and wore a denim jacket—the clothing, Woodroof knew, that the gunman had worn. She also said Dana owned some camouflage clothing, and that he used to shop at army surplus stores.

That could explain the camouflage jumpsuit he was wearing when he was arrested in Pembroke Pines, and possibly the black nylon military SWAT belt, Woodroof thought.

She also said Dana used to do work for Chuck Panoyan. However, she had never heard of James Malcolm.

Explaining later why he didn't jump onto the Dana Williamson leads faster, Woodroof said: "You can't throw out a year's worth of investigative work over an anonymous phone call. That's not good investigation."

✦ Thirteen

Peter and Christy Wagner

When Woodroof circulated the name Dana Williamson around the Davie Police Department, it sent some shivers down the necks of the old-timers.

In February 1975, fifteen-year-old Dana Williamson and a friend beat four-year-old Peter Wagner to death and left his six-year-old sister Christy for dead. Three days after the murder, a local newspaper reported that Davie police were baffled at this "most heinous crime conceivable." The day he was apprehended he admitted he and his pal had done it "just for fun."

Only three months earlier, Joseph and Josephine Wagner had moved their family of six children from New Jersey to Hollywood. They liked their new home because there were stables nearby in Davie where they could board a horse and pony.

The Wagners went to the stables every day to feed their animals, as they did at 4:30 P.M. on Monday, February 17. About an hour later Josephine noticed that Peter and Christy were missing and sent her fourteen-year-old son Mark out on a pony to look for them. As darkness fell, Joseph, their ten-year-old son Brian, and Davie police joined the increasingly desperate search.

Joseph called out Peter and Christy's names as he entered a horse trail leading into the dense pine and melaleuca woods. He heard Christy scream from a distance, near an orange grove.

Together, Joseph and Brian ran toward the drainage canal, then crossed over two large pipes to get on the other bank.

122

There they found Peter and Christy lying on the ground. Peter was unconscious, his face bloody, but he was still gasping. Christy was screaming, her face badly pounded. She was wearing only her red top; her underwear was folded, lying on top of her pants, also folded. Two hours later, Peter died from complications compounded by a fractured skull.

"The man who did this is sick, sick," Josephine Wagner said in tears to *The Miami Herald*. "There is no cure for such a person. The key should be thrown away."

Davie police assigned an officer to stay at the hospital with Christy Wagner, who suffered brain damage, until the killer was apprehended. He stayed five days straight with her. During that time he was able to get a few words from her about the incident: "The man knocked me down and held his foot on my neck." She also said the man wore black boots.

Virtually the entire Davie police force worked on the case. Nearby the site was the Nova Living and Learning Center, a residential home for problem boys. That evening, a lieutenant checked to see if they had any runaways. They did: thirteen-year-old Roland Menzies and fifteen-year-old Dana Williamson. The school had reported them as runaways the day before.

Five days after the murder, Officer Russell Elzey (still on the force in 1988) spotted one of them. It was Dana Williamson, on a bicycle. Dana jumped off the bicycle and got away, but Elzey caught him an hour later. He was wearing a pair of black lace-up military boots.

The police advised Dana of his Miranda rights, then he spoke anyway. At first his story was that he had merely seen the children crossing the pipes over the drainage canal. But later he volunteered that he had lied, that he and Menzies had chased them "to have some fun."

"Roland and me started hitting and punching the kids, and then Roland knocked the girl down and took her pants off.

"Then Roland said, 'Let's kill them.' I chased the boy and hit him and kicked him in the head. Then I stood on the girl's throat and neck. Next I took off my shirt and wrapped it around the girl's neck. Roland kept hitting her with his fist."

Later that night, Roland Menzies was arrested. He didn't believe that Christy was still alive until police let him see the news report on television.

Roland's version of what Dana did was rougher. "I punched the boy in the chest a couple of times. I then hit the girl and she fell down and didn't get up. I then took off her pants and underpants. Dana stood on her neck and then put his tank shirt around her neck and choked her. Dana then twisted her head. We thought they were both dead when we left them."

But prosecutors were afraid that Dana and Roland's confessions might not stand up in court. "It was a horror scene," said retired Broward Circuit judge Louis Weissing, years later. "It was one of those [cases] no judge wants to see come down his way. The law puts a lot of restrictions on children that age, and you have to be very careful."

So instead of getting convictions of first-degree murder and aggravated assault, Dana and Roland were allowed to plead guilty to the lesser charge of manslaughter. They were sentenced to seven years beginning August 1975. Both were out by 1980.

Ironically, just when Dana Williamson's name was first linked to the Decker murder, Roland Menzies was again arrested for murder. In December 1989, he was charged with picking up a forty-six-year-old postal worker at an adult book store, promising him sex, then stabbing him to death in a secluded area in Fort Lauderdale and stealing his van and credit cards. (A year-and-a-half later he would be convicted of first-degree murder and sentenced to life in prison, which means he will have to serve at least twenty-five years before he is eligible for parole.)

✦ FOURTEEN

The state originally thought they would be celebrating Charles Panoyan's indictment on December 21. Instead, Bob and Clyde Decker, Brian Cavanagh, and Kelly Woodroof met together at the Davie police station.

Bob Decker said that during an afternoon two or so weeks before, Chuck had driven up to his construction site wanting to talk. He said, "The cops are no good," the case was "drug-related," and "Maybe we'll pay this guy off and he'll get out of town."

Decker reacted bitterly. He wanted no part of Panoyan anymore and told him "Get the hell off my property, you're trespassing." When Panoyan, instead of leaving, pled for Bob to talk to him, Decker dialed 911. Then Chuck left.

On December 26, Woodroof sent a teletype request for assistance to the Cincinnati police. He had a phone number for Dana Williamson from directory assistance—could they get him an address?

Within short order, Cincinnati responded. Williamson was listed at 1811 Cleveland Avenue, but that was in the city of Norwood, Ohio, a suburb wholly enclosed by the city of Cincinnati.

The next day, December 27, Woodroof contacted Norwood police and asked if an officer would drive by the address, but without contacting Williamson. By 6:30 P.M., Sgt. M.F. Wheeler wired back that he had done so. The house was a duplex, and there were two vehicles parked in front. One was a 1974 red VW bus with Colorado plates registered to Rodney Williamson.

Wheeler had also checked Dana Williamson on his computer. He had been issued a traffic ticket in April 1989 for improper display of license plates. On the ticket, Williamson had signed his name and put his address as 1811 Cleveland Avenue.

Woodroof did an FCIC request the same day for Dawna Williamson. He found she had been arrested three times in the eight months between July 1987 and March 1988: twice for possession of cocaine, and the third for violating probation.

On December 28, Woodroof brought a copy of the Crimestoppers tape to Dawna, Vernon, and Charlie Williamson, hoping they could identify the voice. Only Charlie had a guess; he thought maybe it sounded like his son Rodney, disguising his voice.

On January 3, 1990, Woodroof drove to Port St. Lucie to tell Bob and Clyde Decker the latest news. He also showed them a booking photo of Dana Williamson.

Both said they'd never seen him before.

Because Dana Williamson was a convicted felon, his fingerprints were on file. On January 17, BSO crime lab latent examiner Fred Boyd compared Williamson's prints to the seven fingerprints and one palm print still unidentified from the crime scene. There were no matches. That wasn't surprising, since all the witnesses said the gunman was wearing gloves.

Boyd informed Woodroof that neither Bob nor Clyde Decker's prints had ever been submitted for elimination in the fourteen months since the crime. Woodroof requested St. Lucie County detectives to take imprints, and within five days, the Broward crime lab had them.

On January 22, Boyd positively identified Bob Decker's prints as all of the remaining fingerprints. That still left a palm print on a check stub. St. Lucie had sent fingerprints only, no palm prints.

Although Brian Cavanagh and Woodroof had never held much hope that fingerprints were going to lead them to a positive ID of the suspect, they were at least optimistic about a DNA test of plaque scraped from the inside band of the cowboy hat. They sent it to a lab in Maryland, which reported back about this same time that the testing was inconclusive.

Woodroof had Dawna come to the police station on the afternoon of January 22 to give a taped statement.

Given the opportunity, Dawna went on a tirade about her brother Dana. He was supposed to be the primary caretaker for her invalid father, but he took inadequate care of him while he was there, then deserted him without telling anyone he had left. In addition, he had conned his father into signing over the deed to the family house to him, and now Charlie Williamson wanted it back.

"He wasn't giving him his medication—he has high blood pressure and an ulcer. He kept him in a very filthy environment—it was cleaner than the rest of the house, but sanitary-wise it was not clean. He just wasn't making sure my father got the proper care," she said.

For the week or so until the family realized Dana was gone, Charlie Williamson received hardly any care at all. "He was given one drink of water a day and one meal a day, and that was being given to him by Dana's oldest girl."

Woodroof asked Dawna to detail the violent criminal activity in which she believed Dana had become involved.

"Dana told me that he was going to do a job for a friend of his, he was going to go rough some people up for some money that they owed this friend of his, and the man couldn't go to the police because the money wasn't for something exactly legal. He didn't intend on hurting anyone, but if someone got hurt, oh well."

Woodroof asked if Dana owned weapons. Dawna remembered that Rodney kept a semiautomatic assault rifle, and that he and Dana liked to talk about killing.

"Rodney has an IQ higher than Einstein's, he can tell you how to make a nuclear bomb out of things around the house. They would tell me one time about a .22 rifle, they could take the shells for a .22 and hollow the tip out, its lead tip, and you hollow the tip out and put mercury in it. If you shoot someone with it, they'll die, because they'll get mercury poisoning."

Dawna had earlier told Woodroof that Dana had filed divorce papers against Sandy at the Broward County Clerk's

Office, but had never told her. Woodroof had since obtained a copy of the final decree, which was prepared without an attorney.

"Dana told me that he couldn't tell her they were divorced because she knew enough to put him away for a long time—not just a brief stay in prison for somewhere around five years, but he said a long time. More like life."

"When did he mention this?"

" '88, it was while he was living at my father's house, before they left."

"Would it be fair to say it was fairly soon before they left, or several months before?"

"Within two months that he left."

"Did Dana ever say anything about Sandy that you interpreted as being threatening, that he might be threatening her safety in any way?"

"Oh, yeah, he said that one of the guys she was going out with had a friend that was in prison who was a crack addict, and [Dana] was waiting for [this] friend to get out of prison, and he was going to have him take her out to the alley and make sure she didn't come back."

Dawna said Dana once attacked her.

"Dana has a nasty temper, he tried to choke me, and my [half-] brother Jay hit him over the head with a solid steel bat to get him off me. I kicked him between the legs and he let go, then he came right back, had me up against the wall by the throat."

"Would you say Dana is a violent person?"

"He can be."

"Do you think he would be capable of the sort of crime that we're investigating?"

"I wouldn't put anything past him."

✦ Fifteen

After listening to the Crimestoppers tape a few times, Woodroof thought he had heard that voice before. Was it on the wiretap? Checking, he compared it to the person named Winston or "Winnie" who'd called Panoyan's line twice. To Woodroof's ear, it was the same voice.

The wiretap had included a trap and trace of phone numbers, both incoming and dialed out. Woodroof checked Winnie's number in a cross-reference directory and found the corresponding name Winston Marsden, with an address listed in Hollywood.

Just to be certain that he was right, Woodroof called a criminologist in Miami who performed voice comparisons. But his fee was $500, which Woodroof's bosses nixed.

Instead, Woodroof asked Brian Cavanagh to subpoena Marsden. When Woodroof took an evening run at Marsden to serve him, Marsden got annoyed.

"I thought calling Crimestoppers was supposed to be confidential," he said.

Woodroof chuckled to himself. It was until now.

Marsden came to the courthouse on January 29 to give a sworn statement. To protect his identity for the record, they referred to him as "Confidential Informant 101."

Marsden took his subpoena as an opportunity to tell everything he knew—and to tell off the police for investigating his friend Charles Panoyan.

Marsden, sixty-one, a builder himself, said he had first met Chuck twenty years before, when Panoyan—then just a carpenter's helper—began to build his own house in the Tropical Valley subdivision of Miramar. That was where the Williamsons lived, and Marsden had a home there, too. Back then it was on the very western edge of the city; water and sewer services hadn't yet been installed.

He said Panoyan had poured concrete for his floor so unevenly that it was a near disaster. At sunset that day, while it was still wet, he introduced himself to Marsden and asked for help. Marsden got it straightened out best he could, and in doing so, the two men became friends.

Over the years, Marsden had often subcontracted construction work to Panoyan. As friends, they talked often, but it was weeks after the murder before Marsden got the chance to ask Panoyan what he knew about it.

"He told me you don't know what it is like to have somebody hold a pistol to your head with the hammer back. Your life passes before your face.

"He told me this guy, he don't know where he came from, was in the house with a shroud on or something, and had a gun on him. He thought it was a joke that Bob was pulling on him. Bob thought it was a joke [Panoyan] was pulling on him. But then it got to the point, he says, when the guy started kicking him in his ribs and legs and it was not a joke anymore.

"He told him that he was going to let him go, that he knew where he lives, he knew where his wife worked, and that he knew his kids, and that if he went to the law or turned around and didn't get straight out of there that they would be wasted."

Marsden said Panoyan got almost home when "he came to his senses and realized that he had to call somebody."

That was a different story than Panoyan had given to the police on the night of the murder and had stuck to.

"Say a mile south of 84 and Hiatus to Panoyan's house—how long does it take to drive out there?" asked Charlie Vaughan.

"I would say it must be, oh, like eighteen miles, and I know his truck. He is probably lucky if he made thirty miles an hour with it."

Woodroof asked Marsden if he thought Panoyan was an honest person.

"Definitely."

"You have never known him to lie?"

"Never. I would be very surprised to find out he did anything dishonest, to be honest with you."

"Can you think of any reason why he would willfully obstruct this investigation by not telling the truth?"

"If that is the case, the only thing that I could even suggest he would do that for would be to protect, you know, his children and his wife."

Woodroof tried a different tact.

"This may seem like a silly question, but have you ever known Mr. Panoyan to hallucinate?"

"No."

"To see things that nobody else sees, seeing things that aren't true?"

"If you mean is he a little bit flaky at times, yes."

The investigators wanted to know how Marsden knew that Dana Williamson was the killer. His answer was a little disappointing. It was thirdhand, at best. He had heard it from a friend named Allie Kittle, who still lived in Tropical Valley. Marsden had moved away years before.

"He said, 'I know who killed that guy out there that they're trying to hang Chuck Panoyan with.' He said it is the Williamson kid."

Marsden said he had asked Kittle how he knew, but Kittle said his information was secondhand too. He wouldn't be more specific.

"I said, 'I want you to call Crimestoppers.' He said it is too close to me, they'll know that I heard it. And he says, they'll get me and my family."

"What did you think when you first heard Dana Williamson's name mentioned in connection with this?" Woodroof asked.

"I made a suggestion to this one time before to Chuck. I am trying to think of anybody he knew, because I said to myself, Why would he not be shot when everybody else was? It does look a little strange, okay.

"So I said to him, the only explanation I have for it, I said, 'Chuck, it must have been somebody that knew you.' "

"What was his response to that?" asked Brian Cavanagh.

"He says, 'I have no idea.' He says, 'I wish the hell I knew who the hell it was.' "

Marsden said he had told Panoyan that he knew the killer was Dana Williamson.

"I said, 'I bet you money that is the man.'

"He says, 'How do you know that?'

"I said, 'Well, I have been told that by a reliable source.'

"So, he says to me, 'I don't believe it.' He said, 'That is a hell of a thing to say about somebody if you don't know.'

"I says, 'As far as [Williamson] is concerned, I really don't care; if it was a decent person I may not even say anything. But this guy, as far as I am concerned, should be behind bars anyhow.' "

"Did he know Dana Williamson?"

"Yes, sure. He grew up right out there with us in the valley. You knew everybody. It was only about eight families out there in that valley and everybody knew everybody."

In fact, Marsden said Panoyan wanted him to hire Dana on a construction job sometime in the middle of 1988. "When I found out who it was, I told Chuck to get him out of here, 'I don't want him around here. You have a lot of nerve even bringing him on my job.' "

"What do you know about Dana Williamson?" Woodroof asked.

"I know that he is a killer. I know he is not to be trusted from the time he was this big." Marsden gestured to a height of about three feet off the ground.

Marsden said Dana as a child had been a problem to him twice. When he was about six, he had climbed over a chain-link fence onto Marsden's property, then grabbed his German Shepherd guard dog around the neck. Marsden hollered at the child to let him go, but the dog reacted in defense first, slashing Dana's throat open "from ear to ear." He had to be rushed to the hospital, and Marsden's homeowner's insurance paid the bills.

A year later, Dana again trespassed onto Marsden's property and rode a horse without permission. Marsden considered it stealing and called the police, but didn't pursue charges.

"Was there anything else in his childhood before he got into serious trouble that you remember?" asked Charlie Vaughan.

"No, other than the fact from time to time you hear in the neighborhood he has done this, done that, he hurt somebody's animal or something. Just a mean kid, a no good [kid]. When the mother died, these kids all went down the drain. All of them.''

"Did you tell Mr. Panoyan that you called Crimestoppers?'' Cavanagh asked.

"Yes.''

"What did he say?''

"He says, 'Oh my god, you have done it now.'

"I said, 'What do you mean?'

"He said, 'You are stirring up a hornet's nest.'

"I said, 'Hey buddy, something has to put a stop to it, you're never going to get any relief.' ''

That evening, Woodroof called Allie Kittle to tell him that he should expect a subpoena as well. At four o'clock on January 30, Woodroof delivered it himself.

Kittle, an older man, lived about three blocks from the Williamson house. He told Woodroof that he got his information from another neighbor named Wanda Sullivan, who owned a fruit stand.

Woodroof got Wanda Sullivan on the phone at 7:15 that evening. Her information was secondhand, too; she mentioned Ginger Kostige as her source.

I've been running around in circles, Woodroof realized.

✦ Sixteen

On February 1, Ginger Kostige came to the courthouse to answer her subpoena.

She told investigators Dana had left the state sometime after Halloween 1988, alone, then returned for his wife and children about a week before Christmas. She herself saw him loading his car the second time.

She specifically remembered him being home at Halloween, because she had asked him if she could take his two girls trick-or-treating. That was Monday, October 31, 1988.

The investigators were interested in the clothes Dana commonly wore. Kostige said blue jeans and T-shirts, as well as a denim jacket. He also wore work boots; in fact, she remembered he had shown her, at around Halloween, a new pair of brown six-inch hightops he had just bought.

Woodroof had signed the cowboy hat out of the police evidence room so that he could show it to her. He pulled it out of a brown paper bag.

"Do you recognize that hat?"

"Yes, sir, I do."

"Where have you seen that?"

"On top of Dana Williamson's head."

Nervously, Woodroof asked her to be even more positive.

"Can you tell me what stands out? What things about it make you believe that it's his hat?"

"This particular feather here and the holes in the hat here. I remember because I remember seeing him wear this hat many times."

"Are you saying that's roughly the same color hat that he wore?"

"Yes."

"Is it roughly, or the same color?"

"It's the hat, okay?"

Next, Woodroof showed her the SWAT belt. She recognized that too. One evening she had seen Dana wearing it as part of a Ninja outfit.

Woodroof asked her to describe the Ninja outfit.

"It was camouflage and it had—it had like a hood that you put on top of your head, but I don't know if it was connected with the shirt part. And it had the Ninja mask to go with it, and he had black slip-on shoes."

That sounded to Woodroof like the same as the "camouflage jumpsuit" the Pembroke Pines officer described Dana wearing on the night he was arrested for driving with a suspended license.

"Was it a one-piece outfit?"

"It was a two-piece outfit because I remember him having the belt on the one piece, so this went around here like this."

Kostige said it wasn't unusual for the Williamsons to show her new things they had just gotten. She remembered in particular the day Dana and Rodney showed off their new Ninja suits.

"[Dana] had had the Ninja outfit on, and he had come across the street, but I didn't know that he was at my house. And he was by one of our bushes by the corner of the garage, and as I turned around to walk out he tried to scare me with it. But I knew it was him."

Kostige said that incident was in keeping with a loud conversation she had overheard at the Williamson house on the Saturday two days before Halloween, after midnight. That was the colloquy—after she had repeated it and it found its way through the grapevine—that resulted in Marsden's call to Crimestoppers.

Dana and Rodney were having a beer party with two friends in their living room. Their window was open, and Kostige, who was outside looking for her cats, could easily overhear.

"They were talking real loud and they were partying and I had heard someone say that 'We could jump on the roof.'

"And then someone said, ''Well, we can stab 'em.'

"And then I went into the house to tell my husband about

it. I shut the porch light. I had goose bumps because I thought they're talking about doing something to somebody.

"That's how I thought. They could have been talking about going hunting, I don't know. When I went back out I heard them mention something about mesh, but that was it."

"Did you recognize the voices?" asked Brian Cavanagh.

"Yes, I did. Rodney was the one that said 'We can jump on the roof,' but I don't know who the other person was."

"Did you ever hear Dana mention anything about harming or killing any other person at any other time?" Woodroof asked.

"Well, it's only through family. He mentioned when he'd get mad at his sister how they were going to do away with her."

"Did he mention any specific way?"

"Well, they were specific, with chemicals. You mix these chemicals and you can create a bomb with this. I can't remember all of what they said because I don't understand it. You can order stuff through stores and get it."

Cavanagh asked if she knew Charles Panoyan.

"We bought our house from him, but we also met him when we moved out there because he was friends with Charlie Williamson."

"Did you ever see him with Dana Williamson?"

"Yes, I have. I've seen them talk together about work, you know, him picking Dana up and taking him to work because he would have Dana work with him sometimes."

Cavanagh asked whether she had seen Panoyan there in the fall of 1988.

She had. "The one time he was over there he also came over to our house to say hi to us."

✦ Seventeen

The next step in the investigation was clear: a trip to Ohio.

That, of course, was going to cost money. Anticipating that it was going to take a sell to get Davie to pay for Woodroof's freight, Brian Cavanagh wrote a letter on January 25, 1990, to Woodroof's commander, Lt. John Sciadini:

"As you know, Det. Kelly Woodroof has located the suspected killer, Dana Williamson, in that region. We know that he is dangerous and has committed at least one other homicide (of which he was convicted). Unfortunately, although we have an articulable suspicion of his guilt, we are still short of probable cause on which to arrest him or to predicate an indictment.

"Among the reasons the investigation must proceed to Cincinnati are:

1. To establish when and why he went there (i.e., possible flight after the crime);
2. To interview his associates and neighbors for the purpose of not only cultivating leads, but ascertaining any admissions about his commission of the crime;
3. To interview Dana Williamson himself, in a noncustodial situation prior to our reaching a critical stage of prosecution where he might invoke his right to counsel;
4. To determine whether there is probable cause to believe that Williamson has possession of physical evidence which connects him to the crime (e.g., the stolen guns or other items from the Decker house-

137

hold, as well as anything which matches what was worn or used during the crime.''

The trip was approved, but didn't begin until May 1. Accompanying Woodroof were two members of the State Attorney's Office—investigator Dave Patterson, and Assistant State Attorney Tony Loe.

Woodroof had long since elicited the help of Norwood, Ohio, police. Once the Floridians arrived, the Ohioans were extremely cooperative, offering to put the entire detective bureau at their disposal.

On the afternoon of May 2, Norwood detective Steve Daniels took Woodroof to the Williamson home at 1811 Cleveland Avenue, a rickety white and green wood frame duplex with a cupola. Dana wasn't home, but Sandy Williamson was.

She let them in the house. Inside, Woodroof and Daniels were overwhelmed by the disarray and filth. Sandy seemed to fit in well. She was short, very heavy, wearing ratty clothes, and she didn't seem concerned about either her appearance or that of the house.

Woodroof asked her to come to the Norwood police station, and there he told her what the investigation was about. But to first put her in the proper mood, he asked if she had seen the dissolution of marriage document that Dana had filed in Fort Lauderdale on January 14, 1987—more than three years before.

She didn't believe it, even after Woodroof showed her the document. Then he read it out loud. The decree gave Dana sole parental responsibility for both of their children—seven-year-old Jessica and four-year-old Erica.

Dana had even denied Sandy visitation rights, writing that ''Shared parenting would be detrimental to the children because Petitioner fears the respondent will physically abuse the children,'' Woodroof read.

The news sent Sandy into a rage. Her sister-in-law Dawna had told her about it, but Dana denied it was true. As a result, they had lived together as husband and wife for the last three years, but weren't actually married.

By 4 P.M., Woodroof turned on his tape recorder so that Sandy could make a statement for the record.

* * *

She said Dana first left Florida a week or two before Thanksgiving 1988 so that he could help remodel her parents' home. There was no plan back then to move, but on December 10 he returned to take her and the children to Ohio.

She knew Charles Panoyan. Once at the Miramar house she overheard Dana and Panoyan talking about two people being killed. "I didn't know if the guy was joking or not." She also remembered Dana telling Panoyan not to talk about it around his house.

Sandy's suspicions were aroused when Panoyan called her parents' house in Norwood around Christmas 1989, asking for Dana.

"He kept on saying that he was somebody else, disguising his voice. We got into a big old argument, so later on he called Dana at my parents' house again and Dana turned around and met him at Frisch's [Big Boy Restaurant] over in Covington, Kentucky."

Sandy asked Dana why Panoyan was in Ohio, and Dana told her that Chuck was there to talk about Dana's dad.

"I thought it was unusual for him to be coming all the way up here to turn around and talk about his dad."

"What else did they talk about?" Woodroof asked.

"That's all I knew of, other than, you know, I finally confronted Dana, it was also about a case going on down there—that I didn't know was a case, I thought it was just, you know, a practical joke he's been playing, two people being killed and somebody's after him for it."

Woodroof asked her if Dana ever had a cowboy hat, and if so, could she describe it.

"It's like an old straw cowboy hat, and from what I understand, he had it since 1972, which is before I met him."

"Did you ever see him with that hat?"

"Yes, I have, he wore it a lot, and the girls—my two kids—used to wear it all the time, too."

Woodroof had a number of Polaroid pictures of the hat, which he then brought out to show to Sandy. Before she could figure out why a police officer investigating a homicide was trying to get a positive identification of something of her husband's, Woodroof asked: "Does that look to you like the hat?"

"Yes, it does," she said.

The trip to Ohio had just paid for itself.

Woodroof continued. He asked, "Is there anything about the hat that really stands out and really catches your attention?"

"I used to like the hat myself, it looked good on him, but it just looked like it, it was his type."

"Do you believe that's his hat?"

"From the way it looks, it looks like it is."

Woodroof asked the last time she had seen it.

"Just before we moved up here."

That made sense, too.

Woodroof next showed her a picture of the nylon SWAT belt taken from Panoyan's truck.

"Have you ever seen your husband Dana with a belt like that?"

"Yes, I did."

"Okay. Tell me about it."

"Well, [to] the best of my knowledge, I think he bought it through a magazine article thing, 'cause I used to take it with me to a dart place—you know, shooting darts—and that [I] didn't have nothing else to use so I used it."

"Did your husband Dana ever own any handcuffs?"

"No, not that I know of. His brother owns a pair."

"Who is his brother?"

"Rodney Williamson."

"How do you know Rodney owned a pair?"

"Because he used to wrestle around with me, putting them on and that."

As the interview was ending, Sandy volunteered something without prompting.

"All I know is, ah, one time my husband was low on money and we didn't have no money or anything, and all I know is we talked about him going and robbing somebody for some money to get money for the rent and everything because it was behind. And he talked about rolling somebody over on University [Drive] and Hollywood Boulevard at a bar, and he was talking about taking a Ninja outfit to do it in so nobody wouldn't recognize him.

"And at that point Chuck Panoyan might have been the one going over there with him, all I know is he's either

supposed to have picked him up and take him there, or picked
him up from there and bring him to the house—''

"Mr. Panoyan was supposed to pick him up at the house?"

"I don't know if he picked him up in the street from the
house, but all I know is he had pulled right up in our driveway when my husband left. But all I know is I feel bad that,
from what I understand, my husband robbed somebody for
money, you know, this drunk guy, that's all I knew, I didn't
know somebody else was kilied.''

Woodroof asked how much Dana got from the robbery.
She said three or four hundred dollars. He threw his disguise
in a canal near a commuter airport nearby, she said.

"When he discussed committing robberies with you, how
did he say he was going to do it?"

"He had, ah, what he'd call a stun gun, it's the only thing
I knew he carried with him at the time.'' She also said they
kept a .22 rifle at the house, and Rodney owned a .22 pistol
as well.

Woodroof prodded her for details of the robbery scheme.
She said it was precipitated by family arguments with Dawna,
who didn't work but insisted on sharing Dana's paycheck.

"We got into an argument about it, and Dana went and
was talking about robbing somebody. And I felt that—I went
along with it because my kids had to get something to eat
and the apartment paid because welfare turned us down because my husband was supposed to be working at the time.''

✦ EIGHTEEN

DANA WILLIAMSON

After Sandy's statement was concluded, she asked Woodroof about the hat. He told her that it was found at the murder scene. Only then did she realize she had been tricked.

While Sandy flew into another rage, Norwood police informed Woodroof they had Dana outside. Before Woodroof had brought Sandy to the police station, she had called her parents so that Dana would know where she was. Her stepfather, Rick Schulze, had brought him to the station.

Woodroof and Patterson rushed Sandy out a back exit so that she wouldn't see Dana; then they brought him in.

Dana Williamson was about 5' 10" with a solid build. He looked scraggly with an uneven handlebar mustache and an unshaven beard. He wore a green plaid flannel shirt, halfway unbuttoned, revealing a gray undershirt. His hair was greasy and combed back off his forehead.

He fits the description, thought Woodroof.

Before Woodroof began recording, he flipped the Polaroid pictures of the cowboy hat on the table toward Dana, with no introduction. Without looking the least bit surprised, or asking where police had found it, he volunteered, "That's my hat. And the last time I saw it, Vernon was over at my house."

It sounded prepared to Woodroof. Had Dana long since thought out the eventuality that he might someday be confronted with his lost hat?

At 7:08 P.M., Woodroof read Dana his Miranda rights, then had him sign an acknowledgment. At 7:10, the taped statement began.

*   *   *

What was striking about Dana Williamson was his affect— or lack of it. He had a gentle voice, but he spoke mostly in a monotone, without emotion. He wasn't afraid to talk, but he gave off a sense of being detached that was somewhat otherworldly, like he wasn't really there.

As the interview went on, Woodroof realized he was showing absolutely no sympathy for the victims of the crime. He had no warmth at all, no proffer of even "I'd like to help you, but I can't."

Dana began the interview by denying knowledge of the homicide or knowing the Deckers. But he did admit that Chuck Panoyan had mentioned the murder to him.

"When's the last time you had visible or personal contact with Chuck Panoyan?" asked Dave Patterson.

"Um, late October, early November of 1988," said Dana.

"When's the last time you talked to Chuck Panoyan?"

"December of '89 or January of '90."

"OK. Tell us how that conversation came about."

"He called my father-in-law's house and left a message for me to call. Said he had to talk to me. He left several messages."

Dana said he couldn't recall the area code of the phone number he was supposed to call back, but the number wasn't in Florida. When he rang it, from his father-in-law's house, Panoyan answered.

"What did Chuck say?"

"That he would be in Cincinnati in a few hours and that we had to meet."

"What did you say?"

"I told him no. I asked him, 'Why do we have to meet?' And he says, 'Because we can't talk on the phone.'

"I said, 'Why? Nobody's here, nobody's listening.' [He says,] 'Because they might have the phone bugged.' "

Dana said Panoyan then gave him another phone number, somewhere in the Cincinnati area, and told him to call it in a few hours. To make that call, Dana said, he went to a phone booth at Frisch's Big Boy Restaurant across the state line in Covington, Kentucky. It was only about two miles away.

"Why did you go to Frisch's Big Boy in Covington, Kentucky, to make that phone call?" Patterson asked.

"Because my wife was on one of her binges of being upset about a bunch of different things. And I didn't want to have to argue with her while I was trying to talk to him to find out what was up."

Panoyan answered the phone when he called. "He told me that my sister and my father was going to run an ad in a local Cincinnati paper, he didn't know which one, and that if I answered the ad, they were going to have me arrested for attempted murder on my father for withholding medication—which happened to be blood pressure medication—credit card fraud, and a few other things that they could make up, and that if I didn't answer the ad, they would get the house put back in my father's name and my sister's name.

"More power to them. I'm not even going to bother answering it. And then he said that somebody down there called Tips [Crimestoppers] and said that they overheard me talking on the phone to someone about shooting some people and shooting into a safe and then I said, 'Chuck, did you do it?'

"He said no. I said, 'Well, I didn't do it, so I don't have nothing to worry about. They can make all the accusations they want. They can't hurt me if I didn't do it.' "

"Did Chuck mention that your name was mentioned in the phone calls to Tips?"

"He said that they told Tips that they overheard me on the phone talking to somebody, that I had shot some people and then shot into a safe and that they did not come forward before then for fear that I would kill them."

"Prior to that, did you ever discuss this incident with Mr. Panoyan?" asked Kelly Woodroof.

"One time, he said that 'They're following me,' and I said, 'Who?' And he said, 'The cops.' He says, 'They got me pegged as the inside guy when my friend got killed.'

"And I said, 'Who got killed?' He says, 'A very close friend of mine.' He says, 'I can't talk no more about it because they told me not to.' "

"Where were you when this conversation took place?"

"In front of Apollo Auto Parts [in Hollywood]. He drove me up from my house to get parts for a car to fix."

"OK. And when was this?"

"Late November ... uh, early October ... late Nov[ember], late October, early November. Of '88."

"And you're certain of where you were when Mr. Panoyan discussed this with you the first time?"

"Yeah. It was the first time I seen him paranoid."

Dana said he didn't meet with Panoyan when he came to Ohio.

"I had the feeling that he might have my brother or my sister with him, setting me up, so that they could take a potshot or something at me."

"Why would you have that feeling?" Patterson asked.

"Because my sister and my brother are back-stabbers. My sister's a crack addict. She's tried to have me arrested. She's tried looking for a gun that she couldn't find after starting an argument with my wife, knowing she would aggravate me. Then when she couldn't find the gun, she called the cops and reported the gun stolen."

"Why would you have the feeling they would be with Chuck?"

"Because he's known my father longer than he has me. He's been friends with my father longer than he has me."

"When you say you were concerned about one of them coming up with Chuck and taking a potshot at you, what do you mean by a potshot?" Woodroof asked.

"With a gun."

"OK. From Mr. Panoyan, does it seem to you like that would be kind of a risky thing for him to do?"

"Not if he thought that he would not be connected."

"But then you said, earlier, that Chuck is definitely not a risk taker, he's not a man to take risks."

"No," said Dana. "I don't think he is."

"But you still feel that way, that he was trying to set you up with other members of your family?"

"No. But like I said before, he was paranoid and whenever somebody's paranoid, they won't talk on the phone for fear it's bugged. I'm going to be paranoid, 'cause most people, when they're paranoid, they're paranoid for a reason."

"Had you ever been to the Decker residence in Davie, Florida?" Patterson asked.

"Not that I know of. I've been to a lot of different places in Davie. I was raised basically in Davie."

"And you never heard of the Decker family?"

"No. I was out of town for a while. From '75 to about '80."

"When did you first meet Chuck Panoyan?"

"I got out of prison and I was staying with my dad and my dad tells me that Chuck's known me since I was about eight or nine. Chuck and his wife say they've known me since I was about eight or nine."

Woodroof took out the photo of the cowboy hat again.

"That is a hat I used to have that came up missing from the house in Florida," Dana said, referring to his house.

"OK, describe that hat," Patterson asked.

"It's a plastic cowboy hat, made to look like straw. It's kind of rugged and it's got a couple of grouse feathers on it, on one side."

"OK. Are you positive that's your hat?"

"Yeah. Looks just like the hat that I had."

"OK. When's the last time you saw that hat?" asked Patterson, with that warm, giddy feeling of imminent triumph in his stomach, the same stirring that Woodroof had.

"About September of '88."

"Yeah. Why do you remember September 1988 as being the last time you saw that hat?"

"Because I went looking for it one day to wear. I was going to be painting outside and I went looking for it and couldn't find it and I asked everybody where it was. I asked my brother Rodney, who was staying in the house with me. I asked my wife. I asked my daughters. And I did not ask my dad because he wasn't in, he wasn't out, his body is confined to his bed. And nobody had seen it, and the only other person that had been around the house was my brother Vernon."

"You suspect Vernon took your hat?"

"Yeah."

"Why do you suspect Vernon took your hat?"

"Why would an alcoholic steal anything? If he's not smoking pot or popping pills or drinking. He can't hold down a job because of it. I know a couple cases where he took pants from my brother and said that somebody gave them to him. Who gives you a $100 pair of nylon jump pants?"

"Did you ever confront Vernon?"

"No. I chalked it up as an experience of not letting him near anything that I wanted."

Woodroof then showed Dana a picture of the SWAT belt. He asked him if he had ever seen a belt like that before.

"In an ad for Asian World of Martial Arts, at the Immortal Dragon Martial Arts Supply over on 56th or 58th and Johnson," referring to an address in Hollywood.

"Is that the only place you've ever seen one?"

"My brother Rodney has one that looks similar."

"Have you ever owned one?"

"No."

"Has your wife ever owned one?"

"No."

"Have you ever seen your wife wearing one like that?"

"No. Not unless she had one of my brother's."

"When is the last time you saw that belt with Rodney?"

"About a month ago."

Dana said Rodney had bought the belt by mail order from Asian World of Martial Arts. Dana said that he too had bought martial arts paraphernalia from the Immortal Dragon: blow guns, blow gun tips, blow gun darts, and throwing stars.

"Have you ever owned handcuffs?"

"No."

"Has Rodney ever owned handcuffs?"

"He owns a pair now. Smith and Wesson High Security."

"Did he own other handcuffs?"

"No."

Dana said Panoyan never mentioned the name Donna Decker to him. "Not even when he called you to tell you about the phone call to Tips—you didn't ask who was murdered?" questioned Patterson.

"No. I didn't want to."

"Why?"

"Didn't need to know."

"It didn't make you curious to know who you were being kind of accused of being involved in the murder of?" Woodroof asked.

"If somebody accused you of doing something you didn't do, would it bother you?" Dana returned the question to Woodroof.

"Well, I'd want to know what the circumstances were," Woodroof responded.

"Well, I don't. I didn't do nothing. I have nothing to hide, so why would, why should I want to know? I've been accused of trying to murder my father by withholding his blood-pressure medication to cause him to have to die, but when the directions on your blood-pressure medicine says to take this, that your blood pressure goes above 140 over 80, take the medication. If it's below, do not take it. If your blood pressure's below 140 over 80, do you want somebody to give you the medicine, which could cause you to die? Which they were very clear about at the hospital."

"So when Chuck warned you that you had been accused of talking over a telephone about shooting people and shooting into a safe, your curiosity was not aroused?" Patterson asked again.

"No. Because if Dawna, who I believe did it—she could accuse me of anything, including trying to assassinate the president of the United States."

Taking that to mean he thought Dawna was the tipster to Crimestoppers, Patterson asked him if he was sure of that.

"Not for a fact, but I was told three members of my family called."

"Who told you that?"

"Chuck Panoyan."

"Did you ask Chuck Panoyan how he arrived at that conclusion?"

"He told me that somebody we know told him that—a member of my family. The person I assumed said it, told him that, was Dennis Mayo [Dana's oldest sister Renee's husband], who Chuck talked to on a regular basis because they were renting to own a house from him."

Patterson asked Dana if he suspected anyone in the murder of Donna Decker.

"I don't suspect Chuck. I may be wrong, but I do not suspect Chuck."

"Do you suspect anyone?"

"Not that I know of."

Then came the showdown. Patterson asked, "I just wonder what your reaction will be when you are told your hat was found in the Decker residence the night of the murder."

"I don't know what to think."

"Can you explain how that hat would get there?"

"No. Not unless somebody put it there."

"Who do you suspect would have put it there?"

"Dawna, Vernon, Jay, Dawna's boyfriend, just to name a few."

"Do you think that's reasonable?" asked Woodroof, surprised at the answer.

"I wouldn't put nothing past Dawna. Dawna is a schemer, a conniver. One on one, she'll needle you and aggravate you; let a third party come up, she acts like Miss Priss. She [says,] 'Me—do something like that? No way. He's imagining it.' She's a con man from the word go. She's a crack addict."

"Can you think of a reason why she would be involved in this home invasion robbery?"

"If there was drugs around, I'd say yeah."

"Does Chuck know Dawna?" Patterson asked.

"Yeah."

"And does he know all the members of your family?"

"Yes."

"And Chuck was a victim of this home invasion robbery?"

"What little bit he has said, yeah."

"Wouldn't he have recognized the member of your family being there?"

"I don't know."

"Well, he knows them, doesn't he?"

"He knows them, but I don't know. I don't know. There, there's several ways to disguise yourself, that even, you wouldn't even know a member of your own family."

"Would he—"

"You might recognize the voice," Dana added.

"Would he know a male from a female?"

"Yeah."

"OK, it was a male that went into the house wearing that hat."

"Then I guess that lets Dawna off the hook," deduced Dana.

"That leaves now—who?"

"As far as I'm concerned, it could be Jay, Paul, or Vernon."

"Now tell us who Jay is."

"He's my youngest brother—half brother."

"Who's Paul?"

"Dawna's boyfriend. A self-proclaimed coke dealer."

"Who's Vernon?"

"My youngest brother."

"Now, found in Chuck's truck is the utility belt. Can you explain how the utility belt got into Chuck's car?"

"Not the faintest idea."

"Did Chuck tell you about the utility belt being found in his truck?"

"No."

"What has Mr. Panoyan told you that he's told the police?" Woodroof asked.

"Nothing."

"He didn't mention anything he said to the police about this?"

"He said something that somebody close to him had died, and that somebody cut—that the person that had been in the house had everybody tied up, or handcuffed or whatever, and that they let him go and something to him threatening him, and that he jumped in his truck, left, got home and called the police and that he couldn't talk about it."

"You said cut," Patterson noted.

"Turned him loose. He said cut me loose. He didn't, you know—as far as—I took that as turn him loose. If he was tied up, handcuffed or whatever, he cut him loose."

"Did he mention anything about anyone in that house being cut?"

"No. He said that they were secured and that he was secured. The guy had his wallet and that after a while the guy cut him loose, made threats against him and his family."

Woodroof asked when Dana moved from Florida.

"The early part of December of '88."

"And had you been staying up here prior to that?"

"I came up before Thanksgiving to help my father-in-law, mother-in-law fix up their house."

"How did you come up here?"

"By Greyhound bus."

"And how much before Thanksgiving was this?"

"About a week at least."

"How long had you been planning to go up here?"

"My wife's mother and father called and asked if I could come up—if they'd pay the bus ticket—could I come up and give them a hand with the house for a week or two. And I asked my dad if he minded me going away for a week or two."

"So how soon after that did you leave?"

"The very next day."

"And at that time, were you planning on staying up here?"

"No."

"When did you decide to stay up here?"

"I got a call in the first part of December saying that HRS and two Miramar police took my daughters from the house while my wife was getting prescription medicine for my father, and that they were told that there had been several complaints that the girls had been mistreated, locked out of the house, locked in the room, punched in the face, not clothed, not fed, and that they came out and took the kids as a precautionary measure. Later that evening, they were returned under condition that they wouldn't stay in the house with their mother until after I got back.

"When I got back, I talked to the lady, who came out, and all she would say was, a lady called and said that if Dana found out who called, he would kill me. And since I had been having trouble with my sister—who says she's going to teach me hardball—I assumed it was her."

"So that's when you made the decision to move?"

"Yes. A person can only go so long without family cooperation before they snap, and I'd reached my point."

✦ Nineteen

When the statement was over, Kelly Woodroof called Brian Cavanagh to tell him the news. After listening, Cavanagh agreed that they had enough, at last, to make an arrest. And they had to do it immediately, with Dana Williamson still at the police station. Otherwise, he was a flight risk and a danger to Sandy Williamson, who was now a state witness.

Woodroof spent the evening writing an arrest warrant and reading it to Cavanagh and William Dimitrouleas, the duty judge that night in Broward County. Once they agreed on it, Woodroof faxed his draft to Det. Bob Spence, who was sitting by the phone at the Davie Police department. He copied it onto the proper form and drove it to the home of the judge who signed it at 12:30 in the morning.

Once Spence had the signed document in hand, he called Davie Police and had them teletype a message to Norwood police. Right then, Norwood officer Steve Daniels arrested Dana Williamson for first-degree murder and attempted murder and booked him into the Norwood jail.

Next morning, May 3, Woodroof, Cavanagh, and Charlie Vaughan decided they had probable cause to arrest Charles Panoyan as well.

In an unmarked car, Davie detectives Spence and Sylvestri waited for Panoyan to come home from work in the evening. When they spotted his truck a block away from his house, they flashed their blue light from the dash to pull him over.

"We've got some news for you," said Spence, once out of the car. "We've made an arrest in the Decker homicide."

Panoyan looked relieved. "I'm glad it's over with," he said, meaning at last the police would be off his back.

"He's a friend of yours."

Relief turned to shock. He asked who.

"Dana Williamson," said Spence.

"Oh my God!" said Panoyan, shaking.

"How long has it been since you've seen him?" Spence asked.

"It's been a while," he said.

Spence asked how long was "a while," but Panoyan ended the conversation by saying he wanted to talk to his attorney. At that point, Gary Sylvestri placed him under arrest.

When Sylvestri searched Panoyan, he found a .25 caliber semiautomatic handgun in his front waistband. However, Panoyan had a current Florida concealed weapons permit for it. Both the gun and the permit were taken into evidence.

In the car on the way to the Davie Police station, Panoyan insisted he was innocent, but an hour later, walking between the detective bureau and the booking cell, Spence said Panoyan made a different comment, also unsolicited.

"You guys are doing a fine job. You finally got your men."

Spence took it as an admission of guilt.

Then later that evening, when Officer Mark Ray transported Panoyan from Davie to the Broward County Jail in downtown Fort Lauderdale, Panoyan began humming to himself. Then he stopped for a moment and Ray said he told him, "I'm glad I got arrested. Now I can get this over with."

When Panoyan's lawyers David Vinikoor and Paul Stark heard about the arrest, they were burning. They had a standing offer to surrender Panoyan in case the state ever wanted to arrest him. But they realized an ambush gave police a chance to get a statement from Panoyan before they informed him of the arrest.

Woodroof spent the morning in Ohio writing an application for a warrant to search Williamson's house. It was signed by a local judge at 1 P.M., and the search began two hours later.

The house was a disaster area. There was junk everywhere. They kept a huge garbage can in the bedroom, the beds didn't have sheets, and the attic had a rope with little girls' clothes hanging from it.

However, after four hours of searching, Woodroof and the Norwood officers had compiled a number of interesting things: Dana Williamson's address book, with Chuck Panoyan's name and phone number written in it; a catalogue of Ninja wear and accessories from Asian World of Martial Arts; a green camouflage Ninja suit, size medium; a grappling hook and black rope; and five boxes of .22 long-rifle ammunition, quickly determined to be similar to bullets removed from the base of Bob Decker's skull.

Also, Charlie Williamson's undated and unsigned last will and testament, leaving Dana his car, electronics, tools, and a .38 pistol; a quitclaim deed to Charlie Williamson's house in Miramar, now placed in Dana and Crassandra's names, signed and executed August 26, 1988; an invoice for a one-way Greyhound bus ticket, from Fort Lauderdale to Covington, Kentucky, dated November 17, 1988; and a school notebook with GED lecture notes, found inside a bookbag. One page of it was extremely tantalizing: it was blank except for three words, one of them misspelled: "frist degree murder."

While Woodroof was searching the house, Dave Patterson took a sworn statement from Sandy's stepfather, Fred Schulze, who preferred to be called Rick. The main topic was a set of phone calls Panoyan had made to his house in Covington, Kentucky. (Norwood, Ohio, was just ten miles away.)

Schulze, a muscular but soft-spoken forty-five-year-old, whose temples were graying, had met Panoyan once, during Christmas 1987 at the Williamson house in Miramar. When Panoyan called his Covington house in December 1989, he gave his name as Eddie Roberts. He said he was calling from Virginia, but that he would be in Kentucky the next day.

Schulze told him Dana lived elsewhere, but he could get in touch with him. He asked if Schulze could arrange for Dana to be at the house the next morning; then he would call again. Schulze did, and the call came on schedule. He answered the phone and handed it to Dana.

"Did you hear Dana's side of the phone call?" asked Patterson.

"I heard parts of the conversation. I understood him to say that he was gonna meet him at Frisch's on Fourth Street, in Covington, Kentucky. Dana talked with him for a while after that, and then he left. And his wife wanted to go with

him and he wouldn't let her, he told her to stay there."
Schulze said the restaurant was about ten minutes away, and
Dana was gone for about forty-five minutes.

"Did he ever tell you why he was going to meet with
Eddie Roberts or Chuck Panoyan?"

"No, he just said that he wanted to talk to him about
something about his situation with his father and his sister
down in Miramar."

"Did you ask Dana why Chuck Panoyan was using the
name Eddie Roberts?"

"When I asked him why was this person calling my house
using the name Eddie Roberts, when [Dana] in fact told me
it was Chuck Panoyan, he said that quite a while back that
[Panoyan] had been involved with something in Florida, that
it was, ah, a family killed, and the way I understood it the
whole family had been involved as far as a victim, and that
the person had come in and killed the family and took his
wallet and told him to leave, and that they had his name and
that if he ever went to the police or anything they'd kill him,
and then he left. And that there's some kind of investigation
going on that he didn't want to be involved in something,
that's why he was using that name."

Patterson asked what that had to do with any discussion
about Dana's father.

"Dana had been taking care of his dad since he brought
him home from the nursing home, and there was a conflict
between him and his sister as to who was gonna live in the
house and who was gonna take care of him and everything.

"When Dana and his sister got into it, [Dana and Sandy]
moved up here and his sister moved into the house, and then
they were telling different relatives that they were gonna take
out a warrant on Dana for attempted manslaughter, trying to
kill his dad, saying that he wasn't feeding him, wasn't taking
care of him, and this is what this Eddie Roberts or Chuck
Panoyan, whichever you want to call him, was supposedly
coming up here to tell him."

"Okay, when Dana left your house, were you led to believe that he was going to go meet with Mr. Panoyan?"

"Yes, I was."

"And were you told anything different?"

"Not until when I spoke to Dana this morning. He said

no, that he didn't go meet him, that he went somewhere to make a phone call to another phone to talk to him.''

In the afternoon, Woodroof's commander, Lt. Sciadini, suggested they keep a lid on the story for a day.

''I'm afraid that might be impossible,'' said Woodroof. ''There's a TV station here broadcasting live from the front yard.''

That night, all the south Florida local media covered Panoyan's arrest. Included in some of the TV coverage was video from Ohio. Woodroof's wife saw Kelly on one station.

The next morning, the *Fort Lauderdale Sun-Sentinel* headlined its story: ''Invasion 'victim' arrested; Davie home robbery killed woman, wounded 3 in 1988.''

''I'm innocent,'' the paper quoted Panoyan. ''I was a victim then and I am a victim now.''

The Miami Herald wrote that the police said Panoyan had acted as if he were cooperating with the investigation, even reenacting the crime for them.

''I cannot believe it,'' the *Herald* quoted Bob Decker. ''In my own mind, I thought it was him, but I didn't really want to believe it. It's something that has been a long time coming. I hoped and hoped.''

✦ TWENTY

RODNEY WILLIAMSON

Once back at home on May 5, Woodroof called the toll-free order line for Asian World of Martial Arts, in Philadelphia. Within a half hour, proprietor George Ciukurescu called back with information that Rodney Williamson had ordered from him twice in 1988. The second time, in August, he had ordered two "Ninja black utility belts" at $5.95 apiece; two "Camo Ninja uniforms," one small and one medium, at $19.95 apiece; and a book called *Deadly Karate Blows*.

The catalogue described the belt: "One size fits all, easy to adjust. Belt loops made of durable black nylon webbing. Five different pockets with velcro closure." Woodroof compared the catalogue picture to the belt taken from Panoyan's truck. It was the same.

However, he didn't quite know what to make of the Ninja suit they had seized. It sounded like the same one seen by Ginger Kostige and the Pembroke Pines officer. It also came with a "two-piece Ninja hood" and a nylon mask. That was suspicious; Bob Decker had described the gunman wearing something like a woman's stocking to conceal his face.

The next step was to find Rodney Williamson. Both Sandy and Rick Schulze had said they had seen him with an old .22 pistol, which sounded to Woodroof like it could have been the gun used to shoot the Deckers.

Schulze had told Woodroof that Rodney was in Golden, Colorado. Based on that tip, Woodroof contacted local police there and got his address: 718 Park Street.

On May 9, Woodroof and Patterson went back on the road, this time to Colorado.

Golden police Sgt. Robert Tortora drove them to the Park Street address that morning. It was a small house that looked like someone had built it himself. An American-Indian girl answered the door and let them in. Patterson asked where Rodney was, and she pointed to a cluttered couch.

"Where?" asked Patterson.

The girl walked over and gave it a jolt. From inside a sleeping bag emerged Rodney Williamson.

Unquestionably the most remarkable feature of Rodney Williamson was his huge red muttonchops. "It was Yosemite Sam," Woodroof said later. "I thought he was going to say 'Great Horny Toads!'"

Rodney agreed to go to the police station to give a statement. Woodroof started his tape just before 12 noon.

"OK. Mr. Williamson, when we were talking earlier in the day, I showed you two photographs of a hat. Can you describe that hat for me?"

"It's a straw, Western hat, it's crumbled up pretty badly from being sit on and it's bent down and tore in half. It's bent up and in on the sides and has a gray and black kind of a feather design on one side, which I gave my brother."

"Do you recognize this hat?"

"I recognize it as being one very similar to, or belonging to, my brother."

"Which brother is that?"

"Dana Williamson."

"OK, and when was the last time you saw that hat?"

"Uh, probably November or December of '88."

"Where did you see it?"

"In the house at 1711 S.W. 99 Terrace, Miramar, Florida."

"OK. And has that hat since been missed?"

"Yes, it has. My brother was asking his wife one time where it was. She said she thought it was in the attic, and he said like hell it was, because he looked through the whole attic and could not find the hat anywhere."

"When was this? Do you know?"

"This is, uh, summer of last year."

"OK. I also showed you three photographs of a belt."

"I described it as a Ninja utility belt, similar to one that I ordered two of, and my brother got one and I wound up with one."

"Where is your belt now?"

"It's packed away in my belongings at my brother's house in Ohio."

"And what happened with the other belt?"

"Uh, to the best of my knowledge, my brother still has it."

"Explain to me about the order."

"OK. The order came about—I had got a catalogue from Asian World of Martial Arts and I was looking through it, and my brother was looking through it. Uh, and there was a few things that I wanted to get, but I didn't have the money at the time. My brother had a paycheck. It was a pretty good size paycheck, and he made a deal with me, that to go ahead and order and get everything we wanted together, and then the things I wanted to keep I could reimburse him for later. He gave me the money to buy a money order. I went down to the post office, bought a money order and sent this order in to Asian World of Martial Arts."

"OK. And what items did you keep?"

"A, uh, Ninja outfit, complete from the, the head mask all the way down to the, the boots and socks and uh, he got a couple books and uh, uh, a grappling hook and a, a Ninja outfit."

"What size Ninja outfit did he get?"

"He got a medium and I got a small."

Rodney said the last time he saw Charles Panoyan was January 1989, as Rodney was packing to leave Florida. Panoyan had come by the Miramar house asking for Dana. Rodney told him Dana had moved to Ohio.

Woodroof asked about the day Dana was arrested by Pembroke Pines police.

"Uh, Dana and I were putting on the uniforms to see how they fit and see if they were comfortable, and Dana was playing with the grappling hook in a holly tree. Chuck Panoyan pulled up and wanted to talk to Dana, and Dana took off with Chuck Panoyan.

"A little while later, Chuck Panoyan came back and said Dana was in jail and Chuck went into my dad's bedroom, talked with my dad and evidently got the money from my dad to bond my brother out of jail.

"Dana told me later that they were sitting on the side of Douglas Road in Pembroke Pines and a police officer pulled up behind them because it looked suspicious sitting out in the middle of nowhere, two men in a car, talking. And he got arrested because he was dressed in, in a Ninja outfit, and I had told him before he left that he had no business wearing that out unless he was going to go to a Ninja class or something like that.''

"Did Dana say what he and Mr. Panoyan were talking about?''

"No, he didn't.''

"OK. Why did Mr. Panoyan want Dana to go for a ride with him?''

"Uh, Dana said that it was because he didn't want Sandy to know how much money Dana was making. Sandy had a habit of spending money all the time, as fast as Dana could make it, and I assumed that would be a logical reason for them to ride off together.''

Rodney had earlier mentioned to Woodroof that Panoyan had said he wanted Dana to do a favor for him.

"Dana did say that, uh, Chuck did say he wanted Dana to do him a favor before they left. Uh, he never specified in my hearing what kind of a favor and Dana never specified later on if they got to the favor or not.''

"OK. We discussed earlier an incident where some party visited your brother Dana while you were living in the house. Tell me about that.''

"Uh, somebody had been trying to get ahold of my brother Dana. His phone was cut off. They, they were trying to get ahold of him at his mother-in-law's house.''

"And who would that be?''

"Rick and Fran Schulze. In Covington, Kentucky. Uh, so Dana went to their house one night and he came back and he said he had to meet somebody who's coming in from West Virginia to see him. He never specified who it was.

"I asked him if it was anybody that I might know, and he said no, I don't think you know him. The next day, uh, we met this per—or Dana met this person at a restaurant, Big Boy's Restaurant off of I-75 in Covington, Kentucky. I never got a look at the man. I don't know who it was, how old he was or whatever. Uh, I was sitting in the truck reading a paperback book and drinking coffee out of a thermos.''

"Did Dana actually go inside the restaurant?''

"Uh, Dana got out of the truck and went in the restaurant, yeah."

"How long was he inside?"

"Uh, half an hour to an hour."

"Did he indicate that he had actually seen somebody in there?"

"He never discussed it with me afterwards."

"He never discussed it. Never told," repeated Woodroof.

"I never asked him. He told me it wasn't anybody that I—he didn't think it was anybody I knew, so I never was curious about it."

Rodney said he had owned a pair of handcuffs but had sold them. He still owned a Ruger Mini-14 rifle that he kept in Ohio.

"Do you own a .22 pistol?"

"Uh, I had a .22 pistol, yeah."

"When did you have this .22 pistol?"

"I got a .22 pistol from a friend of mine for $20 in 1989."

"When did you get it? When in 1989?"

"Uh, June or July."

"Who is the friend that you got it from?"

"A guy named Fabian, uh, in some warehouses over on Palm Avenue in Miramar."

"In 1989?"

"Yeah."

"When were you in South Florida in 1989?"

"January. Let's see. No, it would have been '88 that I got it."

Rodney said he couldn't remember Fabian's last name. Woodroof asked him to describe the gun.

"Uh, it was a .22, it said 'HS,' I believe, on the plastic handle on the grip. It was a little .22 pistol with about a six-inch barrel." He said it was a six-shot revolver, rusted, and one of the side handles was broken.

Woodroof knew that description was very close to the gun Bob Decker had described—the one used to shoot him and his family.

"What happened to this weapon?"

"Uh, the last time I seen it was in Cincinnati. Uh, it was in my camper, in my brother's garage now. It was parked in my brother's yard."

"Did anybody else ever have access to this weapon when you owned it?"

"Uh, no, I scrupulously kept my keys in my pocket. Uh, once in a while, I'd leave them laying around the house, but nobody else knew where the gun was at in the van. I kept the cylinder in the glove box and I kept the pistol itself, behind, a, a, a furnace thing in a, inside the engine compartment."

"Did Dana know that you owned this pistol?"

"Dana knew I owned a pistol, yes. Dana owns a .22 rifle also."

"Have you seen Dana with any other weapons?"

"A .22 rifle and a BB gun, that's it. That and, uh, some throwing stars and a blow dart gun."

When the statement ended, Woodroof asked Rodney to sign a consent to search his house. Rodney agreed, excluding the search from the parts of the house his roommate lived in. The search turned up nothing.

✦ TWENTY-ONE

On May 10, BSO latent examiner Fred Boyd received via fax a palm print of Dana Williamson to compare to the last remaining latent from the crime scene—a palm print left on a check stub. Again there was no match.

When Panoyan was arrested, a magistrate refused his request for bond. But on May 15, he was offered a bond hearing in front of Broward Circuit Court judge Richard D. Eade.

Before the hearing, Brian Cavanagh met with Dawna Williamson. She told him some provocative new things: Dana had talked to her about how to kill someone with a .22 handgun; he used aliases; he had robbed drug dealers; and that Rodney had a machine gun in November to December 1988.

Dawna also remembered that Panoyan came to her sometime in November 1989, asking where Dana was. Panoyan told her that he had called Dana and left messages, but he wasn't returning the calls. Panoyan said he wanted to visit him; that way he might be able to talk him into signing the house back to their father. Dawna took out a map of Ohio and showed Panoyan the area where Dana was.

She said Rodney and Dana shared everything. That may have included Rodney's .22 pistol, and definitely included Sandy; one of her two children was Dana's, and one was Rodney's.

Panoyan was represented by Paul Stark and David Vinikoor, both former prosecutors. Stark had been an assistant district attorney in the Bronx, and Vinikoor had been a state attorney in Philadelphia, as well as in Broward County, where as the number three man in the office, he was chief of the organized crime division. A taste of just how good they both were would come out at this first hearing.

The defense brought three character witnesses for Panoyan, including his wife Darla. The prosecution had Kelly Woodroof, Dave Patterson, and Bob Spence.

On cross-examination, Paul Stark asked Woodroof how many times Panoyan was told he was going to "burn or fry in the electric chair."

"None in my presence, sir," said Woodroof.

Stark asked if Panoyan had been a flight risk during the eighteen months he had been a suspect in the case.

"No concrete evidence, no, sir."

"He gave you a statement of his version of the events, isn't that true?"

"Yes, sir."

"And one of the things that you omitted to put in your probable cause affidavit is that Mr. Panoyan told you, did he not, that this masked intruder told him that he recognized him, knew him, knew where his family lived and would kill his family if Mr. Panoyan told the police?"

"Mr. Panoyan testified—or has said that, yes, sir."

"But you didn't put that in the probable cause affidavit, did you?"

"No, sir."

"And if Mr. Panoyan knew Dana Williamson, and if, in fact, Dana Williamson was the shooter in this case, then that statement may well not be inconsistent with Mr. Panoyan's version of the events, right?"

"Objection," said Brian Cavanagh.

"I don't quite understand your—your question, sir," stuttered Woodroof.

Cavanagh asked Spence about a phone call he had received from Dawna while Woodroof was in Norwood.

"She was very upset, stating that Charles Panoyan was just at her residence and asked her, 'Why don't you just slip your father something so he won't wake up in the morning?' "

On cross, Stark asked Spence if he had any reason to believe that Panoyan would do harm to his friend, Charlie Williamson.

"Well, the fact that he wants to slip him something where

he can't wake up the next morning doesn't speak highly for Mr. Panoyan's relationship with Mr. Williamson,'' Spence said.

Judge Eade denied the motion for bond, ruling that the police probable cause affidavit showed numerous inconsistencies between Panoyan's version of events and the other witnesses.

"Taken on isolation, any of these inconsistencies doesn't amount to much, but in the aggregate the circumstantial evidence in this case [shows] that proof is evident and presumption is great that this defendant conspired or was an accomplice of the actual trigger man in this fatality.

"It appears that eighteen months ago the biggest question looming for the State of Florida was: If he was simply allowed to leave the residence with only the intimidation of 'Well, we know where you live, we know where your house is,' the question that loomed large at that time was: Why would a cold-blooded trigger man who had no hesitation to put the bullet in the right ear of a two-and-a-half-year-old boy allow an adult to escape and be a vivid live witness to give testimony, possible testimony, against the assailant?''

But now the answer was clearer, Eade said. Williamson and Panoyan knew each other. "It appears quite clear to this Court that this defendant, although he told the police that he never knew who the assailant was, knew who the assailant was even if the assailant was wearing a mask.

"It appears they've been friends at least for a considerable length of time; friends enough that they shared the same car two months before this murder.

"And even with a mask, I never heard of any testimony or anything in the probable cause affidavit to indicate that the assailant ever camouflaged his voice. Certainly, friends would know each other's voices. There is just too much here.''

That same day, Norwood detective Harry Schlie obtained another search warrant, this time for Rodney's VW van only. They were looking for the .22 pistol, but it didn't turn up.

At the bond hearing, when Charlie Vaughan had crossexamined Darla Panoyan regarding her husband's risk of flight, she said that he had visited a friend named Louis Praino in Washington, D.C., around October, to go deer hunting.

It immediately struck Woodroof that Darla might have mixed up October with November. First thing the next morning, Woodroof called the West Virginia agency that licensed hunters, but found no information on either Panoyan or Praino.

Two days later, with the help of the Virginia State Police, Woodroof found an address and phone number for Praino in Dumfries, Virginia, a Washington suburb. That evening Woodroof called him.

Praino said that he and Panoyan had been friends for more than twenty years. He confirmed that Panoyan had in fact visited him at the end of November.

He said Panoyan had called him during the summer, asking if he could get time off from his job to hunt deer in West Virginia's Blue Ridge mountains. In early November, Panoyan called to remind him.

Then, on Friday, November 25, Panoyan called to say that he was flying to Washington to attend a Sunday wedding in Maryland at which his father was presiding. However, Panoyan didn't show up at Praino's house until 10 P.M. Monday night. When he got there, in a tan Chevy rental car, he was tired and unshaven. He explained that he had been driving around the area for the previous eight to ten hours, contemplating things.

Rick Schulze wanted to get to the bottom of the pistol controversy. Even though Dana had divorced his stepdaughter without telling her, he believed him innocent of murder, though he wasn't as certain about Rodney.

After Norwood police searched Rodney's van without success, Schulze called Rodney and directly asked where the gun was. He told Schulze it was on the blower motor in the back of the van.

Schulze searched the van himself on May 21, with Sandy and his wife Fran watching. They didn't find the .22, but it was amazing what had suddenly appeared in it: five vials of .22 bullets under the front seat; the Ruger Mini-14, which Rodney had told Woodroof he owned, covered by papers on the floor under the rear seat; another black Ninja belt, on top of a mattress in the rear; a full Ninja suit with hoods; two hunting knives; and several typewritten pages. Schulze then called Dave Patterson in Florida, who got Norwood Police to arrange to take it all into evidence for Davie.

Just after the arrests, Brian Cavanagh scheduled a grand jury presentation on May 23 to indict both Panoyan and Dana Williamson. Kelly Woodroof outlined the case. If the case had any problems, he thought, it was that the grand jury might think that Dana Williamson had been framed.

The night before, Cavanagh's mother Isabelle died. As a last minute substitute, Charlie Vaughan took his place, successfully. By the end of the day, the grand jury returned indictments on both men for first-degree murder and three counts of attempted Murder One.

On May 25, Kelly Woodroof got a warrant to search Charles Panoyan's impounded 1979 Ford pickup truck. The vehicle was in the worst condition imaginable: a square wood board covered the driver's seat because the upholstery had worn through to the foam; the driver's side door didn't shut completely; and there was garbage and papers and junk throughout.

Woodroof conducted the search. Among the intriguing items seized were a receiver handset to a cordless telephone, which Woodroof thought might have matched the one taken from the Deckers' bedroom (but turned out not to); a yellow paper with Dana Williamson's name and address on it, found on the cluttered dashboard; a newspaper clipping of the homicide; blank quitclaim deeds; a 9-mm shell casing; a single yellow and black metal earring; and some rope, found in the bed of the truck.

Later that afternoon, Woodroof called all the large rental car agencies to see if they had a record of Panoyan getting a car on Thanksgiving weekend. He struck pay dirt at National Car Rental. Panoyan had taken a car at 3 P.M. on November 25 at Washington National Airport, returning it on November 28 at 9:30 A.M. with 1,296 additional miles on it.

Woodroof also reviewed Dana Williamson's Ohio telephone bills and found more engaging material. Williamson had called Panoyan's home on February 19, 1989, at 9:35 P.M., and spoken for six minutes. Six days later, at 8:30 P.M., he called again and spoke for thirteen minutes. Also, on February 10, 1989, at 8:07 P.M., he had called a feed store in Davie and talked for sixteen minutes. Woodroof interviewed the store owner, Bill Sirola, who said he had hired Panoyan to do late evening renovation work that month.

Also singular on Williamson's phone records were two calls in February 1989 to the main Fort Lauderdale number of the Broward Sheriff's Office, one for five minutes and the other for sixteen minutes.

✦ TWENTY-TWO

Summer 1990 was a time for Kelly Woodroof to try to tie up some loose ends.

He subpoenaed Panoyan's travel records from National Car Rental and Eastern Airlines. Next, he tried to see if Panoyan had used his credit cards while on the road (for example, to buy gas). Woodroof had a list of those cards from his earlier credit inquiries, but they showed no activity.

On June 14, Dana was booked into Broward County's custody after extradition from Hamilton, Ohio. Dawna Williamson called Woodroof that night. She reported that Dana had called a cousin earlier that day and said that Panoyan must be trying to blame the murder on him.

On July 2, Dennis Mayo—Dana's sister Renee's husband—called Woodroof. Dana had called their house twice from jail, trying to keep Renee from talking to the police. It had the opposite effect on her. That evening, Renee called Woodroof, and after work on July 6 she came in to Davie Police to give a statement.

At the time of the murder, Renee Williamson Mayo was renting a house in Davie that Chuck Panoyan had built and still owned.

She first learned about the murder the Monday after it happened. She was a supervisor at the Davie Post Office, and the carrier who delivered mail on the Deckers' route told her some of the details.

Woodroof asked if Panoyan ever talked with Renee about the murder.

"Yes. He came over about a week after the murder, and he wanted two months advance rent from us and told us that he was in a real tight bind for money, which was not unusual. He told me that he needed to get a lawyer, he needed $1,500 for a retainer.

"We had just paid the rent about a week and a half before that, and it was right before Christmas. 'What, are you crazy, Chuck? Who can come up with that kind of money?' He was very insistent, he was desperate, he needed the money.

"I asked him if it was about the investigation that was going on, because I assumed that he was trying to be protected from the killer who had eyewitnessed him. He said no, he had a story to tell that I would never believe.

"He said he couldn't tell me anything at that time, that someday when it was all said and done, he would tell me and I would never believe it."

Renee said she didn't know that Dana had left Florida until Thanksgiving 1988. Dawna had come to take their father to holiday dinner at a relative's, but Rodney—who fought constantly with Dawna—wouldn't let her in the house.

Hysterical, Dawna called her aunt, Billie Melton, who Rodney allowed into the house. She found Dana missing and Charlie Williamson in neglected condition—underweight and looking ill. Immediately she called for an ambulance.

Sometime later, someone else (Renee thought Dawna) called the state child abuse hotline. When social workers arrived, finding the house in filth and chaos, they removed Dana and Sandy's two children, Jessica and Erica. Later they placed them in their aunt Billie's care.

"The next morning my aunt got a phone call from Dana in Ohio, wanting to know who took his kids and what was going on. He seemed surprised that my father was sick and in the hospital. He couldn't understand why everyone was upset that he wasn't there and that my dad wasn't being taken care of."

Shortly after that, Dana returned from Ohio just long enough to gather Sandy, the kids from Aunt Billie, and his possessions, and drove them all north.

Renee described some of the family problems: Arguments ensued on who could enter the house to see their father. Dana and Sandy didn't get along and didn't sleep together. Dana complained that she didn't take care of the kids, didn't clean the house, and didn't even practice personal hygiene.

That left Dana as the primary caretaker of his father and his children because neither Sandy nor Rodney helped. On top of that, Dana worked full-time in construction, while neither Sandy nor Rodney had a job.

"So, it would be somewhat unusual for him to leave the kids and your father in a position where they might not be attended to?" Woodroof asked.

"Oh sure. Dana wouldn't leave the house overnight because he was worried that Sandy wouldn't feed the kids or my father—well, she didn't. He was the only one who held everyone together. He was the only one who fed the kids, bathed them, the only one who did any housekeeping at all, which was minimal. The only one who took care of my dad. Shaved him, bathed him, helped him go to the bathroom, put a bedpan underneath him.

"Dana was always there for my father, and he was always there for the girls. He was the only stable thing in their lives. He was the one constant that remained no matter all the problems everybody had."

"To your knowledge, before he left, did he provide for anybody to sort of pick up the slack?"

"No. Nobody even knew he was leaving."

"So that would seem a little unusual?"

"Extremely unusual, because when I say no one fed the girls, I'm not exaggerating, no one fed them at all. And Erica was a baby. If Jessica didn't get it out of the refrigerator or out of the cabinet—she was about three, almost four—neither one of them ate.

"Sandy did not cook. Sandy did not get them food, she wouldn't even go to the kitchen and fix something up out of the cabinets—here, eat it. She would not do anything—period—nothing, zero, nothing at all.

"The sight of my father repulsed her—she wouldn't go in the room with him, she said that he smelled, with everything that's coming up out of him. And Rodney reacted to the kids, how should I say, they were a nuisance, they were in the way. Playing with them he didn't do, he would push them out of the way if they came near him."

Bob Spence asked Renee if she ever found out why Dana left.

"Actually my aunt asked him, because I wasn't civil to

Dana at this point. I was totally furious that he left my father
and left the girls under the care of those two idiots who
weren't competent. Dana said that he had to go to help his
father-in-law work, and it was something only he could do.
I said, oh right, sure—bull.''

Woodroof asked her what she knew about Dana and
Sandy's divorce.

''Dana had been complaining that he was having problems
with Sandy. Before my father had the stroke, my dad and
Dana were very close. They worked together. Everywhere
my dad went, Dana was there.

''So Dana was always complaining to my dad—Sandy this,
Sandy that—and my dad told him if he didn't like things that
were going on in his life, do something to change them or
shut up and stop complaining. If you can't change her behavior, divorce her.

''I believe Dana talked to my father's lawyer and found
out about do-it-yourself kits for divorce. Dana sat down and
started planning how he was going to get a divorce. He called
my brother Rodney and asked if he would come and take
Sandy to Colorado and dump her, just leave her there.

''So Rodney came over and he asked Sandy: Did she want
to go on a vacation, get rid of the kids for a while?—and
Sandy ate up the idea. Here was another man paying attention to her and her husband wouldn't talk to her.

''It was a family joke that Sandy and Rodney had a long-
standing affair, anyway, that they had been sleeping together
for quite some time. So when Rodney asked Sandy if she
wanted to go away on a vacation, she just went, Let's go,
let's go now.

''So from what I understand, Dana told Rodney to keep
Sandy away for at least six months. While Sandy and Rodney
were gone, Dana filed for the divorce on grounds of desertion.

''Rodney was supposed to dump Sandy and leave her
someplace in Colorado. Well, he brought her back. And when
she came back, it was like, oh no, what are we going to do
now? She came back and moved back in like it was nothing.''

Renee said Dawna got a copy of the final divorce decree
and showed it to everyone in the family.

''To my knowledge, Dana never told her they were divorced. My sister repeatedly threw it in Sandy's face that she

wasn't part of the family anymore, and Sandy never believed Dawna. Dawna at one point showed it to Sandy. I was witness to this. I saw her wave the divorce papers out in front of her and say, Look, idiot, you're divorced.

"And Sandy looked at it and said, That doesn't mean anything. Now, whether she couldn't read or whether she didn't believe it or didn't think it was legal, I don't know. So Dana and Sandy were back living together again, and it was shortly after this time that my dad had a stroke, and then Sandy was like a permanent fixture again."

Woodroof brought out his deck of Polaroids of the cowboy hat and showed them to Renee. She confirmed the hat was Dana's.

"It's got a unique style that he formed to fit his own personality. He's got the sides curled up so they fit close to the head, the back curled down a little bit, and the front is curved at the sharp angle to come close to the face. And the feather on the side."

✦ Twenty-three

Vernon Williamson was Dana's youngest full brother, who sided on most family issues with Renee. On July 12, Woodroof went to his house to take a statement.

Vernon was short and thin, with dark hair, and wore a trimmed Fu Manchu mustache and beard. He was an auto mechanic.

He said that there had been a lot of family conflict over the quitclaim deed that Norwood police had found. Charlie Williamson had executed it to Dana and Sandy in the fall of 1988, but as Vernon recalled, it was only so the family could improve its chances of getting a second mortgage, to pay some bills. Dana was employed, Charlie was not.

Once they got the loan, Charlie Williamson asked Dana to sign it back. Dana refused. When Vernon protested that Dana was welshing on a deal, Dana told him to shut the hell up.

"When Dana left he left in [such] a big hurry, he didn't even clean the house, and I assume that he just was pretty ticked off at my father because at the time I thought, maybe he feels that Dad was stabbing him in the back after everything he has done for him, and now my father wants the house back.

"But when he left, the house was in such a mess—there was trash piled up hip-deep throughout the house, literally knee-deep. We found gowns that my father wore that were stained like he had worn them for at least a month without bathing.

"Every time we went over there, Sandy wouldn't let anyone in except my Aunt Billie, and she wouldn't go over there 'cause she couldn't stand to see my father that way. When-

174

ever I'd go over there, she wouldn't let me in, she'd call the police."

"Now, was Dana basically the one taking care of your father and his two children?"

"Yes, he was the primary. Sandy spent too much time drinking, going out—she slept all day and would go out all night. Rodney slept all day and stayed up all night."

"Was Dana pretty conscientious about taking care of the kids and your father?"

"Yeah, I called him a very good father. I mean, he protected the kids when Sandy got angry. He would bathe the kids, or make sure they—one daughter was old enough to bathe the youngest, so usually they bathed each other. Dana treated them exceptionally well, and my father too, he did everything he could to take care of my father. More than I could do myself. I don't think I could take the pressure."

"Does it seem a little unusual that he would leave then— in a situation where they wouldn't be taken care of?"

"Definitely, definitely unusual. It seems strange he wouldn't at least have my father move in with my Aunt Billie, who was taking care of my grandmother, anyway. She was there all day and it wouldn't have been that much trouble to help take care of my father too."

On July 17, Cincinnati Bell turned over records of Rick Schulze's telephone bills, as required by a subpoena, and Woodroof got them the next day. By far the most interesting entry was a call on November 26, 1989, at 7:34 P.M., to a number in Washington, Pennsylvania.

Woodroof checked a map. Washington was a small town on the western edge of the state, on Interstate 70. That road west, then I-71 southwest at Columbus, Ohio, was the logical route between Washington, D.C., and Cincinnati. What must have happened was Panoyan called Williamson, who called him back.

Immediately Woodroof called police in Washington, Pa. They told him the phone number corresponded with a truck stop called the Toot 'n Scoot, on I-70. When Woodroof called the truck stop, he found that the phone number was for a pay phone.

On July 28, Woodroof sent a teletype message to every

county sheriff's office between Washington, D.C., and Cincinnati that those interstates crossed, asking if they had any contact with Panoyan, or knew the tag number of the rental car he was driving, and he asked for names of roadside hotels in their jurisdictions.

The ambitious search turned up no new leads.

Nor could Woodroof get long-distance records from that pay phone. The security department of Bell of Pennsylvania told him that records were erased once cash was collected from the phone.

On August 20, Rodney Williamson consented to a polygraph, administered by Golden Police detective Roger Key. Woodroof wanted to know if Rodney was withholding information about Dana's involvement in the homicide; whether or not he had hidden the .22 pistol; and if it had been used in the murder.

In the pre-test interview, Rodney reiterated to Key that neither he nor Dana were involved in the murder. But he did change his story about where the .22 was located.

He had told police he had hidden it, in two parts, in his VW van parked in Norwood. This time Rodney said the gun had been in a locked box he kept in the trunk of his 1974 VW Dasher, in Golden. On the day Woodroof and Patterson searched his house, he hadn't been able to locate the key. But he found it two days after, unlocked the box to look for some papers, and found the gun. He had forgotten it was there. Then he recalled that in January 1990, he had put it there to use in case he had to shoot rabbits for food.

In an affidavit, Rodney handwrote: "I got scared because I told the officers it was in Ohio in my camper, having had experiences with police in Florida. My first instinct was to hide it because I thought if I turned it in, I would lose everything I gathered up to that point over a several year period."

Rodney said he took the gun to the mountains in Clear Creek County, Colorado, and hid it under a large boulder on a hillside next to U.S. 6 between the Blackhawk cutoff and I-70. Then, on a trip to Ohio to help Sandy move and to collect his things, he visited Dana in jail and told him what he had done.

Rodney said Dana told him to retrieve the gun and turn it

over to the police because it could clear him. Rodney said he went back four or five times, but wasn't able to find the same spot again. He volunteered to go back again with police.

"Williamson's description of the area is so vague and general in nature that he could not narrow the area down to four or five acres," Key wrote. "If in fact the weapon is hidden in there, I think it would be impossible to find."

To determine whether Rodney would be a suitable subject for a polygraph, Key asked him questions about his mental health.

"The subject stated he had gone through sanity hearings in Florida as a juvenile, and during evaluations by three different psychologists he had been diagnosed as a paranoid schizophrenic, a pathological liar, and as sane.

"Williamson denied having any psychological problems and stated that he played around with the psychologists during those interviews."

Key's first thought was to stop the procedure at that point and recommend a psychological evaluation, but then he rationalized that police might not ever see him again. Expectations lowered, he continued.

Indeed, the test was a failure. "After administration of two charts," he wrote, "the physiological responses [i.e., blood pressure, etc.] of Williamson's are such that they make it impossible to render an opinion as to to his truthfulness regarding the issues under investigation."

At the courthouse, Brian Cavanagh was having his own problems. Panoyan's counselors, Paul Stark and Dave Vinikoor—two attorneys Cavanagh respected greatly—were now playing dirty, in his estimation.

Stark sent Cavanagh a letter on August 2 complaining that he hadn't been forthcoming in providing discovery materials that the defense was entitled to. Stark called Brian negligent, irresponsible, arrogant, and intimidating.

When Stark came in for a conference, Cavanagh blew up. "Paul, you know that's not true," he said.

"Well, we have to do what we have to do to represent our client," Stark answered.

That's when Brian lost it. At the top of his powerful voice, he screamed, "No, you don't have to do that. That's not zealous representation of your client. That's persnickety hard-ball. You're playing legal games.''

Then he threw him out of the office. Secretaries and other prosecutors in the office were shocked.

In a letter a few days later, Cavanagh channeled his anger into elocution: ''Never before in my professional career have I received correspondence with comments not only so inappropriately vituperative, but fraught with confabulation, factual misstatement and outright falsehood. Such malevolent averments are not commensurate with the caliber of counselor and gentleman which I have otherwise known you to be.

''Anticipating the very sort of shenanigans in which you and your co-counsel are now engaging, I meticulously prepared a thorough and precise catalog of all discovery materials. . . . Shame on you, Paul. You are hitting below the belt, under the misapplied guise of zealous advocacy.''

✦ TWENTY-FOUR

STEPHEN LUCHAK

During a discussion with Brian Cavanagh in July, Kelly Woodroof said that according to what Dana had told his Aunt Billie, Panoyan was trying to make contact with him in the jail through an intermediary. At that time Woodroof raised the thought that a jailhouse confession might be in the works.

It turned out that he was right. On August 24, Dana Williamson's cellmate, Stephen Luchak, a robbery suspect and drug abuser, called Dave Patterson. He explained that he had seen Patterson's business card that he had given Dana in Ohio.

He said Dana had talked to him at length about his case. Dana insisted that he was innocent, but after a while, Luchak realized that he knew far too many details about the crime scene not to have been there. Dana always referred to the "gunman" in the third person, but Luchak theorized that he was really talking about himself.

When Patterson told Brian Cavanagh about Luchak, the prosecutor's first thought was how wary he was of jailhouse snitches. They always carried a lot of baggage; in general, their motivation in coming forward was to swap information for leniency on their own cases. And very often, snitches embellished and invented information outright to sell their tales.

In court, defense attorneys are obliged to sneer and ask the snitch about his sordid criminal record during cross-examination. Even the judge instructs the jury before they begin deliberating a verdict that they should be cautious when weighing a snitch's testimony.

Given all that, Cavanagh also knew that sometimes snitches reporting jailhouse confessions—despite all their problems—told the truth and were thus invaluable.

On September 14, 1990, Woodroof taped Luchak's statement. He was college-educated and well-spoken, about thirty years old. He said he considered himself guilty of his crimes and blamed them on his drug addiction. Predictably, he did want help in his case, but added that his statement wasn't contingent upon it.

He hadn't thought of snitching until Dana told him about his previous manslaughter conviction. From then on, Luchak began taking clandestine notes of their conversations—always keeping them in his pockets—and looking through Dana's files.

Luchak narrated from his notes for much of the statement:

"He knows there is a push-button alarm. He is saying there are three phones in the house, an island kitchen. One time he tells me Decker is shot two times in the back of the head, Decker's father is shot in the mouth, and the boy behind the ear. He talks about the gun misfiring and it being a .22 caliber revolver, and I don't know how he knows it was a revolver.

"He talks about the people shot in the master bedroom. Lady in a closet. She comes home, sees Chuck. Chuck was sitting in a chair. Gunman hiding and got the lady and Decker to sign papers, and he uses drivers' licenses to check the signatures.

"He talks about the victim crawling out and seeing Chuck talk with the gunman on his hands and knees. See, at this time I don't know how he has got any information. He stated he hasn't seen his lawyers."

If that was true, it made Luchak's information blockbuster. All of the verifiable information so far was right, and many of the details were not made public until discovery. But Woodroof knew it would be difficult to prove that Dana hadn't gotten it from his attorneys sometime in the past two months.

However, what Luchak said next wasn't on public record because only the gunman knew for sure.

Luchak said Williamson contradicted himself on the issue of whether the male Deckers were shot before Donna Decker was stabbed. One time he said it that way, another time the reverse. Once Dana said he described to Panoyan exactly which of Donna's knife wounds were fatal.

Even more interestingly, Luchak said Williamson told him that Mrs. Decker was stabbed in two places in the house.

"The lady got out of the office or is caught somewhere in the kitchen area or somewhere, I am not certain. She's decided to fight for her life or something.

"What happens is the gunman goes berserk. He stabs the lady, and I am under the impression they are in the front—in the front living room near the door. They had taken her back to the office and stabbed her more in the office—in the closet type office."

Police did have blood spatter evidence found in the foyer near the front door, however, they hadn't been able to say for certain Donna had been stabbed there because there were no witnesses.

Luchak said Williamson talked about how he could neutralize the evidence against him at trial. He admitted the cowboy hat found at the murder scene was his, but he had two possible explanations why it was there. Both ways suggested he had been framed: either his brother Vernon had stolen it with the intention of leaving it there during commission of the crime; or Panoyan had it inadvertently because Williamson's daughter had left it in the back of Panoyan's truck while he and Dana went fishing together. He said the hat had been missing for two months before the murder.

They also talked about the thirty-minute delay between Donna Decker's 911 call and Panoyan's arrival at the Xtra shopping center. Luchak had his own theory to explain it.

"See, I think they think the lady is dead, everybody is dead, and they left way before the lady called. He leads me to believe that there was fifteen minutes or so before the lady had called and that the people had left.

"And he said, 'I will give ample time for Chuck to drive them home' or whatever."

At that point, Luchak said Williamson made a faux pas.

"He kind of slips and says, 'Belts should never have been left in the truck.' He caught himself immediately. You had to be there to see it. His mind started thinking. His eyes got wide. He changed the subject immediately."

Williamson made a second slip talking about Panoyan, he said.

Luchak said he had seen Williamson and Panoyan talking together in the rear rows of the jail chapel. "I was talking to another inmate about this. When they first were put in the cell, he didn't want anything to do with Chuck.

"We had asked him why. He says, 'Well, if I see him, I will kill him.' This was over a conversation about somebody turning against him. When he first came in the jail, I think he had thought that Chuck might have turned on him.

"And eventually he meets with Chuck in the church, and now they are friends all of a sudden again."

Luchak said Williamson told him that Panoyan's testimony was the key to the case and that Panoyan had been offered immunity to testify against him, but hadn't accepted any deal.

"I think he is under the impression that on this case, they don't have anything on him. And that just as long as Chuck maintains silence, they can't get a conviction."

He said Williamson told him that Panoyan "is afraid of the gunman, that he will do something to Chuck or his family.

"Then he just paused, and walked over to the commode and stated, 'If he ever rolled on my brothers, I know that at least one of my brothers would kill him.' The conversation changed immediately, like he caught himself."

Luchak also offered Woodroof and Patterson personal letters Dana had just gotten from Sandy.

In one, undated and filled with spelling and grammatical errors, she wrote:

"I feel bad because they want me to testify against you, I thought you had a ninja belt, and everything I said to the police looks bad on you and I didn't mean it to be that way.

"You know if they get me on the stand they will jump all over me and have me scared to death you know they will pull me apart peace by peace until I brake down. You know I don't want to testafy against you. I just want you to know that. Please don't hate me. I need you too. It is hard for me to write because I am crying, I wish I were dead so I couldn't testafy against you.

"I will allways love you even when I do something in the trial. I don't mean to hurt you in any way, you know I don't know very much about all of this, I don't know if you have ninja utilaty belt but I told them you did and you wore a ninja alfet [outfit] the night you robbed some guy in a bar on night.

"I was all in tears and shook up from the divorce papers and some one dead and three people shot in the head and being on my medicine earlyer and not having it and being in pain from my teeth being pulled out that Friday before and them pulling me in different directions, I don't know if I was coming or going or who to believe, you or them."

On September 10, 1990, the Smith & Wesson .357 stolen from the briefcase in Bob Decker's van finally surfaced.

A twenty-one-year-old man named Pedro Marin walked into a Metro-Dade County police station to register two guns. But when an officer checked the serial number of the .357, it came up stolen. Immediately the officer called Davie Police, and within half an hour, detectives Spence and Sylvestri arrived to ask Marin about the gun.

Marin told them a homeless man named Papucho—a Latin nickname equivalent to "Pops"—had approached him a week before with an offer to sell the gun for $200. Marin had seen Papucho a few times before, hanging out and drinking beer near a Hialeah supermarket with other homeless friends. Marin worked as a mechanic a few blocks from there.

He described Papucho as a Latin, late forties, short, dark skin, mustache, receding hairline, and dirty looking.

Marin said Papucho told him that someone was going to bring the gun over. "He said I shouldn't, you know, get involved with the man. But I didn't see no problem with it because I was going to go to the police station and get the gun checked out.

"I asked Papucho to come with me. He said, 'That's okay. You have it checked out and you bring it back.' " That morning, Papucho gave him the gun. Marin was impressed that it was all greased up and immaculately clean.

Spence and Sylvestri took the gun and asked Marin if he would help them find Papucho. In two cars, the detectives following Marin, they drove to the supermarket, but Papucho was gone.

Marin said Papucho was always at the supermarket on

Saturday mornings. Spence asked him not to look for Papucho until then. That Saturday, Spence, Woodroof, Dave Patterson, and a Hialeah police officer tried again. Once again they were unsuccessful. If Papucho was suspicious before this interview that something was up, he certainly would have felt that way after three Anglo cops came barging into the Spanish-speaking neighborhood, asking questions.

Briefly, the .357 had been a hot lead, but now it was cold. Woodroof gave it to the crime lab, and they lifted two latent fingerprints from it. But neither matched Dana Williamson or Charles Panoyan.

Trying not to admit defeat, Cavanagh brought Marin in for a polygraph to ask if he was telling the truth about getting the gun from Papucho, or if he knew where Papucho lived. Marin answered yes, he did get the gun from Papucho, and no, he didn't know where he lived. In the examiner's opinion, Marin was lying.

In October 1990, Woodroof and Patterson retraced Charles Panoyan's trip north to visit Dana Williamson.

They flew to Washington National Airport and rented a car, noting the mileage. Their first stop was a place called Eighty-four, Pennsylvania—a truck stop on I-70 called the Toot 'n Scoot. There they found the telephone booth corresponding to a phone number on the Schulzes' November long-distance bill. It confirmed that Dana called Panoyan at that phone booth, or at least returned a call to him after Panoyan ran out of change to feed the phone.

From there, the investigators drove on to Covington, Kentucky, where they found and photographed Frisch's Big Boy Restaurant. While in the area, they met again with Norwood detectives and picked up the property taken in May from Rodney Williamson's van.

Returning to Washington, D.C., they noted their round-trip mileage as 1,126. On the same trip, Panoyan had logged 1,296 miles.

Back home, Woodroof had a chance to read Rodney's papers, which had been found in the van. He was a prolific writer, if not somewhat disturbed, typing letters, diary entries, and paranoid short stories involving himself and sometimes Dana as characters.

In one story, Rodney wrote about vagabonding through the country in his Volkswagen camper, making a few dollars at odd jobs here and there to sustain himself.

"I got to the truckstop when I heard some people at a table arguing over drugs. I'd gotten up and one of the men at the table got up and followed me toward the rest room. I started thinking he was going to jump me, so when I walked into the men's room I stepped to the side behind the door after it'd closed. He came through next and was reaching into his jacket, so I cat-footed behind to see what he was getting and when he pulled out a pistol I almost ripped off his head.

"He dropped the .380 auto when I hit him, after I picked it up I pulled him into the closet behind the door, and as I closed it someone came in from the hall. I turned on the light in the closet and search[ed] his pockets to see what else he might be carrying. I found another .380 and several more clips for them and $390 in cash. He was carrying a small bag of cocaine and no I.D., so thinking he might have been sent after me I decided to leave after I tied him up."

So began the first-person character's descent into a profitable life of ripping off drug dealers. He trailed the other men who had been discussing drugs at the truckstop table to a series of houses that were their drop-off locations.

"I parked a block away and put on a set of cammo ninja togs and stuffed the gloves and hood in a jacket pocket. I took a small backpack and set out to do a recon of the house on a bicycle I had mounted on a rack on the camper. I rode past the house and hid the bike in an alley then removed the jacket and put the hood and gloves on. I crept down the alley into the backyard of the target house, listening at a window in shrubbery I heard some drug deals go down and decided to hit them.

"I zip-stripped the people in the house and removed all the ammo, guns and cash from the premises. The drugs I piled in the front room neatly and left out the backyard to the bicycle."

It wasn't hard to realize the similarities to the Decker murder. Woodroof asked himself, Was Rodney somehow part of it? Bob Decker had said the gunman was looking for drugs.

The ninja clothes, the hood, the stealth in surveilling the house, a car parked a block away, and tying up the people in the house all rang true. But most suspicious of all was the tone to the story that made Woodroof's skin tingle.

In another short story, Rodney imagined himself committing violent acts against drug dealers and petty thieves who had robbed him.

"The police suspected he'd been beaten by a potential victim who had martial arts training. I'd dropped the gun in a mail box on a corner after I'd soaked it in gasoline then wiped it with transmission fluid on a rag. I sometimes wonder if it'd been used in any murders." That sounded like it could have referred either to the .357 just found, cleaned before Marin got it, or maybe Rodney's .22.

There were other typed papers, too. Most interesting was a letter from Rodney to Dana dated October 27, 1988—eight days before the murder. In it, Rodney talks about an unspecified business he and Dana are supposed to begin.

"Another good reason I'm going on with it tonight is we are having a cash flow problem .... You bought the stunner [stun gun? thought Woodroof] to make money with, before you do something, try thinking about the consequences, all of them, of your actions. Then ask yourself if it's worth it. Dad once said if it isn't worth the risk it isn't worth doing. He also counselled us, 'If a thing is worth doing, do it right the first time so you will not have to do it again.'

"Remember, you are setting an example for two children, are you doing something you will want them to do also/ there are no secrets if more than one person knows! And if you are illegally doing things there can be a lot of trouble ...

"I'm capable of keeping silent, but will tell the exact truth if asked for it, except when I'm directly involved, I then extemporise it may be heresay, therefore rumor and rumor might not be truth, therefore not worth a mention in a question of truth.

"You like to brag about things you've done, everyone does to a point, but you do not realize if someone gets a case of oral Diarreah, a snitch only has to be able to prove 1 thing the rest are brought as confessions and a snitch could be 3rd hand information (do you realize what time we could do for things Sandy knows?) ... By the way, I heard Vernon questioning Sandy about Arson ..."

The snitch reference two years prior to Luchak was prescient. Also, Rodney's description of how he would answer police questions sounded like just the way he handled them in his interviews.

There were also pathetic letters and jottings Rodney made regarding his hate for his family. In "An Open Letter to the Williamson Family," he wrote:

> First I regret to inform some of you that I consider this a rotten excuse for a Family unit ... I feel shamed for being unlucky enough to be born into your Family. That I can not change, but I can deny you the ability to walk the streets ...

In a letter to "Dad, Grandma and Aunt Billie," he wrote:

> Dad, I'm not as sorry for you as the normal son would be, you lived long enough to let me know you have feet of Clay. I used to HATE YOUR GUTS, then I became indifferent toward you when I realized you were not worth it. The only reason I stayed after you had the Stroke was I felt Guilt over my having hated you when I was a child.
>
> I'm not so sure I was Guilty of the feelings I held for you, I realize you never in your life had an Honest bone in your body. I remember the times I helped you cheat, the I.R.S., the Union, and the Unemployment Compensation people ...
>
> You sure was a good example for me, of what not to be as a parent, You are probably the reason I've never gotten Married, I do not want to be YOU and I'm afraid I see more of the possible Violent Father you were to me inside me than the father you are to Jay.
>
> I guess you had to have proof that made you change into the Lenient parent you are today, We were it. Every single one of your first brood are somehow twisted, I do not believe it was mom that twisted us ... I had a bout with alcohol and another with Speed, Dana was locked up for a crime he did not commit but was capable of ... You stole our happiness from us.

However, Rodney vented his loudest anger in a letter to Sandy:

> *Sandy, Sandy, Sandy ... you talk your loud mouth shit after you come home, every night I'm awake, some of the time you wake me up at the unGodly hours you come in ...*
>
> *The final fucking straw is the fact I WILL NOT TAKE ANY MORE OF YOUR SHIT! If you do NOT stop running off at the BIG STUPID MOUTH! I will, WILL! BREAK YOUR JAW!!! I despise you and EVERY THING YOU REPRESENT!!! And I've been sick of you long enough to wish I'd never talked Dana out of killing you. You are the type of person who is the best reason FOR ABORTION,,,RETROACTIVE ABORTION.*

Finally, there were two ghastly poems, one about his father, the other about his mother:

> *I hated my Father*
> *with all of my heart*
> *there was a difference*
> *right from the start*
> *it was a disagreement.*
>
> *He whipped and he beat until*
> *from he drew blood and*
> *we wanted to die*
> *or better yet kill.*

And

> *Our mother died one Christmas night*
> *the result of a driver was at*
> *an alcoholic party earlier that day*
> *His Lawyer was a slick one with*
> *a really glib tongue*
> *he lied through his teeth*
> *his client got a slap on the wrist*
> *and then walked free*

Woodroof called Golden police once more on November 8, 1990, requesting that they reinterview Rodney to ask him if he had a stun gun. Five days later, in a taped statement, Rodney admitted Dana had bought one in mid-1988 and gave it to Rodney after they moved to Ohio. He still had it.

Woodroof also got the BSO to find Rodney's prints from their files and compare them to the still unidentified single palm print. Again, no match.

III

Paul Stark and David Vinikoor

✦ TWENTY-FIVE

ALLIE KITTLE
Deposition, December 19, 1990

In Florida state criminal cases, the defense is entitled to examine all of the state's witnesses before trial. These on-the-record depositions are held out of court, but the information that comes out in the process is a precursor of the trial.

The first witness deposed was sixty-five-year-old Allie Kittle. He was part of the twisted sequence of neighborhood gossip that led to the Crimestoppers tip naming Dana Williamson.

This was the chain of hearsay: Kittle worked part-time during the growing season for Wanda Sullivan's fruit stand and nursery in west Hollywood. Both Kittle and Sullivan lived in Tropical Valley, near the Williamsons.

Sullivan also employed a girl named Dawn, who told her that a woman "had heard some people talking about a robbery when she's out looking for her cat, across the street from her house." Sullivan repeated that to Kittle, then he told Winston Marsden, who called police.

The woman Dawn was talking about turned out to be Ginger Kostige. Dawn was her future daughter-in-law.

"What possessed you to tell Winnie Marsden this?" asked Charlie Johnson, a court-appointed "Special Public Defender" for Dana Williamson. Johnson, a private practice attorney, got the case because the state Public Defender's office had a conflict of interest. They had previously defended Dana's sister Dawna on her drug charges, and now she was a state witness against him.

"Well now, the case was dead. It might have been a lead

to it, but I'm kind of doubting now whether I should have even said anything about it.''

"Did you have any idea what the result of this was going to be?''

"No, I sure did not.''

"Did you think it was going to hurt Charles Panoyan?''

"No, I sure did not.''

Paul Stark asked Kittle his opinion of Panoyan.

"To me, he's A#1. He's just a guy that you like. You ever work with a guy that you liked that you got along good with?''

"Is he a violent guy?'' Stark asked.

"Never. Never seen him get mad at nothing.''

Stark asked him if Panoyan was capable of the crime he was charged with.

"He would not do that. Chuck is—though he don't seem like it, he's a very religious man.''

Kittle said there was a lot of talk in the neighborhood about the murder. Stark asked for specifics.

"Well, the only rumors that I heard of was how they let Chuck go.''

"It seemed unusual, right?''

"Yeah, it sure did. Don't it to you?'' Kittle asked.

"Well, it is unusual,'' Stark admitted.

"They said that he must've knowed whoever done it, or they wouldn't have let him go.''

"Did you have an explanation for that, as to why they let him go?'' Stark asked (the largest question for which he himself didn't have the answer).

Kittle was no help there. "No, I don't.''

GINGER KOSTIGE
Deposition, December 19, 1990

Next up was Ginger Kostige. Living so close to the Williamson family was a trip, she said. For eleven years, she had lived either next door or across the street from them, so she was never surprised to hear commotion coming from the house.

Dana and his wife Sandy fought constantly. On Halloween

night in 1988, Kostige reported, "I went across the street and asked Dana if I could take his two little girls down the street to go trick-or-treating, because everything was bothering him. Everything was on his nerves. He was screaming and yelling at the kids continuously.

"I knew how his temper was. I told my husband—I said, 'Let me go over and ask if I can take the kids and give him a break.' "

Halloween was just two nights after she had overheard yelling about stabbing and jumping on the roof, so Paul Stark asked if she had mentioned what she had heard to Dana.

"No, I did not mention anything."

"Why not?"

"It's really none of my business—I mean, if you've lived across the street from them like I have, I think maybe you wouldn't ask either.

"When we first moved out there (we bought our house in 1979), and after we're living there six months or a year, we find out that Dana Williamson was serving time in jail for killing that little boy and injuring that little girl.

"Then when he gets out and we find he's going to live there for a while, well, you try to get along with everybody. Okay?

"But then one night he comes to my open picture window and he shows me what he had just killed. He found an opossum or something. Then he was standing by the window with the blood on his shirt and on his hands and he had the knife there and he had skinned it.

"So I mean, you try to ignore him, but you try to get along with him. You try to be nice."

Paul Stark paused while he tried to figure out what he wanted to say.

"Is what you're telling me that you're living across the street from somebody who you obviously fear as being almost a psychopathic killer?"

"I do not—I do not fear him. He lived with his father there. Okay? It was not a fear, it was just—we tried to keep our distance, but it was like—when we'd come home from work, we could not step out of the car. Either we were walked from our mailbox, or from our car, to our front door. This was an everyday thing."

← Twenty-six

KELLY WOODROOF
*Deposition, December 27–28, 1990
and January 3, 1991*

The first real indication of just how difficult it was going to be for the state to win this case came during Kelly Woodroof's eleven-hour, three-day deposition.

Going in, Woodroof and Cavanagh thought they had their defendants down cold. Instead, Dave Vinikoor and Paul Stark exposed them on seemingly every loose end, assumption, and inadequately contemplated logic. When it was over, they could not help but be impressed by the magnificent lawyering they had just witnessed, even if it did come at their expense.

Vinikoor's opening question belied the scrutiny and torture he was about to put Woodroof through. He simply asked him to recount the evidence against Charles Panoyan.

"Well, the first thing that comes to mind are the numerous contradictions between his account and Bob Decker's account, Clyde Decker's account, and general things that simply go against common sense," said Woodroof. There was also the belt found in Panoyan's truck.

"Does the belt show that Charles Panoyan aided, or solicited, or both, a person to murder Donna Decker?" asked Vinikoor, reading from count one of the indictment.

"Objection to the form of the question," said Brian Cavanagh.

"You're asking me an overly simplistic question. There is no one piece of evidence that's—"

"I didn't ask for one piece. I've asked for any. Any and all. So far you've given me two. You've said inconsistent statements and you've said a belt. And then as to the belt, I asked you whether that supports the conclusion that Charles Panoyan aided and abetted, or does it support the conclusion that he solicited another to murder Donna Decker?"

"It adds to it."

"Adds to what?"

"It adds to the proof."

Vinikoor changed his tack, dividing up the allegations. He asked if there was evidence showing that Panoyan solicited Donna Decker's murder, as opposed to him merely aiding and abetting it.

"The only thing that I can think of that falls under the ambit of that would be the unusual meeting between Mr. Panoyan and Mr. Williamson on the second of September," Woodroof answered.

"That had something to do with the soliciting to commit a murder on Donna Decker, to your knowledge?"

"Well, we think it may have."

"Objection to the form of the question," said Brian Cavanagh. The rules of interrogation are different in deposition than at trial. Since judges don't referee depositions, objections don't prevent witnesses from answering, they just preserve an attorney's protest for the record.

"Do you have any proof of that?"

"We don't know what was said during that."

"So, the answer is you have no proof of that," stated Vinikoor.

"Objection to the form of the question," said Cavanagh.

Vinikoor asked which of Panoyan's inconsistent statements and omissions told Woodroof about the manner of Panoyan's involvement in the murder.

"One thing that springs to mind is Mr. Panoyan's glaring omission of the fact that he left the house to get the venison."

"What's the significance of that?"

"Objection to the form of that question," said Cavanagh.

"My interpretation, coupled with the rest of the evidence in the case, indicates to me a knowledge of what was going to happen beforehand. In other words, entry into the residence would be a significant hurdle."

"That suggests that Panoyan was involved early on in the incident, right?"

"Yes."

"Was that it?" Vinikoor asked.

"Of course not," said Woodroof. "I think that when you put the whole thing together you have a very clear-cut picture. It's a little like a jigsaw puzzle. One piece out of a 600-piece jigsaw puzzle doesn't mean a great deal."

That answer would have made a good sound bite for TV, but it didn't wash with Vinikoor. Once more he demanded Woodroof to itemize all the evidence that proved Panoyan solicited someone to murder Donna Decker.

"I'm not sure I can give you an answer," said Woodroof.

"Is that because there is no evidence to support the conclusion?"

"He's here to tell you facts, not theory," interrupted Brian Cavanagh.

Vinikoor snapped at Cavanagh. "Please, if you have an objection, note an objection. I don't need you to tell me why he's here."

"Mr. Vinikoor, I'm a police detective," Woodroof said. "I'm not an attorney. I don't prosecute the case. I put together the evidence."

"Fine. What's the nature of the evidence to support the conclusion that Charles Panoyan asked anybody to murder Donna Decker?"

"Objection to the form of the question," said Brian Cavanagh.

"To break it down like that, I just can't do it."

"Are you aware of any such evidence?"

"Objection," said Cavanagh.

"If I asked you the question: Are you aware of any evidence that Charles Panoyan pulled a trigger and thereby killed somebody?—you'd be able to answer that question, wouldn't you?"

"Yeah."

"So why is that any different?"

Woodroof didn't respond.

Frustrated, Vinikoor asked still again.

"Are you aware of *any* information or evidence that Charles Panoyan asked somebody to murder Donna Decker?"

"Objection to the form," said Cavanagh.

"No," said Woodroof.

"Thank you," said Vinikoor.

Flushed with a victory in his first challenge to the indictment, Vinikoor next asked whether there was evidence of solicitation of the attempted murders of Bob, Clyde and Carl Decker, as referred to in counts two, three, and four.

"Objection to the form of the question," said Brian Cavanagh. "You're dealing with circumstantial evidence, of which there hasn't been any inferences that may be drawn of probative value that go to what you're asking, but there are things that depend upon other evidence that's deduced. It's the whole smorgasbord of different evidence taken together from which a reasonable conclusion can be drawn."

There's your sound bite, thought Vinikoor. The state's case against Panoyan was a smorgasbord of evidence scattered in 600 jigsaw puzzle pieces that all depended on each other.

Vinikoor asked if Panoyan had been a suspect almost from the start of the investigation.

"I would view it differently," said Woodroof. "The way I would view it is that he was someone who was at the crime scene at the time of occurrence. We attempted to eliminate him from consideration and simply couldn't."

"Did you, as lead investigator, consider any reasons, other than Panoyan being involved, which would explain why he was released unharmed?"

"Yeah, we discussed it."

"What other reasons did you discuss?"

"Well, there are a handful. The first one that comes to mind is the fact that somebody had a specific grudge against either Bob Decker, Donna Decker, or Clyde Decker. I think we can assume that nobody had a real heavy grudge against Carl.

"We discussed the possibility that somebody might be trying to set Mr. Panoyan up. We really didn't put any validity to that, but it was something that was considered."

"Why didn't you put any validity to that?"

"Well, because if they're willing to shoot a thirty-month-old infant, they probably weren't going to leave a competent adult witness."

"But the possibility that somebody was directing their anger only at the Deckers was something that you did seriously consider?" Vinikoor said.

"That was an early consideration, yes."

"You thought there was a real possibility to that?"

"It was something that we considered and ruled out."

"How the hell did you rule that out?"

"Well, namely because we found such glaring inconsistencies in Mr. Panoyan's account."

"How were those inconsistencies inconsistent with the theory that it was a hit on the Decker family?" Vinikoor asked.

"Objection to the form," spoke Brian Cavanagh.

"Would you agree that inconsistencies in an account may be because somebody's lying throughout, correct?"

"Yeah."

Then Vinikoor suggested: "Another reason why there's inconsistencies might be that somebody is the world's worst accounter of what transpired in front of them."

"That's true," said Woodroof.

"Do you know which of the two it is as to Charles Panoyan?"

Woodroof jumped on that one.

"Yeah, Panoyan's lying."

"Objection," said Cavanagh, too late.

"Well, I know that's your feeling," said Vinikoor, "but do you know for a fact whether that's the case?"

"There is one incident in the inconsistencies that I think is very glaring to that point," said Woodroof.

"What's that?"

"Mr. Panoyan's assertion that Donna Decker was grabbed right in front of him. In the videotape he points out right in front of the hearth. You know, within steps of it."

"Right," said Vinikoor.

"Contrasted with Bob Decker and Clyde Decker's independent recollection that Donna was grabbed near the foot of the bed, coupled with the shoe that Bob Decker saw her lose and that we found at the scene. The two points are not visible with one another. Either Mr. Panoyan saw that, or he didn't."

"Well, isn't it a fact that Bob Decker said under oath that

Donna Decker lost her shoe the *second* time she came into that room?"

"I don't believe that's correct," said Woodroof.

"Any other theories that you can think of that explain or could possibly explain why Charles Panoyan was released unharmed that you explored?"

"Yeah, that he's part of the crime."

"Anything else?"

"I can't think of anything else."

Vinikoor paused. "Did you explore the reason that the assailant knew Charles Panoyan, even though he may not have been involved, to explain his being released unharmed?"

"Well, once Dana Williamson's name came up, yeah, we considered that possibility. Yeah, I see where you're driving."

"Did you dismiss that possible theory?"

"Yeah. That was a theory that, like I said, we considered, but when we spoke with the various parties in Norwood, we ruled out."

"Why did you rule that one out?"

"Because of some unusual contacts between Panoyan and Williamson."

"Well, let's phrase it this way: Did your investigation reveal any evidence to *disprove* the theory that Panoyan was released unharmed, but wasn't involved, even though he knew the assailant?"

"Yeah, I believe there's evidence to refute that."

"What evidence is that?"

"Well, as I stated earlier, Panoyan's omission of leaving the house to get the venison, providing an entryway for the assailant; and that Bob Decker has no knowledge of Dana Williamson."

Vinikoor asked Woodroof if he was suggesting that the only way Dana Williamson knew about Decker was through Panoyan.

"Yeah. Coupled with the fact that the assailant, Mr. Williamson, knew that there was a floor safe; compared with the fact that Mr. Panoyan indicates that Bob mentioned that there was a floor safe and the fact that Mr. Panoyan assisted in the building of the house and would be aware of the floor safe, or presumably would be aware of the floor safe.''

''Anything else you can think of?''

''Not right off the bat.''

''Did your investigation reveal any evidence to disprove the theory that Panoyan was released unharmed because this was a hit on the Decker family?''

''Well, essentially, we couldn't find anybody that had a grudge with Bob Decker.''

''You couldn't find *anyone* who had a grudge with Bob Decker?''

''A grudge of that magnitude.''

''You did get from Bob Decker a number of people that had threatened him in the past?''

''No.''

''You did not? Did you get anybody? The name of anybody that had threatened him in the past?''

''He mentioned a couple of people that he had had problems with.''

''But no one that had threatened him?'' asked Vinikoor.

''Not that I can recall at this time.''

''From experience—investigator experience—in what context are family hits most common?''

''I suppose there are several of them. Organized crime comes to mind, and narcotics.''

''Is it a fair statement that the very first night of this incident that you believed that this was a contract hit?''

''No, I think it was one of those things that we weren't quite sure of.''

''Detective Mocarski had expressed that opinion the very first night, did he not?''

''I don't remember Detective Mocarski saying it. The sergeant who was on the scene—the road patrol sergeant—told me that he thought it was a professional hit.''

''Who was that?''

''That was Sergeant Michael Allen.''

''Did he tell you why he thought that?''

''I think he was specifically citing the site of the gunshot wounds.''

*　　*　　*

Vinikoor asked if Woodroof believed that Panoyan knew in advance that these crimes would occur.

"Yeah, I believe he did. I believe he knew that some crimes would occur."

"Namely, a robbery?"

"And grand theft and burglary—armed burglary."

Since Woodroof left murder out of his answer, Vinikoor asked him directly if he believed that Panoyan knew in advance that a murder or attempted murder would take place.

"Investigatively, I can't say. I don't think the evidence really provides an answer for that," Woodroof said.

"As lead investigator, is it your position that Charles Panoyan actually participated in the crimes charged?"

"Inasmuch as I believe he's a principal, yeah, I believe he participated."

"Well, do you believe that Charles Panoyan robbed anyone?"

"I believe his actions facilitated the robbery, the thefts, the kidnappings, and the murder and the attempted murders."

"Although he did not personally do it," suggested Vinikoor.

"Objection to the form," said Brian Cavanagh.

"I don't know everything Mr. Panoyan did. There's certain areas that the evidence just simply does not address," said Woodroof.

"As lead investigator, is it your position that Charles Panoyan, after the fact, assisted in the avoidance of detection of an accomplice?"

"Absolutely, yes."

"Can you tell me of any evidence or proof that was revealed through your investigation that suggests that Charles Panoyan planned the crimes?"

"Objection to the form of the question," said Brian Cavanagh.

"Well, I think inasmuch as he is the only person involved in the crime who knows the Deckers, that certainly suggests an element of planning," said Woodroof. "The fact that he is the only one who knows the layout of the house and knows the location and existence of the floor safe."

"Can you tell me what evidence or proof was revealed

through your investigation that Charles Panoyan knew that these crimes were going to occur in advance?"

"As I said, the evidence suggests that he facilitated the entry. He enabled it to occur."

"So, that's by leaving the door unlocked when he went to get the venison?" suggested Vinikoor.

"Yes."

"Any other evidence?"

"The fact that he arrived at the house before the Deckers suggests that he brought the assailant with him."

Vinikoor asked how.

"Well, if he came afterwards, it would be a little difficult, because then Mr. Williamson would have to get out of the vehicle. If he was there before, Mr. Williamson had an opportunity to hide [somewhere] in the ample backyard."

"Did you uncover anything to suggest that Charles Panoyan knew that the Deckers weren't going to be home that night?"

"Being a close friend of the Deckers, I believe he would know that Bob and his father and the baby generally go out to eat on Friday nights and then come home shortly—"

"Did you even determine whether Bob Decker and his father and son customarily go out to dinner on Friday nights?"

"Yeah."

"They said the answer to that is yes?"

"Yeah. I believe the owner of the restaurant that they went to said that they were generally there on Friday nights."

Vinikoor asked about James Malcolm, who Bob Decker had obliquely led police to by saying that the assailant's build reminded him of Panoyan's electrician. Woodroof said Malcolm, at 6'1", fit the physical description of the assailant, then was quick to say that "Generally speaking, the description of Mr. Williamson and Mr. Malcolm are pretty much the same."

"What are the other reasons that caused James Malcolm to become a major suspect?"

"We considered Mr. Malcolm further because he had spent time away from the area with Mr. Panoyan shortly before the homicide. I believe they returned from a hunting trip about a week prior to this happening." Woodroof added that Malcolm had seemed evasive when they talked to him.

"He remained a suspect for over one year, correct?"

"He was somebody that we had some suspicions over. We never—"

"Well, it was more than suspicions," Vinikoor interrupted. "He was a major suspect in November of 1989, one year later, was he not?"

"Objection to the form," said Brian Cavanagh.

"He was somebody that we hadn't cleared from suspicion," said Woodroof.

"More than that, he was the focus of a major part of your investigation even a year after the date of the incident, was he not?"

"Yeah, he was a focus, however, we never felt that we had accumulated a great deal of evidence against him."

For Woodroof, backtracking from Malcolm was another problem. A year before, he and Cavanagh had considered taking Malcolm as well as Panoyan to the grand jury. Only when Woodroof discovered Ginger Kostige did they dismiss Malcolm as a suspect.

"One of the first investigative steps that was taken was to ask Bob Decker who he thought could have committed these crimes, right?"

"Yeah."

"Who did Bob Decker name?"

"Actually, we asked him if he knew who had committed it."

"What did he say?"

"He said, 'No.' "

"Bob Decker was asked for leads as to who you ought to look at, right?"

"Yeah."

"Who did he give you other than the person that turned out to be Jim Malcolm?"

"Well, he felt—he was extremely concerned about Mr. Panoyan. Yeah, he felt that Panoyan had had a hand in it."

Vinikoor attempted to shift the focus of suspicion onto Bob Decker. He asked what Woodroof knew about Decker's lawyer, Daniel Guerrieri, visiting the hospital on the morning after the crime, when he told the police officer guarding Bob not to talk to his client.

"This is news to me. Obviously, though, even if that warning was given, it was something we paid absolutely no attention to. As soon as Mr. Decker was conscious, we were speaking with him."

"As the lead investigator, do you try to determine what life insurance policies existed concerning Donna, Clyde, and Carl Decker?"

"I believe all of Bob's were directed to Donna."

"How about Donna's?"

"I believe hers was directed to Bob. I believe."

"Do you know the amounts?"

"No."

"Do you know if there were more than one?"

"No. I remember discussing the matter briefly with Bob and there not being anything unusual, but I don't remember if any checks were made."

"Again, did you rely entirely upon what Bob Decker said as to whether or not there existed life insurance policies?"

"No, I think—yeah, we did rely on it."

"Did you investigate extramarital affairs by either Bob Decker or Donna Decker?"

"We attempted to check the best that we could. We couldn't find any evidence of them."

"Again, did you rely on Bob Decker, or did you use other means?"

"No, we asked people outside the family, friends, acquaintances. Interestingly enough, the only person who said there was any problem in the marriage was Chuck."

"Chuck Panoyan," inserted Vinikoor.

"Yes. When we asked Bob if he ever had any suspicions that Donna might be having an affair, he said, no, none, but if she were and he didn't know about it, probably the one person who would know would be her sister. We spoke with her."

Vinikoor asked why Woodroof polygraphed Bob Decker in March 1989.

"The reason that was done is at that point we really weren't getting anywhere. There was some evidence against Chuck, but there was a desire to clear out a concern that everybody had voiced."

"What concern had everyone voiced?"

"Not so much a concern over Bob, but most everybody that we had brought in—Bob's friends—the thought was, 'Well, if this happened to me, the police wouldn't have to worry about it, because I'd take care of it myself.'

"We wanted to, as much as we could, insure that Bob wasn't withholding any information from us, either for fear of prosecution for some sort of misdeed that he might have been involved in, or just biding his time until he was recovered enough to go out and take care of the matter himself."

"Those things don't come out of the blue. What was uncovered that gave rise to that kind of concern?"

"Nothing was uncovered. Again, the investigation was essentially at a standstill."

"Yeah, but when investigations are at a standstill, you don't always go and polygraph a guy that got shot in the head and is listed as a victim," said Vinikoor.

"Well, this case has some rather strange nuances to it."

"Were there specific things that you thought he wasn't being truthful with?"

"We wanted to make sure that he didn't have any narcotic connections. We wanted to insure that there weren't any major business problems that we weren't being told about."

Woodroof said he also had Det. Sylvestri—a Davie narcotics detective—check if any drug investigations had been done at or near the Decker house. There hadn't been any. Sylvestri also checked with narcotics detectives at all the neighboring Broward County police departments, as well as the Florida Department of Law Enforcement's database. In addition, he asked his confidential informants whether they had ever heard Decker's name.

"I don't work narcotics. But my experience is that, as a general rule, persons who have engaged in the narcotics trade, even if they have no record, somewhere, somebody has mentioned their name. It's not a hard and fast rule. It's not absolutely foolproof."

Decker passed the polygraph, and his name did not surface anywhere in the drug intelligence. That reinforced Woodroof's belief that Decker's information was in fact totally credible.

Vinikoor was amazed to find that some basic crime scene leads hadn't been followed up. For instance, blood evidence found near Donna Decker's body had never been compared with Dana Williamson, or after two years, even eliminated by a comparison with Donna's blood.

"We have been attempting to get the lab to get started on that. They say they no longer do typing," complained Woodroof.

"I mean, it dawned on you, did it not, as the lead investigator from looking at the scene, that it's possible that the assailant got injured in the course of this attack?"

"Yeah, that's always a possibility in a stabbing."

Vinikoor asked if the crime lab had matched up any hair evidence removed from Donna Decker's body.

"To my knowledge, none of the hairs have attempted to be matched yet. That's one of the things that—"

Vinikoor was incredulous. "None of the hairs—Two years after the investigation, that nobody has attempted to match the hairs removed from the crime scene? I heard you right on that?"

"The lab will not make comparisons until there is a suspect," said Woodroof.

"So, we've had a suspect since April. In the eight-month period since we have had suspects, have you asked the lab to tell you whose hairs were found on Donna Decker's body?"

"No, we haven't, but as I'm sure you probably know, hair analysis is certainly not held in, say, the esteem that fingerprints are."

"Well, whether they are or aren't, it's obviously something that you're going to want to know. I mean, if you have a red hair or a black hair, and it can't be matched to anybody in the household, and it's found on Donna Decker's dress, that's something you're going to want to know, isn't it?"

"Thanks to you, after this, we may reconsider it," piped in Brian Cavanagh.

"I hope so," said Vinikoor.

"Then you'll let them go," suggested Paul Stark.

"We may," said Cavanagh.

"Then we'll finally do some investigation that's directed towards finding the truth, rather than pinning it on the guy that was released unharmed," said Vinikoor.

"Maybe it's just a red herring," said Cavanagh.

"Maybe it is," said Vinikoor. "And I'll bet it's a red *hairing*. It's a red beard hairing from Rodney."

Next Vinikoor asked Woodroof if police were able to determine whether any documents were missing from the house.

"Well, we were unable to. We don't know what should have been there. Relying on Bob Decker's memory and ability to put things back together, he wasn't able to place anything that was missing."

"We're talking, though, about what? Thousands of pieces of paper? Maybe tens of thousands of pieces of paper?"

"It wouldn't be that many pieces of paper, but there were a lot of them. It is entirely conceivable that certain things could be missing without Bob realizing it. Some of the things that we found there were charge receipts. Things like that."

"Did you notice, for example, hypothetically, that one file cabinet drawer that contained property documents had been disturbed, whereas another file cabinet was not disturbed?"

"We were able to say definitively that some of the records for property closings had been disturbed. One of the envelopes of property closings."

"Was there anything unique about that particular envelope of property closings in terms of time or description?"

"I don't remember anything significant about it. The one thing that does stand out is that there was a document that we recovered very close to the body. It was completely blood-soaked. I believe it's been destroyed. It was putrefied. There was no way you could really do anything with it. But it was a quitclaim deed between Mr. Decker and Sam McFarland. That's another reason that Sam McFarland's name jumped out at us."

Sam McFarland was a mystery man to Vinikoor and Stark. A lot of suspicious things kept leading to him; but after Davie detectives did what seemed to be a cursory investigation of him, then administered a polygraph, which he flunked, they had dropped him as a full-fledged suspect.

Woodroof said he gave McFarland a polygraph "not so much because of anything concrete, but [because] Mr. Decker owed him a pretty reasonable size sum of money."

"Over $25,000?"

"I think the original debt had been about thirty, and that Bob had paid back about ten thousand shortly before this happened."

"You learned, did you not, Sam McFarland had intensified his efforts around November of 1988 to collect that debt?"

"No, I don't recall that being mentioned."

"Did you learn that Sam McFarland was told by Donna Decker that she had the money that Bob owed Sam?"

"No."

Woodroof said he discussed the quitclaim deed with both Decker and McFarland. McFarland said he and Decker had bought the property together. But Woodroof couldn't remember the direction which the deed went—to or from McFarland.

Vinikoor, however, knew which way the deed went. "Do you know why McFarland would quitclaim property to Decker at a time when Decker owed a lot of money to McFarland? Did you ask those questions of McFarland?"

"No, I don't recall asking those questions, no."

Nor could Woodroof remember when the deed was signed.

"Well, I mean, as a lead investigator, when you were attempting to discount Sam McFarland as a suspect, would it have been important to you to know whether or not this property deal between McFarland and Bob Decker had occurred right during the same period of 1988?"

"At the point in time we're talking about, I was not the lead investigator, and I don't remember."

"When you did become lead investigator, had Sam McFarland already been dismissed as a possible suspect?"

"Yeah, we were reasonably comfortable that he hadn't had anything to do with it."

"That determination was made without specifically determining the nature of his property deal with Bob Decker," Vinikoor said.

"Like I said, I don't recall the exact nature of that particular deal. Mr. Decker and Mr. McFarland had had dealings for quite some time."

Vinikoor asked whether Davie Police had been able to determine where the SWAT belt found in Panoyan's truck, and the handcuffs used on Bob Decker, were purchased.

Donna Decker bathes her son, Carl, a year before
the fatal attack. *(Courtesy of the Decker family)*

The house at 1651 Southwest 116th Avenue, Davie, Florida.
(Courtesy of the Broward County Sheriff's Department)

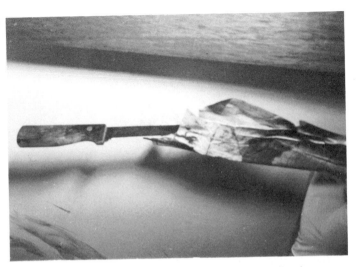

The knife Dana Williamson used to stab Donna Decker to death. *(Courtesy of Art Harris)*

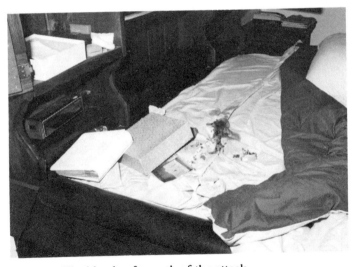

The bloody aftermath of the attack.
(Note Clyde Decker's shattered dentures.)
(Courtesy of the Broward County Sheriff's Department)

The incredible interior of Charles Panoyan's truck.
(Courtesy of the Broward County Sheriff's Department)

Panoyan at his arrest.
(Courtesy of the Broward County Sheriff's Department)

Panoyan on the stand.
(Courtesy of Art Harris)

Dana Williamson
in 1969 at age nine.
*(Courtesy of
Renee Williamson)*

Dana and Jessie, his grandmother.
(Courtesy of Renee Williamson)

Dana's battered cowboy hat became an important piece of evidence. *(Courtesy of Art Harris)*

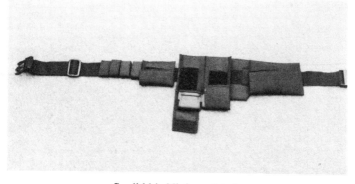

So did his Ninja web belt.
(Courtesy of Art Harris)

Prosecutor Brian Cavanagh and his father, ex-New York City Police Department lieutenant, Tom Cavanagh.

(Courtesy of Art Harris)

"The Over the Hill Gang." *Left to right:* Chuckie West, Tom Cavanagh, Jr., Frank Boccio, John Mandel.

(Courtesy of Thomas Cavanagh, Jr.)

Woodroof said no, but he had found identical belts at a number of army-navy surplus stores in Davie. The handcuffs, he said, were even more common: they could be purchased at convenience stores.

Woodroof said that he had contacted the manufacturer of the belt—Rothco—which mailed him a computer printout of all their Florida retailers.

"Do you know how Rothco describes the belt by either lot number or name?" Vinikoor asked.

"It has a lot number. The product name they use is 'SWAT Belt.' "

"Is that the same or different than the descriptive name and lot number that the Asian World assigned to that item?"

"Again, it has a lot number that I don't know, but they advertise it as a Ninja utility belt."

"Same belt, different name?"

"Yeah."

"Is that belt sold in police supply stores in Broward County?"

"I can't vouch for all of them. I don't believe I've seen it in any of the ones that I've been in. Basically, it's a very cheap, garbage-type belt. It's certainly not something I'd want to carry my stuff in."

Vinikoor asked if Woodroof had found any person who thought Panoyan was capable of committing these crimes.

"The only person who indicated that they thought Chuck could be involved in this, or the only persons, were people in the Decker family. In all honesty, I think that's based on the events, not prior knowledge," said Woodroof.

"Is there anything other than people's opinions that you uncovered in the course of your investigation that reveals the capability by Charles Panoyan to be involved in the crimes that he's charged with?"

"Objection to the form of the question," said Brian Cavanagh.

"There's nothing in his criminal record," Woodroof continued. "The financial records that we have assembled indicate a man who has some severe financial problems. That would be the only thing as far as Mr. Panoyan's background goes."

Vinikoor asked Woodroof to detail those problems at the time of the murder.

"My knowledge is based on the records that were received from various credit card companies and from Hollywood Federal [Savings and Loan]. If I recall correctly, he bounced several checks during that period. He missed some payments to various credit card companies, and he had past due balances.

"If I recall correctly, his line of credit on his equity on his home was generally right at the upper limit. His wife had a certain amount of money being taken from her check and put into the credit union into a savings account and it was drawn out almost as soon as it went in, I believe, on several occasions that I saw. In addition, I believe that the children's accounts had been depleted."

"Well, do you know if Charles Panoyan's assets far outweighed his liabilities in November of 1988?"

"No."

"Are you aware of how many checks Bob Decker was bouncing at or around the same time?"

"No, I am not."

"Are you aware of how much money, if any, Bob Decker had in any account?"

"I never subpoenaed his bank records or credit card records. I will save you some questions."

"Did your investigation reveal a motive for Charlie Panoyan being involved in these crimes?"

"Financial gain."

"Is there any other motive?"

"From some of the people we spoke with, it appeared that Bob treated Mr. Panoyan at times like his court jester, sort of held him up to ridicule."

"Were you able to trace any of the funds from the Decker home to Charlie Panoyan?"

"No, but since cash was taken, cash is not easily traced."

Vinikoor questioned why Woodroof waited until August 1989 before he began to assemble Charles Panoyan's financial records.

"During that time period is when I began attempting to put together the circumstantial evidence that existed that I believed might be enough to convince the State Attorney's office that this matter should be pursued."

"By pursuit, you mean prosecuted," said Vinikoor.

"Yeah. In addition—"

"Because your department decides which investigation gets investigatively pursued, so the only thing that the State Attorney's Office would be involved in was whether it got prosecuted or not."

"Well, no, that's not strictly true. This is an extraordinary case. This is not a common homicide. It's extraordinary in its complexity. While—"

"Well, by that do you mean it's extraordinary in the number of unanswered questions?"

"Objection to the form of the question," said Brian Cavanagh.

"No, I wouldn't say that. I'm just saying it's complicated."

"Well, what's complicated about somebody getting stabbed and three people getting shot in the course of a home invasion robbery?"

"Nothing in itself, but when you factor in that a friend of the family is released unharmed, what's complicated about it is the vast majority of the evidence is circumstantial in nature. Those cases are complicated. The State Attorney's Office is not always willing to prosecute circumstantial cases, particularly if they don't come up to a certain level—if there's not a certain amount of evidence. Add to that the fact that, as I understand it, they have an ethical duty not to prosecute cases that there's not a reasonable chance of success."

"That's only on paper," said Vinikoor.

"It's my understanding," said Woodroof.

"Objection to the declaratory statements," said Brian Cavanagh.

"If this were only a robbery, can you think of any reason why everyone except Charles Panoyan was either shot or stabbed?" Vinikoor asked.

"An effort to eliminate witnesses," Woodroof answered curtly.

"Do you have any other reason that explains that?"

"Some event during the course of the robbery arousing the assailant's ire. In other words, him becoming angry."

"Now, if it's a robbery, can you think of a reason why the baby would be shot?"

"Well, I—"

"Given the two reasons that you just gave."

"I think given the age of the child you can discount the child being a witness. If something happened to arouse the person's ire, I think it's reasonable that the baby would come under the brunt of that. There's some basically just genuinely vicious people in the world. I don't think the fact that they were all shot or stabbed indicates that this is more than a robbery."

"Can you think of reasons why—if this were *not* a robbery—why the baby would be shot?"

"I think if this were something other than a robbery, the reason that would jump to mind is an effort to wipe out the entire family."

"Well, what was the most unusual fact concerning the conduct of the assailant, in your estimation?"

Woodroof thought about that for a moment. "It's a bit of a task," he said. "Given a robbery just chock-full of unusual things, I would say, releasing Mr. Panoyan."

Vinikoor tried again, asking what the second most unusual thing was.

"Again, speaking strictly hypothetically, the signing of the papers."

"That's something you've never seen nor heard of before in a home invasion robbery, have you?"

"I haven't."

"Have you found anybody who has?"

"No."

Woodroof said he had asked Bob Decker to describe the documents, then unsuccessfully looked through the house to find them or similar documents. He reasoned that the signed but otherwise blank documents might have been the beginning of a quitclaim deed, but then again, it could also have been intended to be any number of other documents.

"Do you know for a fact if the document Bob and Donna Decker signed was ever filed after she was killed?"

"We found no record of it."

"Did you ever look?"

"Bob hasn't been notified that any of his property has been transferred."

"I didn't ask you that. I asked you if you ever looked to see if a document signed by Donna and Bob Decker was filed after the date of her death."

"No, and to be honest, I have no idea where one might look to see if a document signed by two parties was filed."

As the exhaustive deposition drew to a close, Vinikoor took to pointing out a large number of smaller flaws in the police investigation. His manner became similar to a pool sharp dispatching a young hotshot he had patiently toyed with for most of the contest, if only to raise the stakes. In rapid fire, Vinikoor cleared the ivories remaining on the table, dropping each with a crack and a thud as it fell into a pocket.

"Now, is it a fair statement that as to material facts Charles Panoyan has told substantially the same story since the date of the incident?" Vinikoor asked.

"Objection to the form of the question," said Brian Cavanagh.

"I think there are some differences, but, yeah, I think probably as a general rule his account has been substantially the same."

"Is it a fair statement that of all the people you interviewed, the story they related having received from Charles Panoyan has been the same from day one?"

"Objection to the form of the question," said Brian Cavanagh.

"I can think of a minor variation. There may be some inconsistencies that I'm not calling to mind right at the present time, but as a general rule, yeah, the account that he's given to other people has generally been consistent with that account that he gave us."

"What's the minor variations?"

"He indicated to us that the assailant only had the one weapon, the weapon that was actually used. I believe Mr. Leech indicated that Mr. Panoyan indicated that he did see him with the Uzi."

"How many times has Charles Panoyan told you, or some

other police agent of which you're aware, that he—Panoyan—feared for his safety and that of his family?''

''I couldn't give you a number, but I will concede it's several.''

''Bob Decker said that he will never forget the voice of the assailant. Have you done anything to try to test Bob Decker's ability to identify the voice of Dana Williamson?''

''No, I haven't.''

''Now, you thought it was significant that Charlie Panoyan omitted from his statement the fact of his going out to his truck and getting venison,'' stated Vinikoor.

''True,'' said Woodroof.

''Did you think it was significant that Bob Decker omitted in his walk-through signing the documents that were presented by the assailant?''

''I haven't seen the walk-through in a while. I don't recall that.''

''Did you think it was significant that Clyde Decker omitted in his walk-through that he was shot in the head?''

''I haven't seen it in a while. I am not aware of that.''

''Did you ever investigate if Charlie Panoyan was delivering venison to other friends that night?''

''That particular night?'' asked Woodroof.

''Yes,'' said Vinikoor.

''No,'' replied Woodroof.

''What was the paper clutched in Donna Decker's hand?''

''Some sort of a charge receipt. It actually stuck on the blood on her hand. It was a tissue paper. It would be sticky.''

''Did you make a record of what specifically it related to?''

''I don't remember making a specific record of it. It is in the photo, I believe. It was some sort of Penney's charge. Without the photograph, I am not certain.''

''Are you aware of the robberies in South Florida referred to as the 'Ninja robberies'?'' Vinikoor asked.

''I think I have heard of them. I don't know a great deal about them.''

''Are you aware of a robbery in Miami that a robber dressed in a Ninja outfit did a home invasion, taking drugs and money?''

''Objection. Be more specific,'' said Brian Cavanagh.

"It happened where a gun and knife were used and occupants were handcuffed."

"I am not aware of that, no."

Vinikoor asked whether Panoyan's credit cards had ever been used after the crime. Woodroof said no, they hadn't surfaced, but they were in fact reported to the credit card companies as stolen.

"Now, Panoyan claimed that his license was stolen during this incident. Did you also attempt to verify whether or not Panoyan got a new license after November fourth of '88?"

"Yeah, we ran his license, and he had had one issued after that. The teletype reveals a date of issue."

Vinikoor asked Woodroof to outline the major inconsistencies in Panoyan's statements versus the Deckers' statements.

"The first one I recall is in Mr. Panoyan's taped statement. He indicates that upon arriving at work on the fourth of November of 1988, that he was speaking with Bob, and Bob indicated that the house they were working on had just been sold."

"Decker denied it had been sold," said Vinikoor.

"That is correct."

"What is the significance to you of that alleged inconsistency?"

"I think that Mr. Panoyan is showing that Mr. Decker has said in public in the neighborhood that he has come into a large sum of money."

"Okay. So the significance of it relates to the common knowledge of there being money at the Decker home," said Vinikoor.

"It invites Mr. Decker as a target to anyone in that area," said Woodroof.

But Paul Stark saw through the logic of that. "The only thing that causes me to wonder about that is that you said Mr. Panoyan said that Decker said he sold the home."

"That is correct," said Woodroof.

"Decker denies he said that," said Stark.

"That is correct."

"If Decker's version of the events were true, there would be no reason to think that Panoyan thinks he came into money," said Stark.

Woodroof thought about that for a moment. "I don't believe Mr. Panoyan is saying he thinks Decker came into money through the sale of that house. He is providing Mr. Decker as a target. In other words, he is saying that Mr. Decker had said something to set himself up as a target.''

''He said something publicly to set himself up as a target?'' repeated Stark.

''Yeah, because he was shot in the back of the head and should be dead,'' said Woodroof.

Continuing, the next major inconsistency was Panoyan's inability to distinguish the assailant's voice, Woodroof said. ''He was the only person in the house who says he can't tell.''

''What is the significance of that?'' asked Vinikoor.

''To cover for the fact he is the assailant and not to provide any information that is not absolutely necessary. At the time Mr. Panoyan gave the statement, I believe he was under the impression there would be no living witnesses to contradict him.''

''If he were right,'' pointed out Vinikoor, ''and he was the only living witness, then, the only way you would have learned anything about who the assailant was, was through Charlie Panoyan.''

Woodroof agreed.

That was a set up. ''Who was the very first person that told law enforcement about the assailant wearing a cowboy hat?'' Vinikoor asked.

''I don't recall if it—well, it had to be Mr. Panoyan. I don't believe Bob said anything about that.''

''Did Charlie Panoyan tell law enforcement about the cowboy hat at the time he felt Decker was dying and he was the only surviving witness?''

''In my belief, yes, but at some point someone would have discovered Mr. Williamson no longer had his hat on his head.''

Of course Williamson's identity wasn't discovered for a year.

''Do you have a theory,'' asked Paul Stark, ''as to how the hat came to be left in the room, based on your investigation?''

''There are numerous ideas that have been kicked about, but I don't have a definitive answer,'' said Woodroof.

"What would you say?"

"For whatever reason the assailant took his hat off during the course of the crime."

"He just took it off and put it down?"

"Yeah."

"Where was the hat found?"

"It is depicted in the picture. It is found in the room where Mrs. Decker's body was found."

"On the floor?"

"On the floor, I believe it is going to be, the west edge."

"Is one of the theories that he took his hat off and put it on the floor?" asked Stark.

"I don't believe I would characterize it as a theory."

"Would it be a reasonable theory to assume that the hat might have been knocked off the assailant's head by Donna?"

"That is another one I would have suggested."

Woodroof said other major inconsistencies concerned the conversation Panoyan said he and Bob had (which Decker denied), asking each other if they knew the gunman; whether it was Bob or Chuck who had mentioned the floor safe to the gunman; and Panoyan's assertion that he was taken into the bedroom when Bob and Clyde Decker said he wasn't.

"I have no idea why he would lie about it."

"What does it tell you investigatively? What is the significance about that other than it is inconsistent?"

Woodroof didn't have a good answer, but the question did give him a chance to blow off some steam in the defense attorneys' direction.

"It shows your client is a liar, and it is hard to understand why a man who is a victim/witness would be untruthful— would go so far out of his way to obstruct the investigation into the murder of his best friend's wife. It gives rise to suspicion."

When Woodroof ran out of inconsistencies in Panoyan's statements, Vinikoor and Stark presented some of their own in the police theory of the case.

"If Charles Panoyan was involved, can you explain why he was tied up with the Deckers soon after the assailant entered?" Vinikoor asked.

"Object to the form of the question," said Brian Cavanagh.

"Again, it is strictly my speculation," said Woodroof. "We don't know if the plan from the very beginning was to kill everybody. And if it wasn't, if this was something that just happened as a result of Dana Williamson acting strictly on his own, or something that happened during the course of the robbery that forced a change in plans, then it would enable Panoyan to participate without being obvious."

"Is it a fair statement that Panoyan being tied up was an indication that suggests no one was to be killed?"

"I think that is a possibility, but I don't think it suggests [anything] to the exclusion of everything else."

"If there was intention to kill, there was no reason to go through the charade of tying up Panoyan," said Vinikoor.

"Objection to the form," said Brian Cavanagh.

"You don't know what Dana Williamson was thinking," said Woodroof.

"Or whoever was under that cowboy hat," said Vinikoor.

"As I said, we don't know what Dana Williamson was thinking," Woodroof repeated.

"What is your theory, or what do you feel the evidence shows, as to why Mr. Panoyan would call the police, if he believed that all the people in the house were dead?" asked Paul Stark.

"There is a point in his videotaped statement where he said—I forget the exact words—'. . . as I was going out, that is when you guys were coming in.'

"My interpretation of that is since the other three people in the room were police officers, as he was leaving the area, the police were coming in. It would be easy to pick out the police coming in because it was a Code 3 run, meaning lights and sirens, you know."

That didn't make sense to Stark. He asked why Panoyan would have called police if he had seen them going to the house.

"It would have come to mind that somebody might have seen his truck or that perhaps somebody had lived," said Woodroof.

*   *   *

"Do you have any explanation for why Charles Panoyan was segregated from the Deckers?" Vinikoor asked.

"In my opinion it is so that he can basically act as a lookout and be there to prevent anybody from escaping through the southernmost door with a special eye toward the arrival of Donna Decker."

But if Panoyan was the lookout for Donna, why didn't they just wait for her to enter the house before they began the home invasion, Paul Stark wondered.

"Bear in mind that as the crime unfolded, Mr. Panoyan and Mr. Williamson only had to contend with two adults, whereas if Mrs. Decker had been there, it would have been two people involved in the crime dealing with three victims," said Woodroof.

But that neglected the fact that Donna's entrance surprised the gunman, Stark pointed out.

"By the time that they had to deal with Mrs. Decker, Clyde Decker and Bob Decker were bound and gagged and they were no longer a security risk to the assailants," Woodroof replied.

That still didn't ring true to Stark. "So, in other words, what you are saying to me is that it made more sense to be caught by surprise by a person they knew would be coming later than to wait for her to come?"

"Object to the question," said Brian Cavanagh. Stark didn't insist that Woodroof answer it. They had made their points.

◆ Twenty-seven

Det. William Coyne
Deposition, January 18, 1991

Bill Coyne was one of the two Davie officers who questioned Panoyan on the night of the murder. His deposition began badly: when Vinikoor asked whether he had had any conversation with Panoyan before he and Det. Spence turned on the audiotape at 1:22 A.M., he said no. Yet it was 11:30 P.M. when they took Panoyan from the crime scene and drove him to the police station.

Proceeding, Vinikoor asked, "Did you have any suspicions that he was more involved than he claimed after you finished his statement?"

"It seemed to be that he had more knowledge of what was going on, but there was nothing conclusive. There were just some inconsistencies that were given."

"They were inconsistent with what?"

"Inconsistent with the mannerisms and actions of an individual that had just been present and witnessed people being shot and murdered around him," Coyne said. That assumed that Panoyan had witnessed the stabbing and shootings, which no one had ever alleged before.

"Inconsistencies with how he stated that the female Decker came inside the home, yet when I mentioned the Burger King bag—inconsistent with someone arriving and walking in on a crime in progress. The way she set her stuff down, having to pass by somebody who supposedly is tied up on a couch and walks by calmly, didn't seem to be consistent with his story."

"That didn't make sense to you," said Vinikoor.

"No, sir. It also didn't make sense why he was let go and all the others shot."

More than anyone else, Coyne seemed to have made a few leaps in judgment, Vinikoor thought.

Both Coyne and Spence were detectives assigned to burglaries, so they didn't play the largest follow-up roles in this case. But the next day, Coyne was assigned to rummage through Bob Decker's files to develop leads, such as phone numbers of associates or evidence of recent construction deals. He found "thousands and thousands of papers" in both the office/closet and the bedroom.

"The way those files were scattered all over the room, I couldn't make much head nor tail of any of the documents, to be honest with you," he said.

Davie Police had kept a twenty-four-hour guard on the Deckers even after they were released from the hospital. Coyne spent a day shift (he called it) "baby-sitting" them. While there, he and Bob Decker got to talking about the case.

"He thought that [Panoyan] had some kind of involvement in it, but he didn't have any reason for it. That was his gut feeling," Coyne said.

"Did he comment on the fact how could a good friend of his like Charlie do something like this?" asked Paul Stark.

"That was basically what he intimated, but then again, it was based upon his anger. It was unsubstantiated. He didn't have any real reason."

Dana Williamson's attorney, Charlie Johnson, asked if Coyne had any ideas about the crime's motive consistent with the home invasion and the blank documents Bob and Donna were forced to sign.

"I figured it was that Panoyan had some sort of business dealings with the Deckers that either he was cheated out of, or thought he was owed some monies on some kind of land deal or something that didn't pan out, and as a result decided to get even, based upon the attack of the family."

"Well, ordinarily, home invaders don't kill all the victims, do they?"

"No."

"And they don't shoot them behind the back of the head, right?"

"Execution-style. That's why it seemed like it was a retaliation for some wrongdoing. They also don't let one go when they shoot everybody, either.''

DET. DENNIS MOCARSKI
Deposition, January 22, 1991

Dave Vinikoor asked Mocarski, the original lead detective in the case, why he ordered a polygraph for Jo and James Zazzo, Donna's sister and brother-in-law.

"During our conversations they seemed to be more concerned about the child and who was going to get to take care of the child. And we had learned of the fact that they may have had a falling out with Bob at one time."

(In 1975, the Zazzos allowed their daughter Gail to live with Bob and Donna; the child was killed in a car accident while in their care.)

"So, you thought there may be a revenge angle there?"

"Again, everything that—we spoke and we discussed it indicate that—"

"But you had enough doubts to want them to be polygraphed, right?"

"Again, to eliminate them as suspects, yes."

Vinikoor found contradictions in Mocarski's memory and theories of the case. The first issue was whether Panoyan, on the morning after the murder, had been given Miranda warnings before Mocarski got him to sign the consent to search his truck. Mocarski said Panoyan had then already been informed of his Miranda rights, but Woodroof said—and wrote in his notes—it didn't happen until an hour and a half later.

He asked about the background check on Panoyan police had done. "Did you uncover in the course of your investigation one human being who said that they believed Charles Panoyan was capable of being involved in these kinds of crimes?"

"We had spoken to a number of people, and a number of people felt that he was capable, yes."

"Who, specifically?"

"Ricketts, I believe, we spoke with."

"Anybody else?"

"Ricketts stands out in my mind."

Another discrepancy he had with Woodroof regarded whether James Malcolm was a prime suspect during the time Mocarski was lead detective.

"No. I think Malcolm was eliminated after the poly[graph] was given, in my mind, anyway. I don't know [about] Kelly, but in my mind he was eliminated from suspicion." In fact, Woodroof had continued believing Malcolm might be the gunman up through and even after the Crimestoppers tip. Also, Malcolm was said to have been deceptive in that polygraph.

"Did you ever conduct an investigation to determine if Chuck Panoyan was delivering venison to other friends on that same night as the Decker homicide?"

"As far as my investigation revealed, he was only delivering venison to the Deckers." That may have been as far as Mocarski knew, but it wasn't so.

Woodroof had made a point that one of the most suspicious things about the murder was the gunman's segregation of Panoyan from the Deckers in the house. Vinikoor asked Mocarski if he had an explanation for why that happened.

"Do I have a reason?" Mocarski answered.

"Yeah."

"That's what we tried to find out—why he was segregated from the other three males."

"What did you come up with?"

"No reasonable explanation whatsoever."

Paul Stark followed that up with a point that no one had thought of before.

"Why was Donna Decker segregated from the males?"

Mocarski drew another blank. "I don't know. I couldn't answer that."

"I mean," said Stark, "that was no different than Panoyan being segregated, right?"

Caught off guard, Mocarski eventually responded that Donna was put in the closet alone because she was fighting with the gunman.

"Why was she stabbed and the other three men shot?"

"Objection to the form. He wasn't there," said Charlie Vaughan.

Stark rephrased. "Did your investigation reveal why she was stabbed and the other three were shot?"

"No."

"Do you have a theory as to why she was stabbed and the other three were shot?"

"Objection to the form of that, also," said Vaughan.

"Yeah, I have my own theory," said Mocarski. "He took the knife out of the kitchen, or she took the knife out of the kitchen, and there was a struggle. The struggle began in the hallway and then went into the hall closet. Either he originally had the knife, or she had the knife and was trying to protect herself when the stabbing went down. Then she was placed into the closet and then the others were shot. But again, that's only my opinion."

JAMES WACHTSTETTER
Deposition, January 23, 1991

Officer Wachtstetter had actually known Charles Panoyan for a few years before the Decker murder and considered him a casual friend. In fact, Panoyan quite often had invited him to go hunting with him. Of course, Panoyan invited almost everyone he ever met to go hunting with him.

"Why would he think that you would be a hunter?" asked Paul Stark.

"I think I told him I was going to north Florida to deer hunt, and he says, 'If you'll go that far to hunt large game, you should really go out west where it's really beautiful, and you can'—I ride the police horse in Davie—he says, 'You can ride horses there and hunt and go out in real wilderness where you don't see any houses.' "

"Would it be fair to say the guy's a friendly guy?"

"A very friendly guy," said Wachtstetter.

Wachtstetter said he first got involved in the Decker case when he was assigned to guard Clyde Decker at Hollywood Memorial Hospital, and later he guarded the family at home after they had all been released from the hospital.

Clyde told him that Panoyan had been at the Decker home

the night of the murder, delivering some deer meat from his hunting trip.

"Did Clyde Decker ever tell you that he was under the impression that Mr. Panoyan was involved in the incident?"

"I don't believe he ever did," said Wachtstetter.

"Did he describe to you what he felt the nature of Mr. Panoyan's relationship was with his family?"

"I think he said that they were in a similar business. Chuck had been building houses and his son, Bobby Decker, had been building houses, and they would kind of trade labor with each other. When you had one coming out of the ground, one of them would come over and help the other one until the house was completed. They weren't in the position to just go out and hire labor, so they'd trade with each other. 'If you help me lay blocks, I'll help you put in your electric.' "

Wachtstetter said he saw Panoyan a few times after the incident as well. "He'd see me in the street and he'd wave to me—wave me over. I explained to him that I wasn't involved in the investigation, and I didn't know any more facts than they had let me know on the case, and I didn't know if he was a target or if he was a victim. And he explained the first couple of times that he was very, very distraught that Bob could even think that he was a suspect.

"Chuck had this real bad feeling, that he wanted to talk to Bob Decker just to see where Bob stood on where Chuck was. And the next time I talked to him, I guess he had talked to the police, and he took a dislike to a couple of our detectives."

"Did he tell you why?"

"He just didn't like their attitude, he didn't like their tone of voice, and I guess they had basically told him he was more than just a person over there to drop off deer meat."

"Did he tell you that they had told him, for example, that he's going to go to prison for this?"

"He might have said that."

"Did he ever indicate to you that he was very concerned for the safety of himself and his family? Or primarily his family?"

"There was something about—we had a detective that was keeping an eye on his house, and I think he told me he put the detective in the cross hairs of his rifle because he didn't know if this guy was a policeman or if this guy was a bad guy, and he didn't know if the people that would do this to the Deckers would come over and do this to the Panoyans.''

"So there's no doubt that he conveyed to you—"

"He was in fear."

Wachtstetter said Panoyan also complained to him about the time Woodroof and Spence interviewed Panoyan's children at school. Wachtstetter had sat in on the interviews.

"What did they ask them?"

"Just simple questions. 'Your daddy was involved in a problem at his friend's house. Has he said anything to you?' They said no."

"Now, that bothered Charlie?"

"It bothered his wife. He said that he didn't feel that the school should be a place to do a criminal investigation."

"Did he ever make any statements to you to the effect that he wanted to get this over with once and for all, one way or the other?"

"I think he might have. I think he said that—he basically prayed that some day the facts would come out and he would be cleared."

← TWENTY-EIGHT

Charles Panoyan had insisted to his lawyers that he had never seen the Ninja belt before the Davie Police showed it to him. He inferred that police planted it to frame him after he left his truck at the Xtra parking lot on the night of the murder.

Stark and Vinikoor depositioned seven witnesses to ask them when, where, or whether they saw the belt. Six were Davie police officers, one was the private security officer assigned that night to the shopping mall.

To the attorneys' amazement, almost every statement concerning the belt contradicted every other statement.

In the order the statements were taken:

Officer David Pavone, one of the first Davie officers responding to the crime scene, had been ordered at about 11 P.M. to respond to Xtra to guard Panoyan's truck. Pavone said he stayed there until 4:30 A.M., but since the incident had happened two years before, his memory wasn't clear.

Asked whether he remembered other officers at Xtra that night, he answered a very surprising no—except for some coming by to see if he wanted coffee. He didn't remember anyone at all searching the truck with the legal consent form. Nor did he look inside the truck for the five and a half hours he was guarding it.

However, he had written in his police report that he talked to two Marill Security guards, both of whom had talked to Panoyan. One was Jay Greenfeder, another was someone a bit more mysterious because Davie hadn't taken his formal statement—Michael Masi.

*   *   *

229

Det. Jo Ann Carter, who first responded to the Xtra call and brought Panoyan to the crime scene, said Sgt. Allen had ordered her to return to Xtra at about 11:10 P.M. She said Officer Pavone arrived at about the same time. She didn't stay long, leaving Pavone in charge, but first she looked inside the truck with her flashlight. She didn't recall seeing anything specific in it.

Sgt. Rein worked the midnight road patrol shift on the evening of the murder. He said the first place he went coming on duty, at 11:30 P.M., was the Xtra parking lot.

He looked inside the truck without touching anything (the windows were rolled down) and saw the belt lying on top of the seat "in plain view, very obvious to me as soon as I looked in there. I don't know how anybody would miss it."

The belt was on the passenger side spread out, he said. One end was dangling over the front of the seat, the other end wedged between the backrest and the seat.

"I keyed on the belt because I had heard there was a shooting," he said. The Davie SWAT team, which Rein supervised, used similar utility gunbelts. He added that no one had told him prior that they had seen it first. He said he left the scene to tell Lt. Wollschlager what he had found.

Lt. James Wollschlager, the highest ranking Davie police officer at the crime scene, said he got to Xtra at 3 A.M., but no one had told him anything about a belt. He remembered Det. Spence arrived about the same time he did, although Wollschlager didn't recall that Spence was carrying a signed consent to search. Therefore, no search was carried out while he was present, he said. However, they both looked through the open window and each saw the belt.

Det. Bob Spence said Panoyan had signed the consent to search at 2:25 A.M. (which was documented), then Spence took it to the Xtra parking lot, arriving at about 3 A.M. When he drove up, Pavone and Carter were on the scene, and Wollschlager was looking inside the truck's windows, which were closed.

"He was looking in and I went ahead and opened the door

and that's when I saw the belt." Until then, he said, no one had told him about a belt.

But a little later in the deposition, Spence retreated. The truck was cluttered with junk and litter. "I remember saying, Oh my God, this is going to take forever to go through this thing. Well, to be honest with you, I didn't even see the belt at first. I was going through the stuff on the dashboard, through the glove box."

Spence said it took twenty minutes to do that. "Actually, I was leaning up against the belt. As I was going through everything, I was moving stuff around and as I backed up to get into the back, that's when I saw the belt sitting there on the seat." He said the belt was hanging over the seat toward the passenger door, not toward the front windshield.

And in fact, he didn't consider the belt significant when he first saw it. Even after he pulled out the handcuff keys from the pouch, he still didn't make the connection that they may have fit the cuffs used on the Deckers. A few days later, Spence talked to Marill Security officer Mike Masi, but reported Masi hadn't been at the scene and had no information to provide.

Sgt. Ed Taylor had been out of town when the murder occurred and didn't know anything about it until he listened to his answering machine messages at about 2:30 A.M. Immediately he went to the Xtra parking lot. He remembered seeing Wollschlager, Spence, and Pavone.

Before the search began, he said Spence told him that he had spotted the belt on the front seat. Then, "when I looked in, I saw it sitting on the seat," unobscured. The belt was hanging over the front of the seat toward the windshield, not over the side toward the passenger door.

Once Vinikoor and Stark realized Michael Masi existed, they hired a private investigator to find him. Masi had since left his job at Marill Security.

In a sworn written statement, Masi said he was Marill Security's supervisor on duty that night, and Greenfeder radioed him for backup just after Panoyan arrived. It took Masi less than five minutes to respond.

"The defendant appeared to be in shock, was very messed up and confused. I, being a former fireman, saw the defen-

dant's behavior to be consistent with someone scared to
death, psycho, or on drugs.

"The defendant could not even tell us his name and was
unable to verbalize practically anything. The defendant kept
muttering someone was breaking in or robbing his house and
after about ten minutes I contacted my dispatcher and requested she call the [Davie] police."

Just after Det. Carter took Panoyan away, Masi flashed his
light through the truck's door, which was open.

"Although the vehicle was filled with junk, I am certain
that there was no belt on the front seat of the truck. Realizing
there was a robbery involved, I would have been alerted if I
had seen a SWAT type belt."

Masi then left Xtra, but Greenfeder called him back fifteen
minutes later. "When I arrived back at the shopping center,
I saw numerous police officers searching the defendant's
truck. One of the Davie Police officers advised [me that] the
defendant was a suspect in the case."

Jay Greenfeder backed up much of what Masi had said,
although Greenfeder didn't remember Masi present while Panoyan was there; therefore, it was he who called Marill dispatch. Also, before Carter arrived, Greenfeder said he looked
inside the truck several times with his flashlight and saw only
junk and clothing. He said had a SWAT belt been in obvious
view, he would have recognized it because of his familiarity
with military police paraphernalia.

Could Panoyan have been right, that officers did plant the
belt? It was funny how the two sergeants and one lieutenant
saw the belt in the truck in obvious view, but no one else did.

If in fact it was planted, the attorneys now knew that the
Davie SWAT team used belts like that. Certainly the discrepancy between Rein and Taylor, who both saw the belt hanging over the seat toward the windshield, and Spence, who
saw it hanging over the seat toward the passenger door, further suggested at least that it might have been moved.

But perhaps most intriguing was Masi's statement that he
saw Davie police searching the truck three hours before Panoyan signed the consent to search.

The defense attorneys now wondered if they were looking
at a partially dirty investigation, and they didn't think the

prosecutor was aware of it. Brian Cavanagh didn't have a reputation for that sort of thing. In fact, he was known as the cleanest, most aboveboard prosecutor in the Broward State Attorney's Office.

◆ TWENTY-NINE

DANA WILLIAMSON
Hearing on motion for bail reduction
January 28, 1991

Dana Williamson's motion to reduce his bail from No Bond gave a glimpse at the issues that would be fought at an upcoming trial.

First and foremost, Brian Cavanagh had the cowboy hat found at the scene, positively identified by Dana, his wife Crassandra (Sandy), and Ginger Kostige. Bob and Clyde Decker both had said earlier it belonged to the killer.

The state also presented the police report from Pembroke Pines Police officer Thomas Vogel, putting Charles Panoyan and Dana Williamson together in the same car about two months prior to the murder date. That was the night Dana, dressed in a Ninja suit, was arrested for driving with a suspended license.

The black nylon belt found in Panoyan's truck on the night of the murder was identical to a second belt taken from Rodney Williamson's van in May 1990; the state also had a completed order form in Rodney's handwriting for two belts, a shipping receipt for them from Asian World of Martial Arts dated August 1988, as well as Rodney's admission that he gave one of the belts to Dana.

That prompted a rebuttal from Charlie Johnson: "Your honor, the proof is also going to show that Dana Williamson never had a belt for his Ninja suit; and secondly, the belt we are talking about is the common kind of Ninja belt or SWAT belt. It is really a SWAT belt, and I think the members of the Davie Police force wear them."

Cavanagh also placed into evidence the reports of Kelly Woodroof and Dave Patterson, who traced the phone and travel records of Charles Panoyan a few days after the Crimestoppers tip was made.

"The evidence and the circumstantial evidence in the case all point to the fact that this was in the nature of a continuing conspiracy between Charles Panoyan and Dana Williamson to avert justice, that Dana Williamson was led into the house by Charles Panoyan, who had come, according to the statements of the surviving witnesses, to the Decker residence shortly before 9 o'clock on November 4, 1988," Cavanagh told Judge Richard Eade.

"Not long after his arrival, he had gone out to the truck to get the venison, supposedly, and returned and came in with the masked intruder. Mr. Panoyan was kept in the living room. The others were all taken into the master bedroom. Bob Decker recollects him coming up at one point and seeing the killer leaning over, talking, whispering with Charles Panoyan.

"The evidence further shows that not only did Williamson leave his hat at the scene, but that [the] Ninja utility belt corresponds to the one found in Charles Panoyan's truck.

"[Panoyan] suggested various ways that it might have gotten there, from 'Oh, I thought I saw it at Bob Decker's house.' Bob Decker is prepared to testify that he never had such an item in his house or his garage—"

"Objection, your Honor, and this goes to the heart of the case," said Johnson. "This is Dana Williamson's bond hearing. It is not Charles Panoyan's bond hearing."

"Judge, there is an overlap because of the integral relationship between the two," Cavanagh explained. "It is the evidence against Charles Panoyan that goes against Dana Williamson as it does against Charles Panoyan himself."

Both sides brought testimony. Johnson's star witness was Dana's wife, Sandy. He showed her a picture of the cowboy hat, which she had identified as Dana's six months before, and asked her again whether she could say it was Dana's hat.

"No, I cannot," she said this time.

"Why not? In fact, do a lot of people in Davie wear that kind of a hat?"

"Yes, they do."

"How many people would you say that you know have those kind of hats?"

"More than fifteen people."

"Now, previously, when you made your statement before the Norwood Police Department, did you say that you thought that was Dana's hat that they showed you the picture of?"

"Yes, I did."

"But now you are not so sure?"

"No, I am not."

Moments later, Crassandra also retracted her statement that Dana had a Ninja belt; the belts were Rodney's, she remembered now.

Assistant State's Attorney Tony Loe handled the cross-examination.

"You had indicated on May 2nd, when you were spoken to or interviewed by Detective Woodroof and Investigator Patterson, you were mad; is that correct?"

"Yes, I was."

"Pretty much you were mad at everything that day, weren't you?"

"Yes, I was."

"That day did you lie? You were mad, but did you lie?"

"I was hurt and angry, but as far as I don't, you know—"

"You didn't lie that day, did you?"

"No."

"Do you remember when he said, 'Do you swear to tell the truth, the whole truth, and nothing but the truth, so help you God?' "

"Yes."

"Do you remember what your answer was?"

"That I would tell the truth."

"Similar to the oath you took before you took that chair today, right?"

"Yes."

Loe showed her the Polaroid of the cowboy hat again.

"And you indicated to Detective Woodroof or Investigator Patterson that Dana Williamson owned the hat that just looked like that; do you remember?"

"Yes."

"And you have before you another photograph. If you would be so kind, will you take a look at the photograph here, inside the doorway, past the lady that's lying on the floor and blood. Do you see the straw hat?''

"I can't positively identify that as his hat."

"Isn't it true when you were shown the Polaroid photograph by the Norwood police that you were able to say that's his hat?"

"No, I did not. I said, it looks like his hat."

"Okay. And does the hat in that photograph look like his hat?"

"It looks similar."

At the end of the hearing, Judge Eade issued his ruling. Dana Williamson would not be offered bond, which meant he would stay in county jail until trial. The judge's words were unambiguous: "The Court finds that the proof is evident and the presumption is great that the defendant in this case, Dana Williamson, committed murder in the first degree."

← Thirty

Frederick Schulze
Deposition, January 29, 1991

Since Rick Schulze was in Florida for Dana's bond hearing, the defense attorneys took the occasion to depose him.

Schulze said in 1988 he tore down his old house in Covington, Kentucky, and built a new house on the same land. In October 1988, with winter fast approaching, he said he asked Dana to come up north to help him finish. He hadn't yet installed either the windows or insulation.

"I asked Dana if he would be able to get away from taking care of his dad for a couple of weeks and he said he would." Dana came a month later, in mid-November, after Schulze was able to scrape up enough money for a one-way bus ticket.

In December, when Dana moved his family and possessions north, Rodney came along too, although he and Schulze didn't get along. In fact, Schulze hadn't allowed Rodney in his house for seven years, "since the day I have seen him bringing drugs to my house to my youngest son."

He said Rodney was "always coming up with different schemes of how to do things, how to blow up a house. He would sit there and turn around and say you can put chemicals on the house and be five hundred miles away and nobody would be able to accuse you of it. And I'm asking where the hell do you read something like that.

"I know he had all kinds of books. I don't know exactly what you call it—star inside a circle. Some type of satanic—"

"Cult," finished Don Carpenter, investigator for Charlie Johnson.

"Yeah. Satanic books and stuff like that. I found him to be an off-the-wall type person."

Schulze also despised Rodney's attitude toward women. "He was on a job that we were on, and he started in with my other son-in-law, explaining to him that all women are bitches, that anybody that is married is sick, stupid and crazy, every man is a wimp that is married to a woman because they live like lowlife bitches."

Schulze said when Panoyan called his house, and Dana took the call, Rodney was waiting outside in Dana's truck, and they left together.

Afterward, Dana explained to Schulze that Panoyan came to see him because Dawna had threatened to swear out an arrest warrant against Dana for starving his father.

"I said, that don't make sense. I said the man could call you from Florida or anywhere and tell you the same thing he told you here. He said, yeah, it didn't make sense to him either why he would come up here just to tell him that."

Nor did Dana's explanation wash that Panoyan was in deep trouble for witnessing whoever had killed a family.

"I said, Dana, that don't make sense. If somebody's going to come in and shoot everybody in the house, they're not going to let one person walk out the door that could identify him. They would kill that person too. Dana said it didn't make sense to him either."

On his own, Schulze called Rodney on the phone to ask where his .22 pistol was. Norwood police had searched for it without success. Rodney said he had left it in his van. Schulze knew the gun they were looking for; he had even held it once.

Schulze then looked through Rodney's possessions. He didn't see it, but instead found—which Norwood hadn't found before—the two Ninja outfits, a Ruger Mini-14 handgun, boxes of .22 shells, knives, and Rodney's papers. Schulze then called Dave Patterson, who got Norwood police to collect the additional evidence.

"Do you think Rodney might have had some involvement in this?" asked Johnson, whose strategy was to shift the blame for the murder from Dana to Rodney.

"I do."

"Why do you think that?"

"Like I said, his outlook on life, and several things I found in his van, such as his papers.

"There was a diary in there and there were several—I guess you would call them some kind of novels or stories or something he wrote up, and one of them particularly had a lot of instances referring to this particular case." Schulze thought it might not have been coincidental that in Rodney's story, as well as in the murder, people were handcuffed, "zip stripped," and assaulted in the head.

"Is Rodney known to play with cuffs?"

"Constantly wearing them, putting them on people as jokes and locking the things," he said.

Johnson led Schulze back to why he thought Rodney might be guilty. "Somebody lives with somebody for several years and all of a sudden Chuck Panoyan comes to Ohio and Rodney takes off and goes to Colorado and leaves all his things here, but a .22 pistol turns up missing. I believe I got a reason to feel that way, yeah."

However, when Rodney came back to Norwood, he and Schulze together looked for the gun where he said he had left it. It wasn't there.

"He walked to the back of his van and said, 'Somebody must have stole it.' "

CRASSANDRA WILLIAMSON
Deposition, January 30, 1991

The next day was Sandy's turn. She remembered wearing Dana's Ninja outfit to a Halloween party at a bar in 1988.

"I wore the pants, the shirt, and the face-mask-looking thing, and the camouflage-hat-looking thing that goes with it," she said.

She also admitted wearing the black nylon belt to the bar, to hold her darts, but she repeated that it was Rodney's belt, not Dana's. "[Rodney] turned around and loaned it to me and told me not to get anything on them or nothing. As far as the other one, I don't know where it was at."

"They were both his belts?" asked Charlie Johnson.

"Yes, they was."

"Now, you said in your statement you've seen Dana with a belt like that. Is that true?"

"No, it is not."

"Why is it not true?"

"At times I get Dana and Rodney mistaken, and then I was also on medication, which is [a] painkiller."

"So you just made a mistake there?"

"Yes, I did."

Johnson asked her about a robbery conversation she said she had overheard between Dana and Panoyan.

"Is there a way I can take back my statement, because I didn't really hear that conversation. I was hurt and angry at Chuck and Dana."

"So why did you say that you heard that?"

"To get back at Chuck and Dana."

"So the statement wasn't true?"

"No, it wasn't."

"Was any part of the statement true?"

"No."

Since Sandy had already raised the issue of confusion between her husband and brother-in-law, Johnson asked her who was the father of her second child. "The second one is Rodney's, but Dana has always claimed her as his," she said.

← THIRTY-ONE

PATRICK O'BRIEN
Statement to State Attorney's Office
March 18, 1991

On March 14, 1991, a second jailhouse snitch called the State Attorney's office.

Patrick O'Brien—a tall, stocky, thirty-three-year-old with dark blond hair that fell over his forehead—told Dave Patterson that he had been moved onto Dana Williamson's floor the previous day. Just as soon as he got there, Williamson introduced himself and began speaking to him about the Decker murder.

O'Brien cautioned that he had to be vague while speaking on the telephone, which was monitored by the jail, but in person he could say a great deal more. Patterson said he and Woodroof would arrange to meet him.

After O'Brien impatiently made a few more collect phone calls to ask when the meeting would happen, Patterson had him brought across the street to the State Attorney's Office in the courthouse. By then, O'Brien had notes from five days of conversations with Williamson.

The first thing Brian Cavanagh noticed about O'Brien was that they were the same size, and, of course, that both were Irish. He was also very cool and intelligent—maybe too smooth. He sounded like Cliff Claven, the know-it-all postman in the television show *Cheers*. Luchak had earned Cavanagh's trust with his modesty.

Perhaps what convinced Cavanagh that O'Brien was telling the truth was the sheer volume of information he provided.

Although he gave them a great deal that added to what police already knew, enigmatically, O'Brien had much they knew wasn't true. Who was muddying up the field: O'Brien or Dana Williamson?

But right off the top there was a close similarity in the stories O'Brien and Luchak told. Luchak had said Williamson talked about the "gunman" in the third person, but added it was obvious he was referring to himself. O'Brien said that, too.

O'Brien said not two hours after he was moved to Dana Williamson's floor did Williamson approach him, asking about his height and weight.

"I asked him why he wanted to know. And he said that the witnesses against him described him as between 5'6", 165 pounds, and 5'9", 180 pounds, and his age from anywhere from thirty years old, forty years old, to fifty something."

O'Brien asked him about his charges. Williamson said he had thirteen capital offenses against him, including a first-degree murder, three first-degree attempted murders, an armed burglary, and three armed robberies.

"So I said, 'What the hell's the case?' He said that three people were shot with four bullets and a woman was stabbed to death at a house in Davie. He said the police had no witnesses and no motive, and no weapons."

O'Brien asked about the weapon. Dana told him it was a long-nose .22 caliber antique handgun. "He then said to me, 'Can you understand why someone would shoot four bullets and then stab somebody?'

"I said, 'I don't know.'

"And he said, 'Oh, but the weapon misfired.' "

O'Brien speculated that the police must have the casings. Dana answered him, " 'They didn't have the casings because it was a revolver.' And I'm saying to myself, how did he know it was a revolver unless it was his gun?

"He said, 'All they have of mine is my straw cowboy hat, which they can't prove is mine, and a belt that carries ammunition for hunting. The gunman had a nylon stocking and boots on.' "

O'Brien asked if his co-defendant had described him differently than the victims had.

"He said, 'The gunman was much taller than I am and

much heavier. The confidential informant said the gunman had red hair. My brother has red hair.'

"I said, 'Why wasn't your brother arrested?'

"And his quote was, 'Well, they arrested me first.' "

O'Brien asked what had happened to the gun.

"He said, 'The last I heard my brother had it in Colorado, but he sent me a note saying 'No gun, no murder.' I want the gun because it's the only way they can do a ballistics test. The only way they can do a ballistics test is if they operate on the child, because the only bullet [as evidence] is in the child's head.'

"I said, 'Why would anyone—your brother, your co-defendant, or you—shoot a thirty-month-old baby, anyway?'

"His quote: 'I can't say. You might be an informant for the state.' "

At noon the next day, O'Brien said Williamson approached him again and asked him directly if he were an informant.

"I said, 'Hey pal, I think you're innocent until proven guilty, okay?' "

But then O'Brien pried further into the mystery of why three people were shot and the fourth stabbed.

"He said, 'She surprised the gunman and the .22 misfired.' She came at him with a knife first. She came home early, said 'Hi' to Chuck, was grabbed by the gunman and tied up in a closet.

"I said, 'Who grabbed and stabbed her—Chuck or the gunman?'

"He said, 'Apparently she came home when the gunman was in the bedroom. Decker yelled for her to run. She dropped the groceries and was grabbed and tied up in the closet.' "

O'Brien protested that the story was changing.

"But yesterday you told me that the gunman let Chuck go as soon as he came in the house, with the warning to keep his mouth shut or his family would suffer. He should have been gone before she came home.

"And his quote is, 'I really don't know why he came back, or if he came back to help her with the groceries.'

"I said, 'Bullshit, he was just as involved as the gunman. If someone stuck a gun in my face and said get out and keep your mouth shut, I wouldn't stick around to help with the groceries. I'd warn the lady and get the hell out of there.'

"He laughed and then he said, 'I never said Chuck was smart, did I?' "

O'Brien said just before he left to give this statement, Williamson told him that the knife that stabbed Mrs. Decker came from a wood block in the kitchen.

"I said, 'How'd you know where the knife came from? How do you know it wasn't in a drawer or on the kitchen table?'

"He goes, 'Well, that's in the Deckers' statement.'

"I said, 'Oh. Well, it better be. Because if you say that in court, and it's not in the Deckers' statement, that'll fry you.'

"And he ran right upstairs—he goes, 'I'll find it for you.' And he came back and he said, 'You're right, it wasn't.' "

On Friday, March 15, O'Brien asked why no one had heard any shots.

"He said, 'A pillow was used to muffle the sound and there was no house real close to hear anything. Plus the windows were shut and the heater was on because it was cold as hell that month.' "

That was partial misinformation. A pillow had been used, but in fact the temperature at 9 P.M. on the night of the murder was 79 degrees, according to the newspaper.

Then came something else that gave investigators more pause. O'Brien said Williamson told him that the gunman had found two kilos of cocaine inside the Decker house. They were hidden underneath construction materials, in the bottom of a full ten- or twenty-gallon plastic bucket of drywall paste. The Deckers had put it there so police dogs wouldn't be able to sniff it.

"I said, 'So the people were tied up and questioned for the dope which you found?'

"His quote: 'I didn't find it—the gunman did.' He also got two thousand in cash—two thousand in the safe.''

Williamson told him the Deckers "warehoused" coke. That meant Decker stored it for someone else, he didn't deal it or do coke himself. Therefore, he wasn't suspicious to the police.

Police had been suspicious early on that drugs might have

been involved in the robbery, but they had never found any evidence to substantiate it. They did know that building contractors often hid drugs in materials, but there had been no reason to believe Decker was doing it. Nor had they any reason to believe Decker wasn't telling the truth that his safe had been empty.

"I said, 'So the motive for the whole thing was to rip off the coke and leave no witnesses. But she came home, got tied up and got free. Went at someone with a knife to try to save her family and got killed doing so.'

"His quote: 'That's how I see it, too, and that's why the Deckers are in hiding.'

"I said, 'Why are they in hiding?'

"His quote was, 'The police aren't really sure [whether] it's me or my brother, or other suspects of which there were six to ten of them. So they have to make sure they're safe until the trial is over.'

"I said, 'Don't you think they've been through enough? First, the baby is shot in the head. Then someone is shot in the face, the other guy gets two bullets in the back of the head, and the mother and wife is stabbed to death.'

"His quote was, 'You'd think that would keep 'em quiet, wouldn't you?' "

O'Brien said Dana told him his brother hid the gun in a paper bag under a rock on a Colorado mountainside. But O'Brien couldn't understand why they would even keep the gun. He said Dana told him that the state [prosecutors] didn't have any case, besides, Dana said, "The gun's worth a lot of money."

O'Brien asked if Dana's brother was involved in the murder.

"I said, 'Was he keeping the peace?' which is a slang saying for keeping watch outside.

"He goes, 'No, supposedly my brother was at the shopping mall, waiting for us in case we had to switch vehicles.' And he goes, that's when the brother took charge of the weapon.

"I guess the brother was the one who took the coke. And the brother drove Dana back to his house in Miramar. I'm not sure if this is all nonsense, but this is what he told me. And then Chuck waited five or ten minutes after they had left to talk to the security guard and then to dial 911, saying his friends had been robbed.

"I said, 'Your brother's out there free. How could he not get arrested, nothing?'

"And he says, 'The state has a weak case. They know it, they'll drag it out for as long as possible. They'll probably offer my codefendant immunity.' And he said they already offered him second degree to tell them exactly what happened."

O'Brien said Williamson figured Panoyan would have already cooperated with the state had he not been certain his wife would leave him if he acknowledged his guilt. "That's the only thing Williamson is saying that's keeping Chuck's mouth shut.

"And I said, 'Well, if Chuck cooperates, pal, you're all frying. You're all toast. The missing link is your brother and the gun. Those cops ever come across the gun, you're fried.'

"He goes, 'Doesn't make any difference, there's no prints left on it. There's no prints on the knife.'

"I said, 'How do you know there's no prints on the knife?'

"And he said, 'Wouldn't you wipe the prints after you did it?'

"I said, 'Yeah, I suppose.' I said, 'I can't see myself shooting people in the head and them not die in the first place.'

"He goes, 'Well, it was only a .22.'

"I said, 'You're smart, you're articulate, you seem to be pretty well versed in the law 'cause you go [to the law library] six hours a day. But when it comes right down to it, you're gonna slip up. They're gonna bury you.'

"And he goes, 'How are they gonna bury me? All I have to do is get reasonable doubt and set myself up for appeals.'

"And I said, 'Well, good luck to you.' "

O'Brien said it was frustrating listening to Dana tell the details without admitting his guilt.

"He never comes out and says, 'I did it,' but he knows so much about it. I said to myself, if I could get over with Chuck, if I could get put over there, I could put two and two together and get the whole scenario.

"I said, 'For someone that didn't do it, you seem to know an awful lot about it.'

"He goes, 'If you were charged with it, you'd know an awful lot about it too.' "

Woodroof returned O'Brien to Dana's statements about the shopping center.

"He was talking about a thirty-one-minute gap between the time that Mrs. Decker dialed 911 and the time that Chuck or the security guard or the security guard dispatcher dialed 911. He goes, 'You can imagine it'd take a couple minutes for Chuck to tell the security guard what's going on, security guard to talk to a dispatcher, and his dispatcher to dial 911.'

"I said, 'Yeah, that must take like thirty-five seconds.'

"He goes, 'The only problem we have is establishing the thirty-one-minute gap, because the shopping center was only a mile to a mile and a half away. What they're thinking now is that Chuck took me all the way to Miramar and came back to the shopping center before he notified the guard. That's about fifteen miles.'

"I said, 'That doesn't make any sense. First of all, you gotta be speeding.'

"He goes, 'Yeah, and that road's real busy on Friday nights and they have a lot of policemen doing roadblocks, testing for drunk drivers and things like that.'

"I said, 'That doesn't sound like the kind of road that you can go sixty miles an hour.'

"He goes, 'You'd have to go about eight-five miles an hour to really pull it off.'

"I said, 'Well, the police don't know about your brother being there. That kind of makes it all fit together. You get down there, you clean up the truck real good, you wipe everything down, you get rid of what you got to get rid of, you give your brother the gun and the stocking. That takes a few minutes and then you sit down and you plan on what the hell you're gonna say, you and your brother split, and Chuck goes and does the rest.' "

"What did he say to that?" Woodroof asked.

"He said, 'Well, they have no idea my brother was there,' nice and cool. And I said to myself, Boom—Gotcha."

O'Brien said he asked Dana why he shot the baby.

"He goes, 'The grandfather was shot first, the baby was shot second, and the father was shot third.'

"I said, 'How do you know that?'

"And he goes, 'I must have it in the statement or my lawyer has it in the statement.'

"I said, 'If I was gonna fry, I'd try to beat it too, but don't bullshit me. I'm on your side.' "

O'Brien then theorized that the three consecutive shootings meant that the Deckers didn't have drugs in the house, although Williamson thought they did.

"I said, 'If I was Decker and I saw someone shoot my father, I think I'd tell them what they want to know. I could stop right there, I wouldn't have to go on to the baby. Matter of fact, if you pointed the gun at that baby and asked me a question, I think I'd answer it.'

"Then he goes, 'Yeah, they should've answered, but apparently they didn't.' "

If the shootings took place before Donna Decker was stabbed, O'Brien's logic was possibly right. But if the stabbing was first, and hadn't been planned, then the shootings might have been to eliminate witnesses. On the other hand, O'Brien reported Dana told him that the Deckers eventually admitted the drugs were in the drywall paste.

"There's no doubt that the whole thing was planned, okay? The guy Chuck definitely was the inside guy, setting the whole thing up, but I guess he didn't do his job good enough to find out where the coke was."

O'Brien said he thought Dana adopted him as his friend because no one else would even talk to him. "People give me dirty looks in there. They're starting to wonder what the hell I did.

"But it gets to the point—he was talking about the baby and the bullet in the baby's head. I tried to picture someone putting a pillow over a baby's head and then pulling the trigger. And I'm saying, what kind of a demented—then I felt nauseous to myself.

"Then I said, 'All these guys in here think you killed all these babies and stuff.'

"And he goes, 'Well, they know I killed one and that's enough to keep them away from me.'

"I said, Jesus, he's admitting it to me."

However, O'Brien was unaware at the time that Williamson may have been referring to the Wagner murder.

O'Brien said he advised Dana to cop a plea to avoid the electric chair. Dana laughed.

"He goes, 'I'll get the ACLU, the anti-death penalty people, people come out of the woodwork when you get sentenced.'

"I said, 'Well, Jesus, nice to know you got your future planned.' I mean, this guy is crazy."

As further evidence of that, O'Brien said Williamson was a born-again Christian who prays all the time.

"He came to me this morning, he goes, 'I've really enjoyed talking with you the past couple days. I feel like I've given witness. I've talked to you about the case and you didn't go running to the D.A., and I feel like my soul's been cleansed.'

"I said, 'Get away from me, you're wacko.' And then he came about ten o'clock and he's trying to convert me.

"I said, 'Look, you've got a better shot at lotto. It's amazing how you guys go to jail and that beam of light hits you right between the bars and all of a sudden you're saved.' "

Realizing he had won over his audience of police and prosecutors, O'Brien created a bit of a soap opera. Each of the next two days he called with updates of what Williamson had just told him, and each day he was brought over to the courthouse to receive an afternoon audience.

On March 19, O'Brien reported that Dana had mentioned Panoyan's visit to Ohio, and how Panoyan had used a pseudonym on the phone.

"I said, 'Well, if you didn't do anything, why would Chuck use a different name?'

"Then he said, 'Well, just because I didn't do anything doesn't mean Chuck didn't do anything.' And I said, 'We're going back to that crap again, huh?'

"He goes, 'That's my only out.' "

O'Brien said he met Panoyan and talked with him about getting transferred to his block.

"I said, 'Maybe I can talk to the deputies and sergeants and see what can happen, because I've been talking to [Dana] so much now. I'm sure people are wondering if I'm an informant.' "

Panoyan then answered, " 'Oh, don't worry about that,

they got him cold. I know some things that he doesn't know that they have on him.'

"I said, 'Aren't you supposed to be co-defendants? If I were in your position, I'd do anything to get along, to make sure that we stuck through thick and thin.'

"He said, 'Dana is extremely manipulative. Don't fall into his trap.'

"And I said, 'Well, jeez, you know, he did say you were kinda crazy, but just saying that, you know, you can't be too dumb, 'cause I agree with you.' "

O'Brien said Dana's father-in-law was the go-between for Dana and Rodney. The last time Rodney called Rick Schulze, he asked if he found a "Black and Decker package."

"I said, 'What the hell is a Black and Decker package?'

"He said, 'The Deckers.' So they're definitely, seriously looking for those people, and I think those people should be at least warned about that. If there's no Deckers, there's no case."

O'Brien asked if Dana had found out where the Deckers now lived. "He goes, 'I don't want to send this. You know that newspaper article I showed you? I don't want to send that out in the mail. You know what happens if they look at it.' "

Dana admitted that both the cowboy hat and the nylon belt found in Panoyan's truck were his, O'Brien said.

"I got the quote wrote down. He said, 'My hat was found at the murder scene near the body of the lady in the same room.' "

As for the belt, it was one of four Dana said he bought to play Paintball. "They run through the Everglades and they shoot people. If you get hit with the paint, you're dead."

Woodroof asked if Dana ever mentioned how the hat left his head.

"Yes, he got in, she resisted, she broke free or something and was trying to fight him and came at him, and during the scuffle the hat came off.

"I said, 'Why didn't you pick up the hat?'

"He says, 'If you've ever been in a scuffle with somebody, like you've had a baseball hat on or something like that and it comes off and you don't even realize it came off. That's what I think happened.' I said, 'Oh, okay.' "

After six days, O'Brien said he had begun to consider Dana a pest. "I am getting kind of tired of him, 'cause I can't lose him. The door opens up and zoom, he's right down where I am. I don't know if he looks at me as a friend or protection or what.

"I guess he wore his roommates here out, there's a couple other guys that he talks to, but they kind of blow him off. He's kind of obsessed with this reasonable doubt issue.

"I asked him, 'How do you feel about this whole thing, anyway?' He goes, 'I'm gettin' screwed.'

"I said, 'What do you feel about the Decker family—don't you think they got screwed a little bit?'

"And he goes, 'They're not here.'

" 'No,' I said, 'the child is growing up now without a mother, the husband buried the wife.'

"And he goes, 'Well, it doesn't mean anything to me. I don't even know the people.'

"I said, 'You're one cold fish, pal.' I said, 'One thing about the sentences they hand out, they look for things like remorse, and you got none.'

"He goes, 'Well, why should I have something for something I didn't do?' "

On March 20, O'Brien called Brian Cavanagh once more and breathlessly told him that Williamson had just confessed to him that he was in fact the gunman at the Decker house, and that Brian should bring him back to the courthouse as soon as he could to give another taped statement.

Cavanagh balked. He said he didn't want it to look like O'Brien was an agent for the state. The investigators had been very careful to tell O'Brien they would listen to anything he had to say, but he couldn't legally be under the impression he was doing work for the state.

"Bullshit," said O'Brien. "Get me over there." Late that afternoon, they did bring him back.

With his public defender present, O'Brien made it clear that he wasn't snitching in order to make a deal for himself.

"Okay, anything that I'm involved in, that I'm charged with, number one, I am guilty of. I know I'm screwing up and I pay the price." He said he was admitting that, although it would be contrary to any attorney's advice. Still, "I feel that with the things that I've been told and what I've been hearing, there are people's lives at stake, and, therefore, time cannot be wasted.

"An individual approached me and probably told me one of the most horrible things that I've ever heard in my life to the point that—even though I'm presently incarcerated on stuff like this and I don't want to prejudge anybody—this guy's gotta go.

"This is not the first time he's killed somebody, and he's still planning on killing people. He shows absolutely no remorse whatsoever for shooting a baby in the head and a grandfather in the face and a father in the back of the head and stabbing the mother to death.

"He talks as we're talking now, very clear, smiles on his face. I don't know why I attract these people or something. I'm the only one that he talks to there because everyone else on the cell block hates him. When I start listening I say, Oh my God, you know this stuff has to passed on to authorities—society does have to be protected.

"We're talking about a very, very intelligent individual who is just setting up a nice little reasonable doubt for himself, and is trying to have witnesses disappear. This man is planning on trying to kill witnesses, and these people have already lost a life, and people shot in the head.

"Today he told me he's guilty of the crime. Today was the first time that he told me that he did it. Before he would refer to himself as the gunman; this morning he said, 'I am the gunman.' I said I figured that out a few days ago, but if you want to tell me that, fine.

"One of the things that he said today was he handcuffed these people behind their back and tied the people up with some sort of cord and tied the mother up and stuck her in a closet and stabbed her. Today he told me that the reason he stabbed her with the knife is she resisted being tied up, and he went to the kitchen and got the knife.

"Previously he had told me that she was surprised coming into the house and dropped the groceries. Today he said the groceries were, in fact, placed on the counter, and that's when he grabbed the woman and brought her into the closet."

O'Brien said he asked Williamson if it was supposed to be a drug robbery and had he planned to shoot his victims?

"He goes, 'No, I think if they cooperated and the woman didn't come home, they wouldn't have been shot and they would have played it off as Chuck being just as much a victim as them.'"

Williamson said his plan was to hogtie Panoyan to make him look like a victim, then take the Deckers into the back and ask them where the drugs were. But then, unexpectedly, Mrs. Decker came home.

"With her husband yelling at her, warning her, he came out and grabbed her and he said, 'I lost it.' He said, I quote, 'I just lost it.'

"Then he goes, 'Then I had to take out everybody.'"

O'Brien said Williamson mentioned that "Chuckie didn't know I was coming that day."

"I said, 'If he's your inside guy, why wouldn't he know?'

"He said, 'You talked to Chuckie for a couple of minutes the other day, you saw how crazy he is, I can't trust him. He doesn't stand up under that sort of stress.'

"And I said, 'I imagine Chuckie's lucky you let him out of the house without putting a bullet in his head.'"

Then O'Brien said Williamson responded with a chilling remark.

"He said, 'Well, the gun did misfire on the woman.'" He took that to imply that Williamson would have shot Panoyan as well, had only the gun been more reliable.

"Another thing he said, 'I'm not one for leaving witnesses.'

"I thought, 'Oh my God.' I said, 'Why did you attempt to kill the baby? He's thirty months old, there's no way a baby after like a month [had passed] would ever recognize someone with a stocking mask over their head.'

"He said, 'You don't understand how the police work. The police can bring you in and put a stocking mask over you and get the reaction from a little child. The little child could possibly act real terrified and that would be circumstantial evidence.'

"His sister Dawna, he said that before he did the crime he stated to her that he was gonna take out the house, and the people in that house were doing something illegal, therefore they could not call the police. Her response was, ''What happens if they resist?' He said, I quote, 'Oh, well.'

''I said to him, 'Does that mean you'd be prepared, if they had guns or something, for violence?'

''He said, 'Of course. You don't do something like this unless you're ready to go the whole way.'

''I pointed out to him, 'Look, they got your father testifying for the State, they got your sister testifying for the State, your brother's given up a few statements, Chuck's given up a few statements, what do you think the jury's going to think when your own family is testifying for the State?'

''He said, 'It doesn't matter. All I have to do is establish reasonable doubt.'

''I said, 'You're telling me this stuff here is awful dangerous to yourself. So what are you trying to do, say a confession or something because I used to be an altar boy as a Catholic? I really don't want to hear this.'

''He said, 'Who else can I tell?'

'' 'So tell the police, tell your lawyer, he'll advise you,' I said. 'Maybe he can save you from the chair.'

''He goes, 'If you were the judge and I pleaded guilty to this, what would you do?'

''I said, 'I'd fry you. I have a conscience. Just for the fact that you tried to kill the baby. I can't see any excuse for doing what you did.' ''

O'Brien said Williamson told him he sold the two kilos of cocaine for $20,000 and split the money evenly with his brother. Dana gave some of his money to a real-estate investment firm.

''I said, 'That's nothing for a couple of kilos. Jesus, you gave the stuff away.'

''He said, 'You have to understand that less than two weeks after the murder occurred I was in Ohio. I got a legitimate excuse—I helped my father-in-law build a house and then I came back down in the beginning of December and I got my wife and kids and a couple of my belongings and got back up there, and I dumped the kilos. I didn't really have a choice and I couldn't take a chance of having anybody find out about it.' I believe they told Chuck they just got rid of the kilos because they were too paranoid.''

O'Brien said the confidential informant's knowledge came indirectly from Dana's next-door neighbor. Days after the murder, the neighbor was out after midnight searching for her cat and overheard Rodney say to Dana and a friend named Larry, "Why did you have to kill the kid?"

Although Williamson said the neighbor didn't repeat that in her statement to police, he gathered that she told it to someone, who passed it along until "it got to a man three or four or five people later named Mr. Kettle [Kittle]. Mr. Kettle talked to the confidential informant who knew Dana Williamson because his white German Shepherd chewed up his face—Dana Williamson's face—when he was younger.

"He said the confidential informant's testimony won't stand up because he informed the police that this kid shouldn't have been let out of jail before on the manslaughter case—they should have let him rot in jail the first time.

"I said, 'Maybe the confidential informant just doesn't want a murderer in the neighborhood. Did that ever dawn on you?'

"He said, 'Most people out there mind their own business.'

"I said, 'Most people out there don't witness and don't hear about babies getting their heads blown off either, or living the rest of their lives with bullets in their head.' "

O'Brien said he taunted Dana with what he now knew. " 'How do you know I'm not going to go over to the State Attorney's office this afternoon and fill them in? I'll have my lawyer go over there and fill them in and cut a deal.'

"He says, 'You're guilty and you can't get a deal anyway.' "

O'Brien agreed, but that wasn't entirely true. With Brian Cavanagh's help, O'Brien was soon to get his bond dropped, which would release him from jail.

O'Brien did tell Williamson he expected to be released out on bond soon, but didn't say how. He asked Dana if there was anything he could do for him on the street. O'Brien had mentioned that he had a family friend from Massachusetts living in Golden, Colorado (where Rodney was now living) so Williamson asked if he could go there and get the gun from Rodney.

"He said, 'You could go out there and talk to my brother and bring him a letter, and in the letter will be instructions.'

"I said, 'Why don't you just tell me what you want your brother to do?'

"He said, 'It has to do with the witnesses.' "

O'Brien said Dana told him he could pay for the errand out of about $17,000 he had hidden. Dana said he was saving the money because "If I get time I'm going to need it to exist in here and I'll have to pay a street lawyer for my appeals." He said the money came from refinancing his father's home and vague "things he had done in Ohio."

O'Brien said Williamson told him he had the Deckers sign a deed before he tried to kill them.

"I don't know if this makes sense, gentlemen, but he had them sign a paper. I said, 'What was it?'

"He said, 'The police think it was a deed or a mortgage type thing or something like that. But who the heck is going to have someone sign a paper and then shoot somebody?'

"I said, 'Didn't you say that Mr. Decker was a contractor?'

"He said, 'Yeah.'

"I said, 'Didn't you say that he just got paid to do a bunch of houses?'

"He said, 'Yeah.'

"I said, 'Don't you think that maybe you got the deed on one of those houses and you had him sign it over to you? Which contractors do all the time to hide money.'

"He smiled at me and he goes, 'You have a background in mortgages?'

"I said, 'Yeah, I've worked for a few banks in my day and I've written about $30 million worth of mortgages as a broker up in Massachusetts. I know all about that. You want me to fill you in on the ABCs about how to do that?'

"He goes, 'I know everything about it.'

"I said, 'Don't you think that they're going to check? They have to file those things in the registry of deeds and they hit a time clock that the mortgage is recorded on the book and page.'

"He says, 'I haven't recorded it yet, besides, Decker and his father didn't know where to sign.' "

Given so much contradictory information, O'Brien had trouble deciding to what extent Panoyan was involved in the crime, although he still considered him guilty of something. He believed that Panoyan hadn't shot or stabbed any of the Deckers; didn't know violence was going to occur; and, unlike the Williamson brothers, didn't even know that the crime was going to happen that night.

The crime's genesis, O'Brien presumed, was when Panoyan, possibly innocently, mentioned to Rodney that the next day his boss, Decker, was going to get a draw against some houses he had contracted to build.

"Rodney told Dana, and Dana said, this is a quote, 'There's a bonus, let's go do it tonight.'

"I said, 'Didn't Rodney say let's get in touch with Chuck?'

"He said, 'You don't know Chuck like we know Chuck, we couldn't tell him that we were coming that night, and we did try to contact him and we found out that he was already over there.'

"I don't know if that lessens the responsibility of the other guy. From reports in the institution and the people that know him—three people to be exact that know Dana Williamson and know Chuck—they say that [Panoyan] wouldn't hurt a fly. He wouldn't kill a butterfly."

O'Brien concluded that Panoyan was out of the house when the shots took place. However, he also believed Panoyan was in the house when Donna Decker was stabbed to death and knew about it. He asked Williamson what Panoyan's reaction was when that happened.

"He said, 'He didn't see me off this lady because it was around the corner, down the hall and in a closet.'

"I said, 'I never knew it was a closet. Boy, I thought you told me that the hat was in the room where the lady was murdered. You know, I don't know why you're telling me, you should want me to testify that you're a nice guy and that you just lost it for a day.'

"He said, 'I think I can influence one of the deputies to get you moved over to Chuck's cell and you can talk to Chuck.'

"I said, 'What in the hell do I want to talk to Chuck for? You're both guilty and your brother is guilty, too.'

"He goes, 'Yeah, but the worst they could do to my brother is accessory after the fact.'

"I said, 'Wait a second now. He was down the street with

you, he dropped you off at the house, and he went to wait for you at the shopping center. That means he knew what was going to go on, so he's involved in the thing from the jump, I don't care what you say. You know he's got to do life without parole too when the cops find out what's going on.''

"He goes, 'Well, they will never find out.'

"I said, 'You're crazy. They probably already know. You don't know what your brother's saying up there or not saying.'

"I said, 'Do you actually think that your brother is going to come down here and kill the Deckers—locate the Deckers and kill them—you actually think that he's going to do that?'

"He goes, 'Of course.'

"I said, ''Haven't these people gone through enough?'

"He goes, 'I'm facing the chair, why should I give a fuck?'

"I said, 'Well, I guess when you put it like that, you got nothing to lose, but your brother ain't facing the chair. Do you think he's gonna come down here, do three more premeditated murders to get you out of jail? Think about it—that doesn't make any sense, and you said your brother has a real high IQ and he's extremely eccentric and people think he's mentally deranged, but I think it might just run in the family. The fact that the incident took place at all, I think you're all fruit loops, you don't belong existing with the rest of us.'

"He goes. 'Well, you're already here too.'

"And I said, 'Yeah, and I'm an asshole for being in here. Hate to clue you in, but everyone in these rooms, we're all assholes.'

"I said, 'You run this Bible banging bullshit to me all day, you try to get me to go to church with you, and today you tell that God talked to you, God gives you visions, that you call this church up in Ohio and all these people are behind you 100 percent. You gotta come back down and deal with reality because you're on the edge. You're not playing with an insanity defense, are you?'

"He goes, 'No, it wouldn't work.' ''

O'Brien said he had saved Dana from injury twice in the past two days.

"I said, 'Yesterday, I just did it because I didn't want to

see you get hurt, maybe it was a spontaneous reaction on my part, if you can save someone from getting hurt, you just do. I know that's kind of alien to you because you like to just go in there and whack people out,' and he started laughing. I said, 'Oh, Jesus.'

"He said that you guys, the police, have a picture of him and Chuck at an ATM machine. He goes, 'Supposedly I took the ATM cards and we banged them at a Publix [grocery store].'

"I said, "How much money did you get there?'

"He goes, 'I don't remember.'

"I said, "Was it Decker's card?'

"He said, 'I can't say that.'

"I said, Jeez, you just told me that you killed the woman—why give a fuck about an ATM card? Do me a favor and tell me why the fuck you're telling me this shit, what did I do to deserve this privilege?'

"He said, 'You are no doubt the most intelligent guy in here besides me. Besides you, they're nothing but a bunch of illiterate white trash and niggers. I think my jury will be a lot of people like me, a lot of people like you.'

"I said, 'You don't want that because they'll fry you. They'll fry [you], they won't even wait for an appeal, they'll torch you right in the stand.'

"He laughed and said, 'You think so? Let me tell you what my jury is gonna be. This is south Florida, my jury is going to be a bunch of old Jewish people.'

"I said, 'Yeah, God forbid, the Jews don't know what suffering is. God forbid they hear about this. They'll have flashbacks of Auschwitz, pal, and they'll just gas ya right there. Now, if you get twelve Irish guys like me, you're fucked. We wouldn't even let you on the stand. We'd probably kill ya during recess or something.'

"He goes, 'Do you know what happens in the electric chair?'

"I said, 'No, tell me.' That was a bad move on my part, this was after lunch.

"He goes, 'They pack your ears, so your brains don't come out your ears. They put a hood on you. Do you know why?'

"I said, 'I imagine they don't want the people witnessing

the execution to see the different contortions of your face from the electric shock they're going through.'

"He goes, 'No, your eyes blow out of your head.'

"I said, 'Jeez, that's lovely.'

"He said, 'Oh yeah, and of course they make you wear a diaper.'

"I said, 'Why is that?'

"He goes, 'Because you end up defecating and urinating when you're dead.'

"I said, 'Jesus, you know a lot about that, huh? What'd you have, visions of your future?'

"He goes, 'Exactly.' "

O'Brien said Williamson told him he didn't have any friends on the outside, but that he now considered O'Brien a close friend with whom he wanted to stay in contact.

"I said, 'Yeah, you've known me five days.'

"He goes, 'Would you ever be with me on the street?'

"I said, 'If I knew you killed someone, would I ever be with you on the street? No, I'd spit in your face. You don't belong out there. And the worst thing about it, Dana, is that you're intelligent but you're not crazy. You did a very crazy thing but you're not wacko. You're just one of those individuals that comes along very rarely that is just plain and simple a sick bastard. You just have no conscience about it.' "

✦ THIRTY-TWO

DET. GERALD TODOROFF
Deposition, March 26, 1991

The defense attorneys would not become familiar with Patrick O'Brien for more than a month, when his statements would be transcribed and mailed out as part of ongoing Discovery. Meanwhile, they continued with depositions.

Gerald Todoroff was the one Davie detective Charles Panoyan liked. Todoroff was in the process of studying for an advanced degree in psychology.

Todoroff had walked Panoyan through the videotape at the Decker house. Dave Vinikoor asked him about discrepancies he felt existed in Panoyan's story.

The first thing, said Todoroff, was the problem with where Donna was confronted by the suspect.

"Chuck said Donna came in, and he'd indicated that he was handcuffed and sitting in a chair in the living room. 'Donna came in'—and these were his words—'and I said Hi and she said Hi,' which kind of threw me off right there, because why would you be so complacent when you know that there's this bad guy in the house with everybody tied up?

"And then he says [from] where he was sitting in the chair he could see the bad guy down the hallway, and the bad guy could see him. But in the re-creation, he had to move the chair halfway across the room because it appeared that he realized that what he had just said wasn't possible. So that kind of threw us right there.

"The other unusual part was the fact that I knew that there were groceries neatly sitting on the kitchen counter. I knew that from being told about it by other officers. So when he indicated that she was attacked right there as she walked in the door, I couldn't figure why somebody would neatly stack groceries in the kitchen after confronting—I mean, you know, you would think she would drop them and things would spill, and it would not be one of those things you would mess with. So that was kind of unusual."

"So you discounted the reasonableness of somebody having a gun pointed at them and walking to the kitchen and putting the bags down?" asked Vinikoor.

"Did I discount that? No, I didn't discount anything. You just asked me what struck me as strange. That struck me as strange."

"What else did you find unusual about Chuck Panoyan's re-creation on video?"

"His periodic stops to see what's going on—think about what's happening."

"As opposed to being able to give a continuous account of what transpired?"

"Yes. Yes."

"Now, you talked to Charlie Panoyan enough to get a feel for his style of speech and the way he answers questions. I mean, is it a fair statement that when talking even about innocent subjects, Charlie Panoyan has a manner of speech that is not consistent with giving a coherent answer to a specific question?"

"Objection to the form of the question," said Brian Cavanagh.

"All right. Let me rephrase it. Does Charlie Panoyan tend to ramble on when telling a story or giving you an answer to a question?"

"At times, yes, he does."

"I mean," Vinikoor tried to explain, "if you were to ask Charlie Panoyan 'Was the shirt red?' it's not unlike Charlie Panoyan to begin by telling you the conversation he had, and how he got into his truck and filled it with gas before he finally gets to, 'Yeah, the shirt was red'?"

"Objection to the form of the question," said Brian Cavanagh, again.

"That's too hard for me to answer," said Todoroff.

Paul Stark attempted the same line of questioning. "If I

asked you to describe Charles Panoyan, the manner in which he looks, the manner in which he speaks, the manner in which he conducts himself, what would you say?''

"I don't think that I could fairly characterize him in any particular way only because I never knew the man prior to the incident," said Todoroff.

"I'm not asking that. I mean, from what you have been able to see, from what you have been able to note about him—his ability to converse, his ability to verbalize, his ability to conduct himself, his ability to stay on track—how would you characterize him?''

"Objection to the form of the question," said Brian Cavanagh.

"What's wrong? I mean, what's wrong with that question?'' Stark asked him.

"Oh, I just want to—" Cavanagh started.

"If I was going to describe Mr. Cavanagh, I would say verbose and loud—" Stark offered.

"I just want to preserve an objection so in the event that you're going to use it for some sort of impeachment at trial, that I can argue that it shouldn't come in," said Cavanagh. "That he shouldn't be able to read the deposition in front of the jury.''

"All right. Okay," conceded Stark. Turning back to Todoroff, he asked again, "You can't describe Mr. Panoyan?''

"Not in one or two words. And it depends on the situation. You know, you're asking me for my opinion, which means little or nothing. My opinion is that the man basically has difficulty getting communications across to others.''

"That's all I'm trying to understand. Why do you say that?''

"Because he has a tendency not to stay on the subject, for whatever reason. For what reason, I don't know. If you let him talk and not interrupt him, he'll bring himself back on track. We are not accustomed to that, as individuals, listening to someone ramble like that. He is, apparently, quite accustomed to it.''

"To rambling?''

"Right. But he will get back on the subject, and he will give you the answer. He thinks out loud sometimes.''

"In the course of thinking out loud, do you find sometimes

he says things that either don't make sense or that he wants to retract or he does retract? I mean, when you say, 'He's thinking out loud,' in essence what you're telling me is—''

"That's why he rambles."

"—that his brain process is coming through his mouth."

"I couldn't say that," said Todoroff. "No. You need a neuropsychologist for that."

Vinikoor asked whether Todoroff felt that Panoyan's emotions were genuine on two occasions: the fear he showed when Todoroff first met him at his house two days after the murder, and his tears at Donna's funeral. Todoroff said yes both times.

"I mean, he didn't look like he was acting to you at all?"

"I know Charlie Panoyan. He does not impress me as a guy that can act."

HOWARD LEECH
Deposition, April 23, 1991

The police had considered Howard Leech to be sort of a snitch on Panoyan, but Dave Vinikoor reversed the tables during his questioning.

In the weeks after the murder, Panoyan had approached Leech—a Broward County building inspector with whom he was friendly—and told him his story. Leech had once been involved in a murder investigation years before and observed then that no one had wanted to get involved, so he decided this time he would call Davie police and tell them what he had heard.

"Basically he had told me that he was a police suspect in a homicide where a friend of his was murdered, and they attempted to murder the remaining [members] of the family," said Leech. "He was at the scene when the assailant came into the house. Threats were made. Apparently the assailant knew him and threatened him and released him.

"And I remember he said he hid for about twenty minutes and finally he overcame his fear and went back to the house or called the police."

So there—from yet another unlikely source—was a second answer to what might have happened to most of the missing thirty minutes between Panoyan's departure from the Decker house and his arrival at Xtra. Perhaps, thought Vinikoor, the truth lay in a combination of Leech's answer and the Marill Security guards' answers: that Panoyan got to Xtra sooner than detectives believed.

"Did Charlie Panoyan tell you that he felt like a coward because he hid for that period of time?" asked Vinikoor.

"Objection to the form of the question," said Brian Cavanagh.

"You're jogging my memory. Charlie's statement was he was scared to death," answered Leech.

"Did that fear seem genuine to you?"

"Objection to the form," said Brian Cavanagh.

"If you're calling for a conclusion?" Leech asked. "At the moment, yes."

Vinikoor asked if Panoyan had taken any precautions in view of that fear.

"I cannot remember any exact statements he had made, but I'm aware that he was afraid and he had loaded guns and he was always watching over his shoulder."

"In discussing the incident with him, he told you that he did not give the full account to the police?" Paul Stark asked.

"Correct."

"Did he tell you why he did not give the full account to the police?"

"He was in fear of his life and in fear of his family's lives."

"Did he tell you specifically what type of things he omitted to tell the police?"

"No, sir."

"Did he ever indicate that beyond not giving the full account to the police, that he may have intentionally given the police inaccurate information?"

"No, sir."

Vinikoor asked him his personal opinion of Panoyan.

"Personal opinion? As far as I know, he's a lonely person who'd like to have a friend. I don't—I've never seen any violence from him or heard of any violence."

✦ Thirty-three

ROY DAVIS
Deposition, April 23, 1991

Roy Davis said that up until the murder, Panoyan and Bob Decker had been each other's closest friends for years, and that he had been friendly with both. When Davis heard about the murder the morning after, he first called Bob's house, getting an answering machine, then called Panoyan, waking him up after his long night at the police station.

In fact, Davis had gotten past police guards at the hospital twice to visit both Bob and Clyde Decker. He saw Clyde the day after the shooting—the same day, police first interviewed him, and Bob on the day of Donna's funeral.

"How did you get in to see Clyde on that Saturday?" Vinikoor asked, a bit astounded.

"Walked in there like I owned the place—I just kind of walked right on in."

"There was a cop standing guard outside," said Vinikoor.

"He about shit when I came walking in there," Davis said. But he let him stay.

Clyde was coherent and asked if Donna was dead. Roy told him so. "And he said he thought so, because he heard horrible screaming."

He used the same routine to get to visit Bob. "I guess once I found the room he was in, I just walked right on in. Don't ask questions. Just keep walking."

"Also, a cop outside guarding his room then," added Vinikoor, impressed.

"Yeah, when I talked to him, I guess Bob heard my voice and Bob said it was all right, yes."

267

Roy had been shocked to see Bob's condition. His head had been shaved, revealing stitches in his scalp. It was obvious he was in pain, and Bob even cried during the visit. But he, too, was coherent—besides some stuttering—and his memory seemed intact.

When Davis was given a polygraph in February 1989, Det. Charles Forrest wrote in his summary that Davis "feels that Bob Decker knows who murdered his wife and that Chuck Panoyan is involved."

Vinikoor referred to that, but Davis denied saying it.

"No. I don't even know myself, so I don't know how Bob could have told me. No. I don't recall saying that at all. No."

"Did Bob in any way indicate to you that he thought Panoyan was in any way involved in this thing?" asked Steve Hammer, recently appointed co-counsel for Dana Williamson.

"Objection to the form of the question," said Brian Cavanagh.

"No," said Davis.

"Were you and other members of the group [of Bob and Panoyan's mutual friends] somewhat surprised that the police suspected Chuck Panoyan in this incident?"

"Yes."

"And are you still surprised at that?"

"Yes."

"When was it then, if you recall, that Bob started thinking that Chuck was involved?"

"Probably after he got out of the hospital. I know that one time [Chuck] went over to Bob's duplex and tried to make a truce with Bob, and Bob told him to get the hell off his property. I don't know whether he suspected him as doing it, or knowing something that he isn't saying."

Vinikoor asked if Bob ever told Roy who he suspected was the gunman.

"Some guy that did work on a roof for a house," Davis said.

"Barry Drovie?"

"Barry's a contractor, but this guy was working for Barry. A real mean-looking guy. That's all. Raggedy. Bob said if anybody did it, you know, it would be him. That's the biggest guy Bob suspected."

"Did Bob Decker verbalize any reasons why he suspected that fellow?"

"I think Bob shorted him some money or something; didn't pay him."

"Did Bob Decker have some kind of financial problem with Barry Drovie as well?"

"He owed Barry money maybe for the roof or something, and Barry never paid the guy, so the guy was wanting Bob to pay or some kind of garbage."

Davis described his business dealings with Decker and Panoyan: He had loaned $4,500 to Panoyan, which still remained unpaid after almost two years—this after Decker said Chuck was good for the money. He often did plumbing work for Bob, who always paid in cash, though usually late, because Bob was financially overextended from buying new properties.

However, Davis said Bob was not known as a guy who kept a lot of cash on him, although Davis did know that Decker had a safe in his house. Paul Stark asked him how he knew that. "It was not the kind of thing he kept secret, right?"

"Yes, because he would say he had to get the money out of the safe or something like that."

That contradicted what Bob had told police many times, that he hadn't used his safe since the house was built, and he had even forgotten in which corner of the closet it was hidden, under the rug.

Stark asked Davis to describe Panoyan and what it was like to have a conversation with him.

"Down to earth, regular country boy like the rest of us."

"No problem relating a story or telling a story?" asked Vinikoor.

"No, no."

"It must be our problem because we're city slickers," remarked Vinikoor.

"Right," agreed Stark.

"Yeah, we talk on the same level. He does in a way kind of talk in circles. He—Chuck is Chuck," said Davis.

"What does that mean?" asked Stark, hoping for some insight into his maddening client. "That's what I'm trying to get you to say. I mean, I'll be quite frank with you. My conversing with you is not the same as my conversing with Chuck. What do you mean, 'Chuck is Chuck'?''

"Chuck is happy-go-lucky—I don't know if he's ever had all the marbles there," answered Davis.

"What do you mean by that?''

"Chuck's crazy. Not as far as pure old nuts. He's different. Everybody likes Chuck.''

TRISHA TENBROCK
Deposition, April 30, 1991

Trisha, who was fourteen at the time of the murder, said she was a friend of Donna Decker as well as a neighbor. Donna used to cut her hair, and once Trisha baby-sat for Carl.

She remembered Donna getting a threatening phone call that foreshadowed her murder by only a few days. It came after Donna had finished cutting Trisha's hair:

"We were just sitting there and the phone rings and she picks it up. I had my head turned toward her. I looked around and she has this look on her face like she was scared. I was like—she was like, 'Trisha, Trisha, listen.'

"I got on the phone and the person wouldn't talk to me, whoever it was. She hung up. She's like, 'I'm scared.' I'm like, 'What's wrong?' She goes, 'Someone just crank called me.' She said they had a real deep voice and that they were disguising their voice and said that they were going to kill her; that they knew Bob was out of town, getting his father wherever he lived up in—I don't know. Wherever he lives upstate or something.''

"Did Donna tell you how many people would have known that Bob was out of town?'' Paul Stark asked.

"All she said to me was, 'I don't know who would know that Bob was out of town.' ''

"Did she have any further conversation with you about the call at all?''

"After the phone hung up, she said, 'Trisha, I'm really scared. Bob's out of town getting his father and I'm really scared. I don't want something to happen.' ''

"In your mind, do you have any doubt that what happened to her was related to that phone call?"

"Objection to the form of the question," spoke Brian Cavanagh.

"Yeah," answered Trisha.

Depositions
Gary Jones—*April 30, 1991*
Jim Westcott—*August 5, 1991*
Doug Amos—*September 10, 1991*

Three other persons who knew the relationship between Bob Decker and Charles Panoyan contradicted things Bob had told police.

In both of Decker's November 1988 taped statements to police, he left the impression that Panoyan was a rare visitor to his house. On November 11, from his hospital bed, Dennis Mocarski asked Decker, "Was it unusual for Chuck to be at your house like this?"

"Yeah, it was," he said.

And on November 19, during the videotaped walk-through of the crime scene, Bob volunteered to Gerald Todoroff that "I thought it was weird that he was here. I see him twice a year for about two minutes. He come in like he made himself at home and was going to spend the night. I thought it was real strange because I see him every day, I don't need to see him at night."

But Gary Jones and Jim Westcott, neither of whom were friendly with Panoyan, gave testimony to the contrary. Westcott, who had met Panoyan at the same time as Decker when he and Bob worked together at W.T. Grant's automotive department in 1970, said whenever he would come to Bob's house, Panoyan would be there. That was once every week or two.

Jones, a mason who once employed Decker and still employed Westcott, said Bob told him that Panoyan was a regular, if sometimes undesired, visitor to his house.

Jones recalled an incident two years before the murder. Donna was cutting his hair at her home beauty salon when Bob came home. "I don't know if he looked out the front window or he heard his truck. He says, 'Don't answer the door. It's Chuck.' He says, 'Chuck's a pain in the ass. He comes here every night while I'm trying to eat my supper.' He said, 'He'll come back,' and he laughed.''

"Every night?" Paul Stark reiterated.

"Yeah," said Jones.

Doug Amos, a Davie general contractor who had been a neighbor of Panoyan for a dozen years and had also employed Bob Decker in the years before he worked for himself, disagreed that Panoyan could have been involved in the murder.

"They were always buddies and doing stuff together," Amos said. "Chuck would do anything for Decker." Even when Panoyan had hired himself out to work for Amos and his partner, "If he [Chuck] knew Decker was in a bind and needed some help, he'd always say, 'I got to go help my daddy,' because that's what he always called him. Kidding around with him."

Amos said it was beyond his comprehension that Panoyan could hurt a flea, much less be involved in shooting a child. He remembered when a friend of Panoyan's daughter died of a brain tumor or heart condition Panoyan "was in the flower shop buying flowers for her and he was crying.

"And you know Chuck was always good with kids. And when I heard what happened to Bobby's little boy—getting shot and stuff, I just—to this day I still don't believe that Chuck would hurt a kid. I don't believe Chuck would hurt Donna. And I just can't believe that he would even have something to do with anything that would happen to hurt the family.''

✦ Thirty-four

Richard Ricketts
Deposition, May 2, 1991

Richard Ricketts was the first civilian witness the defense attorneys found who didn't like Chuck Panoyan.

Ricketts, a huge forty-two-year-old contractor in Davie who knew Panoyan and the Deckers, explained why he was at the Decker house on the Saturday evening after the murder.

"I became more like an acquaintance-friend type with Bob. Saturday night I started bringing my kids over and we'd play on the swings with his kid. Well, this was the next Saturday, and I'd just go over to bring the kids over to play. And here's yellow ticker tape all around. And I spoke with a policeman there and he said, 'There's been a shooting here.' "

Ironically, Ricketts said he had been listening to a friend's police radio the night before.

"And I heard something about a shooting, and that address flicked to my mind. And I said Decker."

"So you heard this transmission. Did you in fact put it together with the Decker home?" asked Paul Stark.

"Well, let's get back. I heard that transmission, and I heard something Decker residency, and it just kind of hit me that he might have got shot or something. It was a little confusing, but in my mind, for some reason, it just related that Bob got shot."

"Did you call Bob's house to find out if everything—"

"No."

"Did you do anything at all to find out whether or not—"

"No, it went over my head like, nah, couldn't be."

273

"And now you get there and you see what?"

"I saw the yellow ticker tape there and I seen—I believe it was a truck/car, unmarked or marked, whatever, and I pulled over. I says, 'Is everything all right over here?' He [a policeman] says, 'Some of them got shot.' And then it just— Donna got killed or whatever, you know. So the guy there asked me a few questions and everything. Asked for my driver's license. And it went on from there. It was like a total shock to me at the time."

Ricketts had mentioned "Warren" to the police as a possible suspect, but he told Paul Stark something else.

"In my mind, for some strong inclination, I felt Chuck did it," Ricketts said.

"Why did you feel Chuck did it?"

"Well, just a vague reason of guilt. The way he was— just a hunch, so to speak. Riding around like—real nervous reactions—body sync. Two and two don't make two when I saw him afterwards. I wanted him to stay away from me. Because one time he had confronted me and asked me did I think he did it."

"Did you ever get together with some of your buddies or some of the guys in Davie who knew the Deckers, or people who were builders, and say, 'Listen, what do you think happened at the Decker house? Here's what I think happened at the Decker house.' Did you ever do anything like that?"

"Not that I can recollect. There was one time when I did feel that it was one of the guys that worked for us."

"That's Warren, right?"

"No. It's Barry Drovie."

Stark asked Ricketts what he told the police.

"Basically, what we're discussing here. The last bottom line was who would I feel would have done it. Who do I think. And I told them who I thought."

"Who did you tell them?"

"Chuck."

"Who else did you tell them?"

"I said at one time there that Barry Drovie had owed Bob some money. There was a little bit of a disagreement of some sort."

Ricketts said he had hired Bob as subcontractor to build two or three houses, and Bob had hired Drovie to do the roofs. Ricketts didn't think Bob paid Drovie the money he had expected—he thought the amount was $1500. "This guy was getting a little bit raw, I could feel it," Ricketts said.

"You used the words, 'That you had a strong inclination that it was Barry Drovie,'" said Dave Vinikoor. "What caused you to have a strong inclination that it was Barry Drovie?"

"Like I says, I'm nobody but a contractor, but when I get these little gut feelings—he had—too guilty. I don't know if it's in his personality, and even to this day if I said something to him, he couldn't open up and say nothing to me. That's why I was kind of picking his brain to see if he had anything to do with it. This guy's working with us. I'm asking him, 'What do you think? What do you think?' I'm asking him these questions. He's turning red in the face."

"Barry Drovie's turning red in the face?"

"Yeah."

"What questions were you asking Barry?"

"I said, 'Who do you think did it, Barry? Did you go down to the police department? You did?' He'd get nervous. Well, I guess we all get nervous if we're in front of the police department."

"Did Bob ever tell you why he woke up thinking it was Barry Drovie that was involved?"

"Because of that money that he might have paid him or owed or—you see, that's the part I don't know about."

"Because of the money dispute," prompted Vinikoor.

"Well, it wasn't a dispute. It was just an ordinary when-are-you-going-to-pay-me routine. One guy is supposed to get paid and he's always wanting to know when he's—it's simple, basic."

Ricketts said he knew Donna, and she also used to cut his hair.

"What kind of person was Donna?" Stark asked.

"Well, to be honest with you, one week, I guess, before this happened, I was sitting down and getting a haircut and Bob was going to come in within an hour or so. She's cutting my hair and for some uncanny reason, she asked me if I was religious. And I says, 'Well, yeah, I'm religious,' but I says, 'I'm not no, you know, practice-what-I-preach individual.

I've got deep, inner feelings of religion, and you'll see me apply them somewhere.'

"She says, 'I like that.' She says, 'I'm going to spend more time with my kid.' She said, 'I'm not going to be like Bob.' I said, 'What do you mean?' I said, 'Bob's just busy working, you know.'

"She said, 'I'm going to enjoy my kid. I'm going to be with him a lot of times.' I said, 'Hey, nothing wrong with that.' And she said, 'I might even go to church.' She bought a little cross for her and Bob—her and the little boy. And then, boom, this happened."

"Was there anything that you can point to which might indicate that their marriage was in trouble?"

"I didn't feel their marriage was in trouble. I just felt it was just like anybody else struggling to get ahead. Bob has his faults like us all. He worked hard, physical work. If someone told me he was a drug dealer, I'd say, 'No way.' There's no indication of any type of drugs in his house or selling of any drugs that I would ever suspect Bob to be."

"Why would you bring that up?"

"Because that's all there is in Davie is drugs—West Davie. Drug dealers."

"You mean where Bob lives?"

"All of West Davie. It's all around there."

"What do you base that on?"

"Just by knowledge."

"This is like news to me. Your knowledge based on what?"

"Just on basic common knowledge of, say, every five years my next-door neighbor, or my cross-the-street neighbor, or the guy behind me—forty-five years. What's happening? You know."

"Was there ever any indication that Donna used drugs?"

"No."

Stark returned Ricketts's recollections to Warren.

"Warren is another individual I felt did it. There goes the third one I felt did it. Warren was a big fellow. I'm 6'5". He's littler than me but he's built, and he's big. College education. He had little problems in there with his mother and leaving Ohio. He was the biggest sort of nothing-type individual I ever seen. And when you looked at him you'd think he'd break you in half, but he just don't have it.

"And Bob and him went round and round at times where I felt Bob went past the human concept of people and pushing these wrong buttons and maybe getting him a little aggravated. But the guy can't say it right to you. When it first happened, I thought he did it. Yeah, I had very strong indications, I believe, of him. Yeah. Definitely."

"Rather than describe it as pushing buttons, because truthfully, that doesn't mean anything to me, can you be specific as to what you're talking about? What did Bob do to Warren which caused you to feel that Warren would want to do something like that to Bob?"

"Well, basically, word-for-word verbatim coming from Bob's mouth—on top of my mind, I'd say, 'Hey nigger, don't do that.' "

"That's what Bob said to Warren?"

"You asked me about pushing the buttons. This is the button."

"Is there anything else you can think of?"

"Bob was good to him. Deep down in his heart Bob helped him. Bob gave him a place to stay and a job. Listened to his so-called sob story. Got his foot in the door, renting one of Bob's places down there. Bob opened his heart and gave."

"Well, apparently, you didn't think that must have meant too much because you thought Warren might have wanted to kill Bob, right?"

"After he tore the place up."

"Tell me about that."

"Well, he was renting to him, and they must have had some type of disagreement. I don't know the details. But the place was left like all tore up, from Bob's description."

Ricketts said he changed his mind that Warren did it while he was questioned at the police department. He told them he thought that Panoyan was involved.

"How did that happen?" asked Dave Vinikoor.

"Because Warren wasn't around town."

"Where was Warren?"

"Up in Ohio. I guess he went back home."

"How did you know that?"

"From hearsay. You know, people talking."

"What, if anything, did the police tell you during that meeting at the Davie Police Department that caused you to begin thinking it was more likely that Chuck was involved?"

"Well, there was nothing that the police had stated to me that would make me have any inclination that Chuck did it."

"Did you specifically ask Bob whether the gunman was white or black?"

"I can't remember. I think I implied about this character Warren to Bob. He says, 'I don't know. I don't think. It could have been Warren the way he whispered.' Because Warren had a high-speaking voice for such a big dude."

"So Bob had not, at least according to your conversation, discounted that it may have been a black man?"

"Well, he didn't know. He couldn't tell."

That contradicted what Bob told police. Both he and Clyde were certain the man was white, and that's why police eliminated Warren Smith as a suspect.

"Do you know Sam McFarland?" asked Stark.

"Yes."

"How do you know Sam?"

"Reputation."

"What's Sam's reputation?"

"Poor."

"What is it?"

"Okay. As far as financing or as far as moral character?" Ricketts asked Stark.

"Yeah. The whole nine yards. Anything you know about Sam."

"Thief," Ricketts said.

"Who does he steal from?"

"Well, you know, getting back to Davie. Small place, everybody talks, knows everybody's business. He stole some Creepy Crawlies [a pool maintenance item] and a detective knocked on the door and said, 'I want to buy this Creepy Crawlie.'

"He said, 'Sure, come out back. I got them all here.' And there's all these stolen Creepy Crawlies."

"What have you heard about his moral character?"

"Divorced here and there. Maybe drink, whatever. If that adds to morals."

"Does he have a reputation of being a tough guy? A dangerous guy?"

"I never heard that. I've heard more thievery than anything."

"Do you know if Bob had a relationship with Sam?"

"Yeah, there was something there."

"What was there?"

"Friends, I guess, or something. It was hidden from me. I know that."

"Why do you say hidden?"

"Bob never said to me, 'Sam's my friend.' Because Bob probably felt that he knew that I'd disapprove of some of those things that Sam would do. And I always keep myself away from those characters."

"Do you know if Bob and Sam built [houses] together?"

"I think Sam had pulled some permits for Bob."

"Why would Sam pull permits for Bob?"

"To get some money, because Bob is a classified unlicensed contractor. And if Sam's a licensed contractor, some guys just use their license and say, 'Here, hold me a permit.' And then you supply the supervision, and the guy pays you for supervising the job that he pulled the permit."

"Except that what happens in reality is that the license contractor doesn't supervise. So what's happening is really illegal, right?"

"Objection to the form of the question," said Brian Cavanagh.

"I don't know," said Ricketts.

Ricketts said he didn't visit Bob in the hospital, but saw him right after he got home. Stark asked about their first conversations.

"Well, when he got out of the hospital the first day, he's back to his quadruplex, building it. He couldn't see good. He asked me for a little help. He had a very high inner feeling of hate. Well, I guess you got to be. Lost his wife, kid shot in the head, him shot twice in the back of the head, and his loving dad shot twice in the face. He's burning inside, that guy."

"Was he burning at anybody at particular?"

"He was burning over all this work he'd done, and to have someone in a half hour destroy what he worked for and had."

"What was he most disturbed about?"

"He thought it was Chuck. But when he first woke up in a hospital, the very first time he woke up, he thought Barry Drovie did it."

"What disturbed him the most out of all of those things?"

"That he thought Chuck did it. That burned his ass because it was like a friend of his. And he felt very strongly Chuck did it because he whispered. When he was whispering, he thought there was a connection between this guy with the hat and the mask, and Chuck there. And that's what burned him. It got him going. He couldn't stand it."

Stark asked Ricketts to recount what Bob told him about the actual incident.

Ricketts began with the man in the cowboy hat entering the house, and Bob first believing it was part of a joke. "But he wasn't joking when he had a gun. And he asked, 'Is there any drugs in here?' Bob told me he said, 'If you could find an aspirin in this place, you'll find all the drugs that you'll ever find in here.'

"So Bob told me the guy tied him up with electric cord. He got out of it. Walked in and saw Chuck, basically, whispering to someone. The guy caught wind of it, put the handcuffs on him in the back of him and put him down—well, his wife walked in at nine o'clock, Bob said—"

"How did Bob know it was nine o'clock?"

"Well, that's the time she gets off, I guess."

"Objection to the form of the question," inserted Brian Cavanagh.

"Go ahead," instructed Stark.

"Well, nine o'clock—" began Ricketts.

"Make sure you're accurate about these things," said Cavanagh, knowing that the time was a bit off, "because he's going to ram this down Bob's throat at trial. So make sure you're accurate."

That froze the air. "You know what?" asked Stark.

"That's an outrageous comment," said Vinikoor.

"I really object to that," said Stark.

"Make sure you're accurate," repeated Cavanagh.

"Absolutely outrageous comment," repeated Vinikoor.

"I really object to that," repeated Stark.

Cavanagh defended himself. "It's a truthful comment. It's not outrageous at all."

"Jesus, Christmas. That's terrible. You have an objection to make, make an objection. Stop interfering with the witness. That's ridiculous. That's beneath you," said Vinikoor.

After a break to cool off, Ricketts continued his recollection of what Bob had first told him

"Donna had come into the situation. She looked at Bob down on the ground and said, 'My God, my husband.' Saw the back of a man standing over her dresser. Went into the kitchen, came out with a kitchen knife, walked in, and, like Bob said, 'foolishly jumped him.'

"Bob was kind of disgusted that she just couldn't relax and take it easy. She was a little cocky. He might have had it deep down inside himself, 'I wish Donna would have stayed over here, because they would have got what they wanted and left.'

"But she interfered and something happening there. That if she could have just—you know how you would rethink something and do it over again. If Donna would have just came over to us, but she saw her husband tied up and her kid down there and she saw this guy, and out of her personality she jumped right in on the situation.

"He turned the knife on her, stabbed her, and threw her in the office, shut the door.

"Then Bob said the pillows went over his dad, shot him in the face twice. Shot the kid—the kid stood right beside Bob like this, which Bob prayed to God the kid wouldn't jump to the mother and get killed with her. Stayed right in here and the kid got a shot. I don't know if it was intentionally involved for the child, but the child got it in the temple. Then the pillow went over the back of Bob's head. He felt like he jumped off—three feet off the ground. Next thing he wakes up in the hospital."

There were two remarkable things here. If Ricketts had accurately recounted Bob's words, this was the first time anyone had said that Donna was stabbed before the rest of the family was shot.

Also, the order in which they were shot contradicted both

Bob's and Clyde's account to police, which had contradicted each other.

(In Bob's police statement of November 11, 1988, he said: "I got shot first, then the baby got shot second and my father third and Donna was fourth."

In Clyde's police statement of the same day, he said: "He shot the baby. Then he come over and put the pillow on Bob and shot him two or three times. I don't know. I lost track of it. . . . Then he done that and went around Bob and come in here and put it in me with a pillow over.")

"Did Bob Decker carry, to your knowledge, some sort of rifle or firearm around for protection the week before this incident occurred?" Vinikoor asked.

"Well, he always carried a firearm."

"Do you remember like a week or two before this incident Bob Decker telling you anything about a special need that he thought he had to carry a firearm?"

"No."

"What kind of guns did Bob Decker own?" asked Charlie Johnson.

"Well, I knew he had a .357 Magnum. Later I found out he had an Uzi that they stole and the clip wasn't in it and he would have got shot by that. He mentioned that in conversation. They took off with a shotgun and went out to his van and got his .357. That's why he figured it was something inside, because the guy knew he had a gun inside his van."

"Why did Bob own a .357?"

"I have no idea."

"It was a stainless steel model, wasn't it? Did you know the gun?"

"Well, I knew of the gun when he told me he'd shoot Chuck. Afterwards he says, 'I'm going to take that .357 and I'm going to blow his brains out.' Then [Chuck] did come on the property and Bob called the police at the time. He got a warrant for Chuck to stay off his property. Chuck wanted to come around and say, 'I didn't do that' and kind of converse with him."

"Why do you think that Bob Decker owned an Uzi?"

"I don't know. I didn't never think he would own an Uzi."

"It's not a collector's item," stated Johnson.

"You're looking at me and an Uzi. I can only think of one thing and an Uzi, but we don't tend to—"

"What do you think of—" began Johnson.

"Anybody tells me they've got a gun for target practice is lying. A gun is to kill somebody. I carry a concealed weapon myself. If I had to use it, I'd have to kill somebody. I respect it."

"Bob never told you why he had his guns?"

"I never knew he had an Uzi."

"He never told you why he had guns, though, to begin with?"

"No, just like out in Davie everybody's got a gun. It ain't nothing for a guy to have collectors' guns or something. Guys in construction always—businessmen always make sure they have a gun somewhere. It's in the house or something."

"Now, when you told us the details of what Bob Decker told you concerning what happened on November 4, 1988; are there any other details that he told you that you forgot to tell us that you now remember?" asked Vinikoor.

"No. There was other incidents where we discussed different things and basic relations of—'I'm going to murder Chuck.' I says, 'What do you want me to do, raise that kid for you?' Get him to think."

"How about the incident itself? Are there any other details that Bob told you about the incident that you didn't remember to include when you were talking about it a few minutes ago?"

Ricketts recalled something about the papers the intruder wanted Bob to sign.

"He picked him up and threw him on the bed or something. He got aggravated because he got out of his telephone cord and he picked him up, threw him on the bed. It was a big guy, he said."

"Bob Decker told you that he was on the bed as opposed to being on the floor?"

"Yeah. It was right on the bed. He asked him to sign something or Bob introduced some paperwork of, say, property he owned to get rid of the guy."

This was yet another major contradiction. Bob had told police he stayed on the floor, and his father was on the bed.

Panoyan's two police statements were contradictory: once he said Bob was on the bed and Clyde on the floor, the other time the reverse.

"What did Clyde Decker have to say about what happened that night?" asked Johnson.

"He said that it all happened so fast, put a pillow over my head, shoot me twice. He said, 'I thought it was my time to go.' But he says, 'I woke up.' Then he talked about having the bullet lodged in his nose. He was a little remorseful too, because his mother—Bob's mother—she's deceased—had said, 'Don't hang around Chuck.' The dad probably said, 'Don't hang around Chuck, either.' "

Johnson asked if Ricketts knew his client, Dana Williamson.

"Now that I think about it, from hearsay, he was in 1975 convicted of killing a girl possibly, sent to—in Davie, sent away for five or seven years and now he's out, supposedly hanging around with Chuck and trying to plan something together."

"Where did you learn that?"

"From hearsay."

"When did you learn that?"

"Three months after it happened."

"What did they say they were cooking up?"

"A robbery."

"How did they get that idea?"

"Well, riding around and they got stopped or something. Chuck was hurting for money, but that's every day."

"Do you know Don Wetz?" Paul Stark asked.

"That sounds familiar."

"Wetz-Zz's Restaurant?"

"Yes."

"What do you know about Don Wetz?"

"I'd say—reputation from hearsay I hear—that he deals drugs."

"Would you say that's common knowledge in Davie?"

"I've got a family at home and I'm not the type of guy— I mind my own business. Okay?"

"Okay," said Stark. "Enough said."

Before dismissing Ricketts, Brian Cavanagh had some questions.

"You mentioned that Chuck came up to you one time and confronted you and asked you if you thought he did it. When did he come up to you and confront you with that?"

"Oh, say three months after it happened, somewhere to that. He was waiting out near my truck. So, I just go up to my truck. He said, 'Ricketts, you don't honestly think I would do something like that?' I says, 'I don't know, Chuck. I don't know.' "

"He brought up the subject?"

"He brought up the subject. He says, 'You've known me for a long time, Ricketts.' I said, 'Look, you want to clear yourself with me, you want me to be your friend,' I said, 'go down to the Davie Police Department and take a polygraph. Then I'll be your friend.' That's the way I dealt with him. He never touched me or come around me that day after."

"Did he respond to that when you said that?"

"No, he didn't. He didn't say nothing."

"What kind of look did he have on his face? How did he act?"

"He had a blank look, just like stare in space look."

Paul Stark interrupted the questioning. "Did he tell you what Sam McFarland did on the polygraph?"

"No."

"Ask him," said Stark.

"That's not in the questions. He's got to give me the question," Ricketts protested.

"You ask us and we'll give you some answers," said Vinikoor.

"Yeah, man. I don't know. I just don't want to have nothing to do with it. As long as justice is done, this guy right here will be happy."

"You're going to be happy," said Vinikoor.

"That's what I would like to see, justice. Fair, honest-to-goodness, down-to-earth justice."

"You're going to be a happy guy," repeated Vinikoor.

✦ THIRTY-FIVE

BOB DECKER
Deposition, May 14–15, 1991

Vinikoor asked Bob Decker about an auto accident he had been in a month after the murder. He had been cited for failure to exercise care.

"I was turning to go into the house with the new van. And this white Cadillac come up the road and it was either hit the white Cadillac or the telephone pole, and I took the pole. Needless to say, the white Cadillac took off and I don't ever—I never seen it again."

"Did you get hurt?"

"I bumped my head on the windshield and cracked it and—"

"Did you get medical attention?"

"I went to [Dr.] Gieseke again." (An emergency medical team came to the scene, but he drove himself to the doctor.)

Vinikoor asked him to describe his relationship with Chuck Panoyan before the incident.

"We were friends. There's no two ways about it. We were good friends and everything. Everybody couldn't quite understand why we were friends because of his nature."

"Because you're different kind of people," suggested Vinikoor.

"Definitely," said Decker.

Questioned, Decker said that Panoyan was honest, trustworthy, mostly reliable, loyal, and not violent. He said he had loaned money to Panoyan about ten times—from a few hundred to possibly $5,000—and each time Panoyan had paid him back.

"If you had to describe Charlie Panoyan to me," asked Paul Stark, "and I did not know Charlie Panoyan, how would you describe him?"

"A very, very unusual person," Decker said.

That begged a follow-up. "Just his nature. That's the way he is. He'll come up to you and go, 'Roses are red,' and in the same breath 'Hi, how you doing?' He's friendly. There's no two ways about that. He's very friendly."

"So is what you're saying to me that he's unusually friendly?"

"Yes. Yeah. Everybody would like him being friendly, but immediately everybody would also know he's an odd type of person."

"What was odd, in your opinion, about him?"

"Just about every single person he ever talked to or knew, he would go that 'Roses are red' thing, or say something that was off-the-wall, so to speak. Just everybody you would meet wouldn't say that. Matter of fact, you'd probably only know one person like that in your lifetime. I mean, you can't help but like him, but right away you would know he's an odd person. I mean, everybody that knew him knows that. I wouldn't be surprised if even his own wife has said that, too."

"In your opinion, do you believe that Charlie Panoyan went to your house that night in order to steal money from you and your father?" Stark asked.

"My opinion?"

"Yes. Do you believe that?"

"Mm-hmm."

"In your opinion, do you believe that Charlie Panoyan went to your house for the purpose of having you shot and having your son shot and having your wife shot?"

"No. No."

"Why do you feel Charlie Panoyan would want to steal money from you?"

"I know for a fact that he was in financial trouble and—"

"Let me ask you—how do you know that?"

"He worked like I did at one time—seven days a week, fourteen to fifteen hours a day—to get payments up because he was behind on them payments in Davie. Black Town.

"What do you mean, 'Black Town'?"

"Them houses that he built in Black Town. He owed quite a bit of money on them. He went to United Mortgage and literally borrowed a maximum on them houses, and he wasn't even getting that for rent."

"You're not telling me that he could come out of his financial difficulties by going to your house and stealing money from you, right?"

"No. No."

"So why would you think he would want to steal money from you?"

"The biggest thing was I opened my mouth before—I mean, about the time my mother had died and that I was going to get some money when she died. He was one of very few friends that I would say anything to."

"What was the figure that you were going to get?"

"Well, I was going to get $20,000. It was in a trust in my name."

"When did you first provide that information to Charlie Panoyan?"

"Before she had died. Just guessing, about October. I told him I was going up to get some money, and that I was going to drive the van back to bring my father back."

"Did you tell anybody else other than Charlie that you were expecting to inherit money?"

"Just my wife."

"So, in the entire world, the only people you thought close enough to tell this to were Charlie Panoyan and your wife?"

"Objection to the form," said Brian Cavanagh.

"Well, is that right?"

"Yes."

"Now, you're convinced that Chuck Panoyan was involved in this, right?" asked Vinikoor.

Decker nodded.

"When did you become convinced?"

That night, said Decker. "I could tell [by] the look on his face, because I knew him for quite a while. And I have always said this right from day one—he knew who it was and the deal went sour. He might not have planned on anybody getting hurt, but I could tell [by] the look on his face he definitely knew who it was. I didn't want to believe it, but, yes."

"And the look on his face—when are you talking about in time?"

"I'm talking about fifteen seconds, maybe, after the gunman come in."

"So once the gunman's in your house, then there was something about Chuck Panoyan's face that caused you to believe that he was involved?"

"He's like this"—Decker made a face—"all the time. And that's very unusual. He pretended he didn't know nothing."

"The expression. Put that into words," Vinikoor asked.

Decker explained. "What happened? He didn't know nothing."

"Like, 'What's going on here?' " Vinikoor tried to clarify.

"Yeah. Really."

"Did he look scared?"

"No. It definitely wasn't a scared look. I could tell [by] the look on his face [that] he was not totally surprised."

"How were you reacting to the gunman being there?"

"I personally thought it was a joke for a minute or so. Knowing [Chuck], that's the type of jokes he would like to play. He would play all kinds of crazy jokes on different people."

Vinikoor pointed out that Decker and Panoyan played jokes on each other. "Well, that day, for example, you had a few jokes, right? Somebody's hat end up in a paint can?"

"Oh, that was every other day," said Decker.

Stark asked him if he recalled an old joke between them involving shooting out each other's tires.

Decker laughed. "I forgot exactly how it started. We were hollering at each other, as usual, and it more or less scared my father. [Chuck] grabbed his gun and was going to shoot up the tires on my new van. I grabbed my gun and was going to shoot the tires out on his truck."

It sounded like Abbott and Costello. "Who initiated these jokes?"

"Oh, back and forth. It was him or I. Even my dog peed on him one time. He raised his leg and he started to pee on him."

"Did you tell the dog to do that?"

"No, I didn't tell him, but he did, I'm glad he did, because we must have laughed for about an hour. One joke after another all the time."

"Now, after this incident, Chuck Panoyan came to your job site, did he not?" Vinikoor asked.

"After? Um-hum."

"And did he tell you that the police lied to you?"

"Um-hum."

"Did he tell you that he was not involved and not to believe the police?"

"That's what he said. He also said it was drug-related. I don't know exactly what he did want me to do—if I was supposed to pay him some money to get rid of this guy or what."

"Did he ask for any money?"

"No. But I don't know what the answer was. He said he wanted to talk to me and I really don't know if it meant paying this guy off or what, but he said it was related."

"Or if it meant, 'Hey, be my friend again. Don't believe the police.' It could have meant that, right?" suggested Vinikoor.

"Objection," said Brian Cavanagh.

"No. He never said that, of course," Decker answered.

"Did you give him a chance?"

"No. I was not in no mood, by any means."

"Chuck Panoyan had also left messages on your phone answering machine, did he not?"

"Once."

"You didn't return that call."

"No. I didn't call him."

"Do you remember him telling you that he loved you like a brother?"

"Yeah. I remember that—I think—I'm pretty sure that was after he'd come by that time."

"Right. He wanted to convey to you that he could never do this to you or to your family, didn't he?"

"Objection to the form," interrupted Brian Cavanagh.

"Well, that's what he wanted to do."

"But you didn't want to hear any of it."

"I didn't believe him, either."

*   *   *

Vinikoor then probed Decker's finances. Decker guessed he had about $150,000 in outstanding construction debt to his bank in November 1988, plus another $28,000 he owed to Sam McFarland. All of the debt was secured by real property.

Decker counted the properties he owned at the time of the murder. He had built two homes next door to each other on Pierce Street in Hollywood that he sold for $84,000 apiece, leaving him $30,000 apiece in profit. He had bought another house two doors away for $18,000 and sold it for $35,000. He eventually sold a house in Miramar for $84,000, leaving him equity of about $40,000.

The house he and Panoyan were working on the day of the murder was elsewhere in Hollywood. He said he sold it for $86,000—less than what it was worth—but he still made a $26,000 profit.

(Panoyan, however, had told police hours after the murder that Bob said earlier that day he had sold the house for $110,000.)

Decker said the only property deals he ever had with Sam McFarland were the two lots on Pierce Street.

"How come you went to Sam McFarland to borrow money?" Vinikoor asked.

"I knew he had gotten some money and I had called him on the phone and asked him if he would back me up with some money if I needed it for sure."

"Is there a reason that you had not gone to the bank for the money?"

"It was vacant land and—"

"Tough to get a loan on it," finished Vinikoor.

"Right. They probably wouldn't lend money on vacant land. Construction, yes. And I was planning on doing construction, but it was one of these deals where I had to move fairly quick or I could forget about it."

"Did Sam McFarland ask for certain terms on the payment of the—"

"Just interest is all."

"In what amount?"

"I think it was 7 percent."

"Over what period of time did you owe Sam McFarland money?"

"I would have said it went about three or four months, maybe. Six months [at] the most."

"During that period of time, did he make any efforts to collect the money from you?"

"No."

"Did there come a point in time when you went up to pick up your dad in New York after your mama died and Sam was asking for the money?"

"No."

"Do you remember ever telling Sam McFarland that when you went up to pick up your dad in New York that you were going to leave the money with Donna?"

"No. Definitely not."

Decker said he finished paying off McFarland in June of '89 when he gave him a Chevy 4-by-4 truck worth $8,000. He said the pickup truck was the final payment—he had made one $10,000 payment and another for an amount he couldn't recall.

"But you ended up paying the full amount of the loan plus the interest?"

"Yeah. I paid him—well, the biggest part was back when I sold the property, of course."

But later, when Paul Stark asked, Decker said he had owed McFarland $12,000 at the time he gave him the $8,000 truck.

"Was there a reason why he made you a gift of $4,000?"

"No. Just like I say, we knew each other for a long time and didn't really write anything down. I mean, it wasn't where I was going to beat him out or vice versa. He knew he would get some money from me for sure."

"So he kind of like washed out $4,000?"

"Yeah. But, needless to say, with his two or three wives, which the first one took him for a lot of money, and to me, it was nothing to him."

"McFarland have a reputation of being a dangerous kind of guy?" Stark asked him.

"Dangerous? No."

"What about violent?"

"No, definitely not."

"Did Sam McFarland ever quitclaim any property to you?"

"I think it was the duplex [on Pierce Street] when all this

happened, of course. I was building that duplex. He signed off from it. He took out a quitclaim to me, signed off from it, because he had that property half in his name and half in mine, of course. And the bank wanted it only in my name.''

Decker said it was October 1988 when he applied to the bank for a construction loan. He said when McFarland quit-claimed off the land, he still owed him between fifteen to eighteen thousand dollars.

Vinikoor asked about Decker's business records left scattered by the intruder. Because his filing system wasn't very good to begin with, he was never certain which papers were missing. Besides, he didn't look very hard.

''So, when you went through all the mess in that room, nothing stood out in your mind like, 'Hey, what in the world is this guy looking for?' ''

''Yeah. And what I didn't file was—we're talking about a stack about this high. So it would be kind of tough to tell exactly what was what.''

(It had been rumored that Donna, when she died, had been holding in her hand a bloody quitclaim deed from Sam McFarland, but that was never confirmed.) Charlie Johnson asked, ''If [Donna] sensed that she was dying and she had a way to indicate who the murderer might have been, do you think that she would have grabbed something that would have had the murderer's name on it?''

''Objection. Objection,'' spoke up Brian Cavanagh.

''My opinion is, I don't think she knew any more than I did who it was,'' Decker said.

''Well, one thing we do know is that she was lying on some papers that had to do with Sam McFarland. What do you think about that?''

''There were all kinds of papers in the office, so that wouldn't surprise me what she'd found—I mean, what she was laying on.''

Vinikoor briefly inquired about property that Decker had constructed in the mid-1970s in Tropical Valley, in Miramar. The Williamsons lived two lots away from where Decker had built.

''Did you ever know Chuck Panoyan's friend, Charlie Williamson?''

''I seen them [the Williamsons] one time for about a few

seconds. I mean, I don't even remember what they looked like. I walked in their house for a second with Chuck, was introduced to them for a second." That was more than ten years ago, he said.

"Right before this incident occurred, had you been carrying a rifle around for a couple days?" asked Vinikoor.

"Me? No. I always said, believe it or not, that if it ever got bad enough where I'd need a gun or to carry it on me or whatever, I'd be out of here. I always said that."

"The .357 [Magnum]—you did carry it on you, though, didn't you?"

"Not on me. It was in my briefcase."

"What did you get the Uzi for?"

"Just to shoot it. Target practice and so on. I went to Markham Park quite a few times and stuff. And then I took the Uzi, as a matter of fact, and one time went up to New York at my father's before my mother died and everything and was shooting it."

"Target practice?"

"Um-hum."

Decker said he had driven to New York on that particular trip, as he couldn't have carried it on an airplane.

"When you were up in New York getting your dad, did Donna tell you about threatening phone calls she received?" Vinikoor asked.

He shook his head no. "And that is very unusual," he said.

"Why do you say that?"

"She would tell me everything and she didn't tell me that—and I don't think it slipped her mind because that would be something she'd definitely remember."

"So you think that Donna intentionally chose not to tell you about that?"

"Objection to the form of the question," said Brian Cavanagh.

"The nearest thing I can figure is that it was a crank call and that's why she didn't tell me, because she told me everything. I'm very surprised. I mean, I'm not calling—I forgot her name. Tenbrock, last name."

"Trish."

"Trish. I'm not calling her a liar, but definitely I don't— I mean, that isn't like her by any means."

"You talked to Donna when you were up in New York picking up your dad?"

"Every other night or every third night or whatever."

Vinikoor asked him if he had locked his van on the night of the murder.

"Definitely. Always. Because there was a lot of stuff in there. There's probably fifteen, twenty thousand dollars worth of tools and a phone and a briefcase and everything else in there. I always lock it."

"What was of most value in the van? The tools?"

"Nail guns and compressor and generator and—"

"Were any of the tools taken from the van?"

Decker shook his head no.

"Was anything taken from the van?"

"Just the briefcase. And the nearest thing I can figure is the radar detector was switched."

"What do you mean by 'switched'?"

"I had one that don't work and mine that I had was a brand-spanking-new one."

"Let's see if I understand you," said Vinikoor. "On November 4, 1988, when you locked your van after coming back from dinner, you had a brand-new, spanking new radar detector, correct?"

Decker nodded yes. "I got it—about a month old, it was. I got it when I flew up to New York and drove the new van back."

"And when you went back to the van to see what was taken after you were released from the hospital, there was a radar detector, but it was an old one and not the new one that you had left," probed Vinikoor.

"I didn't know that, though. It didn't work, I knew that part. I sent it in to have it repaired and they sent me a bill— $25. And mine was brand new. I thought that was kind of unusual—"

"It should have been covered by warranty," Vinikoor said.

"About a week later, I get a call from the Pembroke Pines Police department that said that I had a stolen radar detector.

And right after that—same day—Cincinnati Microwave called me, too, and read my serial numbers off to me.''

"Wild," commented Vinikoor.

"That's probably the most bizarre part of this whole thing," said Decker.

Decker said his briefcase contained his .357 Magnum, two checkbooks, and various business records—important to him, but trash to anyone else.

"Now, if the van was locked, that means whoever switched the radar detector and took your briefcase had to have your keys, right?"

"That was my opinion," said Decker. He said his keys were in fact taken.

"But the van wasn't stolen," said Vinikoor.

"That's what was very unusual. About the first thing or the second thing I said to the police when they came in, 'What is in the driveway? Is my new van in the driveway? Is her new car in the driveway? Is my father's car in the driveway?' ''

"And they were all there. Just the keys missing," said Vinikoor.

Decker said he never kept large amounts of money in the house. His wallet—stolen—had about $200-$300 in it. The $1,700 cash hidden in and stolen from the office/closet was his father's money.

"The only time I would have a little cash on me would be if I would go to the bank—and Chuck was one for wanting cash on a Friday. Normally, I wouldn't have an awful lot on me."

Vinikoor asked Decker about the other people he initially suspected might have been the masked man. When Vinikoor mentioned the name Warren Smith, Decker got confused. He remembered him as Dwight, but couldn't recall the last name Smith. He did recall the run-in the two men had had.

"And needless to say, I went looking for him. I filed a report with the Hollywood Police department when he stole the refrigerator and a stove, of course."

"You had a problem with Barry Drovie?"

"Whatever you call it. I wouldn't say a problem, but I just—"

"Some kind of disagreement of sorts?"

"Yeah. I told him how it was going to be and that was it."

"When did you tell him how it was going to be?"

"I would say about a week—within that week before it happened."

Decker said he had hired Drovie to put roofs on two houses. Decker had been hired out himself, by Richard Ricketts, to take charge of the construction. In the middle of the job, when Drovie felt that he wasn't being paid enough, he went straight to Ricketts to complain.

"I told him, I says, that I don't believe that he went behind my back, so to speak. Because I was literally going to pay him for the job. He took the job for X amount of dollars and that was it. He went behind my back to the contractor, and the contractor didn't want to know nothing."

"So how did Barry Drovie react when you told him the way it was going to be?"

"He wasn't real crazy about it, of course, but I told him that he wouldn't work for me again."

"Now, he had a partner or an associate that you thought resembled the shooter?"

Decker nodded. "I forget his name exactly. I just remember one thing about him: He would have his beer for breakfast and that was all day long."

"In what way did Barry Drovie's associate or partner resemble the assailant?"

"Not the assailant, but Barry. I mean, the guy that was with Barry was not that size."

"Who resembled the gunman? Barry?"

"Just Barry, a little bit. Just size."

That contradicted Decker's earlier statements, including what Roy Davis had recounted in his deposition, that the man Decker first thought was the gunman was Drovie's assistant, not Drovie himself.

"You first suspected that it may have been Barry Drovie, didn't you?"

"Just in my mind. I was literally drawing at straws. I mean, somebody was definitely there."

"Did you think it was Barry Drovie because of the way he looked or because you had had a little run-in with him?"

"Objection to the form," said Brian Cavanagh.

"Just in my mind. I had to think of somebody, of course, right quick."

Vinikoor and Stark then tried to widen a lot of smaller holes in Decker's story. Vinikoor began by asking if Decker had seen a suspicious car while driving home from the restaurant that night. He said he had seen one car parked on the street in front of the vacant lot where Bernie Napolitano was seen sitting in his car at 7:30 P.M.

But Decker said he saw a gray Ford station wagon, backed in. Daniel Metrick, a neighbor, said he had seen a white foreign-made compact car.

"What was suspicious about the car?" Vinikoor asked.

"Well, it's a dead-end street where I lived, and what's suspicious is there ain't nobody that goes there or parks the car there or anything," Decker said.

"Do you think the gunman knew you?"

"Do I? No."

"Why not?"

"Just the way he was to me and everything; very blunt and didn't talk much and stuff." That statement contradicted Decker's earliest articulated thoughts, that the gunman might have been Warren Smith or Barry Drovie.

Next, Vinikoor worked on a story Decker had told about the handcuffs. "Did the gunman tell you that the handcuffs that were used could probably be traced?"

"Yes. Remember we're in the bedroom, so it was a few minutes after we were in there. He said, 'These handcuffs can be traced. I'll take them off you and call 911, the police, when it's all over with and nobody will be hurt.' " Then the gunman repeated that again later.

"Well, if he took the handcuffs with him, then you could have called the police yourself," Vinikoor pointed out.

"Whatever," said Decker. Another hole in the story.

Vinikoor asked who had first mentioned the safe. Panoyan had said Bob mentioned it first, and Decker had said previously it was either Chuck or the gunman who referred to it. But this time Bob said it was the gunman.

"He said, 'Which corner is the floor safe in?' He knew it was in the walk-in closet in the bedroom. And I had probably lived there, just guessing, about three years and I had forgotten because I never use it. I remember being in the closet and I said, 'It was in that corner,' and come to find out it wasn't. He went to pull up the rug and seen it wasn't in that one and it was in the other one.''

"Now, approximately how long were you out of the living room, when they were looking through safes or back in the bedroom or whatever, before Clyde actually got taken into the bedroom?''

"I would say approximately five minutes, the most.''

"Now, when you were in the back of the house with the gunman for that five minutes or so, was there anything that you were aware of that prevented either your dad Clyde or Chuck from going to the south door and getting out of there?''

"No, not really. I mean, they were on the floor with handcuffs on, but to my knowledge, no.''

While the gunman was later rummaging through drawers in the master bedroom, Decker said, "Two or three times I would hear him say, 'Where's your money and drugs?' and so on. And he was a little put out he couldn't find no drugs nowhere. He couldn't believe he couldn't find nothing there. Drugs was the biggest thing for him. I mean, money too, but he was looking for drugs.''

Decker had said a number of times before that the whispering he saw between Panoyan and the intruder meant that Panoyan was in on the robbery. But Stark raised another possibility. Could the gunman have been threatening Panoyan with the same questions about drugs and money?

Decker conceded it was possible. "It was muttering. I don't know what he said. I've no idea.''

Decker said he figured the blank document he signed would be used as a quitclaim deed. "I bought and sold a bunch of property, so it isn't unusual that he would make me try to sign something. The first thing that crossed my mind was my homestead.''

He said both his and Donna's names were on the mortgage for their home, as well as on some other mortgaged properties, including 6109 and 6111 Pierce Street in Hollywood.

Vinikoor made the connection. "Now, forgetting your house for a second—the other properties that you just enumerated—was Sam McFarland involved in any of those properties?''

"No," said Decker. "I mean, he lent me the money for Pierce Street and that was it, but he wasn't involved. I mean—''

Vinikoor realized that Decker had been trying to downplay every relationship with McFarland since the deposition began. He wasn't fooled here by Decker's weak denial.

"So, Sam McFarland loaned you the money for the two properties on Pierce Street."

"Um-hum," went Decker.

The gunman asked for two signatures on the blank document, Vinikoor thought. Did he just figure that a contractor would naturally put his wife's name on a deed, or did the gunman specifically know in advance that he needed Donna's signature?

But Vinikoor also recalled that Donna wasn't present when the gunman first came in. "Now, I don't know if the gunman had thought she wasn't coming home or what, but she surprised him," Bob had said. Another mystery.

"From what you could see and hear, did the gunman release Chuck Panoyan or did Chuck Panoyan run away?''

"Only what I could hear, not what I could see. He left, my opinion."

"As opposed to being released?"

"I mean, I heard the door. I did not see him, of course. I heard him. I heard the door open and shut. So I don't know if he left or if he didn't leave. No idea."

But in his police statements, Decker had said that he was "99 percent sure" that Panoyan had left when the door shut. That was just after the gunman had seized Donna.

When the defense attorneys got to the order in which the Decker males were shot—a disputed point between Bob and his father—Bob recalled it as he had told police in November 1988. First, the gunman shot him, using a pillow, then the baby—with the same pillow—then Clyde. He had also told police that he thought Donna was killed after the shootings.

But to Vinikoor and Stark, and an increasingly nervous Brian Cavanagh, Bob now said he thought the gunman had stabbed Donna before he shot them. That was what Richard Ricketts had said Bob had told him too.

"I don't know what happened," said Bob, "but my opinion was that she went after [the gunman] with a knife and that's when he decided—well, he stabbed her and shot us, because I really don't think in my own mind that that was planned."

Then later, answering Charlie Johnson's question, Decker reversed himself again. "We were shot first and then she was stabbed. That's what I think."

Vinikoor asked Bob about the "picture party" that would have taken place at his house had the murder not happened the night before. It was a Tupperware-style party, except that paintings were for sale. The organizer of the parties was Manny Fernandez, who had played defensive lineman for the Miami Dolphins during their Super Bowl years in the 1970s.

Decker named the people invited: Chris Tenbrock and his wife, Roy Davis and his wife, and Bob's sister-in-law, Jo Zazzo.

Vinikoor then pursued the drug angle. Richard Ricketts had suggested the "wrong house" theory, that the gunman had attempted a drug ripoff, but at the wrong address. Vinikoor asked Decker if he knew of rumors that his neighbors were involved in drugs, and Decker answered yes.

But Decker added that was par for the course, as Ricketts had said. "I mean, it's a little unusual that you don't find everybody in—young people especially—but everybody a little bit involved in drugs or whatever, so they find that I'm a little unusual that I don't. I would say probably 95 percent of the young people here has done something with them."

"You said everybody knew that you were—had nothing to do with drugs," asked Vinikoor.

"I mean, everybody. Everybody."

"Does that everybody include Chuck Panoyan?"

"Definitely."

"Did you ever talk to Chuck Panoyan about your not liking drugs?"

"Many times.

That was another major point for the defense. Why would Panoyan have been involved in a drug ripoff, which Bob suggested it was intended to be, if Panoyan knew he didn't deal in drugs?

Vinikoor had yet another crazy theory—left unsaid, but implied—that Bob Decker wanted his wife dead. He knew there had been tension between Bob and Jo Zazzo, and Chuck had said that Bob and Donna had been fighting, as recently as the week before the murder, at Roy Davis's birthday party.

Vinikoor asked Bob if he and Donna had a fight at that birthday party.

"No, definitely not. Roy and his brother did, but we didn't."

Earlier in the day, Decker had sat in on a court hearing for Dana Williamson. It was the first time he had gotten a look at him.

"Did the Dana Williamson that you saw in court look bigger or smaller than the intruder?" he asked.

"Same size," said Decker.

✦ Thirty-six

Sam McFarland
Deposition, July 17, 1991

The mysterious Sam McFarland had skipped an earlier subpoena for deposition. When he eventually submitted to questioning, he seemed reluctant to cooperate. Dave Vinikoor asked him if he knew Dana Williamson, and he said no—except for being familiar with his name as a co-defendant in this case.

Vinikoor then asked McFarland to recall his police interviews. His answers were curt, making for a difficult interview.

"Just wanted to know my connection with Bob Decker. I don't remember exactly. It's been like—quite a while ago," he answered.

"Did their questioning ever become accusatory?"

"Kind of, yeah, at one time."

"In what fashion?"

"I don't know, but at the end I remember us jumping up together at the same time, shouting at each other."

"What were they shouting?"

"I don't know."

"Did the police ever tell you that they believed you were involved in some way in this case?"

"I think they did. I'm not—"

"Do you remember what they said about your involvement—"

"No."

"—or why they believed you were involved?"

"They just found some papers, I guess on his desk, with

my name on it. You know [what] jerks cops are. I thought they were both jerks. He might have said, I was with his wife or something like that. Anything to get you mad. I don't remember what it was. I guess they try to get you mad to see what they can do with you."

"Did the police ever tell you why they suspected your involvement, other than the fact that there were papers on the desk which had your name on them?" asked Paul Stark.

"I think they were just looking for somebody to put it on. They were looking bad is what I was thinking. They were just using bullshit techniques."

"Did they tell you why they wanted you to take a polygraph test?" asked Vinikoor.

"They said they were giving everybody associated with him a test."

"Did you agree to do it right away?"

"No."

"What was your reluctance in taking a polygraph?"

"I don't know. I just knew I had nothing to do with it. Why bother? Why waste my time?"

"Why did you finally agree to do it?"

"They just kept bugging me."

"Did they ever tell you how you did on the polygraph?"

"They said I didn't do well."

"Did either Woodroof or Mocarski discuss with you why you may have failed the polygraph?"

"No. I remember they told me they wanted me to take a test by another—by a Broward County—but they never—"

"After the first test?"

"Yeah. But they never—Never heard from them again."

Vinikoor then asked McFarland to discuss his business dealings with Bob Decker.

"Have you ever owned property with Bob Decker?"

"Yeah. I don't remember the exact circumstances, but we had bought some lots together."

"As partners?"

"Yeah. First, I was going to build it with him. Then I decided I—I didn't, so I just let him take over the property."

"Is that the only time you've owned property with Bob Decker?"

"I don't know if my name was on the deed. Then I lent him some more money to buy another lot or two lots."

"Do you know if there have ever been any filings with the property office that reflect land owned jointly by you and Bob Decker?"

"I don't know. I think we did it all before they closed on the land. I think I changed my mind. I'm not sure that there was. You might be able to tell me. You probably checked it, right?"

"Somewhere around the time of this incident, there was a quitclaim deed involving you and Bob Decker. Do you know what that was about?"

McFarland's reaction was suspicious. He didn't clearly remember it.

"There must have been—The property must have been in my name then, huh? Then I quitclaimed it."

"To him?"

"Yeah."

"Do you know why you would have quitclaimed land to Bob Decker?"

"I think so he could get a mortgage. I'm not—[It could've been] a construction mortgage. I'm not sure, though."

"Did Bob Decker give you money for your quitclaiming your share of the land to him?"

"I don't know if he gave it to me right then. I don't remember the exact circumstances."

"Well, was it something that you did for money, or was it something that you did just to be a nice guy and give him land?"

"Well, naturally he was going to pay me back."

"In November 1988, did Bob Decker owe you money?"

"Yeah."

"Do you know how much?"

"Well, right before this happened—this happened like on a Friday. He had paid me $10,000 on that Wednesday."

"That was toward a debt that he owed you?"

"Right, um-hum."

"What was the total amount of the debt?"

"I'd say between thirty and forty thousand."

Decker had said in his deposition that the total debt was

about $28,000, plus seven percent interest. He said he had paid McFarland $10,000, but didn't mention that the payment date had been so close to the murder.

"Was the $10,000 payment made that Wednesday the first payment?"

"No."

"He had made prior payments?"

"Well, he had done some work for me and—probably about $9,500, $10,000 worth of work. He probably was like—had paid me around twenty grand."

"So he owed you ten to twenty thousand dollars?"

"I'd guess at that, yeah."

"Do you know for what purpose you loaned him the money?"

"He just came and asked. He said he had a good deal on property. I think at first he said he wanted me to be partners with him. Then I decided I didn't want to be—get involved."

"So you gave him the money and then he bought the property?"

"I think so. I'm not sure. I make so many deals with different people, I can't—I don't—"

"Do you know what year you gave Bob Decker this money?"

"It's probably '88 or '87. Probably '88, I'd say."

"Had you made efforts to collect that money?"

"Not really. Just—"

"So you just relied on Bob Decker coming up with whatever he had whenever he had it?"

"More or less, yeah."

"Well, what does 'more or less' mean?"

"I mean I wasn't worried about it."

"Although you may not have been worried about it, did you make calls to Bob Decker and say, 'Hey, how about giving me some of that money?' "

"No. He just said he'd work it off or pay it off when he could."

Vinikoor said he was confused that Decker owed McFarland money, yet McFarland quitclaimed the deed to Decker. McFarland couldn't clarify, nor could he recall holding any specific collateral from Decker, although he felt sure he must have had some.

"Does Bob Decker owe you money now?"

"Yeah. You already asked me that, didn't you?"

"How much does he owe you now?"

"Well, I said he paid me twenty, and he owed me between thirty and forty."

"So he owes you ten to twenty thousand dollars as of this date?"

"He gave me a truck, which is probably worth four or five grand."

"When did he give you the truck?"

"July of last year [1990]."

"Have you, since obtaining that truck, asked for the balance of the money?"

"Once."

"When was that?"

"Maybe six months ago."

"What did Bob Decker say?"

"That, 'I'll pay you as soon as I get it, and I'm good for it.' "

"If Bob Decker said that he had fully paid you, that would be incorrect?"

"Yeah."

Bob Decker in fact had just deposed that the debt was paid in full, except for maybe $4,000, after he sold his house in Davie.

"If Bob Decker were to die, for example, you have nothing to show that he owed you any money?"

"Not really."

"Now, you say Bob Decker gave you $10,000 on the Wednesday before the date of this incident?"

"Um-hum."

"What did you do with that money?"

"Deposited it in the bank."

Davie Police had never sought out either Decker's or McFarland's bank records.

"Were you aware of Bob Decker's financial condition in November of 1988?"

"The guy was always hurting for money. Had a lot of mortgages."

"Had he approached you on any other occasions to borrow money to help pay those mortgages?"

"No. He was probably doing pretty good then. He was just—you know how some people are with money. He just spends, spends, spends."

"To your knowledge, did Chuck Panoyan know that Bob Decker had just given you $10,000 on Wednesday of the week that this incident occurred?"

"I know he was on the job working, but I don't know if he had knowledge or not."

"You've been arrested before, have you not?"

"Yeah."

"I know that you were arrested for something involving a Creepy Crawlie."

"Yeah."

"Other than the Creepy Crawlie incident, have you ever been arrested?"

"Yeah."

"For what?"

"Traffic, different things."

"Well, let's forget about the traffic and talk about the different things. How many different things have you been arrested for?"

"Assault and battery."

"How many years ago was that?"

"I've been arrested three or four times for that."

McFarland said none of the assault and battery arrests were in the last five years, and none resulted in convictions. He was convicted for possession of stolen property (the Creepy Crawlies). That was odd because McFarland said his annual income was $200,000 to $300,000.

"Do you remember, soon before this incident occurred, Bob Decker carrying a firearm in his van for protection?"

"I think so."

"Do you remember talking to Bob about what had happened that caused him to be carrying that firearm in his van?"

"Yeah. I knew he was having a problem with a black guy that rented one of his apartments."

"Do you remember that black guy's name?"

"If you'd say it, I'd know it."

"Warren Smith?"

"Yeah, right."

"Did Bob Decker tell you that Warren Smith had threatened his life?"

"Somebody did. I don't know if it was Bob or somebody else. I got—I don't know if it was a threat, but—"

"You had heard about that before the incident that involved Donna's death?"

"Either that or shortly after."

"Can you describe Bob Decker's relationship with you back in November 1988?"

"We were going to go to, I think, an art party the next night at his house. I went to a wrestling match with him once; went out with him another night—him and Mike Shope."

In Decker's deposition, he had omitted McFarland's name from the picture party guest list.

"Did you, Bob Decker, and Mike Shope, on somewhat of a regular basis, used to go out socially?"

"Three or four times, yeah."

"What kind of places would you go to?"

"Went to a wrestling match one time. We went to the [car] races in Gainesville a couple of—one year, I remember for sure. Maybe two years."

"Did you ever go to strip joints with Bob Decker?"

"One night."

"Whose idea was that?"

"I don't know. Probably mine."

McFarland said he knew Don Wetz. Vinikoor asked him if he knew any other business Wetz may be in, other than the restaurant business.

"Yeah. I heard—"

"What's that?"

"I heard he was a drug dealer. I don't know."

"That's just scuttlebutt on the street?"

"Yeah. A kid that worked for me told me he heard that."

"When was the last time you saw Bob Decker?"

"Bob Decker, I saw not too long ago. Where did I see him at? Where did I see him? I saw him probably three or four months ago, but I don't remember where."

"Have you ever been to his new house?"

"Yeah."

"What was the occasion for your being at Bob Decker's new house?"

"Just to stop by to see if I could get some money and see how he was going. I think that was the one time I asked him for it."

"And were you successful in getting money from him?"

"No."

Vinikoor asked McFarland to retell what Bob Decker had told him about the incident.

"I remember him telling me that he thought the guy was in a rodeo—had been a rodeo cowboy—because he hogtied somebody professionally. He said the guy looked like a weight lifter."

"Do you remember Bob telling you whether it was a white man or a black man or whether he could tell?"

"He couldn't see. He couldn't see. He was completely covered."

That agreed with what Ricketts had deposed, yet again contradicted what Bob had told authorities—that he was sure the man was white.

"Did Bob Decker discuss an incident involving the signing of some document?"

"Oh, yeah. He said—what did he sign? Yeah, I remember that. A check? I think he said a check. I'm not—I don't know."

That was the most suspicious answer of all, Vinikoor thought. Did McFarland again sidestep the issue of the quit-claim deed? If the blank document was destined to be a quitclaim deed, as Bob thought, it was well within the realm of possibility that the beneficiary was McFarland, Vinikoor thought.

Could he be deposing the masked man right now? Vinikoor knew McFarland fit the broad physical description of the killer.

"How tall are you?" Vinikoor asked.

"About five nine."

"How much did you weigh in November of 1988?"

"Probably about 200, 210."

"Did the police ever actually come out and accuse you of the murder?"

"I think he did say one time, 'Why did you do it?' or something like that, and I just laughed at him."

"Who said that?"

"That Polish—"

"Mocarski?"

"Yeah."

"Have you ever talked to Chuck Panoyan about this incident?"

"Yeah."

"When and how many times?"

"Well, Chuck worked for me part-time occasionally, after it happened and before it happened, and talked about it all the time."

"Do you remember what Chuck said about the incident?"

"I remember him saying that the guy threatened him that if he went and got the cops or ever said anything, that he'd kill his family. I think he said he took his wallet and had his address, and that he was just scared."

"Did Chuck Panoyan genuinely appear to you to be frightened?"

"Frightened? I don't know. I couldn't—I really didn't—Chuck is kind of a funny guy. He's kind of hard to figure out."

"Why do you say that?"

"He's kind of off-the-wall, always goofing around, never serious."

"Does Chuck Panoyan impress you as the kind of person who's capable of being involved in a robbery-murder?"

"No."

"Do you have any reason to believe that Chuck Panoyan is involved in the death of Donna Decker?"

"All the evidence points that way, from what I've heard."

"What evidence is that?"

"Well, that—mainly what Bob Decker has told me: that they found the keys to the handcuffs in his truck; he rented a car to Washington, D.C., and the mileage worked out to wherever this Dana Williamson was; the time that it took for him to get the police. A lot of different things."

"Did Chuck Panoyan ever borrow money from you?"

"Tried once."

"How long ago?"

"I remember it was around Christmastime, but I don't

remember what Christmas. It was either right after that happened, I think—the Christmas after that happened.''

"How much did he want to borrow from you?"

"Just two—two thousand."

"You wouldn't lend it to him?"

"No."

"Why is that?"

"I was tired of lending money."

Paul Stark took over the questions.

"Were you familiar with Chuck Panoyan's relationship with Bob Decker?"

"Well, Chuck had worked for Bob, and I thought they were pretty good friends. I know Bob would kind of put him down once in a while."

"How would he do that?"

"Well, you know, 'You dummy. You can't ever do anything right.' Stuff like that."

"Were you familiar with Chuck Panoyan's financial situation back in November of 1988?"

"I knew he had built some houses there in Davie, in Colored Town, and he had them loaded down with finances. I think that pretty well kept him broke, just cutting the payments on them."

"If you had to evaluate from what you knew of Chuck Panoyan's financial situation in 1988 and Bob Decker's financial situation in 1988, how would you say the two compared?"

"Well, Bob was spec building and he'd get whatever he could make on a job, but he'd just blow it right out again."

"Had a cash flow problem?"

"I'd say so."

"What about Chuck?"

"I'd say Chuck had no cash at all. He was just working ten bucks an hour, whatever Bob paid him. What Chuck had wasn't renting or selling or anything. He built in the wrong part of town. What Bob had he would eventually sell."

"With regard to the $10,000 payment that you say Bob made to you—"

"Um-hum."

"—do you know how he made that payment to you?"

"He must have just sold a property and—he didn't do any work—or maybe he did do some private work, but—I would say he had just sold some property."

That was consistent with what Panoyan told the police in his first statement, hours after the murder. He said Decker told him that morning that he had just sold the house they were still working on.

(Quoting Panoyan's statement: "And he said, 'Well, I just sold this place and I'm taking a vacation.' I said, 'Well, that's great.' I said, 'Well, what did you get for it?' He said, '$110,000,' and I said, 'Man, that's fine,' and he said he bought another lot and, ah, be at work Monday morning.")

Could McFarland have been angry that Decker had used the money he was supposed to repay to McFarland to buy another lot? And that $10,000, as partial payment, wasn't enough?

"Did he make the payment to you in cash or did he make the payment to—" asked Stark.

"No. Check."

"You're positive that was a check that he wrote you out?" asked Steve Hammer.

"Yeah."

"Do you remember what bank that was?"

"I think it was Transflorida. In fact, I might have—I think I took it to the bank and cashed it on the spot, if I remember right."

"That very same day?" asked Charlie Johnson.

"I knew I was worried that it wasn't going to—I was thinking it might bounce, and I know I either put it in my bank right away or took it to his bank."

"Did you ever talk to Donna about the debt that Bob owed you?" asked Stark.

"No. No."

"Did Bob ever tell you that Donna had some of the money and that you could pick it up from her?" asked Vinikoor.

"Yeah, I think he did." (Bob had denied that when asked.)

Vinikoor asked McFarland if he remembered when Bob went to New York to pick up his dad. That was during the time when Trisha Tenbrock said Donna got a telephone death threat. Tenbrock said Donna told her that no one knew Bob was in New York.

"Yeah. I think I was supposed to go by and pick up some money. I think so."

"Did you call Donna and say, 'Hey, where's the money?' "

"No."

Stark then reasoned that if Bob left money for Donna to hand to McFarland, that implied it was cash.

"Well, if it was a check, he could have sent it right to you, right? Nothing to come by and pick up, isn't that right?"

"I don't know. I couldn't tell you if it was a check or cash. I don't even—I didn't remember that until he mentioned it."

Cash payments that large suggested drug-related money.

"Did he ever make reference to the fact that the people who came into the house were looking for drugs?" Stark asked.

"I think he did say that, yeah."

"Did he ever discuss with you why they would be looking for drugs at his house?"

"The wrong house, wrong address. I think he said that once, or I said it."

"You've loaned money to people in the past, prior to the time that you loaned it to Bob. Isn't it a matter of course that you would take back some kind of paper to acknowledge at least that the debt exists?" asked Stark.

"Like I said, I think the property was in my and his name at first, and he had done some work for me and paid like ninety—I think it was around ninety-five hundred off in work and material. Then he gave me ten grand, and I think I might have just signed it over to him then, and then took—you know, I wasn't worried about fifteen thousand."

"You mean with no paperwork at all?"

"No. I trust the guy for fifteen."

Stark asked if an unrecorded mortgage is valid.

"Right. Is it good? I was going to go to my lawyer and—"

"I was hoping you could tell me that. It doesn't lose its validity as a mortgage just because you don't record it," Stark probed.

"I lent this Mike Shope, like I was telling you before, twenty grand, and he was going to pay me back thirty. I think he paid me back around eighteen. In fact, I was going to take all the papers I had on both Mike and some other people—take them to a lawyer and see what he could do with them, just kind of clear everything up, but I haven't done it yet.''

"You mean collect the debt that Shope owes?'' asked Stark.

"Yeah, and other people that owe me.''

"Like Decker, as well?''

"Who?''

"Decker.''

"Yeah.''

"So you're going to attempt to make collection against Decker?''

"The guy is hurting right now. I don't want to push anything. I mean he lost his wife and got shot. I really—I wasn't looking out—I was just looking to do the guy a favor, really. He's a hard—He got up at seven o'clock in the morning, worked till seven o'clock at night, really busted chops.''

"Do you know why he came to you to borrow the money? Were you that close a friend?''

"He had—I had done some work for him, and we were pretty friendly, not real.''

"Did you have a reputation for loaning money to people?''

"No. No.''

"Well, what kind of interest rate were you charging?''

"Whatever. Ten percent.''

"You don't even know the interest rate you were charging?''

"I think we agreed on ten percent.''

Decker had said seven percent.

"Would you know, for example, or did you ask him, why he didn't go to the bank to borrow the money?''

"I think he was probably borrowed out at the bank.''

Stark asked McFarland if he had detected any mental changes in Bob Decker since the shooting.

"Mental, I'd say he's a little forgetful.''

"Why do you say he was forgetful?''

"Just some things he was probably talking about in the past—that happened to him in the past—or just generally speaking. I couldn't put a handle right on it.''

"I mean, for example," asked Stark, "if he told us that he paid out your debt, is that being forgetful?"

"That would be a lie. Did he say that?"

Stark answered that he didn't know.

"Why didn't Bob Decker pay you back the money he owed you when he sold his house?" asked Johnson.

"He told me he had to buy another house or line it up. I don't know. I didn't—I don't really remember. I know I wasn't pushing for the money. I got like more than half of it. He had a tragedy happen in his life. Fifteen grand ain't no big deal."

Stark asked McFarland which version of contradictory information about the case he believed—Panoyan's or Bob Decker's.

"Well, after somebody gets shot and something like that happened to them, then it's hard to say what's going through their head. And Chuck, it's—he's hard to figure anyway."

"In other words," asked Stark, "when you're dealing with someone who's shot in the brain, and Chuck Panoyan, they start off on pretty much an equal footing, right?"

"Yeah," agreed McFarland.

"Did you have any other theory about who is responsible for this incident, other than Warren Smith?"

"Well, everybody—Davie police fluffed it off, Bob fluffed it off, so I fluffed it off."

"But, in other words, you never had any theory about who was involved other than Warren Smith?"

"I've had probably a couple of them."

"What would they be?"

"I would say that Chuck probably mentioned to somebody that he thought—you know how Chuck rambles on—probably mentioned to somebody that he thought Bob had money or was coming into money, and whoever he was talking to might have—"

"Taken it from there?"

"Yeah, took it from there."

"This is what I don't understand. Why would Chuck say that he thought Bob had money when it was obvious to people who knew him that Bob didn't have any money?"

"I think Bob's mother had just died, and Chuck didn't

think like me and you. He would probably think he got cash right out of the bank, he didn't have to go through a will and all this shit—all this stuff—and that he just got cash right out.''

That was another very suspicious reference. In fact, Panoyan said Bob did tell him that he had collected an $18,000 or $20,000 cash inheritance—and that Bob had spent almost all that money on a new Ford van, which he had bought up north when he picked up his father to bring him to Florida.

Could McFarland have been annoyed that Bob had used the money to buy an expensive vehicle instead of paying him back?

McFarland continued: ''Chuck wouldn't—or he might have heard he closed on a house. I don't know. That's what I figured one time. I didn't think Bob would—or Chuck would set him up to have somebody go right in and do a home invasion on him.''

McFarland also had a drug-related theory.

''Then I thought it was a mistaken address. Maybe a guy got the wrong house and went in there for drugs, didn't find any, got mad. Maybe the guy was on drugs and started shooting everybody. I thought maybe that happened. And he felt sorry for Chuck. He looked at Chuck and said, 'Man this guy is'—you know, big glasses—'so I've got to let this guy go. He ain't going to do nothing.' I thought that too. Mistaken home invasion.''

''Is that it? Do you have any other theories on it?''

''Maybe Bob was into something I didn't know about. To me, I knew he got up every morning, hard worker. I never would have lent him any money if I didn't think he was a hard worker. I don't know. It's a real mystery.''

✦ THIRTY-SEVEN

WINSTON MARSDEN
Deposition, August 5, 1991

Marsden—no longer "Confidential Informant 101"—was a friendly witness to the defense. Paul Stark tried to elicit what his relationship with Charles Panoyan had been.

"He's been a good friend. He's helped me out when I was in a jam." Once, when Marsden was between draws on a home and had no money to pay his help, "he probably donated two to two and a half weeks of time."

"In other words, what you are telling me is that, because you were in a jam, Charlie worked for free?"

"Well, he knew circumstances. He's been a builder himself, and he knows what it is."

"Did you know him to do that to others as well?"

"He also did that for my son-in-law. My son-in-law and daughter bought an old house in Hollywood, and it was in pretty rough shape. There was a lot of work to make it liveable. Chuck went over there and helped, and didn't even charge a dime. He must have spent nights over there for about three weeks."

"Is this common in the building trade, for people to work for free?"

"No."

"In other words, Chuck's a special kind of guy?"

"Right."

Stark asked Marsden about Panoyan's reputation in the community and in the trade.

"I don't know of anybody that had anything bad to say about him. Never."

"Was he violent?"

"Never."

"And is he known to have a temper?"

"No."

"And have you ever known him to be dishonest?"

"Guaranteed that's out."

"Did he steal from his friends?"

"No way."

Marsden saved his ill words for Bob Decker. "It seemed like nobody liked Bob Decker that I talked to, and the only person that seemed to like him was Chuck Panoyan. I could never figure that out. Then again, this guy was strange about that. He could not find any wrong."

"Charlie liked everybody?"

"Yeah. You and I would say this guy is a scumbag."

"He wouldn't say that?"

"He would defend them."

Marsden said Decker had had troubles with building inspectors because he was slapdash with details.

Panoyan "would never, ever say anything about the guy when it needed to be said about his business practices. He's told me that he's like his son. He defended him because I said that this guy is a cheap crook."

Marsden said Panoyan was so upset for a month after the murder, "I thought he was going to end up in a mental institution. He was in tears over the whole matter. His wife told me, 'I don't know what's going to happen with him, if he's going to survive. The guy is in tears, he cries all day. I don't know what to do.' " Marsden invited Panoyan to a family barbecue, to cheer him up, but it didn't work. "He was sitting there like he lost his best friend."

Just as upsetting to Panoyan was knowing that Bob Decker thought he was involved in the crime. "And I said, 'It just shows you the caliber of the guy, that he would even think that you have had anything to do with it.' "

PAUL LYONS
Statement to investigators
August 28, 1991

Paul Lyons was the third jailhouse snitch to call the State Attorney's Office about Dana Williamson.

Lyons found himself enmeshed with Williamson simply because he was Patrick O'Brien's cellmate in the protective custody portion of the jail. O'Brien had been released on bond in March, but later re-arrested. By this time, transcripts of O'Brien's March statements had been provided to the defense.

At the end of July, Williamson approached Lyons in the jail's law library. When he found out that Lyons was on the same floor as O'Brien, Dana volunteered that he was going to ask his lawyer to be placed there also.

"I said, 'Why do you want to do that?' He goes, 'I have to take care of him. He's testifying against me and I want to make sure he can't.' "

Lyons said he told O'Brien about the conversation, and O'Brien told him not to worry. Then two weeks later, Williamson asked him to sign a statement saying that O'Brien's testimony was a lie designed to get his own charges dropped. Lyons refused.

"He told me he'll have to try and get up there and kill him then. I said, 'What do you mean? You ain't gonna kill no one in here.' He said, 'No, I can do it, it'll be easy.'

"I said, 'How? There's deputies up there and he's bigger than you.' He said, 'I've had Ninja training, and if I can't do it, one of my friends will. And if you say anything to him or tell anyone, I'll get you too, 'cause I know you're here for kidnapping and you're gonna be up the road, and I'll see you there.' "

What worried Lyons was Williamson's change in demeanor when talking about O'Brien. "He gets red, the vein in his head starts to bulge, his eyes turn glassy, he starts shaking, he's like a Heckle and Jeckle [Jekyll and Hyde], a totally different person. He really gets to scare me when he gets like that."

Just a few days before, Lyons said he had had one more conversation with Dana, this time about Kelly Woodroof.

Woodroof was a liar and inexperienced, Dana said. He threatened to "get even" with him as well, once he beat his case.

RODNEY WILLIAMSON
Deposition, September 17, 1991

Now that Patrick O'Brien claimed Dana had confessed that his brother was also in on the crime, Rodney's deposition assumed the quality of a portent.

Rodney described life as a child after his mother was killed in a 1969 automobile accident.

"My father regularly beat us with a belt. He'd get wild with it. He'd wrap the very end of the belt around his hand and then grab the buckle, folding the belt in half, and he would beat us with it until the buckle would fly out of his hand and wrap around us, and I have scars on both of my hips to prove that."

"Did he beat your sisters, too?" asked Charlie Johnson.

"Occasionally, but not quite as bad as he beat the boys."

"Who did he beat the worst?"

"Me, because I was the oldest. He beat me pretty often. Probably every report card period and a couple times between."

"Who did he beat secondly the most?"

"He beat Dana quite frequently."

"What happened after your mom died?"

"The night my mother died I swore to her ghost that I wouldn't leave the house until A) I finished school; B) I turned 18; or C) My dad kicked me out of the house."

(But Rodney dropped out of school after ninth grade, in 1970.)

"In June of 1970 my father told me he was glad that my mother died so she wouldn't see what bastards and bitches we all turned out to be. I remember him saying that he was going to sell everything he owned, get drunk, and stay drunk as long as it would last, and if he felt like beating us, that would be reason e-fucking-nough. And if we did not like that idea, we could hit the fucking road right then. I left." (He was fifteen.)

"For a long time I was a rebel without a cause against

authority in any way, shape, or form. I instantly had my back up and I was ready to fight.''

Rodney said he had had a number of psychological evaluations as a child, including something called a ''sanity hearing.''

''I know that one of my psychiatrists that looked at me said that I was the most sane person he'd ever met and one of them said I was a paranoid schizophrenic. I don't remember what the third one said.''

Johnson asked Rodney whether he believed he was the natural father to Erica, Sandy's youngest daughter.

''I'm aware that Sandy believes so, yeah.''

''You don't think you are?''

''I'm not positive, but I don't believe so. If I thought she was my daughter, I'd definitely have her ass in court trying to take her away.''

''Do you think Dana's happy about the situation between you and Sandy?''

''Oh yeah. I asked Dana one time did he know where Sandy had spent the night.

''And he said, 'Yeah, in your bedroom.'

''And I said, 'Do you know how she happened to be there?'

''And he said, 'Yeah. She wanted to go in there.'

''And I said, 'And you don't have anything to say about it?'

''And he said, 'More power to her. I hope she gets used to strange dick and decides to take a hike.' ''

Rodney complained about Ginger Kostige. ''Virginia Kostige can say anything she wants about hearing what I say, but Virginia Kostige is a fucking snoop. She likes to eavesdrop on people's conversations. She says she's looking for her cat and then the whole time she's hiding behind bushes by the front windows of the house. I used to say things to irritate her. Like, you know, 'That bitch across the street is a real cunt.' And she would be there listening.''

➤ Thirty-eight

Patrick O'Brien
Deposition, October 2, 1991

In the months since Patrick O'Brien had come forward, he and Brian Cavanagh had developed a relationship; however, Cavanagh was scrupulously careful not to offer O'Brien any background about the case, for fear of tainting his information. He insisted O'Brien tell him the whole truth, as he knew it, whichever way the truth fell.

"I told him, it's very important you don't shade the truth," Cavanagh recounted. "Don't think I'll be pissed at you for not shading it. I have to live, for better or worse, with whatever Dana Williamson says. But I gotta know."

O'Brien had assumed that Panoyan was guilty along with Williamson, but Cavanagh told him not to assume anything. "I can't tell you more than that," he said. "If there's anything exculpatory, let me know."

The first questions the defense attorneys had for O'Brien concerned his pending charges, and whether he had received any deals from the state in exchange for testimony.

"Violation of probation. Violation of parole. Two armed robberies, one robbery, and practicing medicine without a license," O'Brien said, explaining that the probation, in Massachusetts, was for rape and larceny.

As for favors O'Brien was supposed to get, he said he had asked the state attorney to speak up for him at his sentencing. He was pleading guilty to the robbery charges, and faced a guideline prison sentence of seven to nine years. He was hoping for the low end of the guidelines.

In addition, O'Brien said he had received a bond reduction, which led to his release a few days after he gave his taped statements to authorities. However, when he was picked up again three months later, it was for violating probation, as well as a new charge—practicing medicine without a license. That accusation O'Brien denied.

"Is it gynecology you are supposed to have practiced?" asked Paul Stark.

"No, sir."

"Were you supposed to be examining women, posing as a doctor?"

"I am not going to answer that question."

Back in jail, O'Brien said Dana Williamson had made threats on his life in the last two months. Steve Hammer asked about them.

"Just that I will never be allowed to testify, and even if I do testify, he will get me down the road—in reference to prison."

O'Brien said he had recently been in the law library with both Panoyan and Williamson. Although the room was tiny, the two relied on O'Brien to messenger between them.

"You are in the law library and Williamson is in the law library and Panoyan is in the law library?" Stark asked.

"Yes, but Panoyan is deathly afraid of Williamson," O'Brien said, shocking some in the room and pleasing others.

"How do you know that?" asked Stark, one of those pleased.

"Williamson told me. Panoyan stayed the hell away from him, too." O'Brien said Williamson repeated five to ten times that Panoyan was scared of him.

"He didn't make actual threats against Panoyan. On advice from Panoyan's counsel, [Panoyan stayed] the hell away from Williamson, and Williamson was disturbed about that because the only time he could see Panoyan was in church or in the law library. But they could no longer see each other in the law library because Panoyan is assured when he goes there Williamson is not there."

"Did Williamson tell you during these five to ten occasions—when he told you about how Panoyan was deathly afraid of him—did he tell you why he was deathly afraid of him?"

"Williamson was saying that Panoyan would never testify against him."

"Because he was afraid of him?"

"Yeah, and he knew the family."

"Did he say anything about harming Panoyan, if Panoyan were ever to testify against him?"

"Anyone—he said—anyone that testified against him he would get eventually. If not, then the Lord will."

"If he didn't get them first," Stark finished the sentence.

"Right," agreed O'Brien.

"Do you know if that information was ever conveyed to Panoyan that Williamson would get him if Panoyan ever testified against him?"

"I believe it was. I believe that messages were sent across."

"Do you know who sent those messages?"

"I was told one of the people that delivered the message was a guy named Lujack [Luchak]."

"A name I recognize," Stark noted. "Now, you said that in the library, Panoyan was obviously frightened of Williamson."

"Absolutely."

"Why do you say that?"

"He stayed away from him."

"Panoyan stayed on one end of the room?"

"Wherever Williamson moved, Panoyan moved the opposite way."

O'Brien said Panoyan had taken a sodium pentothal test the previous weekend, and Williamson was scared that Panoyan might have said something during it he shouldn't have. (The test was done for the benefit of the defense.)

"You went over to Mr. Panoyan and what did you say?" Stark asked.

" 'How did the sodium pentothal testing go?' " O'Brien answered.

"What did Mr. Panoyan say to you?"

"He said, 'I don't know.' I said, 'Williamson wants to know how the sodium pentothal test went.' "

"What did Panoyan say?"

" 'Are you a friend of his?' 'No, I am with him on the same block. I think he is crazy.' "

"Then what?"

"He said he really is."

"Panoyan said that?"

"He said, 'Watch yourself. He really is crazy.' I said, 'He wants to know the sodium pentothal test results.' Panoyan said, 'I don't know. I was out for a long time after the test and I haven't found out.' "

"I said, 'You are a victim in this case? What are you doing going along with this thing?' "

"Did Panoyan say anything else to you?"

" 'Stay away from him. And watch yourself.' I said to him, 'Why are you in this? You didn't shoot anybody. What the hell are you doing? Why don't you deal with your story and let them know what happened?' "

"He said, 'I will still do time and Williamson can still get me.' I just remembered that, Brian. He is still going to do time and Williamson is going to get him."

"Mr. Panoyan never acknowledged guilt to you?"

"No," O'Brien said.

"Now, Williamson gave you varying pieces of information as it pertained to Mr. Panoyan, isn't that true?"

"Yes, sir."

"As a matter of fact, Williamson told you that Mr. Panoyan was not involved in this incident, did he not?"

"He said he wasn't involved and then he said he was involved."

"All right," said Stark. "I am looking for you to be as honest as you can. Would it be fair to say you didn't write down those parts of Williamson's statements when he told you that Panoyan was not involved because you know that wasn't something really that the state wanted to hear?"

"Objection to the form," said Brian Cavanagh.

"No, sir. I didn't care what the state wanted to hear," answered O'Brien.

"That is fair enough," said Stark. "In terms of what the state wanted to hear, it is obvious the state was interested in acknowledging the guilt and not interested necessarily in information that would tend to exonerate someone."

"Not true, because this man [Brian Cavanagh] told me on more than one occasion if I heard anything that would exonerate anyone not to hold it back."

"He is an honorable guy," said Stark.

"True," said Cavanagh, touched, especially considering the ferocity of his opponents.

Stark asked O'Brien to recount the occasions when Williamson told him that Panoyan was not involved.

"Well, Dana Williamson couldn't trust Chuck. He wouldn't tell Chuck everything that was going to happen when it was going to happen because Chuck was not exactly the brightest bulb on the Christmas tree.

"For example—the cocaine—Chuck never got a piece of that action. He never received proceeds from it."

"You are saying that Dana Williamson told you that?"

"Right."

Nor did Panoyan even know that night that cocaine was in the house, or that Williamson got any, O'Brien said.

Stark prompted further. "You were telling me how he told you that Panoyan had nothing to do with it."

"Initially, Panoyan was a victim like everyone else," O'Brien said.

"In other words, this guy tells you that he shows up at the house and Panoyan doesn't know he is going to show up and he commits a robbery. Panoyan is there, a victim?"

"He releases him because he knows him. He puts a gun to his head and he says, 'I know your family and I can make them suffer so keep your mouth shut.' "

"Williamson told you that he said that?"

"Yes."

"With a gun to Panoyan's head?"

"With a gun to his head, he said, 'I will make your family suffer.' "

"Panoyan recognized who Williamson was and knew he was capable of doing it?"

"Correct. I just thought of something. Williamson told me that one of the reasons that Chuck was in fear of him was Chuck knew his past when he wiped out the kid with the baseball bat."

Stark tried to summarize O'Brien's story for him. He asked him to agree if the following was what Williamson told him:

"That Dana Williamson came to understand that Bob Decker had come into some money, and he may have gotten that information through Panoyan who may have been speaking to the family because he, Panoyan, was friendly with the family.

"Dana Williamson showed up at the Decker home and Panoyan happened to be there. The incident took place and Dana put a gun to Charles Panoyan's head and said, 'If you say anything about this, I will murder your family,' and Charlie was an innocent victim and kept his mouth shut. Is that consistent?"

"I have to say yes and no."

"What is the no part?"

"The no part is Williamson said afterward they were photographed at an ATM machine before Chuck went to the security guard to call 911."

But that was more misinformation on Dana Williamson's part. If an ATM security camera had photographed Dana and Panoyan during a transaction, the police had no knowledge of it. And Bob Decker said he had no bank reports of any such transaction.

O'Brien said Williamson told him he got the card's PIN code from the Deckers. Then he thought, perhaps Dana was referring to Rodney, not Panoyan, at the ATM.

"Williamson had told you that Rodney was there that night?"

"Correct. He said also that Rodney wasn't there that night."

"In essence, what I understand you to be telling me is that out of your conversation with Dana Williamson he made it clear to you that Panoyan never planned this crime to occur, correct?"

"He never planned the murders."

"Did he ever tell you that he planned any of it?"

"No, he said he was in on the robbery and they planned that, but not on that night."

Stark wondered if O'Brien was reaching his own conclusions about Panoyan that might not be justified from what Williamson had told him.

"Let's talk about 'being in on the robbery.' What were his exact words about being in on the robbery?"

"They were all in, including Rodney and Panoyan, yes."

"Did he say what he meant by being 'in' on it?"

"No."

"For all you know, Dana Williamson may have meant that Charles Panoyan, by not going to the police after the fact, was in on the robbery, right?"

"I assume that, yes."

"Williamson never told you that he had planned the robbery in advance with Panoyan? He never said that, did he?"

"He said no, he knew all about it. He just didn't know when. He couldn't be trusted with that kind of information."

"So, for all you know, if Panoyan had provided information and spoken about the fact that Bob Decker was either coming into money or had money, in Williamson's mind, that may have been his involvement in the plan, correct?"

"Correct," said O'Brien.

✦ THIRTY-NINE

THE STENCH OF GUILT

Halloween was Charles Panoyan's fifty-first birthday. Paul Stark hoped that a birthday visit would cheer him up, and more importantly, get him talking. Although Panoyan had constantly insisted he was innocent and a victim, not once in his year and a half of incarceration had he told his full story to his frustrated attorneys. The only time had he come close to breaking down was months before, on his wedding anniversary.

Immediately after his visit, Stark crossed the street from the jail to the courthouse and found Brian Cavanagh in his office.

"I have a crazy idea, and you're probably going to throw me out of the office again," said Stark.

"I can't tell you what went on between my client and I," he said, ethically unable to reveal attorney-client discussions with anyone, especially the prosecutor.

"But we're close."

Cavanagh asked what he meant.

"Let me hypothesize: What if he were able to identify Dana Williamson and someone else we know; he won't, but what if?"

Cavanagh knew immediately this might be the break he was waiting for. He was himself swimming in the horrible problem of what to do about Panoyan. When the depositions started, Cavanagh had thought both defendants were 100 percent guilty. But all the punching Vinikoor and Stark had done to his case had in fact achieved its intended effect. While the argument against Williamson got better, Brian's certainty about Panoyan's guilt slowly dropped. 90 percent guilty. 70 percent guilty. Patrick O'Brien was his star witness; but after his deposition, it plunged below 50 percent—a very unsafe place for a prosecutor to be. If Panoyan was guilty of *anything at all,* it certainly wasn't murder.

In addition, Brian was faced with the dilemma of Rodney Williamson. O'Brien said he was involved, but at this moment Brian didn't have enough evidence even to arrest him.

When Panoyan was first jailed, Cavanagh had hoped he would accept some sort of guilty plea on reduced charges in exchange for testimony against Dana Williamson.

"Talk to him," Cavanagh had told Stark. "See what he thinks he's guilty of." But when Stark had reported back to Cavanagh, Panoyan's answer was he didn't think he was guilty of anything, and he wouldn't take any plea. As a result, no formal offer was ever made.

Trying to force a confession out of him by keeping him locked up—an old prosecutor's trick—clearly hadn't worked.

O'Brien had said Panoyan was deathly afraid of Dana Williamson. Stark suggested they get Panoyan away from Dana, and he asked Brian if he would offer his client a bond.

"You know he's not a danger to the community," said Stark. "Witness after witness said he wasn't. Give Dave and me a chance to work on him together. We're so close."

Problem was, Stark said, Panoyan didn't have any money and wouldn't be able to afford a bond. As it was, he and Vinikoor were working as hard as they were, he said, for 33⅓¢ an hour.

Without skipping a beat, Brian Cavanagh proposed a solution:

"Why don't we ROR him? What do we have to lose?"

Release on Recognizance (ROR)—that meant Panoyan would go from No Bond to a zero bond—a get out of jail free card, someone would call it later. Little could be more unusual than a prosecutor suggesting that his first-degree murder suspect be put on the street while charges were still pending.

Paul Stark's mouth opened. "You're kidding me," he said.

"No," said Brian. "Let's do it."

"That's great," said Stark. "Do you have to run that by anybody?"

No, said Brian, adding that if he did, they'd probably say no. As it turned out, when Brian told some other veteran prosecutors in the office what he was about to do, they tried to make him feel like an idiot. They told him he had a better case against Charles Panoyan than Dana Williamson.

The state couldn't just release Panoyan on their own; they had to ask the judge. Cavanagh asked Judge Eade's secretary for the nearest date she could book for a hearing. That was a week later, November 7.

In the meantime, Cavanagh told Kelly Woodroof what he wanted to do. Woodroof had been reading the depositions and didn't need persuading. Panoyan wasn't a risk, and they needed his testimony, if they could get it. Earlier that year, the Florida Supreme Court had made new case law by over-turning the murder conviction of a Tampa man named Cox that had been won without benefit of any direct witness testi-mony. Woodroof had since convinced Cavanagh that even if they won the Decker case in trial court, it would now risk being thrown out on appeal. But testimony from Panoyan against Williamson, plus Dana's admission that the cowboy hat was his, would be enough, at least to meet that new standard.

Now that Woodroof no longer believed Panoyan was as involved in the planning of the crime as he had once thought, he considered him guilty at most of criminal accessory after the fact. That was worth a prison term of eighteen months. Since he had already served that while awaiting trial, the chances were that he wouldn't be incarcerated again if he pled guilty.

The biggest problem would be convincing the Deckers and the Zazzos that releasing Panoyan from jail was the right thing to do. If the victims didn't agree, the judge's hands would be tied.

Woodroof got on the phone Monday, November 4. In case he didn't realize that that day was the three-year anniversary of the murder, both families knew it all too well.

In those three years, the Zazzos—even more than the Deck-ers—had come to hate Charles Panoyan. Woodroof explained that most, if not all, the reasons they had felt Panoyan was guilty—even months ago—had disintegrated. They were wrong and everyone had to own up to it, hard as it was. All that remained was a vague, unsubstantiated feeling that he was guilty—a stench of guilt. Clutching onto it was like trying to grasp air.

The change in perspective was hard for Kelly Woodroof, too. In March, Davie Police had honored him with "Officer of the Year" for his work leading to the arrests of Panoyan and Williamson. He had even won a cash award, a bicycle, and other goodies donated by local merchants in Davie.

Woodroof had to be vague with the families about what he knew, that Panoyan was close to testifying against Dana Williamson. That made it even harder to sell. But over the three years, he had cultivated the families' trust by staying close with them, and it paid off. Both said they would agree. That night, Bob Decker cried as he fell asleep.

Judge Richard Eade had not been long on the bench, only since November 1991. He had been a Broward County prosecutor, and, therefore, he and Cavanagh knew each other well and had the greatest respect for each other's talents. Nevertheless, Eade was a bit stunned when he realized the request and saw the opposing attorneys in agreement.

Cavanagh asked that the hearing be held *in camera,* which meant it would be closed and the record of it kept sealed. That was to insure that Dana Williamson and his lawyers wouldn't be able to read the transcript and also so the press wouldn't get wind of it. The local newspapers were good at sensationalizing, but not nearly so dependable in giving proper perspective. They would jump up and down if they found out a murder suspect had been let loose.

Cavanagh told Eade that Williamson was a psychopathic killer, but the case against him was meager, at best. He fretted that at trial, after the state presented all their evidence, the court might enter a directed verdict of Not Guilty, which would terminate the case before even jury deliberations.

In effect, Cavanagh was agreeing with Dana Williamson's previous reported assessment, that the state didn't have any case against him, unless Panoyan testified.

Woodroof told the judge that the family had agreed with

Cavanagh's decision. Eade granted the request, but not without noting just how unusual it was.

Brian Cavanagh hoped he was doing the right thing. If he wasn't, he was in big trouble.

The defense attorneys hadn't breathed a word of their ploy to either Panoyan or his wife. As soon as the hearing ended, Paul Stark called Darla Panoyan. He told her, without explanation, that her husband was about to be released, and she should go downtown to the jail and pick him up. In a matter of hours, Panoyan was a confused but free man, although he still remained under indictment.

The story that Panoyan had been released without bond spread like wildfire through the jail. According to Patrick O'Brien, when Dana Williamson found out, he bit his pen in two, and ink flowed out all over his shirt.

Almost immediately, Stark and Vinikoor began working on Panoyan, to get him to spill his whole story. He had never told his wife what had happened that night either, so the attorneys used her as well to try to shame him into speaking.

For about two months, they made little progress. Initially, they reported to Brian that Panoyan was still afraid to tell them, but they were keeping after him.

Then at last, a break. Finally, one night in bed, Panoyan told his wife, then he told his attorneys.

The next step was convincing Panoyan to meet with Brian Cavanagh. Vinikoor told their client "we're not fools who would do this with any prosecutor. We know that Brian won't abuse our good faith."

But Panoyan was still extremely skittish. He insisted on not going to the courthouse. Any meeting would have to be elsewhere.

In February 1992, Stark and Vinikoor invited Brian to Vinikoor's downtown Fort Lauderdale office. "We want you to hear what he has to say," said Stark. "You're going to be astonished."

In preparing for the meeting, Vinikoor gave Brian some ideas on how to approach Panoyan, to gain his confidence. He'd have to break the ice first. Just make small talk for a while, he suggested. Don't talk about the case. Make him see that you're human, a caring person.

"I wasn't going to do this," were Charles Panoyan's first words to Brian Cavanagh.

"I wasn't going to tell anybody. I told them the only reason I'm going to tell you is that they told me you're a good guy.

"But I won't tell anybody else."

Those weren't good ground rules as far as Cavanagh was concerned. "Chuck, you'd have to tell the grand jury," he answered.

"No. Nobody else. You have to swear you won't tell anybody. You don't understand. It's my family, and their lives."

Taking Vinikoor's advice, Brian got Panoyan to talk about himself. Panoyan was a natural chatterbox, so it wasn't hard. The conversation led to Panoyan's father, a prison minister who lived in Santa Barbara, California, and how proud he was of his dad.

Brian just wanted to relate to Panoyan as a friend, which was odd, considering that for two years he had assembled a capital felony case against him. When Panoyan took a rare breath, Brian mentioned that he was proud of his dad, too. He had been a New York City detective who had bucked the entire police force because he believed that an innocent man was headed for the electric chair.

That was a major league segue. Brian said a television movie was made about the case, called *The Marcus-Nelson Murders*. Had he heard of it? It starred a character named Kojak. The real character was his dad.

"You must be real proud of your dad," said Panoyan.

Brian could see Panoyan warming up to him. At last Panoyan agreed to talk.

Stark was right. The story was astonishing.

On November 4, 1988, Panoyan had gone to the Deckers to deliver venison. He went inside the house, then back to his truck to get it. When he did, Dana Williamson—and Rodney Williamson—confronted him at gunpoint and forced him to reenter the house. Rodney stayed outside.

The only reason he could figure why the Williamsons

didn't try to kill him was that he had been a longtime close friend of their father. In lieu of shooting him, the Williamsons threatened in graphic terms what they would do to his family if Panoyan talked. Panoyan knew the threat was good because Dana had killed a child when he was a teenager.

He admitted misleading the police when he said he didn't know who the gunman was. But everything else he told the police was true.

He did go to Ohio after his friend told him he had called Crimestoppers and named Dana Williamson. Panoyan went to tell Dana that he was not the one who called.

Finally, Dana's threats had continued and worsened while the two were together in jail. The threats were even more insidious then before because Panoyan knew that Rodney was still left unchecked on the outside.

Brian Cavanagh was very impressed indeed.

"I need you to tell this to the grand jury," he implored again.

"No! I told you I wouldn't tell anybody else," Panoyan insisted.

Brian told Panoyan he'd have to tell the story to somebody else, just as a sounding board. He suggested Kelly Woodroof. "Absolutely not!" Panoyan said. "He twisted the evidence against me."

Brian tried Dave Patterson's name. Again no. "He took my words out of context at the bond hearing!"

Charlie Vaughan was the worst suggestion of all. "He wanted to put me in the electric chair!" he railed.

Then Panoyan had a great idea.

"But I'd talk to somebody like your dad."

Brian played coy at the suggestion. "Well, I don't know. I'd have to ask him," he said. He didn't let on just then that his dad would be overjoyed to get involved. Although Brian had since grown up, his juvenile pride in his dad as hero had never diminished. Truly, he thought, who better than my dad could interrogate someone to find out if they were telling the truth? He was the world's best in catching liars. Brian had learned early in life never to challenge him.

Meanwhile, he looked up at the defense attorneys. How

unorthodox can you get? thought Dave Vinikoor. A first-degree murder defendant sitting down and discussing his story with the prosecutor's dad.

Paul Stark, the former prosecutor from The Bronx, had known of Brian's dad, Thomas Cavanagh, Jr. He remembered him as an investigator of the highest quality. He thought it was a fabulous idea. So did everyone else.

All along, Brian had been talking to his dad about the case. Part of the reason was to make conversation, part to pick his brain because it had been an inordinately tough case. As a result, he figured that his dad right then was up to speed, equivalent to what he would know if he were still a detective squad commander.

Back in the fall of 1989, when Woodroof had pressed Brian to convene a grand jury to indict James Malcolm and Panoyan, Tom Cavanagh had gotten angry. He told his son he was being too nice a guy, there wasn't enough in the case just then, you have to send it back to the police for more work.

When Brian protested that the police thought they had squeezed everything they were going to get out of the case, Tom told him to delay and wait for something to "drop in from left field." Then he suggested tapping Panoyan's phone.

He was right. The gods from left field gave them Dana Williamson's name just a few months later. And Woodroof traced the Crimestoppers tip to Winnie Marsden because of the wiretap.

But the two years since then had not been kind to Tom. He was now seventy-eight. His health was lousy after a lifetime of smoking, and despite hearing aids in both ears, you still had to talk loudly to him. Worse, since the 1990 death of his wife Isabelle, who he worshipped as the finest person he had ever met, he had been depressed. He didn't like living alone.

Brian knew this news would cheer him up.

✦ FORTY

Tom Cavanagh

Why hog all the fun? thought Tom Cavanagh when Brian told him his idea.

Tom had retired from the force in 1975, but had kept friendships with some of his detectives. Whenever they met they remembered the old days in New York City, the days before search warrants and Miranda readings and back when you could deliver a haymaker punch to impress insolent suspects who had little respect for the badge.

And always, always, they talked about their big cases. Dick Maline had helped collar the most famous jewel thief of all, Murph the Surf, for stealing the Star of India. The stone was said to carry a curse; on the day it was returned to the Museum of Natural History, Frank Boccio was there, and watched a man in front of him shoot two people, then Boccio disarmed the man. John Mandel, coach of the U.S. wrestling team at the 1960 Olympics in Rome, was an imposing brawny figure who patrolled Times Square. Chucky West, who arranged security for Burt Reynolds and Frank Sinatra when they traveled, was so close to the family that the Cavanagh kids knew him as—and still called him—Uncle Chucky. (Twenty years before, one of them wondered out loud why he was Jewish, not Irish.) Together, Tom called them the "Over the Hill Gang."

At Tom's request, they all reviewed the public record case file that Brian had copied, then assembled to discuss their theories. "Imagine the bad press if this doesn't turn out right," Tom told them. "A wrong man indicted on a capital offense? A murder suspect released on his own recognizance? This could ruin Brian's career."

338

*   *   *

1964 was the defining year in Tom Cavanagh's life.

Even New York was a more innocent place then. When two young, pretty career girls from good families named Janice Wylie and Emily Hoffert were killed in their third-floor apartment on Manhattan's East Side on August 28, 1963—the same day as Martin Luther King's Freedom March on Washington, and just three months before the JFK assassination—the story truly shocked the big city.

The crime scene was grotesque. Both girls were bound together and soaked in blood. Janice, a twenty-one-year-old researcher for *Newsweek* magazine and daughter of author Max Wylie, was nude and had been stabbed in the heart and abdomen, which exposed her gas-bloated intestines. Emily, a twenty-three-year-old teacher, had a knife wound in the back, and she had almost been decapitated. But the killer had left no fingerprints or traceable physical evidence at the scene.

The murder had happened in Lt. Tom Cavanagh's jurisdiction; as commander of Manhattan's 23rd detective squad, he was therefore in charge of the investigation. Extra officers from all over the city were assigned to work the case, following every lead and rounding up hundreds of suspects. The story stayed in the headlines for months, which put everyone under tremendous pressure to solve it. But after six months of waiting for something from left field, they still had nothing.

Suddenly, in April 1964, Brooklyn police announced the case was solved. They had just taken a confession from a nineteen-year-old black man with a low IQ named George Whitmore. He had been brought to the police station as a possible witness to a rape, but once there, was identified by the victim as her assailant.

Police seized and searched his wallet, which contained a number of photos. One of the detectives present had worked on the Wylie-Hoffert investigation, and looked closely at a black-and-white picture of two girls in an old Packard convertible in a park. He thought the blond looked just like Janice Wylie. On the back of the photo were the words "George—Love, Janice."

They asked Whitmore about it. After a while, they got him to admit that he had stolen the picture from an apartment house on E. 88th Street. There he had stabbed and beaten two girls. He said he carried the picture around so he could brag that the blond was his girlfriend.

When Manhattan detectives working the case heard about the confession, they rushed to the Brooklyn precinct, but cops there wouldn't let them near the suspect. They even taunted that "you Park Avenue detectives couldn't solve the case," but they had. The only information the Manhattan detectives had came from an old friend of Tom's who worked in the Brooklyn precinct and had called to tip him off.

"I know you can't talk out loud right now, but answer me some questions with a yes or no," Cavanagh said. "Is he a burglar?"

"No."

"Is he a junkie?"

"No."

"Does he have any record for sex crimes or assaults?"

"No."

"My god," said Cavanagh. "You've got the wrong fellow."

"Do I go to the gas chamber today for what I did to those girls?" Whitmore asked Brooklyn cops after an all-night grilling. But in court later that day, he recanted. He said the police had coerced his sixty-one-page statement by beating and threatening him.

As soon as Manhattan detectives saw the transcript of the confession, they found thirteen "glaring errors" in what Whitmore had said. One of them was the sex act he said he had performed on Janice Wylie. It was generally known to police working the case that a sex act had been done to Wylie, but that specific act was known only to the inner circle. In fact, Whitmore had confessed in detail to a sex act different than the one actually done to Wylie.

When the confession was released to the press, all thirteen of the glaring errors had been deleted.

Still, New York City's chief of detectives told the press, "We got the right guy. No question about it."

On close reading, Whitmore's confession appeared prompted and spoon-fed by police. What gives confessions credibility is information that only the killer would know. That was absent.

Worse, the Brooklyn detectives gave the photo to Manhattan cops to show to the murdered girls' relatives and friends so that they could confirm their identities. None of them confirmed it.

That day, the *New York Herald Tribune* wrote: "One of the reasons authorities were certain they had the right man was this: On the suspect they found a snapshot of Miss Wylie which had been stolen from her apartment, police said."

Tom's sergeant, Bill Brent, wanted to raise hell that Brooklyn had the wrong man, but Tom told him to cool his heels. They didn't have any proof. But both men swore they were not going to let Whitmore go to the electric chair.

Only a few others in New York agreed with them: three detectives and two assistant district attorneys. The seven of them took upon themselves the responsibility of proving the rest of the New York City Police Department wrong.

Cavanagh reasoned that if they could prove the real identities of the girls in the photo, Whitmore's confession would be blown apart. But first, the crime lab established that the love message from Janice on the back of the picture was neither the dead girls' nor Whitmore's handwriting.

The challenge was to find the unidentified park where the picture was taken. For a while, detectives searched the entire country. Desperate, they asked Columbia University's botany department if they could identify the location from the foliage. Anywhere in the northeast, they said.

Next they tried state forest wardens and rangers. One thought he recognized the spot—near Wildwood, New Jersey.

Cavanagh recognized the reference to Wildwood immediately. Whitmore had said, early on in his talks with Brooklyn cops, that he had found the photo looking through the city dump next to the junkyard his father owned in Wildwood. Brooklyn cops hadn't believed him.

Cavanagh rushed his team to Wildwood. Police there identified the spot in the photo as in Belle Plain State Park, just outside of town.

They even found the exact spot where the picture had been snapped. Police said it was a popular picnic place for local schoolkids, so investigators showed the photo to teachers at Wildwood High School. One recognized one of the girls as Arlene Franco.

"Where did you *ever* get that?" said Franco when they showed it to her. She knew George Whitmore only as a dental patient in the office where she worked as a receptionist. She had no idea how he had gotten the picture.

Police solved that question when they found the boy who had snapped the photograph. He had thrown it out just before moving to Baltimore, a month before the murder. From his garbage can it would have gone to the city dump—right next to Whitmore's father's place, and just where Whitmore said he found it.

It had never been in Janice Wylie's apartment.

Two days later, a New York junkie named Nathan "Jimmy" Delaney told Patty Lappin—another of Tom's detectives—that Whitmore was the wrong guy for the Wylie-Hoffert murders. A twenty-two-year-old junkie friend of his named Ricky Robles had told him "he had iced two women during a burglary."

Delaney, himself facing murder charges, said that Robles had told him he had entered the apartment through a kitchen window and grabbed a knife when one of the girls heard him. He took Janice into Emily's bedroom, had her undress, then Emily walked in the front door. Janice coolly explained that she was being raped, and Robles lunged for Emily, knocking off her thick glasses.

"You won't get away with this," Emily spat. "I got a good look at you while my glasses were still on."

That's when Robles decided he had to kill both girls, Delaney said.

Robles tied up the girls, said a prayer, then took a thick glass soda bottle in each hand and clubbed both over the head. That explanation of trauma corresponded with the medical examiner's report. Delaney said Robles did it because he had been out of jail a month and didn't want to go back on violating probation for burglary.

On interrogation, Robles told Cavanagh, "I went to pull a lousy burglary and I wound up killing two girls." He was arrested and convicted of murder. Whitmore was cleared within days of Robles's arrest.

A Manhattan assistant district attorney told the newspapers, "I am positive that the police prepared the confession for

Whitmore. I am also sure that the police were the ones who gave Whitmore all the details of the killings that he recited.''

For bucking the entire police force, Tom Cavanagh made a lot of enemies. A friend of his wasn't joking when he suggested at a Brooklyn policeman's dinner that he have someone taste his food.

''Up until that case, I thought only guilty people went to jail,'' Cavanagh said.

Afterward, the New York *Daily News* told the tale in a story headlined: ''The Trees Said: 'Not Guilty.'

''New York detectives, scenting an injustice, ranged the country, hunting a missing park. When they found it, 'confessed killer' George Whitmore was out of the woods.''

Later, the *Daily News* described Cavanagh as an honorable, heroic figure. ''In the sweaty, profane world of homicide detectives, he stood out as a tall, austere figure who never cursed and used courtesy instead of muscle.'' That was his trademark. It earned him a nickname: ''The Velvet Whip.''

The *Marcus-Nelson Murders* script described Theo Kojak very similarly to Cavanagh: ''He is tall and muscular. He gives the impression of having seen and done everything. It is an extraordinary mixture of toughness, forged by a life of what he has seen, and gentleness and sensitivity. It is the picture of the face of a man in conflict with himself.''

The movie's publicity writers called the story ''an indictment of criminal procedures and the structures of justice in our society.''

The reason for the movie's success was its theme of questioning authority; in fact, this was authority—in the person of Kojak—questioning itself.

It was also about the stench of guilt.

As Tom drove his red Cadillac to Dave Vinikoor's law office to meet Panoyan for the first time, he felt an old thrill, that he was back in business doing the work he loved. It had been a while, but what counted in detective work was experience. In fifty years of investigative work, he had seen an awful lot. But every time you thought you'd seen it all, you see something new.

Vinikoor, Stark, and Brian stayed in the room with the two men at first, then left them alone. ''Don't beat him,'' Vinikoor admonished the old man. Both Tom and Panoyan laughed.

Panoyan was genuinely excited to meet Tom and told him that he considered what he was doing a great favor.

At first Tom just wanted to strike up a friendship; he knew Chuck needed a friend. They talked about their fathers. Panoyan said he learned about doing good deeds from his father, who was still dedicating his life to giving prisoners solace. Tom said his father was his role model, too. When Tom was a teenager his dad had him pledge he wouldn't drink alcohol until he was twenty-one. Out of respect for his dad he'd kept the promise his whole life—perhaps he was the only Irish cop in New York who didn't drink.

"Will you pray for me?" Panoyan asked abruptly. Of course, said Tom.

Feeling a bit like a priest hoping for a catharsis, Tom told Chuck how much he admired him for keeping silent so long to protect his family. "In my book, that makes you a hero," he said.

"Do you think so?" Panoyan asked, valuing his praise.

"But now the next heroic thing to do is tell me everything you know," Tom said. "The truth will always stand up. You have nothing to worry about if you tell the truth."

Panoyan repeated again how nervous he was about talking, but Tom assured him that he had never lost a witness before, "and we're not going to lose you. We can protect you in ways I can't explain," he said, and Panoyan believed in him, the voice of authority.

Tom's assignment was to see if he could shake Panoyan into making inconsistent statements—a sure sign of fiction— then trapping him.

For the moments Brian had watched, he thought the process breathtaking, an art form. Panoyan was meandering and disorganized, while his dad was incisive. This man is not chronologically in his prime, Brian thought, but he still knows all the tricks how to catch his subject off guard, and his recall is as good as it had always been.

Tom skillfully loaded his questions, then asked them again from different angles. Each time, Panoyan told the intricate facts the same way. Afterwards, Brian debriefed his dad. Tom's opinion was Panoyan was truthful.

"If he was part and parcel of the operation, he would have gone home and they would have had an unsolved homicide that night," he told Brian. "All he would have to remember is that he went to the Deckers and delivered venison and went home. He would have nothing else to worry about.

"So the story—although there might have been some inconsistencies when you first read it, an element of perhaps stupidity—when you analyze the whole story, it was true.

"As long as Panoyan kept quiet, they had it made. Rodney was never involved and Dana would have blamed everything at trial on poor Panoyan."

After the meeting, Panoyan suggested in a nice way that maybe his dad was getting a little senile.

"He keeps asking me the same questions over and over," he said.

Brian laughed out loud, but kept to himself the method that Panoyan had seen as madness.

Tom and Chuck met four more times, the last with Darla Panoyan present. He asked Chuck if he could talk with her alone, and he consented.

"Did you believe his story?" Tom asked.

"Not from the first moment," she said. "It was stupid, it was crazy. I knew he wasn't capable of committing that horrible crime and there must be more to it. He kept telling me, 'Don't worry, I know what I'm doing is correct.' "

Tom asked Darla what she thought of Chuck as a husband and a father.

"He's a wonderful husband and father. The only thing he does is he plays a lot of jokes on us."

✦ FORTY-ONE

When Charles Panoyan finally consented to testify before the grand jury, Brian Cavanagh and Charlie Vaughan spent the summer preparing to bring a new case. They themselves could have dropped charges against Panoyan, but instead they decided to let the grand jury choose if he should be a defendant or a witness at an upcoming trial. If they believed him, they could then indict Rodney Williamson and bring new extortion charges against Dana.

In the meantime, two more jailhouse snitches came forward. In a brief sworn statement, Seth Penalver said Dana Williamson was now threatening Brian Cavanagh himself:

"He was telling me about the case. What happened [was] three people got shot, a thirty-month-old kid in the back of the head. He said one of his co-defendants [was] in the house the time the crime happened. He told me it was for drugs and money. He told me a .22 pistol was used. It was his brother-in-law's gun. He said his brother-in-law is testifying against him. He said his brother-in-law never gave the gun up because he knew he used it in that crime, so he got rid of it, then his brother-in-law left [the] state not to testify against him.

"Also he told me his state's attorney drives a white Ford Taurus and also a gold minivan. He said he's got both tag numbers. He said he's gonna get somebody to get that motherfucker. He watches him every morning park his vehicle on top of the parking garage. You can see the parking garage from 6-C-1."

* * *

In fact, Brian did drive a minivan, but it wasn't gold. Of course, Penalver also said Dana told him that the person hiding the pistol was his brother-in-law, not his brother.

Then, in July 1992, Juan DeCastro, who had been arrested for grand theft auto, called Dave Patterson to say that he knew Rodney Williamson from the street. He had seen him at a friend's house in Davie where he used to buy dope. Rodney had been slumming there for a few days in mid-December 1991.

DeCastro said his friends Rick and Sheila introduced him to Rodney. Later in the day, after smoking a couple joints and drinking beer, Rodney asked Juan if he would drive to a bar to play pool.

"We started talking, and he told me that he has come from Colorado because he had some problem down here and he stayed up there for a while. He told me that him and his brother went to rob this house and in the process of going to rob this house, there was a shoot-out and they killed this woman and shot a couple people in the house.

"And then he had to leave to go to Colorado because he got afraid and the brother got arrested."

DeCastro said Rodney told him he had stayed outside of the house, entering only once because he knew something was wrong.

"Then he came back out to the car, then he left. The brother came out and they left together, and they took his brother to a shopping center and dropped him off in the shopping center, close to where the house was."

Just before the grand jury was ready to convene, Dave Patterson found Eddie Roberts—the real Eddie Roberts. He was living in a small town in north Florida called Branford, between Gainesville and Lake City.

He had been friends with Dana, Rodney, and Panoyan. Panoyan "wouldn't hurt nobody," he told Cavanagh, but Dana and Rodney were a different story. Dana used to show Eddie his gun collection, which included a .22 pistol he said he had bought from a friend named Vern.

The brothers commonly talked about stabbing, robbing, and Ninja things, he said. Sometimes, Dana would leave wearing his Ninja outfit and come back with things that were obviously not his.

Roberts baby-sat Dana's kids many nights. He thought he might even have been at Dana's house "that night"—the night of the murder.

Also, Roberts said he bumped into Panoyan at a feed store just before Panoyan left for Ohio to see Dana. Chuck was "really scared," he said.

The press at last got wind of the story on August 4, a few days before the grand jury was going to convene. Neither the prosecutors nor Panoyan's attorneys would comment to the *Fort Lauderdale Sun-Sentinel*, leaving only a quote from Charlie Johnson. He said he assumed Panoyan was going to testify against his client, but "It's news to us. It's really very very strange."

Further, the story read: "Defendants charged with first degree murder are rarely allowed to post bail, much less be released on their own recognizance. Panoyan's codefendant, Williamson, is still in jail being held without bond."

Two days later, Rodney Williamson told the paper he was a target of the new investigation, and that he had accepted an invitation to testify.

The *Sun-Sentinel* wrote:

> "The police have been investigating me since they arrested my brother in Ohio" two years ago, said Rodney Williamson, 37. "It's got me really nervous. It looks like they're going to railroad me and stick me in prison, too.
>
> "Dana never planned the crime with me. He never admitted it to me. I really don't know anything about the case, except what they've told me when they questioned me."

The *Miami Herald* picked up on the Kojak angle. Their headline was "Real 'Kojak' helps son solve tough Davie case; Ex-cop persuades defendant to talk."

The grand jury convened on August 12, 1992. Brian Cavanagh brought Panoyan, Eddie Roberts, Bob and Clyde Decker, Ginger Kostige, Patrick O'Brien, Steve Luchak, and

Jan Dubin—one of Panoyan's friends who he had also delivered venison to that night.

Charles Panoyan got an invitation too, but the deck was stacked more in his favor. While they were at it, prosecutors also offered an invitation to Dana, but he refused.

When Rodney Williamson testified, Brian's strategy, which his dad helped him form, was to goad Rodney into making a mistake or at least let the grand jury see the violent side of his personality. To provoke it, Brian knew he would need to confront Rodney directly and loudly.

Brian's most valuable tool was Rodney's own writings that were in police evidence. Brian began by asking Rodney what a "stunner" was, which he had written about in a story.

"A nine-volt battery-operated powered [tool], commonly referred to as a zapper. You hold it in your hand and touch somebody with it, and you press the trigger and it stuns them," he said.

"What did Dana buy that for?"

"He, when he bought the zapper, he told me he intended to rob somebody with it, and I told him I didn't want to know about it first off, and second off, if he did anything that stupid, he would more than likely get caught. He was concerned about his wife abusing his children, and if he got caught and went to jail, she would then wind up with the children by default."

Referring to Rodney's letters, Cavanagh asked him, "Did you say: 'I'm capable of keeping silent, but will tell the exact truth if asked for it, except when I'm not directly involved, and I then extemporize it may be hearsay, therefore rumor, and rumor might not be truth, therefore not worth a mention in the question of truth?' "

"Yes, sir."

"There are a lot of words, and I don't really understand them, Mr. Williamson." Cavanagh's voice raised. "What are you talking about? Are you talking about evading the truth and giving evasive answers?"

"No, sir. Only if I was not involved. If you went out and committed a crime, and I was not involved and you told me later on I committed a crime; if someone asked me, Did he commit a crime? I would say yes, he admitted to me he did it. If they asked me, Do you know for certain that he committed a crime? I would have to say no, it is hearsay because he told me and I wasn't there.''

That got Cavanagh louder and more dramatic. ''Well, if you were outside of a house, and your brother went inside the house and stabbed a woman and shot three people including a two[-and-a-half-]year-old boy in cold blood and you were outside the house, but didn't see it happen, you wouldn't have to give him up, would you?''

That kindled the first defensive reaction from Rodney.

''No, now are you going to stand up and start screaming at me? I am going to stand up and I am going to tell you point-blank that if I knew anything about that fucking crime, I would have left Florida before Dana. I would have left everything I owned—sold or given it away or thrown it away—and I would have left and not let them have a forwarding address for you guys to follow me right to Colorado.''

The tone was set. Cavanagh wanted to box and Rodney only knew how to brawl. Brian did not flinch. He continued: ''Do you remember Eddie Roberts being over at your house when you were cavorting around in a Ninja outfit, along with your brother, talking about stabbing somebody?''

''I was not talking about stabbing anyone. We got Ninja outfits in the mail. Dana had paid for them, and had me order them because he didn't want Sandy to know he was getting them. I had them delivered to a post box that I had a mail drop at, the next street over. Eddie Roberts was over the day we got them. We was showing them to him.''

Cavanagh asked if Rodney was concerned about Dana because of his background. Rodney said he was.

''Were you aware that Dana was a convicted child killer?''

''I was aware Dana was in trouble when he was rather young.''

''What did you think about it?''

''Well, Dana always said that he did not do it.''

''Did you ever question him about it?''

''Yes, I did. Sometimes he would say he did not do it, and sometimes he would be talking to other people, and he would brag that he did do it.''

''Did he tell you—as he did the police—that he did it just for fun?''

"He never told me that. He told me that somebody had slipped some LSD on him, and he had been out drinking that weekend and he ran away from the Nova Living and Learning Center with another guy."

Realizing that both Williamson brothers had decided to show each other in the worst possible light in order to save themselves, Cavanagh decided to take advantage. He asked, "Why would Dana say that you were present at the scene of the crime?"

"I believe you are referring to some conversations he had with some of his cellmates that you told me about."

"Yes. Are you close to your brother Dana?"

"At one time I thought I was. At this point in my life, I am not sure I could trust him."

"Do you have your reasons not to trust Dana now?"

"Well, it looks like to me that if Dana was involved in this crime that he has more or less brought me too close to my being involved in it myself, because I was living with him at the time. I forget which one it was, but it was one of my sisters who said, well, if Dana was involved in it then Rodney knows about it, which is not exactly the truth."

From here on in, Cavanagh decided to see where he could get by provoking Rodney. He began by asking what Dana was going to do with the papers that had Donna and Bob Decker's signatures on it.

"I don't know. I have never seen that paper."

"You have never seen that paper. Did Dana ever tell you about that paper?"

"No, Dana never told me about that paper and I have never seen it."

"Did Dana tell you that the Deckers had come into some money?"

"Dana never discussed the Deckers with me."

"Where did Dana get the information that the Deckers were into drugs?"

"Dana never discussed the Deckers with me. How many times do I have to say it? Do you have wax in your ears? Dana never discussed the Deckers with me."

"Do you remember putting the gun in Charles Panoyan's face, in the driveway of the Decker house?"

"I have never put a gun in Chuck Panoyan's face, or anybody else's face."

"Do you recall your brother Dana putting a gun in his face?"

"I don't recall Dana ever putting a gun in anybody's face."

"Do you recall Dana saying to Charles Panoyan, 'I am going in and Rodney will be watching you through the window, and there is somebody watching your home and is going to take care of your family, if you try anything?' "

"I never recall those words. I was never with Dana when he had those conversations."

"Were you standing outside by Panoyan's truck, when Panoyan came out of that house?"

"I was never at the Decker house."

"Which hand was the gun in when you confronted Panoyan?"

"I was never confronting Panoyan with a gun."

Cavanagh kept this up until Rodney finally exploded.

"How many times do I have to tell you I was never there? You guys have been hounding me. You have been harassing me. You have been making insinuations and innuendoes and threatening me for the last year and a half. Every time you talk to me, you are always telling me, well, if we thought you were involved in it, you would be beside your brother in jail. And then if I don't say what you want me to say, then you say we are going to charge you part and parcel with the crime too. If I wasn't there, how in the fuck am I going to tell you what happened?"

Unfazed, Cavanagh asked about the content of a book called *Deathly Karate Blows,* which Rodney had ordered from Asian World of Martial Arts.

"It is a book that describes the damages possible at approximately what amount of force, anything from just disabling a person momentarily from two to five minutes to internally injuring them to a possible death point."

"What are zip strips?"

"They are nylon slip ties that are used mostly for tying things together."

"What kind of things?"

"Wood, pipe, wire."

"Human hands?"

"They can be used for that. I believe they are called police riot cuffs. There were some in my camper that me and Dana found on a construction site that were approximately forty inches long. They were used for tying big bundles of electrical wiring together."

"Did you write this?: 'The nearest was the third, so I went there and I parked a block away and put on a set of cammo Ninja togs and stuffed the gloves and hood in a jacket pocket. I took a small backpack and set out to do a recon of the house on a bicycle I had mounted on a rack on the camper. I rode past the house and hid the bike in an alley, then removed the jacket and put the hood and gloves on. I crept down the alley into the backyard of the target house, listening at a window in shrubbery I heard some drug deals go down and decided to hit them.

" 'I zip stripped the people in the house and removed all the ammo, guns and cash from the premises. The drugs I piled in the front room neatly and left out the backyard to the bicycle. After getting back to the camper, I drove past the next house, as I figured it was closer and followed about the same routine. I hit three houses that night, and called the Crimestoppers number for the area from a pay phone where I looked up a camp where I could hook up for a day or two. When I woke up, I checked the gun and ammo I took from these drug dealers and put away the ones I was not going to use for hitting them—' "

"Yes, I wrote that."

" '—After I rode the cycle to a restaurant for my breakfast, I went back and counted the cash I got. I got $25,000 in the first house, $20,000 in the second, and another $15,000 from the third. I decided I had a huge grubstake and would not hit the rest of the places, and at a pay phone on the other side of town would be a good place to call in for the rest of the info I had on the gang that I hit. I started a bank account with about $15,000, and applied for a MasterCard and 24 hour card, and had several good reasons for looting the drug houses, and I had with me two Smith & Wessons and a .380 pistol which I took from the man who followed me into the restroom at the truck stop—' "

"Yes, I wrote that."

" '—I figured he would tell his pals my description and would be looking for me, and would tie me in with the houses.'

"Did you write that?"

"Yes."

Cavanagh then showed Rodney a crime scene picture of the bed in the Decker master bedroom. "What is that item on that bed?"

"It is a zip tie."

"That's the thing you use to zip strip people with?"

"Yes."

Totally frustrated, Rodney's answers to Brian Cavanagh's questions became even more aggressive. When Cavanagh asked him where he kept his .22 pistol in the Norwood, Ohio, house, Rodney retorted, "I never carried a gun. I don't need a gun. If I want to threaten somebody I can hurt you with my bare hands. I don't need a gun."

Brian shook off the threat and continued. "Did you also write: 'But remember that a Ninja wears a mask to conceal his identity from anyone who may know him.' "

"Yes. That's the whole theory behind the mask of a Ninja."

"So when you bought these Ninja outfits, you were taking some of your fantasies and putting them into reality?"

"No, sir. When I bought the Ninja outfits, I had the intention to go hunting with them. Have you ever hunted with a crossbow, or a bow and arrow? You have to get right close and personal with the deer before you can get one."

"You have to get up close and personal to that deer?"

"If I wanted to get close and personal, the best way to do it—like with you, for instance—if I wanted to get close and personal with you, I would do it out in the hall out there, and I wouldn't need a mask. I would walk up quickly from behind you and I would get you walking by. Nobody would know a thing until I was already twenty feet down the hall. The only way somebody would know is if you collapsed to the floor."

"Did you ever show Virginia Kostige any of your hunting results?"

"No, not that I know of."

"Did you ever see Dana show Virginia Kostige any possum that he had skinned?"

"No. Oh, yes. He had a possum hatband, yes he did."

"But you don't know if Dana would have threatened to skin a child alive?"

"No, I don't."

"You never heard Dana make that threat?"

"I never heard Dana make a threat similar to that, no."

"Similar to that?"

"I have heard—I have heard him make threats, to break people's arms and ribs. I have heard him threaten to break people's legs, to break people's arms and break people's faces. I have heard him threaten to break people's ribs so that they would remember every time they took a breath for the next couple of months. People would usually get in his face and bother him to death like that, you know, like threaten to take his money from him by not paying for a job already completed. I would rather break your ribs than tear your house down after we had built it, you know. That's the way he thought."

Outside the grand jury room, Rodney blew up again. He had suggested that he might be carrying a tape recorder, so Cavanagh ordered the bailiffs to search him. Rodney cursed Cavanagh loudly.

"I could kill somebody with one finger," Rodney told the *Sun-Sentinel*. "What do I need a gun for? I could kill somebody with an ink pen. What do I need a knife for? I could use an ice pick. I could use lots of methods.

"But I never heard of the crime until the police came to me in Colorado."

The next day, August 13, the grand jury returned the indictment Brian Cavanagh and Charlie Vaughan had wanted: seventeen counts against Dana and Rodney Williamson, including murder in the first degree and three counts of attempted murder in the first degree. They refused to re-indict Charles Panoyan for anything.

Immediately, Davie Police sent four officers to arrest Rodney Williamson. They found him in Davie at Palm Haven mobile home park, working lawn maintenance and riding a tractor. They arrested him without incident.

The Miami Herald's headline the next day was "A 'Kojak' ending: Murder defendant cleared."

"He's been cleared by the grand jury of any criminal charges," was all Dave Vinikoor could tell the *Sun-Sentinel* for print. For he and Paul Stark, it was the remarkable conclusion to two years of brilliant work.

✦ FORTY-TWO

The case would not come to trial for almost another year and a half.

I researched old newspaper clips and found the real beginning to the story: Christmas Day, 1969, the day Rodney Williamson said his mother was killed in a car crash. The Williamson family would never be the same.

After a Christmas dinner and home movies for four of her five children and friends from her job, Ella Williamson loaded up her VW van to take her guests home. All of the kids except Vernon went along for the ride.

Along the way she decided to stop for cigarettes. Conditions were foggy that evening, and before they made it to the convenience store a car ran a stop sign and slammed into the driver's side of the van, knocking it down an embankment. The van flipped over three times before it stopped.

All the kids were pinned in their seats, crying and moaning in pain—except for the oldest, fourteen-year-old Rodney, the only one wearing his seat belt and therefore the only one whose injury was slight. A guest—twenty-seven-year-old Myra Goulding—was thrown through the windshield and out of the van and lay in the middle of the intersection, the bones of her face broken.

Charlie Williamson arrived to find his wife pinned against the steering wheel. She was conscious at the scene, but died at the hospital an hour later of multiple chest injuries.

Dawna, twelve, had a head injury. Renee, thirteen, had a fractured pelvis and a broken back in two places. But Dana, ten, was the most seriously hurt of the children. The impact had crushed the front seat, trapping him, and the rescue squad had to cut through metal to free him. He was bleeding from his mouth and ears, and paramedics couldn't get a blood pressure reading from him.

"I went into the emergency room with him. He was crying. He's only a little boy," Charlie Williamson, crying himself, told *The Miami Herald*.

Dana was bleeding internally and needed emergency surgery to remove his spleen and repair his torn liver. He stayed in a coma for about two weeks. "The doctors told me they didn't give him much of a chance. I was shocked," Charlie said.

Yet another jailhouse snitch came forward in May 1993. Edward Aragones said Dana Williamson first approached him because he noticed that he liked to read books.

"I would read a lot of books in the cell, and Dana Williamson read a lot of books. And the way we came in contact with each other is, he approached me and asked me about the book I was reading. How was the plot, what it was about. I told him about it.

"I asked him about the book he was reading. I was also into studying my Bible in the day room of the cell I was placed in. And Dana Williamson one day approached me, and he sat at the table next to me and he asked me if I had thought God had forgiven me for my sin, the crime I had committed. I told him I believe so.

"That's why I'm praying to God to forgive me for my sins that I committed. His eyes started to water as he was talking to me. And he said to me, 'I hope God can forgive me for killing that kid'—I'm sorry—'for shooting that kid in the head.'

"And I said to him, 'What are you charged with?' I was in shock.

"He said, 'I'm charged with murder.'

"I said, 'What did you do?'

"He said, 'I shot a kid in the head, I shot the mother in the head, and I shot the father in the head.' Or he said, 'I shot the kid in the head, I shot a man and a woman in the head.' I don't recollect whether it was the mother and father, or man and woman. He said, 'I tied them up to a chair and shot them.' And he says, 'I hope God can forgive me for that.'

"I asked him, 'Did the kid die?' He says no, the kid survived, the father survived. But he says the mother died.

"And then he told me, 'The devil must have gotten into me for me to do something like that. I can't believe I did something like that.'

"He says, 'Now they are trying to give me the chair.' I told him, 'Well, let's pray about it.' And he bowed his head, and I bowed my head. I said a prayer for us, for me and him, and then we said the Our Father. We closed the prayer with the Our Father.

"After we had closed the prayer, Dana told me, 'The state doesn't have anything on me. They don't have any evidence.' He says, 'I've been here for two years now, and they have nothing on me.' He says, 'I'm just going to ride it out, and the case will eventually deteriorate.'

"Then later on the same day, he came back to me and told me, 'Don't tell nobody what I told you. Because there is a lot of snitches here, and they can always go back to the state and tell the state what I said.'

" 'Don't worry, I won't tell nobody what you told me,' that's what I said.

"One day we were sitting at the table and we were joking around, goofing off. He got upset and he said, 'I'll stab you.' I told him, 'You are not going to stab me.'

"He went up to his room, he came down with a pen, and he stabbed me in the shoulder. And I looked at him, I was shocked because my shoulder was bleeding. And I says, 'I'm going to tell the guard.'

" 'You don't have to tell the guard, I will tell the guard I did it.'

"He started kicking on the door like a madman. The guard came and said, 'What is wrong?'

" 'I want to be moved. I want you to move me out. I'm going to go nuts if you don't get me out.'

"Then I told the guard this man just stabbed me. And the deputy said, 'I'm going to have to write you a DR [disciplinary report], Dana Williamson. And you too, for horseplaying.'

"I says, 'I wasn't horseplaying, the man just came up to me and stabbed me for no reason.'

"The deputy asked the inmates what happened, they told him that Dana had stabbed me, he snapped. He lost it, he lost his mind and just stabbed me. Then they moved him, they separated us."

Aragones said he had only seen Williamson once after that, and that time Williamson waved at him like they were best friends.

"He's a very intelligent individual, but at the same time, he can be like cynical, like mean, you know? Like cold, real cold. Like distant, far away from reality.

"Like when he stabbed me with the pen, it was like he had a look in his eyes. Like, you know, kill. You know, like, I'm going to kill you."

One of the last investigative things Brian Cavanagh did in the case prior to trial was to send the cowboy hat to the FBI lab in Washington. In the three years since scrapings from the hatband had been tested, unsuccessfully, for DNA comparisons, the technology had improved.

If it worked, the trial would be a slam dunk. But in the fall of 1993, the result came back: even employing the new method, the sample was still insufficient to provide any DNA at all.

IV

THE TRIAL

✦ FORTY-THREE

The trial opened January 28, 1994, on the eighth floor of the Broward County Courthouse in Fort Lauderdale, Florida. Earlier, Rodney Williamson's attorney, Tom Cazel, had moved to separate his trial from Dana's, and Judge Richard Eade granted the motion.

The first day was remarkable for a number of reasons, but the biggest was Dana Williamson himself.

I had seen a number of pictures of him, and he had looked totally different in each set. At age fifteen—the time of the Wagner murder—he looked like a child of ten. Out of prison in the 1980s, he looked like a shaggy longhair. He looked thin in his booking photo in Norwood, unkempt and straggly like a street bum. Just months later, in his BSO booking photo, he was heavier and looked confident, like a career criminal.

Now, almost four years after that, his appearance had turned back to childlike. His hair was short, and his build pudgy. He wore a red plaid cowboy shirt with pearl buttons, a white undershirt visible underneath, and tortoise shell-rimmed glasses. He was clean shaven and his skin was pale.

He didn't look like a murderer.

In his opening statement, Brian Cavanagh wanted the eight-woman, six-man jury (which included two alternates) to understand that Dana's courtroom appearance was worth little in this case. While Williamson chewed gum and exhibited the poker face he would keep all trial, Cavanagh showed a range of emotions rarely seen this side of the Old Bailey—or the Old Globe.

For the day, Cavanagh was a cross between a Greek philosopher and Clarence Darrow. He looked more like Darrow, his open jacket revealing leather suspenders.

As he previewed the facts that the state would bring in the case, he was soft, then he was loud and outraged. He walked back and forth all over the courtroom, twice hulking over the defendant, then played directly to the jurors, even stooping his big frame so he could drop closer to their eye level. His face was animated, especially when he put his finger behind his own right ear, approximating the spot where baby Carl Decker was shot.

Tears rolled (which he had wanted to fight), and he had to clear his throat when he talked about his eighty-year-old dad and how he had played an important role in clearing an innocent man from a charge that had come uncomfortably close to putting him in the electric chair. Thirty years before, as a New York City police lieutenant, he had done something similar; which Brian had watched as an impressionable adolescent.

Williamson would have gotten away with the murder, Cavanagh said, if not for three mistakes: He left his cowboy hat and belt at the scene; he opened his mouth while in jail; and he didn't kill the only witness who knew who he was—Charles Panoyan.

Steve Hammer and Charlie Johnson decided to split up their duties: Hammer would handle the entire trial, and Johnson would do the separate penalty phase if their client lost at trial. In penalty phase, the same jury would have the option of recommending life in prison or death by electrocution; the judge would then make the final decision. The theory in splitting the lawyers' responsibilities in that way was so that if things came to a penalty phase, the jury might appreciate a new face.

Hammer's opening statement harped on reasonable doubt: The Deckers hadn't been able to identify Dana as the gunman; cowboy hats in Davie couldn't be more common; and the DNA test of the hat hadn't concluded that it was Dana's. In fact, there wasn't any hard evidence linking Dana to the crime at all, he said.

But most of all, the state made a mistake by making a

"deal with the devil" when they changed Panoyan from a defendant to a witness.

"Do you know why Chuck Panoyan's here?" he asked the jury. "Because he gets to sit in this chair"—pointing to the witness chair—"rather than what the state was threatening to do to him: put him in a different chair, one hooked up to about a thousand volts of electricity."

Panoyan got off the hook by telling the state what they wanted to hear, he said. Neither Panoyan nor his family was ever in danger.

Hammer admitted he wouldn't be able to compete with Brian Cavanagh's theatrical style, but what was important were the facts—and the state's lack of them.

"No matter how eloquent they are, how dramatic he [Cavanagh] is, how soft he talks, how loud he talks, it's not going to prove that Dana Williamson was there. Because it wasn't him. He wasn't there."

The end of the day was just as good. When Brian Cavanagh walked out of the courtroom, he spat "Psychopath!"—referring to Williamson's lack of emotion during his opening argument.

A few minutes later I walked back into the courtroom to fetch my camera bag. I had to knock on the window because the bailiffs had locked the doors. Everyone was out except for them and the defendant.

To my total surprise, Dana struck up a conversation with me. "How much is Brian Cavanagh paying you for those pictures?" he asked. I had taken quite a few.

I asked if he would pose for a picture. "No," he said. "I'll pose for you when I get out on the street."

He wanted to know who I was, and, I believe, show me that he was intelligent. I thought of Patrick O'Brien and Steve Luchak and realized I didn't want to be a witness. I also knew that had his attorneys been present, there wouldn't have been any conversation between us. After a few moments of small talk, I excused myself.

Moments later, I met Bob Decker for the first time. The defense had invoked the "Rule," which kept witnesses who hadn't yet testified from watching the proceedings. Decker would not testify for another three days; afterward, he could sit in on the rest of the trial.

He was a short, muscular blond-haired fellow, born in Cooperstown, New York, and he still had a Yankee sound. He invited me to feel the depression in the back of his head, where he had been shot, and I did. It felt like part of his bone was missing.

He had a number of unexpected things to tell me. He now believed that Chuck Panoyan was telling the truth all along. "Chuck didn't have the brains to pull off something like this," he said. Nor would he hurt anybody.

He described some Three Stooges slapstick that they pulled on each other at work sites. Bob sounded like Moe and Chuck sounded like Curly or Larry. More than once, Bob painted a horizontal on Chuck's face. If Chuck used the portable john, Bob would tip it over. Another time, Bob snatched the john with a forklift and raised it four stories above the ground. Inside, Chuck screamed for mercy.

Equally big news to me was that the previous night, the prosecution had played for Bob the audiotape of Dana's statement made on the day he was arrested in May 1990. After hearing it, Decker was now prepared to identify Dana's voice as the gunman's.

The next day of trial was a Monday, and I met Bob's new wife, Deanna (pronounced "De-na").

Deanna had met Bob about a year and a half after the incident, and married him in August 1991. She was anxious to tell me the family's progress in recovering from their wounds.

Bob still had problems in his gait. At parties he used to be mistaken for a drunk, the way he bounced off walls. His balance had since improved.

He also had trouble writing legibly; only recently could he even write a check. His memory was fair, but sometimes he would forget the simplest words.

Clyde was in the hospital and would probably not be able to attend the trial. (Prosecutors got the defense to agree that Clyde could give his testimony on videotape from his hospital bed, which would be shown to the jury.)

Carl's problems were something else. As a little boy now

almost eight, he felt guilty for being shot and losing his mother—as if somehow it was his fault. He was now in counseling at school.

He didn't have any recollection of the event besides what Bob and Deanna had told him. Nor could he remember much about his mother, but he kept her picture in his room. He distinguished between his two moms: "Mom Deanna" and "My mom who's in heaven."

Deanna brought the prosecution a copy of a 1993 psychological evaluation of Carl; they placed it in the case file, which made it a public record. In it, a doctor stated that Carl had recovered physically from his gunshot, aside from deafness in one ear, but he still suffered mental trauma from the shooting.

The doctor felt there were indications that Carl recalled the terrible events of November 4, 1988. He may or may not have witnessed his mother's murder, but he clearly saw his father, grandfather, and himself shot. What he saw may have emanated both in a fear of abandonment and in the violent and brutal themes of his fantasy play, which included death and killing.

Mike Shope, a mutual friend of Bob and Chuck who police interviewed early in the investigation, also came to the trial. He now believed Panoyan's story too; although he hadn't at the beginning.

"Chuck was too stupid to think that the Williamsons would overhear him" when he talked loudly to Charlie Williamson, Shope said. Shope did make for an odd character witness.

When Bob Decker took the stand on February 2, Cavanagh had him talk a little about Chuck Panoyan. They met when Bob was working at the auto shop department of W.T. Grant; Panoyan would come in all the time to buy used oil for his pickup truck, which leaked the oil almost as soon as he added it. The joke was—of which Panoyan had no idea of at the time—that the used oil Decker sold him was more expensive than new oil.

They became good friends and worked together in construction. Panoyan was a very hard worker, although "he didn't know what he was doing. He was always losing hammers—that was my biggest expense." And he wasn't very good at hammering nails; he'd regularly bend them.

Decker remembered some of the things the gunman said on November 4, 1988: "Nobody will get hurt," soon after he first walked in; "I told you to stay there," after Bob hopped out of the bedroom and into the living room; "Sign this," and "This ain't good enough. Do it again," when he presented Bob the blank paper with lines on it, demanding a signature; and "Cute. *Real* cute," when he discovered Bob's Uzi he kept in the office/closet.

Cavanagh asked if he would recall the gunman's voice if he heard it again.

"I'll never forget it," Bob said.

With a list of those quotes Bob Decker had just attributed to the gunman, Brian Cavanagh asked Judge Eade to order the defendant to read them for Bob Decker.

The request caught the defense flat-footed. They objected; but in a sidebar, Cavanagh showed case law on the subject. It wasn't a violation of defendants' rights against self-incrimination by asking for a voice sample, he said. Judge Eade said he was familiar with the law, and ordered defense counsel to show the prosecutor's script to Williamson.

They did, then let Williamson make his own decision whether or not to read it aloud. With all eyes on him, he whispered to Charlie Johnson: No.

Outside the courtroom, Brian Cavanagh and Charlie Vaughan high-fived each other. "This was the Gettysburg of the trial," said Cavanagh, grinning. "It was a bad fuck-up," said Vaughan. Even had Decker identified Dana's voice as the gunman, the defense at least would have had an argument that Decker wasn't a reliable witness to it five years after, he said. Now the state would be able to refer to his lack of response in closing argument, and the judge could give a special jury instruction based on it.

Inside the courtroom, as everyone filed out, Dana Williamson had put his hand over his face. It was his first change of emotion. The expression on his face said, I'm fucked.

On February 7, Judge Eade made another ruling that hurt the defense's case.

Cavanagh had hoped he could somehow bring to the jury's

attention Dana's prior manslaughter record. Normally, prior convictions or accusations against a defendant are excluded as prejudicial under Florida law, unless the prosecutor can show a very close similarity between the charges.

The issue, called the Williams rule, had arisen two years before in the William Kennedy Smith rape trial in West Palm Beach. The state had wanted to bring testimony alleging that Smith had sexually assaulted a number of other women in the same manner, but the judge excluded it because she said the circumstances were slightly different.

Dana's prior killing of four-year-old Peter Wagner was relevant to this case, Brian argued to Judge Eade outside the presence of the jury, only because he had threatened to murder Panoyan's family. Since Panoyan knew that Dana had killed before, the threat was very believable. That was why Panoyan misled police as to Dana's identity, even before he found out that the Deckers were shot and stabbed, which compounded the believability of the threat.

Cavanagh maintained that mention of the prior act should come out during Patrick O'Brien's testimony. O'Brien was ready to say that Panoyan told him about Dana's past, and that Panoyan was in fear of Dana because of it. It was evidence to prove the extortion count, Cavanagh said.

That brought another torrent of outcry from Steve Hammer. "There is no way this defendant will get a fair trial once the jury hears about his prior manslaughter conviction," he protested.

But Judge Eade ruled that the mention could come in. (Later, he ruled again it could come in through Luchak's and Panoyan's testimonies as well.) The prior conviction was a fact, he said, and the state was bringing it in through testimony, not by introducing the actual case. He also said it was relevant because the admission was allegedly in the defendant's own words.

When O'Brien testified to the point, his words were:

"He [Dana] said he put a gun to his [Panoyan's] head and said, 'I can make your family suffer.' Panoyan knew Dana had killed before and had no problems killing again. He killed a four-year-old with a baseball bat."

← FORTY-FOUR

RENEE WILLIAMSON

After seeing and reading about the Williamson clan, I was least prepared to meet Renee, Dana's oldest sister. She was articulate, intelligent, and gracious—nothing at all of what I expected from a sibling of someone accused of trying to murder six people in his life.

She took the stand as a prosecution witness on February 8. She talked in complimentary terms about her father. He was "an amiable guy, everyone liked him," she said. But when I talked to her afterwards, her story was much different.

It was true, she told me, people did like Charlie Williamson. He made excellent conversation and was good company. Chuck Panoyan was one of his closest friends.

But after the door to his house closed, Charlie Williamson became Mr. Hyde to his children. His idea of discipline was to beat his children until they bled.

Her story added to what Rodney had written in the papers seized from his camper in Norwood.

Renee remembered two horrific incidents above all others. When Dana was about four, Charlie Williamson had Rodney, then eight, watch over him. Dana wandered away while Rodney wasn't paying attention and was picked up by the shovel of a crane operator, who was excavating a lake.

No harm came to Dana, but when Charlie found out about it, he beat Rodney so hard everyone on the block heard him wail. Rodney had to stay out of school two weeks because he had marks all over his body. Renee remembered that period as the first time she became afraid of her father. She also recalled that from then on, Rodney had trouble with authority and school.

Their mother, Ella, had kept Charlie's most brutal instincts at bay, but after her death in the 1969 Christmas Day car accident, Charlie went to pieces. He had five children and no idea how to take care of them.

In the year following, while the children mourned their mother's passing and recovered from their own injuries, Charlie met Terri Rivers and married her. Terri and the Williamson kids didn't get along. Rather than stick up for her new stepchildren, Terri encouraged Charlie to discipline them harder. Meanwhile, her three young children were treated royally in comparison.

Charlie intensified his beatings, and Terri got into the act, too. Before he had used a cowboy belt with studs; now they both used cat o'-nine-tails, bullwhips, horsewhips, and thorny branches Charlie made the kids select. If the switches broke during their beating, the punishment worsened.

The worst episode of all was when Terri accused Dana and Vernon—then ages eleven and eight—of stealing some of her costume jewelry. The boys denied it; they knew better than to even enter their father and stepmother's room. Terri insisted the boys had done it, all the while defending her children, who probably did it, Renee said.

As penalty for not confessing their crime, Charlie beat both Dana and Vernon and padlocked them in a walk-in storage closet with no ventilation, no light, no food or water, and a bucket to use for a bathroom. It was November, but still hot in south Florida, and the house wasn't air-conditioned.

The boys howled, whimpering to be let out. Renee thought her father would keep them in there for just a few hours, but they spent the whole night. At breakfast the next morning, the other kids asked about it, and were told to keep quiet or they would get the same treatment.

That day, Renee and Terri's kids (Rodney and Dawna had since left the house) crawled under the house to find or create a hole where they could slip Dana and Vernon some food and water. The best they could find was a small crack; from there they forced a straw upwards and placed it in a soda bottle filled with water.

That night, Renee waited for her father and Terri to fall asleep so she could attempt a *Mission: Impossible*. She slipped into their room in the darkness and put her hand into Charlie's pockets until she found his keys. Then she crawled out of the room and unlocked the closet door.

The boys looked terrible. She fed them, gave them water, and let them out to use the bathroom, but realized they'd have to be locked up again or else Charlie would go crazy. Before the night was out, Renee slipped back into her father's room and replaced the keys in his pocket.

The next day, the kids found the keys again. This time when they opened the door, they told Dana and Vernon to run to their aunt and uncle's house. When their aunt saw them, she called police and had the boys taken to a hospital.

Within a year after their mother's death, all five kids were out of the house. Renee, like Rodney, ran away. She lived under a pier for two weeks until she was caught, then was placed in juvenile detention. Dawna, Vernon, and Dana went with relatives. Renee felt herself relatively fortunate: she was fourteen (in 1970) and would soon be able to take care of herself. By sixteen she had her first child, and by seventeen, she was married.

"I've wondered, how did I escape? I've thought about this ever since Dana killed that kid," she said.

Renee thought Dana had suffered the most. As a child he was inappropriate in his need to cling. Ella told Charlie that Dana needed psychological testing, but Charlie didn't believe in it and refused. In fact, Ella did take Dana for some evaluation just before she was killed.

Dana's assault on four-year-old Peter Wagner mirrored what Charlie Williamson was doing to him and the other kids, only Dana acted out too far, she said. The manslaughter conviction in 1975 was like "a wake-up call" for her father. "He realized that his hitting of his children did not produce the adults he wanted."

When Dana returned from prison in 1980, at age twenty-one, he lived with Renee and her husband, in Davie. But to the neighbors, he was a pariah. Parents kept their children inside when he was near. No one would hire him, no one would talk to him, except Sandy, a very shy fifteen-year-old, whose mother insisted on chaperoning her while Dana was around. Dana didn't keep it a secret from her parents that he had served prison time on a murder charge, but he told them he was innocent. He said he had pled guilty only because it saved him from the electric chair. Sandy's parents liked him, saw that he was quiet and had excellent manners, and thought he deserved a second chance.

But Dana also made friends with Sandy's brother, and in 1981, the two boys stole a car and were arrested. Because Dana was a repeat offender, he was returned to prison for a year. In prison, Sandy wrote him and professed her love. They were married soon after he got out.

Ironically, Dana became the child closest to Charlie Williamson. When Charlie was incapacitated by his stroke in 1987, Dana volunteered to be his nurse; Renee believed he did it to gain his father's love. Abused children have that need, she said, to do anything in order to gain love from an abusive parent.

Dana took over as head of the Williamson household, but it soon became an impossible task. From February until November 1988, he worked construction full-time, plus performed all the necessary unpleasant duties caring for an invalid. His days began at 5 A.M. and didn't end until midnight. At the same time, Sandy, Rodney, and Dawna all lived in the house, didn't work, mooched off him, and worse, constantly baited one another. They pitched in to help as little as possible; they'd ignore Charlie Williamson's buzzer when he wanted attention, and they refused to clean the house, which eventually turned into a disaster area. Yet through all the madness, Dana remained calm.

Renee said she believes her brother is guilty of the crime. In fact, she theorized, Dana actually may have wanted to be caught, to get out of his responsibilities. How could he have not known he had left the cowboy hat?

Yet at the same time, Renee hadn't thought Dana would ever try to murder again—especially a child, since he now had two little girls whom he adored.

She considered his denials hollow. He had denied killing Peter Wagner, but when he got out of prison, he told Renee that in fact he had done it. His denials this time sounded the same as after he killed Wagner, she thought.

Renee had mixed feelings for her father. On the one hand, he is her father; on the other, "He should be here on trial," she said. Even after all these years, "He has never been able to say I love you."

✦ FORTY-FIVE

CHARLES PANOYAN

On February 11, when Charles Panoyan was called to testify, he was lying sprawled on the wooden bench outside the courtroom, dressed in the same dark-blue polyester suit and pattern tie he had worn to the grand jury. He had dreaded this moment for more than five years. Now, compounding his nervousness were the effects of a miserable flu and pneumonia. He felt weak and nauseous.

Paul Stark had passed in the hallway moments before, not wishing to miss the testimony to come. "That guy pulled off a major coup in this case," said Steve Hammer, admiringly.

I overheard Brian Cavanagh's last-minute instructions to his witness: "Just tell the truth." Panoyan asked him for a bucket he could keep near him, just in case.

Cavanagh's idea was to take some time and allow the jury to listen to Panoyan ramble on about himself, so they would understand him and like him. It was similar to the strategy Stark and Vinikoor had used on Cavanagh, the first time he met Panoyan. Chuck wasn't hard to like, but until you got to know him, he had a tendency to come off like a scatterbrain.

"How old are you, Chuck?" Cavanagh began.

"Forty-three—no, fifty-three," he answered.

"Only Charlie," whispered Paul Stark, sitting next to me.

He had come from Beirut as a child with his mother, and grew up, from age seven to seventeen, at a boys' ranch in La Verne, California, under the tutelage of a man he called "Uncle Roy." When Panoyan's dad came to the United States, he had twenty-five cents in his pocket, no job, and didn't speak English. He worked for free for two years to learn the language. Under those circumstances, he couldn't take care of his son.

Panoyan moved to Florida in 1969 and met Bob Decker within a year. He laughed when Cavanagh reminded him of the used oil story.

Panoyan was then learning to be a carpenter, and he suggested to Bob in the early 1970s that he build his own house. Bob had no money to pay for building permits. Panoyan asked his father, who loaned Bob $2,000 to get started.

Bob and Chuck became the closest of friends.

"The door was always open to me, any time of night. We'd laugh and joke and have a good time. If he or I were short of money, we'd make fun of each other and give them the money."

He remembered his own set of practical jokes he and Bob pulled on each other. Once, Bob set up an electric fan outside Chuck's cluttered truck and blew all his papers out the other window. Another time, after Chuck put a shovelful of dirt in Bob's new van, Bob warned that he would get even. He did—he dumped a steamshovel load of dirt in the front seat of Chuck's truck.

There were serious moments too. Chuck never forgot that Bob pushed one of Chuck's kids away from danger while they were clearing the lot where Bob built his house, the one where Donna was killed.

Panoyan built a house for himself near where Charlie Williamson lived, also in the early 1970s. Williamson offered to help finish the drywall, even though Panoyan told him he couldn't afford to pay him. That began their long friendship.

Over the years, Panoyan and Charlie Williamson helped each other on projects and picked up each other's kids from school. Panoyan cried the first time he visited him after his paralyzing stroke. His friend was "all twisted up, one eye popped out." He couldn't speak, and the only way he could communicate was by using his right hand.

"Why are you crying, dummy?" Williamson wrote on a message. In relief, Panoyan burst out laughing.

As time went by, Panoyan was Charlie Williamson's only visitor, besides family. Panoyan would ramble on "about everything and anything. I told him about my business, Bob's business, other people's business. You run out of things to talk about.''

The stroke had also left Charlie Williamson almost deaf, so Panoyan had to talk loudly to him. When Dana was around, he would walk in and out of the room, attending to his father. But he didn't have to be in the room to easily overhear what Panoyan was saying.

Panoyan was at the Williamson house the week before the murder. Dana took him aside.

''Hey, what's this about Bob dealing in drugs?'' he asked. It was the first time Dana had ever mentioned Decker to him.

''Bob doesn't deal in drugs,'' Panoyan told him.

''That's not what I heard,'' Dana said.

''I don't care what you heard, Bob doesn't deal in drugs,'' Panoyan insisted.

Panoyan was at the Williamsons again the day before the murder. He told Charlie Williamson he was passing out frozen deer meat, which he had shot during his Utah hunting trip a few weeks before. On an earlier visit, Panoyan had given him a package.

''Dana wanted some more. I said, 'You already got some. Don't be greedy. Other people haven't gotten any yet.' ''

Then Dana told Panoyan he was wrong about Decker. He was so dealing drugs.

Grandpa Clyde Decker was at the job site where Bob and Chuck were working on the morning of November 4, 1988. Panoyan, who liked older people in general, got on well with Clyde. Clyde liked to hunt as well, but hadn't killed a deer that fall because his wife had died weeks before. Panoyan offered to drop off some of his deer meat that evening.

That night, Panoyan made four deliveries of venison. He stopped first at his friends Roger Davis, Mike Sirola, and Jan Dubin, then went on to the Decker house.

Panoyan thought he remembered for sure telling the Deckers at the end of the work day that he would come over that night with the meat. But when he arrived, sometime after eight o'clock, ''There was no one there. I thought they were hiding. I knocked on the door with the venison in hand, and no one answered.''

He called inside. "Man, I know you're in there." There was still no answer. He looked in the front window, went around the back, and saw a light inside.

He decided to wait. He sat in the truck and listened to the radio for about fifteen to thirty minutes, then gave up. Just as he began to pull out, that's when Bob's car pulled in.

"We started yelling to each other—you know, 'Where you been?' "

"We were out to dinner," Bob said.

They all walked into the house, Bob turned on the TV because *Dallas* was coming on, then Bob disappeared into his office/closet for a few minutes. When he came back out, "He said I had to leave."

"I said, 'No, I'm not.'

" 'You are. You make too much noise. *Dallas* is my favorite show.'

"We started wrestling around, and I remembered about the deer meat."

Outside in the driveway, Panoyan noticed someone hiding behind the passenger side of his truck. At first he didn't recognize Dana and Rodney.

"I was surprised. I asked them what they were doing there, and they didn't say anything. I asked how they got there, because I didn't see any transportation. They didn't say anything. I asked if Bob was expecting them. They never said anything. And I says, 'Come on, man, talk to me.' I'm getting kind of nervous, upset. I mean, you know, I don't know what's going on. And he [Dana] didn't say nothing.

"And then [Dana] said he was there to rip Bob off of drugs and money. Well, that threw me back. I said, 'Bob is a friend of mine. You're not ripping him off. He doesn't have any drugs and money.' I said, 'Go home. I won't tell your dad you were here. I won't tell Bob you were here. I won't tell the police. I won't tell anybody. Just go home.' "

When they didn't react, Panoyan got mad and threatened to start screaming and have Bob call the police.

"That's when [Dana] pulled a gun out on me and pointed it right at my face, and his brother pointed a gun at me and [Dana] said, 'You're not going to make a sound.' And I was kind of worried. And he said, 'You're going to do exactly as I say. If you don't, I'll signal the guy in the bushes. And he will make a phone call and your family will get killed.'

"And I said, 'My family?' I says, 'What do they have to do with it?' "

Panoyan didn't see anyone in the bushes, but that didn't make him doubt Dana's word.

Dana told him that Rodney was going to watch what was about to happen from outside, through the front picture window. "And if I did anything out of the ordinary, my family would get killed."

Both Williamsons were wearing dark clothes and white cowboy hats, and both held .22 pistols. When Panoyan could see Dana's gun in the light, he recognized it.

"It was my old rusty beat-up gun. My plunker. I'd pick up bullets people dropped, and my kids and I would go out shooting." Panoyan had kept it in the unlocked glove compartment of his truck.

After Dana walked inside, behind him Bob whispered to Panoyan: "Is this a joke? Do you know this clown?"

Brian Cavanagh asked him, "Did you tell the truth when you answered No?"

"No, I didn't," said Panoyan.

When Dana had Panoyan alone in the living room, he asked him where Bob kept the drugs and money. Panoyan said there weren't any drugs and he didn't know about money; then Dana kicked him.

"He hit me in the stomach, and I bent over, and he kicked me in the knee, and I went down like a rock. It still bothers me now, and that's been over five years.

"I was scared. When he started hitting and kicking me, I said, you know, he enjoys this. I could tell from just looking in his eyes. You could see his lip curl up. I mean, it was scary."

Then Dana got down on one knee. "He said, 'If you don't tell me where the drugs and money are, I'll blow your fucking brains out.' "

He answered, " 'Dana, I just came here to bring deer meat.'

" 'If I find any drugs or money, I'll blow your fucking brains out for lying to me.'

"I said, 'I hope you don't find anything.' "

About that time, Donna Decker walked in the house. When she took two steps past Panoyan, Dana grabbed her.

"I put my head down," said Panoyan, feeling shamed that he wasn't able to warn her.

When Dana came back to Panoyan, he placed him in a chair and hog-tied his wrists, ankles, and neck together. *Dallas* was just ending.

"Dana put his foot on the rope connected to my neck. He got my wallet out and he was choking me. I started seeing stars.

"He was looking through my wallet. And he told me he knew where everybody lived, my relatives, my friends. He said, 'You know who I am. You know what I'm capable of doing. You know my reputation. You can run, but you can't hide. I'll torture and kill any of your friends, relatives, and family to get to you.'

" 'Dana, are you going to kill me?'

" 'No, I just want to get your attention. If you say anything, I'm going to kill your family, starting with your wife.'

"And I say to myself, he did kill them kids, and I wonder how many other people."

Then came the part of the story Panoyan wanted the least to repeat. Up to the night before, he had told Brian Cavanagh he didn't want to say it in public.

"He said him and the boys were going to pull my wife's teeth out. Fuck her in the mouth and the ass. Tie her up and fuck her from both sides. Whip her, burn her. Take her nipples off. Tits off. Skin her. Take her guts out. Break her fingers. Put her on an anthill.

"He said he's gonna do the same thing to my girls. And he said for my boy he was gonna cut his balls off and feed it to him and pull his teeth out.

"I said, 'Dana, I'm not saying nothing to nobody.' I said, 'Just don't kill me.' And he says, 'I'm not gonna kill you.' And he took his foot off the rope."

Dana then untied him and said Rodney would take him. Dana walked him through the house to the in-house beauty salon, and there, sitting in the barber chair, was Rodney, wearing the same kind of mask as his brother.

Dana reminded him there was still someone outside in the

brush (who Panoyan couldn't see) and warned him not to try anything. As Rodney walked him out of the house, Panoyan asked where they were going.

"I'll do the talking," Rodney said.

Rodney ordered Panoyan into the driver's seat of Panoyan's truck, then Rodney got in the passenger side.

" 'Just drive,' Rodney said. 'I'll tell you where to go.' He says, 'We're going to your house.' And that kind of threw me.

"So we got to the end of the block, and he told me to pull over and park, and that's as far as him and I went together."

They stayed in the truck. "He sat next to me and he said, 'I bet you probably think you're better than we are.'

"I just told him, you know, 'I'm not better than you. I just don't go around doing what you do.' I says, 'I don't know anybody that does that.' "

Rodney corrected him. He did know someone who would do something like that—"Eddie"—and he was at Panoyan's house right now. Panoyan asked if he meant Eddie Roberts, and Rodney wouldn't say.

"I said, 'You know, you're nothing but a coward.' Well, that ticked him off. He told me that if he had his way, he would have blown my fucking brains out right then and there, but his brother told him not to. I knew I wasn't gonna get killed, because his brother said not to."

In the left-hand mirror, Panoyan saw Dana running quickly from down the road. When he got to the truck, he grabbed Rodney. He wasn't wearing either his hat or the stocking mask.

"He said, 'Something went wrong'—or there was trouble or something. First thing I was thinking is Grandpa is having a heart attack. That's the first thing that crossed my mind because he didn't look good at all."

Rodney got out, Dana got in, and he put the gun back to Panoyan's head. "He says, 'You do exactly like I tell you. You know what's going to happen to your family.' He said, 'Go straight home. Don't call the police. You're being followed.'

"Buddy, I'm not saying nothing," Panoyan told him.

Brian Cavanagh then showed Panoyan the cowboy hat in

evidence and asked if Dana Williamson had worn it that night.

"That looks like the hat," he said.

As Panoyan left the scene, he constantly checked his rear-view mirrors. He couldn't believe that no one was following him. He was halfway home, then he panicked again when it hit him that he was responsible for getting help for Grandpa if he indeed was having a heart attack.

He doubled back toward the Decker house, stopping at the first place where he could make a phone call. There, he had a security guard call 911, then he called his wife and shouted at her to get out of the house.

Panoyan remembered a female Davie police officer taking him back to the Deckers. "When I saw what happened at the house, I was horrified. There was blood everywhere. I said, 'My God, he's not human.' I knew what was going to happen to my family."

There, and later that night at the police station, "I told them exactly what happened in that house"—except he didn't tell them who the gunman was and he gave them a wrong description.

"What was Dana's reputation?" Cavanagh asked.

"A mean, vicious person who had killed a baby, stomped it to death, and beat another one so it was brain dead," said Panoyan.

At the police station that night, Darla called and asked for him. "She said, 'Charlie, are you okay?' and I said yeah.

"And she said, 'What's this about Donna getting killed?' And I said, 'Who got killed? How did you know that?' She said, 'The sheriff told me that everybody got shot up and Donna got killed.'

"I said, 'Nobody told me that.' I said, 'Look, get out of that house. Your life's in danger.' And so she came down to the police station."

That night, and for the next days, Darla hounded him for details he knew but wouldn't tell her.

"I said, 'I don't know nothing.' I said, 'You don't know nothing. Anything I tell you, you're gonna get killed. What you don't know isn't going to kill you.'"

Panoyan was certain that up to five guys were keeping a

watch on his house. The next morning, while he was in a dead sleep, one of his children spotted a strange car parked thirty feet from the house. "I said, my God, that's one of them." He looked like a drug dealer out of *Miami Vice*.

He called 911 and told them if the man didn't leave, he was going to kill him. A deputy sheriff came quickly, talked to the driver, and the car left, only to return within minutes, parked a little further away. Panoyan called 911 again, and the same deputy came back.

Again the cop talked to the driver, he left, and he came back again, only a block further away.

Panoyan prepared his Browning high-power rifle with a scope, and aimed it out the door. At about that time, Darla came home. "That's him! That's him!" Panoyan told her.

"Who?"

"That's one of them!"

"Call the police," Darla said.

"I did. They were here twice. I'm not going to flag him down. I'm going to shoot him where he sits."

He took Darla's car, with the Browning in one hand and a .44 Magnum handgun lying in his lap, and drove toward the car. As he did, the car began to drive away. Panoyan pursued him for a bit as the first car cut in and out of traffic at high speed.

"It couldn't have been three minutes later I looked out the door and there he was. And my boy says, 'Dad, what's going on here? What are you afraid of?'

"I said, 'Remember when we went deer hunting, there was guts laying all over the place and you threw up? Those could be your guts, your mother's guts, your sister's guts. That guy's a killer. I'm gonna kill him.' And he says, 'Oh, okay.' "

Once more Panoyan approached him in the car, with his cocked .44 pointed out the window.

"He puts up a badge and says, 'I can't talk.' " He was an undercover cop for Davie.

Panoyan's voice quivered as he retold the story. "I started shaking like this. Man, I almost killed a cop. I told my wife, 'This is crazy.' "

*   *   *

Three or four days after the murder, Dana called Panoyan. He needed a ride to a tire store.

"He called me up and wanted me to come over and wanted to talk to me. I told him I didn't want to talk to him, I didn't want to come over. He insisted that his dad needed some medication and he couldn't get it without fixing the tire. I said, all right, I'll be over.

"I came over. He looked down at me. He said I'd been a bad boy, you didn't go straight home, but nobody had come to his house and questioned him, so I must not have said anything."

Panoyan asked where Rodney was. "He's following you," Dana answered.

"Then what do you need a ride from me for?" Panoyan asked.

He asked for his wallet back. Dana refused.

" 'Dana, how in the world could you do something like that? You shot a baby. You killed a friend of mine.'

" 'I don't want to talk about it. Be thankful it wasn't your family.'

"Then he says I want you to come by as often as you were coming by before and visit my dad. I said, man, I'm not coming back here. And he says you're gonna do everything I tell you, when I tell you."

Within a week or so, Panoyan did come to visit Charlie Williamson, but both he and Dana were gone, leaving only Rodney.

He said to Rodney, " 'You're a scumbag. Why did you do what you did?' I wanted to tear his head off right then and there.

"I said I ought to turn you in. He said, 'Don't do anything stupid. There's one of the boys right there.' " Panoyan saw a parked car with a man inside. Since he thought he knew three of the five "boys," he wanted to know who the others were. He got in his truck, maneuvered a U-turn, and drove toward him, but the car left.

Panoyan had wanted to visit Bob in the hospital, but the police said that he wasn't in a stable enough condition to see visitors. But after a mutual friend, Roy Davis, went to see

Bob, Panoyan asked again. "He's a friend of mine and I want to talk to him."

That's when the officer told him, " 'Number one, he's not a friend of yours and he doesn't want to talk to you.' That floored me. I looked at him and I says, 'What are you talking about?'

"He says, 'You know exactly what I'm talking about.' I says, no, I don't. I says I want to see Bob. They said, no, Bob doesn't want to see you. Well, that upset me something terrible."

After Bob was released from the hospital, he went to see him at a job site. "Bob looked me right in the eye and says, 'How could you do this to me?'

"And I says, 'Do what to you, Bob?' And he said, 'My wife's stabbed to death, my baby's shot, my dad's shot, I'm shot.' I said, 'Bob, I didn't do this. I had nothing to do with this.'

"And he said, yes, you did. He said the police said it was an inside job and you did it. I said, 'Bob, they lied to me, they lied to you. How can you believe them?'

"He said, 'Get off my property right now. I should have you arrested.' " When he picked up a phone, Panoyan left.

About a year later, Charlie Williamson asked to see him. Panoyan came immediately. Charlie didn't know why Dana had gone to Ohio. He had Dana's phone number, and asked if Panoyan would call him and ask for both the mortgage loan money and the title to his house back.

"I said, 'What are you telling me?' He said, 'He took my house and $18,000.'

"I got ahold of Dana and I told him that his dad wanted his house and he wanted his money. I said, 'What is this all about?' "

Dana said he didn't want his sisters to get the house and money. "He says, 'I'd kill my sisters and my brothers. They're all a bunch of scumbags.'

"And he says, 'I know you been keeping your mouth shut.' I says, 'What makes you say that?'

"And he says, 'Well, nobody's called me or talked to me.' He says if I get one phone call, if anybody even mentions that they're a cop, he says you know what's gonna happen to your family."

Soon after that, Panoyan's buddy Winnie Marsden called him to say, " 'You're off the hook. I know who did it.'

"I said, who? He said Dana. That floored me."

Marsden said he was going to call the Crimestoppers tips line. "Half of me says, God bless you, go for it. The other half is saying, don't."

Cavanagh asked him about the Ohio trip.

Panoyan said he was supposed to go to Ohio, anyway, for a hunting trip. Instead, he flew to Washington, D.C., rented a car and drove to Ohio. He called Dana from the road and got instructions on where they could meet.

When Panoyan arrived, he was armed with a concealed gun. Dana met him, and let Panoyan see a large knife he was carrying.

"I says, 'What's the knife for?' I put my hand in my pocket and he says, 'It's quieter, it doesn't make any noise.'

"I says, 'What are you gonna do, kill me?' and he says no, no, no."

Panoyan told him about the Crimestoppers call. "I said, 'Dana, I swear, I didn't say anything.' He says, look, don't worry about it. I started to leave, and just then I thought of something else, you know, his dad. So I went back to talk to him and he was talking to somebody else.

"I asked him where his brother was. And he says, 'Well, he could be with a gun in your back or he could be back with your family.' "

In fact he was right there. "I said something to upset him. I called him a coward or a chicken or something, and he pulled his gun out. And Dana said, no, no, I don't want any trouble in here. Dana told me to keep my mouth shut. So I left."

In jail, Panoyan initially was in maximum security, and solitary confinement. When Paul Stark came to visit, "He told me he was totally, utterly helpless unless I told him what happened. And I said I don't know nothing about nothing.

"And he said you're gonna go to the electric chair. I said I'll be going to the electric chair and my family will be safe.

"And he says, what? Boy, they were upset.

"They said they never worked so hard on a case in their

entire career. And they said I was the most baffling case they
had ever had.''

In jail together, Dana renewed his threats. The worst time
was during a court hearing, when Panoyan's daughter walked
over to see him, and Dana whispered to him what he was
going to do to her.

"By this time I was getting madder and madder and I
wanted to choke him right then and there. And he says, 'Just
remember what's gonna happen to your family.' He said,
'Don't do anything, don't say anything, just smile.' And so
I was smiling while he was telling me what he was gonna
do to my family, to my daughter. I couldn't say anything,
do anything.''

After a year and a half in jail, awaiting trial, it hit him that
Rodney was a drug user, and that while on drugs, he would
inevitably spill his story. That person would tell the police.

"I told Dana. I said, 'Dana, I'm going to walk out of
here, and your brother and you are going to end up in jail
for murder.'

"And he said, 'My brother wouldn't say a thing to anybody, because I got enough on him to put him away for life.'

"And I said, 'What do you mean?'

"He said, 'My brother and I have pulled so much shit, it's
not even funny.'

"I said, 'Just you and your brother?'

"And he said, 'Yeah.'

"And I said, 'Was it just you and your brother that night
at Bob's?'

"And he says, 'Yeah.' The minute he said that, our eyes
met and he realized what he said. He said, 'Plus three people,'
but it was too late.''

Freed of the unseen threat, Panoyan opened up just a frac-
tion to Paul Stark the very next day.

A week later, two bailiffs approached Panoyan. "I'm in
trouble," he thought. They walked him away from his food
service job to tell him he was being released.

"Are you sure you got the right guy?" he asked. The
bailiffs laughed, but he insisted they double check their com-
puters. He had no idea what was happening.

*   *   *

After Panoyan was at last done testifying, Charlie Johnson stopped to talk with him in the hallway outside the courtroom. For a year and a half, they had been on the same side.

"You can hold your head up high," Johnson told him. "You did well."

"You're tops," said Panoyan.

✦ FORTY-SIX

My own shining moment came toward the end of the trial.

Brian Cavanagh had Norwood detective Steve Daniels testify in order to introduce evidence seized at Dana's home. That included the Ninja belt, which I had never seen; so at the end of the day, I asked the court clerk to inspect it. Turning it over I saw a white tag with the letters "AWMA," which I recognized as the initials of Asian World of Martial Arts. According to a shipping receipt also seized in Norwood, Rodney had bought two belts from them.

I knew the defense planned to contend that the belts could be purchased at any number of army-navy surplus stores, even in Davie. Just because Rodney had two of them didn't mean Panoyan couldn't have had one as well.

My next thought was whether the other belt found in Panoyan's truck on the night of the murder also had the same tag. In fact it did. Not only did this kill the defense's argument, but it provided perhaps the clearest evidentiary link to Dana Williamson—as good or better than the cowboy hat. Sure, Panoyan could have bought the same belt anywhere, but not one with an AWMA tag. Panoyan didn't playact Ninja warrior, and the Williamsons did.

I hadn't heard any discussion, or seen any reference in the files to this, so I had a feeling the prosecution didn't know about it. "AWMA" didn't mean anything on the night of the murder when the first belt was seized, and detectives must have missed it when they got the second belt in 1990. Since then, the belts had been sitting in the police property room, and probably hadn't been looked at.

It also meant something else. The belt could not have been

planted on Panoyan's truck, as Panoyan suspected, although it didn't preclude it from being moved.

I told Brian Cavanagh. I was right. He didn't know about it, and neither did Woodroof.

When Woodroof testified on February 16, he slammed the point home four times. Steve Hammer didn't even touch it during his cross-examination.

At 3:27 P.M. on February 17, after presenting forty-four witnesses and entering 230 exhibits, Brian Cavanagh announced: "In the case of the State of Florida versus Dana Williamson, the State of Florida rests its case."

The defense would bring no witnesses. However, by declining, they were entitled to sandwich the state during closing arguments: one and a half hours for Hammer, two hours for the state, then the final half hour for Hammer. Normally, the state enjoyed the advantage of the last word.

Closing began the next morning. "You're probably going to have a question of whether Charles Panoyan was involved in this case," Hammer told the jury. "Panoyan was the only man that says, 'Dana Williamson was in that house.'"

The police believed Panoyan was lying from the very beginning, he said. "What happened to make everyone change their mind? Charles Panoyan decided to tell the truth, that Dana Williamson was the gunman, and Rodney Williamson was with him? Is that really believable?"

After five years, the only evidence the state had was Panoyan, O'Brien, a cowboy hat ("It *looks* like Dana's—*and* a thousand others during Rodeo Days in Davie") and the Ninja belt.

Hammer conceded that the belt was Dana's. Now he suggested that Dana had accidentally left it in Panoyan's truck two weeks before the murder, when he was wearing his Ninja suit. That was a reference to Dana's Pembroke Pines traffic stop and arrest.

The first problem in that statement was that the incident was two months before the murder, not two weeks.

The second was pointed out to me by two astute women—Nancy Miller and her married daughter, Christine Kebler—who had watched the entire trial a row behind me in the gallery. They attended at first because they knew Bob Decker;

years ago he had laid concrete blocks for their home, but they kept coming because the trial's drama had hooked them.

Nancy nudged my shoulder, then whispered: Ginger Kostige had testified that she had seen Dana with the belt around Halloween. Either way, that was long after the traffic stop. I checked my notes; she was right.

There was a third problem I noticed afterwards. Panoyan hadn't been driving his truck the night of the traffic stop—he had his wife's car, a 1985 Mercury Cougar.

In his closing, Cavanagh said that Hammer was distorting the facts. He borrowed the shrewd observation of the trial groupies (which left them beaming), then added that Dana's hat was identified as his by Kostige, Renee Williamson, and even Dana himself. In fact, Dana's response to police about it seemed canned. He said he hadn't seen it since September 1988, when Vernon was over at his house, implying that Vernon—who didn't fit the gunman's description—had stolen it.

Panoyan's testimony was in fact consistent with what he had always said. "The only difference is initially he would not disclose Dana and Rodney's identity because he was scared." He told police on the night of the murder that he was afraid for his family's safety, but police made a mistake in choosing not to believe him.

Between a rock and a hard place, Panoyan remained under Dana's coercive influence. "It may not have been a good choice, but it was his choice."

Cavanagh admitted that he came very close to bringing Panoyan to trial. "What happened to Charles Panoyan was a travesty. He was a victim all along. The only bigger travesty would be if the killer, Dana Williamson, would be acquitted."

Cavanagh then advanced to the AWMA tag. "Does this evidence go back to anyone else in the universe besides Dana Williamson and Rodney Williamson?" he asked.

Same thing for Steven Luchak's testimony that Dana told him Donna Decker died near the front door of the house.

"The killer knew!" he trumpeted.

Another question: Why did Dana write the misspelled words "frist degree murder" in his notebook? "He wrote what was on his mind, on his guilty conscience,'' Cavanagh said.

Finally, he answered the question regarding the third and largest mistake Dana made: Why didn't he kill Panoyan, the witness?

"He was left alive because of Charlie Williamson. He wasn't protecting Charles Panoyan, he was protecting his father. Panoyan was the only regular visitor of his father, and that's why he was spared. Rodney wanted to kill him, and Dana said, 'We can't kill him. He's been too good to our father.'

"Even predators in the wild protect their own," Cavanagh said.

In final rebuttal, Steve Hammer tried to list the loose ends the state had never resolved in the case.

He said the biggest fault in Panoyan's story was that Donna Decker had to have walked right past Rodney Williamson— the lookout—in order to get into the house.

He said a lot of people involved in the case disagreed with how it was being prosecuted. There were many Davie detectives, as well as Bob Decker, who still didn't believe Panoyan.

"I submit to you, Bob Decker thinks Charles Panoyan is involved in this," Hammer said.

He also questioned why the state had never done a voice line up for Bob Decker, instead waiting for trial to have Decker identify Dana's voice one on one.

"The state has a lot of circumstantial evidence and innuendo," he said. Hammer referred to a line in Kelly Woodroof's testimony, that once they had the cowboy hat, (like in the story of Cinderella and the glass slipper) the goal was to see who it fit. Hammer then took the cowboy hat, and to his client's apparent surprise, placed it on his head.

"It doesn't fit," he closed.

Jury instructions lasted past four o'clock that Friday afternoon. That was late in the day for deliberations to begin, but since the next Monday was a legal holiday, Judge Eade was prepared to let them stay as long into the evening as they needed, and into the weekend, if necessary.

The vigil began. Chatting with bailiff Bill Meyer, he told me that Dana had boasted early on in the trial that he could slip their handcuffs because he was double-jointed (a fact later confirmed for me by Renee Williamson). As a result, the bailiffs cuffed his ankles as well during transport in and out of the courtroom.

Jo Zazzo and her daughter Chrissie had also been regular attendees of the trial. They asked if I would let them speak to me about Donna Decker.

Donna was bubbly and good-hearted, they said. They were all very close. Chrissie used to sleep at her house three times a week, even though she thought the house was creepy. Just before her murder, Donna had planned a family ski trip to Lake Tahoe, and she was going to pay Chrissie's way. Chrissie gave Donna some cash to keep as her spending money for the trip, and somehow, the robber missed it.

Friday, November 4, 1988, was Chrissie's twenty-first birthday. They had planned to celebrate it on Sunday, two days later. Chrissie and Jo saw her that day at work at J.C. Penney and told her how pretty she looked.

Both had premonitions about her death, they said.

Chrissie had passed near the house late that Friday night, coming home from a nightclub with her friends, and almost stopped over. Earlier, Jo left work with a headache at around 9:30 P.M. and also thought about stopping in. Instead, she went home and went to sleep.

She awoke from a nightmare in the middle of the night, screaming. "No! No!" In the morning, when someone called to say that Donna's house had been robbed the night before, Jo said she already knew.

Chuck Panoyan was nervous and, therefore, his usual talkative self. We talked about a lot of things: While he was under indictment with Dana, "I was scared to death that we would be found innocent," he said. He figured if they were both found guilty, his conviction might be overturned some day, but if they were acquitted, under double jeopardy rules Dana would have forever gotten away with murder and Panoyan would always be under his thumb.

He told me some jail stories. Dana wasn't liked by other inmates, in fact he heard that he was once thrown down some stairs. But Panoyan was never beaten up, and in fact was treated with some respect.

"They respect older men, and on top of that, I was in for murder," he said. He remembered jogging and telling someone about his murder charge, and they immediately backed away, afraid of him. Panoyan told him, it was alright, he didn't do it.

He remembered another prank while building Bob's home. George Williams had stepped on his hat, so Panoyan promised to get him back. He did by pushing him into wet poured concrete. Williams was furious. He promised money to anyone who would put Panoyan in the concrete septic tank.

"When he got to $50, I took off running. I ran six blocks, Bob, Mike [Shope], and George chasing me. But they didn't catch me."

By 8:30 that night, a sinister thought hit Panoyan. If the jury found Dana not guilty, he would have to make arrangements for his family. He ran to the pay telephone.

At nine, Judge Eade called the jury in. They were close to a verdict, they reported, and were ready to keep going until they were finished. And they would have, except that one juror said she was tired. Eade sent them home—with the regular admonition not to talk to anyone about the case—and asked them back at 9 A.M. Saturday.

Saturday, February 19, 1994.
Outside the courtroom, the vigil continued. Panoyan answered some more loose ends for me.

If Bob had come out of the bedroom one second earlier, he said, he would have seen Dana kicking him and pointing his gun at his head. Then there would have been no doubt that he was a victim, too.

He said his life was safe as long as Charlie Williamson stayed alive. But once he died, Dana would have no reason not to kill Panoyan. In jail, Dana once explained: "If anything would have happened to you, my dad would have died. That's why I didn't do anything to you."

Then, further explaining why he thought his threats would be effective, Dana said, "I know you're a caring family man. I knew you wouldn't do anything to hurt your family."

*   *   *

At 11:42 A.M., the jury announced they had reached a verdict. Within a few minutes, everyone was assembled.

I looked to see where the jury's faces were glancing—down, around—I knew what that meant.

"Guilty," the court clerk read, of fifteen of the seventeen counts. They found Dana "Not Guilty" of two counts of armed burglary of Bob Decker's van. That was the weakest part of the state's case.

In the back row, Charles Panoyan sat alone, in tears. Chrissie Zazzo hugged Bob Decker.

At the very instant the first guilty verdict was read, bailiff Earl Aronson came from over Dana's shoulder and cuffed his hands. During it all, Williamson showed absolutely no change in expression. He had kept his poker face throughout the entire trial.

✦ FORTY-SEVEN

RENEE WILLIAMSON

I met with Renee again a month after the conviction. She gave me an envelope full of family pictures, including one I hadn't expected: a circa 1983 shot of Dana wearing a beige cowboy hat in a restaurant, sitting next to Sandy.

I compared the hat on Dana's head to all the pictures I had of the hat in evidence. It was the same color, a lot less battered in the restaurant photo, but otherwise similar. On both were a number of triangular shaped airholes near the top. "It's the hat," said Brian Cavanagh, when I showed it to him.

Renee told me she had had a suspicion that Dana was involved in the murder only a week after it happened. She knew some of the details of it from the newspapers, including that Chuck Panoyan had been inside the Decker house. When Chuck came by her house, which she leased from him, and asked for an advance on the rent so he could pay a retainer for a lawyer, she asked him questions about what had happened.

As Chuck kept refusing to provide any details, she realized he was shielding someone. "Chuck, you have to tell me something," she pled. His answer was that he would tell her some day, but she would never believe it.

After he left, she guessed it was Dana. And if Dana was involved, then Rodney must have been right behind him, in the shadows.

Renee liked Chuck a lot and knew him well enough to know that he couldn't possible be mixed up in a crime, especially one like this. She also knew that Chuck visited her father all the time, though Dana had been acting weird in the week since the murder. Dawna thought so too. He spent a lot of money, and even gave some of it to Sandy to go drinking with. Then, within only a few days, Dana left town without telling anyone, leaving their father unattended to.

Renee had wanted to call the police right away, but her (now former) husband told her no, she had nothing to substantiate it. So she kept it to herself.

Had Renee told police then, I reasoned with her, they would have shown her and Dawna the cowboy hat left at the scene. Both would have identified it as Dana's, and the case would have been solved, at least for the most part.

Dawna hadn't called the police either (most likely because she had a record for drugs and prostitution). But she was more vocal about what she believed. Most probably, Dawna told Ginger Kostige, who sent it down the grapevine, which eventually resulted in the Crimestoppers tip that named Dana. When Kelly Woodroof checked it out, he found Kostige, Dawna, and then Renee.

Woodroof had considered Renee credible, except for her insistence that Chuck Panoyan wasn't the type to mastermind a crime. Woodroof disagreed, saying they had a lot of evidence showing he was involved.

Dawna apparently was Dana's source of information that the Deckers were into drugs, Renee thought. Dawna, then using drugs herself, said all sorts of things like that. Usually they sounded ridiculous and couldn't be confirmed, but often, Renee said, she'd turn out to be right. (Later, Dawna denied to me that she had ever heard of the Deckers before the incident.)

Rodney, who had an IQ of 165, Renee said, was the star of the family growing up. But as an adult he absolutely refused to do any work. She considered Rodney more dangerous than Dana; Rodney was the mastermind who always kept himself in the background, who could always get someone else to do his dirty work. Dana was just his stooge. She compared Rodney with Charles Manson.

After Renee left, I looked at some of the old newspaper clips she had kept about Dana. She had the front page of the March 7, 1975, edition of the *Fort Lauderdale News,* with a five-column banner headline: "CHILD-KILLING SUS-PECTS TO BE TRIED AS ADULTS."

On the same page was another story, headlined "From Rejection to Detention," which detailed at length Dana's troubled childhood to that point. The lead was a juvenile court judge had recommended that the state attorney bring criminal charges against Charlie Williamson for contributing to the dependency of a juvenile. That was for his lack of cooperation with both the court and the State of Florida Division of Family Services (DFS).

(No charges in fact were ever brought.)

The story said Charlie Williamson had twice disobeyed a court order to pay child support, and once he was sentenced to sixty days in jail for contempt. He was released when he coughed up the money.

> Court records repeatedly refer to the father's efforts to rid himself of his five children, all of whom at one time or another have received the attention of juvenile court and DFS.
>
> Counselors and court doctors who dealt with Dana tell a story of a boy burdened with guilt—one who has suffered from repeated rejection by his father and others.
>
> They do not argue that Dana is healthy, but rather that he is a borderline psychotic who responds to stress by engaging in flights of fancy, becoming unaware of what is real and what is not.

The story quoted an unnamed female psychologist who knew Dana:

> He carried with him an enormous burden of rejection. He always wanted to go home. To this day he wants to go home. He was a charming boy, the kind of patient doctors feel for in a special way.

But when Charlie Williamson let Dana come home, for just a few days at Christmas some years before, the result was terrible.

He wouldn't allow the boy to come until Dana got his hair cut, so Dana did that. He and his brother Vernon were in bed Christmas Eve when his father or his second wife apparently overheard the boys saying something uncomplimentary about the wife. They were gotten out of bed and turned out of the house on Christmas Eve.

✦ Forty-eight

PENALTY PHASE HEARING

Persons convicted in Florida of first-degree murder may be sentenced to death by electrocution or life in prison without possibility of parole for twenty-five years. Should the state announce before trial it will seek the death penalty upon conviction (as it did in this case), the judge sets a separate penalty phase hearing after the guilty verdict.

There, the state presents evidence of aggravating circumstances that would call for the harsher penalty; then the defense gets to offer mitigating evidence arguing for the more lenient penalty. The same trial jury listens, then makes a recommendation to the judge. The judge must give "great weight" to the recommendation, but is not obligated to agree. However, in practice, Florida judges do generally follow the jury's recommendation.

Unlike in the guilt phase of trial, a jury need not vote unanimously at penalty phase. A 6-6 tie is a recommendation for lenity, life in prison.

(Although it wasn't clearly explained to the jury, the judge had discretion to stack sentences for fourteen lesser counts on top of Dana Williamson's first-degree murder penalty. If the jury voted for life, in reality, Dana would probably not even be eligible for parole.)

On June 1, after two postponements, the trial reconvened. Judge Eade had last instructed the jury not to discuss the trial with anyone, including other jury members, until after the penalty phase was over. One original juror and one alternate were absent this time, which left twelve, thus making the remaining alternate a voting juror.

The state's most aggravating factors were Dana's previous manslaughter conviction of four-year-old Peter Wagner in 1975, and the argument that the Decker murder and attempted murders were "heinous, atrocious and cruel" and "cold, calculated, and premeditated"—("CCP" in prosecutor parlance).

"It is not within the normal human experience to recommend that another human being be given the death penalty. It is an extremely solemn occasion," said Brian Cavanagh in opening argument.

"I ask that your courage, intellect, and reason rise to this decision."

Charlie Johnson handled the defense this time, as previously planned. His mitigation strategy was to admit that Dana was the masked gunman, then hope to show that Dana's judgment was clouded because of a previous brain injury, possibly suffered in the 1969 auto accident. Dana was in a coma for two weeks afterwards, and an electroencephalogram (EEG) taken in 1971 showed that Dana had an "abnormal" brain, Johnson said.

"The State of Florida has never allowed a brain-damaged person to go to the chair," he told the court.

Johnson brought expert neurological and neuropsychological testimony to say that Dana's brain damage caused him to go into a rage—which he acted out in murderous sprees, and after which he had amnesia. But first, Judge Eade instructed Johnson to confer with his client in the courtroom (but outside the presence of the jury) to make sure Dana agreed with the strategy.

Johnson did, and Dana reaffirmed his approval. Then Johnson protested the judge's request, evoking a Catch-22 scenario. "Mr. Williamson is not a rational person," he said.

Johnson brought a parade of Williamson relatives to the stand to plea for Dana's life, yet it was Renee Williamson who was most effective.

With Charlie Williamson sitting in a wheelchair in the courtroom, Renee, now thirty-seven, talked for the first time in public about what it was like growing up. It was also the first time she had ever faced her father on the subject.

"I thought we were like any other family. Then I learned

in junior high school [in gym class] that other children didn't have bruises like we did.

"He [Charlie] would take a belt or switch and line us up. He would state the offense—someone used something of his, drank up all the milk, left the front door open—and he'd ask, 'Who did it?' If no one confessed, he'd whip the oldest, whip them with a belt, go down the list, ask again, whip again— until somebody would eventually confess, to stop the beating.

"We didn't have the right to question an adult, or show hesitation. We were just supposed to do what they said."

Looking over at Charlie Williamson, I saw him furiously scrawling in his notebook (his last remaining method of verbal communication).

"Terri was our first experience with an alcoholic. She liked to demean people. She took delight in destroying people emotionally. Terri hated us. She got rid of our mother's cat, dog, and kids. She told us that we didn't deserve to live.

"All of us suffered, each in our own way. Why am I able to maintain relationships, jobs? I am clearly fortunate. Dana was not so fortunate—he's had a lot of bad breaks."

Dana had a lump in his throat—his first emotional reaction of the trial—when Renee called him a compassionate person, especially toward the family.

"I don't want to see him die," she said, a tear in her eye.

Tom Cavanagh made one more appearance on the stand. (On the philosophical issue of the death penalty, he and his son differed—Tom was dead against it, and Brian was personally ambivalent or unsure, although his job obligated him to argue for it. Therefore, Tom had volunteered his testimony for the defense.)

"You're the fellow who broke open this case, weren't you?" asked Johnson.

"No, but I participated," Tom answered.

Tom didn't argue that Dana Williamson might not be guilty, but rather that he served more public purpose alive than dead. Tom said that in his career, he had seen a small number of multiple killers, and they had always left a deep impression on him. One was Ricky Robles, of the Wylie-Hoffert case. He was amazed that they could be compassionate to their loved ones, then cold, uncaring killers in their next breath.

"We have to study these people. If we exterminate them, we lose our guinea pigs. I ask the judge and jury to sentence him to life—we'll work out the details [of how to study him] later.''

Johnson ended his case with one last emotional appeal. He brought to the stand eleven-year-old Jessica Williamson, then eight-year-old Erica Williamson.

At eleven, Jessica was the same age as her father when he was thrown out of his house in 1970. Now she and her sister faced similar turmoil. The girls hadn't lived with their father since his arrest in 1990, and soon after, Ohio courts had removed them from their mother Sandy (who had been missing since the guilt phase of trial and hadn't answered her defense subpoena to appear at penalty phase).

Jessica cried as soon as she was sworn in, while Fran Schulze (her grandmother and legal guardian along with husband Rick) stood next to her.

"Do you love your dad?" Johnson asked.

"Yes, sir," she said.

At the defense table, Dana kept his arms folded, his face still without emotion.

"You don't want to see your daddy dead?" Johnson asked Erica.

"No," she said.

"Would you want to go see your daddy in prison?"

"No," she said.

Caught off guard for a second, Johnson returned with "That's because you don't want to see him in prison at all, right?"

"Yes."

"If he was in prison, would you go visit him?"

"Yes."

After Erica left the stand to sit in the gallery next to her grandfather Rick, she handed a bailiff a note to give to Dana. Dana read it, welled up, then tucked the paper away.

In final argument, Brian Cavanagh warned the jury that sympathy for the defendant should not come into play. Dana Williamson does have a compassionate side—that's why he didn't kill his father's friend, Charles Panoyan, Cavanagh said. Then again, it didn't stop him from making graphic extortion threats on the lives of Panoyan's family.

"I've learned the importance of what life is, and what death is," said Charlie Vaughan, closing the state's case. "Death is not laying in the middle of your office on a Friday night. What helped Donna Decker leave this earth was a vicious, evil, wicked act."

For the months in between the conviction and the penalty phase hearing, I also found myself going back and forth on the issue of the death penalty. Tom Cavanagh called it an act of "vengeance"—an eye for an eye penalty that had no place in the modern world. Certainly, he agreed, families of murder victims usually want the killer to get death, but our system of justice puts cooler heads in charge of deciding guilt and punishment.

After listening to Tom, a good closing line for a defense argument came to me, and I mentioned it to Charlie Johnson. I was pleased to hear some of my words back during his final summary to the court.

"Dana has a debt to pay society and Bob Decker's family," Johnson spoke. If Dana dies, he will leave the earth and the debt will always remain unpaid, he said. "Dana can be a patient and he can help us learn to see others like him. He can also realize what he did and say to Bob Decker, 'I'm sorry.'

"Give Dana life—so he can start repaying the debt he owes us all."

The jury deliberated for three hours; then at 8:31 P.M., Friday, June 3, 1994, they signaled they had reached a decision. They had voted 11-1 to recommend to Judge Eade that Dana suffer the death penalty.

Once again, Dana Williamson was stone-faced during the reading of a jury decision.

When Judge Eade finally released the jury, a bailiff escorted them out a back exit. Since I was familiar with Broward County courthouse procedure, I knew I could head them off at the main elevator.

I got to the elevator first, then went down eight floors with the twelve jurors and the bailiff. Over the course of the trial, a few jurors had made small talk with me, though never anything about the proceedings except to grumble how long the trial took to resume after a recess. They had seen me in the front row of the gallery, writing notes, taking my own photos, and now the unanimous first question was from them to me: "All right—who are you?"

The bailiff walked us across the dark street to the parking garage, but before they got in their cars, I got to spend about twenty minutes with them. They were very anxious to talk about what they had seen, especially since they had been restrained until now from doing so.

They said for the three months in between the guilt phase and the penalty phase their minds had sometimes wondered whether they had made the right decision. They were surprised then, at penalty phase, that the defense admitted that Dana was the masked man. That relieved them of any lingering doubts and pleased them that they had, in fact, called it right.

That exchange surprised me. I had thought they had made up their minds that Dana was guilty long before guilt phase deliberations. They said, no, in fact, their initial ballot on the first-degree murder charge was five votes for "Not guilty." Once everyone had a chance to speak, they took a second ballot, then it was 12-0.

Juror Rick Kennedy, president of a microfilm processing lab, reasoned that the case hinged on Panoyan. Leslie Stein called Panoyan "a ditz," but the consensus was that he wasn't the type to be involved in a homicide.

They thought Brian Cavanagh was extremely sincere and wonderfully dramatic, but it was Charlie Vaughan's closing at guilt phase that jury foreman Ernest Cambio brought into the jury room. The line that struck the responsive chord, spoken in Vaughan's folksy manner, was "It just ain't right."

They didn't buy the defense's brain-damage argument as a mitigating factor at all. It turned out that four of the jurors over their lifetimes had sustained brain injuries—Leslie Stein said she had been unconscious for three days after a car accident—yet none of the four had turned into stark raving lunatics.

But the observation that impressed me the most, that showed how intelligent this jury was, was Ernest Cambio spotting that Dana couldn't have left the Ninja belt in Panoyan's truck because his Pembroke Pines arrest was in Panoyan's car. (I myself hadn't caught that until after trial, when I reviewed my notes.) Perhaps Cambio just had a feel for this sort of thing. Two years ago, he wrote a fictional crime book, still unpublished.

✦ FORTY-NINE

CONFIDENTIAL FILES

Juvenile records in the state of Florida are normally sealed from the public, but Charlie Johnson's expert witness, Dr. Antoinette Appel, did a fine job of collecting Dana Williamson's social services file back to 1970; then Johnson placed it all into evidence, making it public record. Many of the pages are marked "Confidential."

I read them after all was said and done.

Marjorie Miller, at one time Dana's therapist, wrote that Dana had been the "favorite child" of his mother.

"Dana had a ruptured spleen as a result of [the 1969] accident and he was hospitalized. For this reason he did not know of his mother's death for several weeks. It always seemed to me that when Dana returned to his home, the rest of the family had lived through their grief concerning the loss of their mother and Dana had never had a healthy opportunity to do this."

Charlie Williamson didn't know how to cope with the loss of his wife. Nor did he have a very good idea how to raise his children in her absence.

Social worker Alma Smith wrote that Charlie Williamson was a "very rigid person who has used extreme discipline on his children." In addition, he was erratic in meting out that discipline. "Some days he beat the children and on other days, he completely ignored them."

While Ella Williamson was alive, she had been able to shelter them from Charlie's most severe punishments, Smith wrote. But after her death, Charlie's temper went unchecked. Things worsened still when Charlie brought Terri Rivers, a barmaid who drank heavily, into the house in August 1970, then married her on November 27, 1970, less than a year after the accident. The children complained that instead of protecting them, Terri encouraged their father to beat them harder and more often.

On November 11, 1970, eleven-year-old Dana and eight-year-old Vernon were beaten so severely, then locked in a closet, that they ran away from home to relatives, who called police. Both boys were put in a children's shelter.

In fact, by then, both Dawna and Rodney were already out of the house. Rodney was a runaway who had been picked up by police and placed in juvenile detention, and Dawna told a judge that her father had ordered her to leave home. At Dawna's court hearing, Charlie Williamson denied he told her to leave, but admitted he might have said she could "get out if she would not obey him."

Broward County Juvenile Court judge Frank A. Orlando set Dana and Vernon's formal dependency hearing for December 14, 1970. Awaiting that, Vernon was placed with his maternal aunt and uncle, and Dana was placed in a shelter home until Thanksgiving, when his paternal grandmother Jessie Smith took him.

Those first two weeks away from home were a disaster for Dana. Division of Family Services supervisor Betty Gunter wrote that he was "hyperactive, and talks constantly to demand attention. He refused to sit quietly in the classroom and crawled on the floor, hid under desks and tables, and actually ran out of the classroom whenever he had the opportunity.

"In the shelter home, he cried frequently, refused to obey the foster parents and did not get along well with the other children. He talks of blood and death and his conversation is often interspersed with threats to kill his father, murder anyone who 'gets in his way.'

"He steals constantly even when he is punished and denied privileges. He lies about where he obtains his stolen goods and will not admit the theft even when he is confronted with evidence proving that he has been dishonest. Relatives tell us that Dana had had the reputation of stealing things that he does not need for several years."

At first, the Williamson relatives were sympathetic toward the kids. Vera Williamson—married to Charlie's brother Bob—argued with her husband that the children were "scared to death" of Charlie Williamson. According to case notes, "She believes that Mr. Charles Williamson might kill the children." Vera added that she believed Charlie Williamson wanted to "get rid of all of his children."

But by December 1, Vera's tone changed. She called the case worker demanding that Dana be moved immediately from the grandmother's home because he was stealing from relatives. Specifically, she said, Dana had taken some jewelry and buried it in the yard, to be found later by his grandmother.

The case worker told Vera the state was powerless to change Dana's placement until the court hearing in two weeks.

On the day of the hearing, the case worker picked up Dana and Vera Williamson to take them to the court house. In the car, Vera told the case worker (quoting from the case notes narrative): "Dana has caused so many problems in the grandparents' home, she is beginning to think that the father was justified in beating the children."

The case worker also wrote: "At this point relatives are unwilling to care for the children except for Mr. and Mrs. Roy Davenport, who have little contact with the other relatives and who are providing a very satisfactory home for Vernon.

"Worker wonders if these children will ever be settled."

That day, Judge Orlando decreed that both boys were legally dependent and placed them in the temporary custody of the state Division of Family Services. Vernon stayed with the Davenports, and Dana was put in another shelter home.

Immediately, an angel came forward for Dana. A former co-worker of Ella Williamson wanted to be Dana's foster mother. Later in December, the court formally gave her temporary custody; but after a month, she called the case worker again to ask that Dana be removed immediately. Dana had stolen her car keys, driven her car, wrecked it, then showed no regret for doing so. That day, Dana had to be placed in a detention home until the state could find somewhere else for him.

The next stop was forty-three days later, at the children's

unit of South Florida State Hospital. In his admission report dated March 1971, Dr. M. Evangelakis found that the "child functions from a well of anger and hostility which may become overpowering with the slightest provocation and result in harmful actions. His anger is directed outward, there is no indication of impulse control, his judgment is directed largely by his emotion.

"According to the father, 'the child lies, steals, and when you approach him of the times, he admits it, then later he will rationalize with himself that he did not do it, and he believes it.' According to the father, when the child was seven years old, he and another boy broke into a house and took lighting fluid and sprayed it, then arrived in the back of a man's truck and set it on fire."

Evangelakis noted that Dana referred to his father as "the old man whom I will kill."

"He seems to have oriented all his thinking around the relationship with his father and it is exceedingly difficult for him to depart from this preoccupation."

Hospital social worker Augusta Zimmerman reviewed Dana's social and psychological history for the files. She wrote that Charlie Williamson "verbalized complete unconcern for his children and their problems and tended to blame the deceased mother of the children for the personality problems which the children have. Since Dana ran away from home in November of 1970 and was removed from his father's custody, Mr. Williamson has 'washed his hands of the child.'

"Mr. Williamson does not seem to understand why any of the children might have run away. He shows very little emotion of any depth when speaking to him. For example, when he noted that his favorite child, Renee, ran away from home just the week before, he expressed no emotion about it. When asked how he felt, he said 'quite upset,' however, he showed no emotion."

("Dana, however, was said by his DFS case worker to have a "strong sense of family.")

After Dana's first months at the state hospital, Dr. Evangelakis reported that Dana talked "blatantly about his housebreaking, lock-picking and stealing in bragging tones."

While the others children played games, Dana desired to

be alone, Evangelakis wrote. "He does not defend himself. Instead he runs, yells and screams and does lots of whining when the children are after him. He resents most of the female staff and prefers the company of a male group worker. Presently he tries to provoke other staff members."

Dana was institutionalized for a year and a half, but his family visited him just once, even though the facility was only a mile from their house. Nor did they inquire about his condition. "It appears they are totally ignoring this child," Alma Smith wrote.

Yet by September 1972, Smith wrote that Dana's condition had "greatly improved"—perhaps a result of twice weekly individual psychotherapy. However, she added that "at this point in his life, Dana desperately needs a positive life experience in order to become a normal functioning adult." The state suggested he be allowed to go home.

If that was Dana's window to return to a normal childhood, it was abruptly and forever slammed shut when his stepmother Terri said no, she wouldn't have him. At that point, the state preferred to put him in a foster home, but lacking an available opening, he was sent to Boys' Town of South Florida, in rural south Dade County.

By the time Dana reached Boys' Town, it was probably too late. Social worker Sister M. Elaine wrote that Dana was "an angry boy who appears to make valiant attempts to cover up his explosive impulses. He has very poor ego strengths and sees himself as 'no good.' Dana can best be described as 'volatile' when he is really angry and disturbed."

He tried once to break into the priests' quarters; then a week later, he ran away with another boy and was arrested for shoplifting. The night he was returned to Boys' Town, he and the same boy ran away again, only much further.

Kicked out of Boys' Town, Dana bounded in between a number of foster group homes in 1973 and 1974. At one, in April 1974, two girls alleged that Dana tried to molest a five-year-old girl in the middle of the night. They ran and told the foster father they saw Dana, wearing no clothing, hiding underneath the child's bed. Moments later, when the foster parents arrived, Dana was back in his room where he "feigned sleeping." The five-year-old child was asleep, but her underwear was down at her ankles. Dana denied the allegations, but that night police removed him from the home and placed him in detention.

After a month in detention, a probation counselor took Dana to Miami for an interview at a group program called Self Help. They told Dana they would accept him, but on the way back to the detention center, he escaped the counselor at a toll booth.

Dana stayed on the run for two months; then in July 1974, he called his case worker from a public phone. He said he was "somewhere in the area of his father and that we better not go out looking for him because he is carrying a .38 and will shoot at anybody who does come after him."

Dana said he had stayed at his father's house for one night. "He was told that his father wanted nothing do with him anymore and it was because of Dana and some of the other children in the family that were actually driving him crazy. Dana was crying on the phone and said that he wants to prove to his father and his stepmother than he can do well and he is going to come back." A day later, he showed up at his case worker's office, volunteering to enter a new residential program.

On October 2, 1974, a prescient doctor sounded the last and loudest siren for Dana.

In an attempt to have Dana placed at Nova University's Living and Learning Center, a progressive alternative school in Fort Lauderdale for troubled kids, psychologist R.K. Berntson was asked to do an evaluation.

He wrote: "It is imperative that this young man be helped to identify with more conventional, conforming behavior, otherwise he might become an anti-social acter-outer."

Dana was assigned to a communal cottage at Nova. According to the cottage parents (quoted by his DFS case worker), "Dana continues to somewhat irritatingly verbalize his super personality, super power, super knowledge."

After two months at Nova, Dana was a runaway problem yet again. On January 17, 1975, he ran with two other boys and was picked up by police more than a hundred miles away. Seven days after their return, Dana and one of the same boys ran away again. While they were gone this time, police alleged they broke into a middle school, shoplifted at department stores, destroyed a golf cart belonging to the high school where Dana was attending, and stiffed several restaurants after being served.

Nova staff allowed Dana to return because they felt he was a follower, not a leader. But on February 12, one of the cottage parents told the DFS case worker that "although Dana is doing fairly well, she truly does not believe that the running had stopped. She stated that she would give Dana approximately two weeks before he would be gone again."

In fact he ran again just four days later, on February 16, with Roland Menzies, a younger boy. Social worker Iris Jones wrote that she saw Dana standing under a canal on Orange Drive in Davie on her way to work that Sunday morning. She reported what she saw to her supervisor.

In the late afternoon of February 17, Peter Wagner was killed and Christy Wagner assaulted near a canal on Orange Drive. Dana was caught on February 22, near Nova, and that night confessed his involvement in the murder to police.

The Florida Department of Corrections wrote Dana's psychological intake report on August 29, 1975. Dr. T.M. Than, a psychiatrist, wrote that "Dana categorically denied his involvement in the crime and instead related in detail of his plans to sue the police officials who were responsible for his arrest.

"He tried hard to impress the interviewer with his cool, smooth-talking and super-knowledgeable attitude which revealed an overcompensated pseudo-maturity rather than emotional stability. He is self-righteous while blaming the society as a whole. Because of his denial and self-righteousness, he felt no reason to be remorseful or repentent."

✦ FIFTY

SENTENCING

In an eighteen-page pre-sentencing investigation written by Florida Department of Corrections probation officer Mark Osowski, placed in the public record on the day of sentencing, Dana Williamson offered his first public words regarding the charges.

"On March 25, 1994, the defendant stated, 'I didn't do it. Simple as that. I've never met the people before we went to court. I never knew their name until I was arrested and told by the cops.' "

There were also statements solicited from the state attorney and law enforcement.

"On April 18, 1994, Assistant State Attorney Brian T. Cavanagh stated, 'Dana Williamson is a bonafide psychopath who knew the difference between right and wrong but deliberately chose to do the horrific wrongs that he visited upon the victims in this case. He plainly executed Donna Decker in cold blood after he tried to eliminate her entire family. Even as she died, her dying words showed that she was cognizant as to what had happened to her husband and child. Dana Williamson's diabolical intent is further underscored by the gruesome threat he made to Charles Panoyan as to what would be done to Charles Panoyan's wife and children were Panoyan to breathe a word about the Williamsons' identities. Society must forever be safeguarded from the onslaught of this predatory man.' "

Kelly Woodroof, now a sergeant, said for the record on April 11, 1994: "He is the most dangerous person I ever met. It appears to me that he felt absolutely no emotion in connection with this case. The two separate crimes that he was convicted of are the most brutal that I am aware of and given those crimes and considering the circumstances of those crimes, if he is not sent to the electric chair then they should do away with it.''

On June 28, Judge Eade held a hearing to hear the victims, and to give Dana Williamson an opportunity to speak to the court.

Bob Decker said, "My wife is gone now. I believe he should not live. He didn't give her a choice, he shouldn't have a choice."

Dana Williamson remained silent.

Once again, on the sentencing date, July 15, 1994, Judge Eade asked Williamson if he wanted to say anything.

"No, sir," he answered.

The judge spent forty-five minutes explaining his findings. He agreed that the state had proved three of four aggravating factors, disagreeing with them only that the murder was premeditated. He also agreed with the defense that some mitigating factors existed, including a "likelihood that Dana Williamson may have some degree of brain damage," although he found no reason to correlate it with this crime. Further, Eade said, Williamson knew right from wrong and appreciated the criminality of his conduct.

While the judge went on, two additional bailiffs entered the rear of the courtroom, making a total of four.

Then, at last, the decision: Dana Williamson would be punished by death by electrocution for the first-degree murder of Donna Decker.

Then Eade read the punishments for each of the remaining fourteen counts: life imprisonment for each of the three attempted murders, one armed burglary, four armed robberies, and five armed kidnappings. For the last count—extortion against Charles Panoyan—Eade gave him thirty years.

Eade set up most of the life sentences to run concurrently; however, four of them were to run consecutively. When counted up, Dana's punishment was death, followed by four consecutive life terms plus thirty years.

The *Sun-Sentinel* wrote the next morning that it was one of the harshest sentences ever handed down in Broward County.

While the judge told him his fate, Dana Williamson predictably kept his poker face. After it was over, as the bailiffs took him out of the courtroom, he walked forward, looking down, and scowled with his upper lip and nose.

But first he walked past Brian Cavanagh, who was visibly affected by the gravity of what had just happened. He had never before sent a defendant to Death Row.

← Fifty-one

Deus ex Machina

Brian Cavanagh gave a speech about his dad at his eightieth birthday party, held at the beach club across the street from Tom's house.

He quoted Cicero that "a life well spent is a life well lived." Besides the positive impact he had had on his family, Tom was in large measure responsible for vindicating three innocent men accused of murder who were well on their way to the electric chair: George Whitmore, New Jersey surgeon Dr. Arsenio Favor, and Charles Panoyan.

He compared his dad to a *deus ex machina*—a god from the machine. He explained that in classical Greek plays, the protagonist on his heroic mission through the unknown would eventually get trapped in a situation in which there was no escape. It could be some sort of enveloping natural disaster, or perhaps his enemies were surrounding him.

Then just in the climactic nick of time, when the situation looked bleakest, Zeus would decide he had to intervene, and so he put down his cocktail. He would lower another god on a pulley from Mount Olympus (a god from the machine), who would rescue the hero from certain death and save the day. To the protagonist, it would look like help arrived out of thin air; but theatergoers got to see the bigger picture.

"As a child, Dad is superhuman. I still have a vestige of blind faith that Dad is always right. Now, I realize that he really is superhuman, and why," said Brian.

"My dad is a vast reservoir of all the attributes I would like to possess, including courage and wisdom. He was always the bravest man I knew. I admired him for standing up

417

to anyone. He made it clear to me that I should always have total integrity.

"He was the greatest detective in the history of New York. I've had the fortune to benefit from his wisdom. He is as decent a man as there is. Thank God for my dad."

Paul Stark and Dave Vinikoor had come too, although it would have been funny to see them at such a party two years earlier. They joked about opposing Brian in the case. He was fun to annoy because he'd get so angry, so easily.

Stark said he was astounded by how much courage Brian had shown in trying to find out where the truth lay in the case. The simplest thing would have been just to bring it to trial, considering that Panoyan had created an ample circumstantial case against himself from the story he had told.

"This was justice at its finest," said Stark. "We all like to believe that ultimately justice will prevail. Those who have worked in it have grown cynical. We know that it isn't always true. This renewed my faith in the system."

"We put our faith in the decency and integrity of the prosecutor," said Vinikoor. "Because we had very special people involved; we had a special result."

Brian wanted to share credit with the defense attorneys.

"We don't always know the absolute truth. We can only be guided by our experience and wisdom. You hope that the testimony you bring is the truth, and the defense is full of cock and bull. But sometimes you get to where you have to decide if you want to vouch for the credibility of your evidence.

"We had invested a tremendous amount of effort in lining up a case. When we realized that Panoyan was totally unwitting in the crime—what a horror. You say, 'It can't be true,' but you have to accept your fallibility and error. It hurts. But we faced up and came to grips that we were wrong. The man was not guilty of the things we fervently believed he was guilty of.

"If you have a conscience, what a nightmare. It's worse by tenfold than a killer going free."

"This was an absolutely unique case," said Tom. "The defense, prosecutor, judge—all working together for justice. The defense and the prosecutor sitting down with the defendant? Letting the prosecutor's father talk with him alone? Never heard of it! You'll never see it again!''

Then Tom turned to Brian. ''I've enjoyed this,'' he said. ''You've added years to my life.''

✦ Epilogue

Rodney Williamson came to trial on March 13, 1995, in front of a different judge, Paul Backman. His attorney, Tom Cazel, said in opening statement that Dana Williamson was guilty of killing Donna Decker, and that most of the evidence in this trial would in fact implicate Dana, not Rodney.

"Do not visit the sins of one brother against the other brother," he asked.

He took aim at Charles Panoyan, whom he said was released from jail because "all of a sudden he was singing the right song.

"Charles Panoyan needed a third man to hold him at gunpoint because that's the only excuse he could give," Cazel said.

Unlike his brother, Rodney took the stand at his trial.

Like his brother, Rodney tried to present a non-threatening appearance at trial. He dressed in sweaters, attempting to achieve the warm-and-fuzzy feel that had worked so well for the Menendez brothers.

Most strikingly, his Yosemite Sam facial hair was gone. To show the jury Rodney's street likeness, Brian Cavanagh entered into evidence a 1992 booking photo of him. Forced to confront his change in appearance for trial, Rodney admitted, chuckling, that there once had been a resemblance between he and Sam.

His chuckle failed to conceal a hiss.

In direct examination by co-counsel Barry Butin, Rodney denied knowing anything about the Decker murder until 1990, when police questioned him. In 1991, Rodney said Cavanagh threatened him during a meeting at the state attorney's office. He said the prosecutor told him, "Your brother Dana's going to prison. Whichever one of you cooperates—you or Charles Panoyan—will go free, the other one is going to jail.''

Cavanagh began cross-examination with a rhyme:

> *Hares they run with hares*
> *and wolves run with their like;*
> *Killers hunt in packs and pairs*
> *and in pairs and packs they strike.*

It came from Rodney's typed papers. Cavanagh asked if he had written it.

Rodney's answer wasn't as telling as how he said it. He leaned forward, his voice rose part of an octave, and he seemed to spit: "Poetry was never my forte. That sounds publishable, and if I had written it, I would have made some money from it.''

Within minutes, two extra bailiffs entered the courtroom, bringing the total to four. When I walked outside the courtroom during a sidebar later, I heard one of them, D.C. Clark, call downstairs on his walkie-talkie: "We have a first-degree murder defendant on the stand in a heated argument with the prosecutor.''

Then Clark turned to me and said, "That guy's dangerous.''

Cavanagh said when police seized Rodney's diaries, they found that three weeks surrounding the date of the murder were missing. He asked Rodney why.

Rodney got defensive. "Are you making an accusation?'' he shot.

"I most certainly am—in the form of a question,'' Cavanagh shot back.

Rodney accused Cavanagh of taking his writings out of context. "You are telling lies by telling half the truth,'' he said. "It's a half-truth, and that's a half-lie, by definition.''

Two days later, April 5, the jury began deliberations in the late morning. At 5:30 P.M., they announced their verdict: Guilty on all seventeen counts.

Ironically, Dana had done better. He won two of his seventeen charges.

*	*	*

At the penalty phase hearing May 9, Judge Backman asked Rodney if he wanted to take the stand. In a deflated voice, he declined. "He'll just make a monkey out of me again," he said, referring to Brian Cavanagh.

It was a wiser decision than he had made at trial. In closing, Barry Butin admitted that both Rodney and Dana were involved in the taking of a life, but he told the jury the death penalty is reserved for only the most egregious and extreme murders. "That was done by Dana Williamson, not Rodney Williamson," he said. Rodney had no expectation it was going to happen, therefore, his crime was punishable by life imprisonment, not death.

When the jury went out, Rodney asked Butin to bet $50 on the outcome; he guessed death. Butin refused the wager.

Less than ten minutes later, the jury came back. Life.

Next morning, May 10, 1995, Judge Backman sentenced Rodney to three consecutive life terms plus thirty years, thus assuring his imprisonment for the rest of his life.

That day I made one last revelation: the murder of Donna Decker had been November 4, 1988. The amount of time that had passed was exactly six years, six months, and six days.

Compelling True Crime Thrillers
From Avon Books

DEATH BENEFIT
by David Heilbroner

72262-3/ $5.50 US/ $6.50 Can

FREED TO KILL
by Gera-Lind Kolarik with Wayne Klatt

71546-5/ $5.50 US/ $6.50 Can

TIN FOR SALE
by John Manca and Vincent Cosgrove

71034-X/ $4.99 US/ $5.99 Can

"I AM CAIN"
by Gera-Lind Kolarik and Wayne Klatt

76624-8/ $4.99 US/ $5.99 Can

GOOMBATA:
THE IMPROBABLE RISE AND FALL OF
JOHN GOTTI AND HIS GANG
by John Cummings and Ernest Volkman

71487-6/ $5.99 US/ $6.99 Can

The Best in Biographies from Avon Books

IT'S ALWAYS SOMETHING
by Gilda Radner   71072-2/ $5.95 US/ $6.95 Can

RUSH!
by Michael Arkush   77539-5/ $4.99 US/ $5.99 Can

STILL TALKING
by Joan Rivers   71992-4/ $5.99 US/ $6.99 Can

I, TINA *by Tina Turner and Kurt Loder*
70097-2/ $5.99 US/ $7.99 Can

PATTY HEARST: HER OWN STORY
by Patricia Campbell Hearst with Alvin Moscow
70651-2/ $6.99 US/ $8.99 Can

SPIKE LEE
by Alex Patterson   76994-8/ $4.99 US/ $5.99 Can

OBSESSION: THE LIVES AND TIMES OF CALVIN KLEIN
by Steven Gaines and Sharon Churcher
72500-2/$5.99 US/$7.99 Can

COMPREHENSIVE, AUTHORITATIVE REFERENCE WORKS FROM AVON TRADE BOOKS

THE OXFORD AMERICAN DICTIONARY
Edited by Stuart Berg Flexner, Eugene Ehrlich and
Gordon Carruth   51052-9/ $12.50 US/ $15.00 Can

**THE CONCISE COLUMBIA DICTIONARY
OF QUOTATIONS**
Robert Andrews   70932-5/ $9.95 US/ $11.95 Can

THE CONCISE COLUMBIA ENCYCLOPEDIA
Edited by Judith S. Levey and Agnes Greenhall
                                  63396-5/ $14.95 US

**THE NEW COMPREHENSIVE AMERICAN
RHYMING DICTIONARY**
Sue Young   71392-6/ $12.00 US/ $15.00 Can

**KIND WORDS: A THESAURUS
OF EUPHEMISMS**
Judith S. Neaman and Carole G. Silver
                                  71247-4/ $10.95 US/ $12.95 Can

**THE WORLD ALMANAC GUIDE
TO GOOD WORD USAGE**
Edited by Martin Manser with Jeffrey McQuain
                                  71449-3/ $8.95 US